Charles K. Whipple

Relation of the American Board of Commissioners for Foreign

Missions to Slavery.

Charles K. Whipple

Relation of the American Board of Commissioners for Foreign Missions to Slavery.

ISBN/EAN: 9783337412401

Printed in Europe, USA, Canada, Australia, Japan

Cover: Foto ©Andreas Hilbeck / pixelio.de

More available books at **www.hansebooks.com**

RELATION

OF THE

AMERICAN BOARD OF COMMISSIONERS

FOR

FOREIGN MISSIONS ;

TO

SLAVERY.

By CHARLES K. WHIPPLE.

BOSTON:
PUBLISHED BY R. F. WALLCUT,
No. 221 WASHINGTON STREET.
1861.

RELATION

"AMERICAN BOARD" TO SLAVERY.

————

At the Annual Meeting of the American Board of Commissioners for Foreign Missions in October, 1860, it was declared by the Prudential Committee that the Cherokee nation was "a Christian people."

When the Board commenced its missionary labors among the Cherokees in 1817, they were a pagan nation, and also a slaveholding nation.

The Prudential Committee (the managing power of the Board) now declares these Indians to be changed from pagans to Christians. But their habit of slaveholding remains unchanged.

The missionaries of the Board strongly opposed some of the vices which the Cherokees had been accustomed to practise, and constantly bore their testimony against these vices, both by preaching against them, and by refusing church-membership to those who continued to practise them. They chose, however, not to preach against slaveholding, and they openly declared slaveholders to be Christians, admitting them to their churches indiscriminately with others.

The Prudential Committee now not only declare this slaveholding nation to be "a Christian people," but they declare the discontinuance of the missionary work among them (first made known to the public at the meeting above mentioned) to have been decided on *because* they were Christianized; because the work undertaken by the missionaries was satisfactorily accomplished, in regard to the Cherokees; and because the duty of the Board was to send its laborers to people who were *not* Christian.

The Prudential Committee further declare—tacitly recognizing the fact that slaveholding existed, unrebuked, among their Cherokee church-members—that the separation in question was *not* made on account of slavery.

They also expressly declare—tacitly recognizing the fact that many complaints had been made in regard to the complicity of the missionaries with slavery—that the preaching of those missionaries has been faithful, and their course of policy satisfactory.

Here is the testimony of the Prudential Committee upon these three points, from their Annual Report for 1860:—

CERTIFICATE OF CHRISTIANITY FOR THE SLAVEHOLDING CHEROKEE NATION.

"1. *The Cherokees are a Christian people.*"—*Ann. Rep.*, 1860, p. 138.

    *   *   *   *   *   *

" The mission is not abandoned ; but *our* appropriate work is done. The Cherokee people have been Christianized, through the divine favor, and what remains for building up and sustaining the institutions of the Gospel—which is every where a work never brought to a close—must be left to others ; for the reason that our appropriate work is no longer there."—*Ibid*, p. 145.

CERTIFICATE OF CHRISTIANITY FOR THE CHEROKEE CHURCHES CONTAINING SLAVEHOLDERS.

" Our brethren declare, that no members have been received into either of our own churches, without first giving what they deemed to be credible evidence of repentance and faith in Christ. In this, there has been exact conformity to the principle recognized by the Board;—' That credible evidence of repentance and faith in Christ, in the judgment of the missionaries and the churches they gather, entitles professed converts from among the heathen to the ordinances of baptism and the Lord's supper ; those ordinances being evidently designed by Christ to be means of grace for such.' Mr. Ranney regards the members of his own church, at Lee's Creek, as furnishing the same evidence of faith and repentance as did the members of a church in Vermont, where he labored as a minister of the Gospel before going among the Cherokees."—*Ib.*, p. 140.

THE DISCONTINUANCE NOT ON ACCOUNT OF SLAVERY.

" The Committee have arrived at the conclusion, that it is time for the Board to discontinue its expenditures among the Cherokees.

To prevent all misapprehension, it should be stated at the outset; — *First*, that this is not owing to the relations of our work among these Indians to the system of slavery." — *Ib.*, p. 137.

CERTIFICATE OF CHRISTIAN FIDELITY FOR THE PRO-SLAVERY MISSIONARIES.

"5. To prevent the possibility of misapprehension, it is farther resolved, that the mission is not discontinued because of any unfaithfulness on the part of our brethren in that mission; they having been exemplary, so far as is known to the Committee, in the discharge of all their missionary duties." — *Ib.*, p. 142.

Mr. James G. Birney, a church-member in Kentucky, having been converted by the labors of the Abolitionists, wrote a tract, in 1842, declaring and proving that the American Church is the Great Bulwark of American Slavery. This statement is even more emphatically true of the Church now, than it was then. And the American Board of Commissioners for Foreign Missions is one of the most popular and influential representatives of that Church. This last unequivocal and emphatic uplifting of the voice of the Board in behalf of slavery will help many Christians to realize how far different is its teaching from the Gospel of Christ. He declared that the Lord had sent him "to preach deliverance to the captives." The Board has not only refused to follow, in this particular, him whom it pretends to call "Lord," but while deserting and betraying the oppressed, it has welcomed the oppressor as "a brother in Christ." And since now, while dismissing churches of slaveholders from its guardianship, it parades before this nation—now agitated as never before by a sense of the guilt and danger involved in slaveholding—its priestly assurance that slaveholding is not sin, it seems a suitable time to trace back the connection of this Board with slavery, and to show how, like the American Church, it has silently acquiesced in that wickedness while silence was possible, has spoken of it, when compelled to speak, in a manner often disingenuous and sometimes deceitful, and, when action could no longer be avoided, has acted in support of slavery, veiling its guilt by a profusion of pious words.

The first *open* action of the Board in regard to slavery — the first direct reference, in their Annual Reports, to their own complicity with it—is found in the Report for 1840, (pp. 63, 64,) under the head, "ON RAISING FUNDS FROM THE HOLDERS OF SLAVES."

It appears, however, from facts derived from other sources, that the Prudential Committee had previously, and repeatedly, been called to act upon this subject; that they had discountenanced the mention of it by missionaries and others; and that they concealed the fact that remonstrances against slavery had been made, both from the Board, at its Annual Meetings, and from the churches, who read their Annual Reports. We know not how many such remonstrances were made, and suppressed by the Prudential Committee, nor do we know when they began to be made. That one was made as early as 1837 is shown by the following letters, and the action of the Board in regard to certain printed documents, sent to this country from the Sandwich Islands mission.

In the year 1837, several of the missionaries of the Board in the Sandwich Islands became deeply impressed with a sense of the guilt of slavery, the danger incurred by their native country in supporting such a wicked system, and the responsibility of the church for its removal. I have now before me copies of letters from three of those persons, one from Rev. Jonathan S. Green, dated at Honolulu, Oahu, in May, one from Rev. Peter Gulick, from the same station, in June, and the third from Rev. H. R. Hitchcock, dated at Kaluaaha in November. They all breathe the same spirit; but to show the strength of their sentiments and the vigor of their language, I subjoin extracts from the last two : —

"HONOLULU, June, 1837.

"DEAR BROTHER WRIGHT, — I can hardly tell whether personal regard, or the warm sympathy I feel for you as one engaged, heart and soul, in the great, the blessed, the arduous cause of abolition, has the greater influence in prompting me to address you. Ever since I seriously considered the subject, my sympathies have been with the Abolitionists, and those for whom they labor. It is, however, but *recently* I have become thoroughly convinced that the system of slavery ought to be *immediately abolished*. And yet this point seems now so clear and plain, that I almost wonder how any *real Christian* could hesitate a moment in coming to a right conclusion. Perhaps one of the greatest causes of delusion in this and similar cases is, our proneness to look at them in what we *call* the light of *expediency*. But what *right* have men, who have the Bible, to follow any other light than of Revelation? I believe, *assuredly*, that abolition is the cause of God, and must, therefore, triumph. The Lord hasten it in his time! I believe, too, that the reproach, abuse and violence which the friends of the cause (and yourself among others) are called to endure, in publishing the truth, will tend powerfully to accelerate the accomplishment of your desires.

"You will perceive by the preceding printed resolutions, that we, as a mission, do not forget our brethren who are in *bonds*. Indeed, the situation of the mass of this nation keeps the subject of slavery almost constantly before our eyes, and in our minds. The condition of the laboring class (which is almost the whole nation) is that of slavery, in its mildest form, however. No corporeal punishments are resorted to, to extort labor, nor are families broken up, and the marriage relation disregarded, as in the slave States of my beloved, though guilty country. Nor do the chiefs, who are the *only masters*, desire to *exclude* mental cultivation; but rather endeavor to promote its general diffusion; still, with these and other palliations, the system tends strongly to idleness, (for who would love to work without recompense?) and is pregnant with evils ruinous to all classes. From the bottom of my heart, therefore, I say, 'God speed the Abolitionists, till every yoke of oppression is broken throughout the whole earth.' Oppression has been greatly mitigated here by the introduction of the Gospel; but much remains still to be done.

P. GULICK."

"KALUAAHA, Nov. 18, 1837.

"To the Editor of the Emancipator:

"Dear Sir,—An accidental perusal of some of the numbers of your paper induces me, though a stranger, to write you. I write on a sheet containing a sort of circular to Christians, in the form of resolutions; not doubting that while you are engaged in the truly philanthropic and Christian work of pleading for the oppressed in the *land of freedom*, you have a deep interest also in the efforts of those who are laboring to break the bonds of pagan darkness.

"Though our fields of labor are at a great distance from each other, and are different in some respects, yet I feel that our object is the same,—that of breaking every bond, of letting the captives go free. Be assured, sir, that in the prosecution of this object, you have my prayers and best wishes for your success. No intelligence from my native land interests me more than that which announces the progress of the cause of the slave.

"I write because it is a privilege for me (as I think it should be for every Christian) to take an open and decided stand in favor of those who are laboring to crush slavery. Especially is this a privilege at a time when morbid prudence or time-serving policy is setting afloat the sentiment that it is a subject with which the missionary should not intermeddle. I must confess, that if the immediate abolition of slavery is a subject in which Christians of every name, circumstance or occupation, whether public or private, individual or corporate, may not and should not take an open, undisguised and active part, then there is no subject in all the wide field of benevolent action in which they should do so. Of all the abominations that have cursed the earth, where is there one more flagrant than that of enslaving and crushing to dust our fellow-men? Of all the sins which Christians are called upon to oppose at the present day, where is there a more heinous one than the one your society are laboring to destroy? The mere fact that insisting upon the immediate abolition of slavery, and that describing in Bible language the odiousness of traffic in human flesh, will disoblige a class of interested persons, however great, is no proof that either sound prudence or the religion of Christ requires one to forbear. A *neutral position* in reference to the immediate destruction of slavery can be justified by the spirit of the Gospel no more than the same position can be in reference to the destruction of intemperance, perjury, or highway robbery. And there can be little doubt, that were those sins as intimately interwoven with the worldly interests and profits of so large a portion of the country as is the existence of slavery, the same policy which now keeps so many aloof from those who are laboring to put down the latter, would do the same in reference to those who should strive to put down the former. Were the sin of holding slaves confined to a few, and those few of little or no wealth or influence, the neutrality which now exists in reference to its immediate abolition would probably be unknown. How disconsonant to the benevolent, but uncompromising spirit of the Bible! *' Open thy mouth for the dumb, in the cause of all such as are appointed to destruction. Open thy mouth, judge righteously, and plead the cause of the poor and needy,'* is a divinely inspired injunction, which no human policy whatever can justify us in evading.

"I am happy to inform you of what I hope you may be officially informed hereafter: that this mission, (so far as I know,) TO A MAN, ARE IN FAVOR OF THE IMMEDIATE EMANCIPATION OF THE SLAVE, and that we of course, as a body, are deeply interested in the success of the object to which your paper is devoted. As we do not get the paper, or, indeed, any other exclusively devoted to the interests of the anti-slavery society, you would do me a favor, and perhaps promote the interests of the cause, by sending us a file. I think good use will be made of it.

"As to the above resolutions, suffice it to say, that however they may fail to recommend themselves to the Christian public, they are the unanimous sentiments of this body on the subjects to which they refer. They were not adopted rashly, or under the impulse of convivial excitement, but after a prayerful and serious discussion. They are sentiments, in the promulgation of which we all feel the deepest interest. Should this strike you, sir, as just, you will do the cause of missions a favor by giving them a place in the *Emancipator*.

"Let the importance of the cause, dear sir, excuse the obtrusion of this letter upon you, and believe me, your cordial and respectful friend and fellow-laborer,

H. R. HITCHCOCK."

These, and others of the Sandwich Islands missionaries, feeling at once the atrocious character of slavery itself, and its detrimental influence upon their missionary work, not only wrote letters like the above to their other friends, but made similar appeals to their employers, the American Board of Commissioners for Foreign Missions, sending them, among other things, two anti-slavery documents printed on the mission press, one a tract, and the other a series of resolutions, printed on a letter sheet, referred to in the two preceding letters, both making a very earnest and affecting appeal to American Christians to apply themselves at once to the work of overthrowing American slavery.

How were this appeal and these documents received by the Board?

They referred the whole matter to a committee, consisting of Drs. Fay and Skinner, Rev. Henry Dwight, and John Tappan and Zechariah Lewis, Esqs., who reported the following resolution, which was *adopted* in September, 1837, and, after discussion, *reaffirmed*, September, 1839, and which *still remains in force:* —

"In general, the sole object of the printing establishments connected with the missions of the Board shall be to exert a direct influence upon the surrounding native population, and NO MISSION OR MEMBER OF A MISSION MAY PRINT ANY LETTER, TRACT OR APPEAL, AT THESE ESTABLISHMENTS, AT THE EXPENSE OF THE BOARD, WITH A VIEW TO ITS BEING SENT TO INDIVIDUALS, OR COMMUNITIES, IN THE UNITED STATES."

This prohibition of the diffusion of such humane and Christian sentiments as, being contained in the preceding letters, we must suppose were repeated in the tract and the printed sheet of resolutions, is discourteous to the missionaries, and shows a despotic style of administration in the Prudential Committee; but the clause, " AT THE EXPENSE OF THE BOARD," is a cruel addition of insult to injury, if we remember that the persons thus rebuked had given *themselves*, with their small worldly possessions, to the Board, and thus had no means of uttering the honest convictions of their hearts to friends at a distance, except by using the paper and ink purchased by the Board with the funds entrusted to them by Christians for the diffusion of Christian light and knowledge. If the missionaries found a fire opened in their rear by the shameless extension of heathenism at home, under the eye, and with the sanction of the Board, why should they not use

1 *

the means furnished them by the Christian public to remonstrate against it?

This rule may be seen on page 27 of the Annual Report for 1837. No reason whatever for passing it appears in that report. I know of no reason for passing it, except the wish to prevent the missionaries from remonstrating with the churches against slavery.

It is a significant fact that, two years before this prohibition of freedom of the press to the missionaries of the Sandwich Islands, the Board gave the following explicit testimony in their favor:—

"*Resolved*, That this Board has entire confidence in the Christian character, prudence and fidelity of their mission in the Sandwich Islands—the unfounded reports occasionally circulated notwithstanding; and that the success which has attended this mission, in the conversion of the heathen, and the great good done to seamen from Christian lands, calls for gratitude to God, and commends this mission to the hearts and the special prayers of all the friends of Christ."—Ann. Rep. of 1835, p. 23.

The following testimony, on page 24 of the same Report, is also highly significant, showing that, until the subject of slavery was brought before them, the Board chose to countenance and commend reformatory activities, at home as well as abroad:—

"*Resolved*, That this Board rejoice and give praise to Almighty God for that increase of Christian activity which is seen in the various institutions established during the last forty years for the prevention of sin in all its forms, and for removing from our guilty and suffering race the evils which sin occasions; that they especially rejoice in the progress of the temperance reform, and of the principles of peace among the nations of Christendom; and that their earnest prayer is, that all these associations may continue to labor with wisdom and energy, and that others may be organized to coöperate with them, until the institutions of Christian benevolence shall present a front as extended as the ravages of sin; and, favored with guidance and power from on high, shall press forward in their joint labors to chase wickedness and misery from the earth."

That the Board then chose also not only to acknowledge, but to coöperate with, reformatory institutions, appears from this statement, page 33 of the same Report:—

"Among the donations from similar sources should be acknowledged a valuable grant from the American Temperance Society, embracing about eleven hundred copies of its annual reports. These have been sent to the several stations occupied by the missionaries of the Board, and circulated with manifest good results, among the settlers and travellers on the frontiers of our own country, and among seamen and residents speaking the English language in foreign parts."

I have said that the vote of the Board in 1837 (forbidding the printing, on the mission presses, of any remonstrance against slavery from the missionaries to their brethren at home) was reäffirmed in 1839. The manner and circumstances of this reäffirmation are significant and instructive. The Prudential Committee chose again to veil this important action in language so carefully guarded that no allusion to slavery appears to the careless reader, either in the text or in the Index. Indeed, without a knowledge, from some other source, of that concerted and unanimous action of the Sandwich Islands missionaries which the votes in question were to nullify, the reader of these Reports of the Prudential Committee for 1837 and 1839 would not discover that either of them made the slightest reference to slavery. The passage in the Report for 1839, in which the prohibition of anti-slavery printing is deceptively placed under the head "RETURN OF MISSIONARIES," is as follows (the *italics* are those of the Report):—

"RETURN OF MISSIONARIES. Memorials from the Mahratta mission, and from that to the Sandwich Islands, relating to the return of missionaries, were read and referred to Rev. Drs. Day, Edwards, and Pond, Hon. Charles Marsh, and Rev. Messrs. Eli Smith and Willard Child. This committee subsequently made the following Report:—

"'The committee to whom was referred memorials from the Mahratta mission, and from the mission at the Sandwich Islands, have attended to the very important subjects submitted to them, and respectfully report:

"'That they see no sufficient cause for suspending or altering a rule adopted by this Board two years ago, in words following, viz.: "No mission or member of a mission may print any letter, tract, or appeal at these establishments" [the mission printing establishments abroad] "*at the expense of the Board*, with a view to its being sent to individuals in the United States." Our brethren abroad have various modes of communicating with friends and the community at home; but the Prudential Committee, obviously, are the proper judges of what ought to be printed, *at the expense of the Board*, with a view to general circulation in the United States.

"'In reference to the other and principal matter complained of in these memorials, viz., *the return of missionaries*, the following statements and recommendations are submitted.'"—p. 38.

These last lines (which are followed by a much more extended report *really* relating to the " return of missionaries ") show that some "other" subject was contemplated in the " Memorials from the Mahratta mission, and from that to the Sandwich Islands." These Memorials are not given in the Report. Wishing to ascertain how strongly and at what length they had urged the subject of slavery upon the notice of the Prudential Committee, I sent the following note, through the post-office, to the senior Secretary : —

BOSTON, Dec. 31st, 1860.

REV. DR. RUFUS ANDERSON :

DEAR SIR, — Will you have the kindness to give me a copy (or allow me to make a copy) of the " *Mem rials from the Mahratta Mission, and from that to the Sandwich Islands*," respecting which a report was made on the first half of page 38 of the Prudential Committee's Annual Report for 1839 ?

Respectfully,   CHARLES K. WHIPPLE.

To this note I have received no answer whatever.

In the Appendix to this Annual Report of 1839, we find— " Instructions given by the Prudential Committee [Oct. 6th, 1839,] to the Rev. Sheldon Dibble, about returning to the Sandwich Islands Mission."

Mr. Dibble was one of that body of Sandwich Islands missionaries of whom Rev. Mr. Hitchcock asserted a unanimous desire for the immediate emancipation of the American slaves, and a deep interest in the abolition movement. (See ante, p. 8.) Of course, in his year's visit to this country, he had seen the utter indifference of the majority of American churches to this subject, and might be expected to speak of the need of further appeals to them by the missionaries. The Prudential Committee provide against this danger by saying to Mr. Dibble (p. 171) —

"Bring not up an evil report of the churches of your native land, in your communications with your brethren."

It must be remembered that this direction was given just after they had a second time voted to smother the testimony of those brethren against slavery, and against the complicity of the churches with it.

It may be worth while to notice, in contrast with this suppression of the testimony of the Sandwich Islands missionaries against American slavery, the fact that the Prudential Committee have repeatedly aided the home circulation of documents written by their missionaries, documents indirectly as well as directly connected with the missionary work. Besides their approving notice, heretofore mentioned, of "a circular letter, printed at the mission-press" in the Sandwich Islands in 1826, and announcing certain facts "to the world"—they published, (p. 52 of the Annual Report for 1852,) a letter written by Mr. Wilson and four other missionaries of the Gaboon station, to Commodore Penand, of the French African squadron, then on that coast, containing this paragraph :—

"We would also express our hearty sympathies in the successful efforts you have put forth to prevent the natives of this region of country from participating further in the foreign slave trade ; and we hope they will not be suspended until this wicked practice is entirely suppressed."

Moreover, in their Annual Report for 1818 (pp. 30–2) is given an abstract of a pamphlet entitled "The Conversion of the World"—"written by Messrs. Hall and Newell at Bombay, and sent home in manuscript." The Report says—"Though this pamphlet has been widely diffused, and will be diffused still more widely, it may be useful to give an abstract of its contents."

So also, in the Annual Report for 1845, (p. 75,) we find mentioned the printing, by the Prudential Committee, of 3,000 copies of a statement and appeal from the mission in Borneo.

It thus appears that the Prudential Committee's suppression of the appeal of the Sandwich Islands missionaries in 1837, and their adoption of a rule for choking off future attempts at appeal or. that subject, and their framing of that rule in language so general as to give no idea to the ordinary reader of the particular object of the prohibition, were parts of a policy which has uniformly been pursued by this body, the avoidance of practical discountenance to that system of slaveholding in the United States in which their contributors were concerned.

It will be perceived by the letters of Mr. Gulick and Mr. Hitchcock, (ante, pp. 6–8,) that even the mild form of slavery then prevailing in the Sandwich Islands was a serious hin-

drance to their missionary labor, and that the publication in
this country of their resolutions in opposition to American
slavery would be (in their judgment) *a benefit to the cause of
missions.*

The very year after the Prudential Committee had smothered this testimony, and suppressed these resolutions, and forbidden the printing of any others, their report respecting the
Sandwich Islands mission contained a division headed " HIN-
DRANCES TO THE WORK." Slavery, however, was *not* mentioned among these hindrances! was not mentioned at all!
Romanism and want of funds were the only topics touched
under this head.—See pp. 117, 118, of Ann. Rep. for 1838.

The significance of this suppression of the testimony of
missionaries in regard to the hindrances to their work among
the heathen becomes very striking when contrasted with the
following declarations previously made by the Prudential
Committee : --

"*Resolved,* That it is eminently desirable that the spiritual condition and necessities of the world be ascertained and spread before
the churches as soon as possible, and that a distinct presentation be
made of all the means which ought to be employed to publish the
Gospel to every creature."—p. 18, Ann. Rep. for 1833.

In the " Conclusion " of this same Annual Report, among
the " General Objects of the Board," occurs the following
passage, p. 141:—

"A joint and solemn responsibility does certainly rest upon the
several missionary societies of Christendom to lose no time in making a full report to the churches of the condition of the heathen
world, *and of all that is necessary for its spiritual regeneration.*"

That there has been (notwithstanding this *general* recognition of the duty of free expression in regard to the obstacles
to success in the missionary enterprise) a steady continuance,
by the Prudential Committee, of the policy of discouraging
any expression of opinion by the missionaries in regard to
slavery in the United States, appears from two letters from
missionaries of the Board, which appeared in *The Independent* of August 13th, 1857.

In that paper, the writers of these letters are editorially
designated as " two of the most able, devoted and successful
missionaries in the East," one " in Western Asia," and the
other " in a neighboring field."

The first of these letters, written from one missionary to the other, is dated May 5th, 1857. The second letter, from the second missionary, and enclosing the letter of the first to some one in this country, is dated June 1st, 1857. We are left in entire ignorance from what particular places, and *from* what persons, and *to* what persons, these letters were sent. Why is this reserve? Is it because both letters express a very strong and heartfelt opposition to American slavery?

The Independent wished these strong expressions of anti-slavery feeling to be heard and heeded, and called attention to them in the following introductory paragraphs :—

"THE TESTIMONY OF MISSIONARIES AGAINST AMERICAN SLAVERY.

"The Christian sentiment of the world, in every form, is arrayed against the system of slavery which exists in the United States. But perhaps no testimony against that system is so strong and so impressive as that which comes from American missionaries, who from their distant fields of labor look back upon their native land. Their love for their country would incline them to look charitably upon her faults, while their relations to the Christian community dispose them always to speak with caution upon home affairs. They are removed from all party and sectional strife upon the subject of slavery, and therefore look upon that subject, not with the excited feelings of controversialists, but with the calmness of impartial observers. As a class, missionaries live near to God, and some of them are eminent for holiness. They are accustomed to look upon every institution, measure, or event, in its bearing upon the kingdom of Christ, and thus their feelings become as sensitive to any thing affecting that kingdom as the barometer to changes of the atmosphere. The churches in this land, therefore, ought to give special heed to the views and feelings of missionaries on the subject of slavery. *They* are not 'infidels,' 'radicals,' or 'fanatics.'

" Formerly, our missionaries looked upon slavery as an evil which they had left far behind them, and with which they had no concern. Now, however, since communication has been so freely opened with all parts of the world, they find the shame and scandal of American slavery a positive hindrance to their work. Converted heathen are amazed that slavery exists in this Christian land, and opposition to the Gospel among the unevangelized is strengthened by this monstrous incongruity. The lamented Stoddard once said, ' We do not dare to let our converts know that slavery exists in America; for how could we reconcile it with our professions as a Christian nation?' "

The language of the second of the letters referred to is so very peculiar and significant that I quote some of its first sentences :—

"JUNE 1st, 1857.

"MY DEAR BROTHER,—The groanings of the missionary over his retrograding country ought perhaps sometimes to be heard.

With this view, I send you the enclosed letter from Mr. —— to my-self, which you are at liberty to publish just as it is forwarded, if you think proper. Names need not be given; for the sentiment of the letter probably represents the feelings of most of our missionaries in these regions. It was of course not penned for the public eye; but the spontaneous gushings of an aching heart, poured into the ear of a brother missionary, are at least as true an index of that heart as any more formal expression could be."

Why is the strong protest against slavery (which is the prominent point in both the letters referred to) thus anony-mously written and published? Why does the missionary say that his complaints upon this subject ought *perhaps some-times* to be heard? Why does he say, in giving permission to publish the letter of his anti-slavery associate, "Names need not be given"? and why does he say, (as if it explained the propriety of withholding the names of persons and places,) "*for* the sentiment of the letter probably represents the feel-ings of most of our missionaries in these regions"? In short, why must the anti-slavery sentiments of American missiona-ries in foreign lands be sent to this country stealthily, and published at second hand, with such precautions, instead of being sent directly to the Board, and published, with their other communications, in the *Missionary Herald* and the An-nual Reports? The answer to these questions will require a careful and extended examination of the past history of the Board in regard to slavery, to which I now proceed.

In 1840, the Prudential Committee found it necessary to make open mention of the subject of slavery in their Annual Report, to indicate this business, as others, by a heading in small capitals, and also to refer to it in the Index. Their action is recorded as follows, pp. 63, 64:—

"ON RAISING FUNDS FROM THE HOLDERS OF SLAVES.

"A memorial from sundry Congregational and Presbyterian minis-ters in the State of New York, on the subject of raising funds for missionary objects from those who hold slaves, and remonstrating against the agents of the Board being sent for that purpose into the States where slaves are held, was laid before the Board by the Re-cording Secretary, and referred to a committee consisting of Rev. Drs. Hawes, and Thomas DeWitt, Hon. Charles Marsh, Walter Hubbell, Esq., and Rev. Messrs. Greene, Hamner and Meigs. This committee subsequently made the report given below, which was accepted and approved.

"'The Committee to whom was referred the memorial of sundry Congre-gational and Presbyterian ministers in the State of New York, respectfully ask leave to report

" ' Your Committee have no reason to doubt that the memorialists are sincerely desirous of promoting the missionary work, and think that their opinions and feelings should be treated with great respect and kindness. That the Lord will not accept the fruits of robbery for sacrifice, we are assured ; nor do your Committee suppose that any gift obtained by means known to the donor to be unrighteous, and in the use of which he still perseveres, will be acceptable to God. Still, they think that much caution should be exercised in judging concerning the character and motives of men who profess to be engaged in the service of Christ, and whose general character and conduct correspond with the profession.

" ' But without deciding in regard to the entire correctness of the principles which are believed to constitute the basis of the reasonings of the memorialists, your Committee are convinced, from a careful consideration of the matter, that the attempt to apply these principles, as proposed in the memorial, would be attended with practical difficulties so numerous and great as to render it inexpedient for the Board to take any order on the subject.' "

The Prudential Committee do not tell us who, and how many, are the "sundry ministers," nor what reasons they allege. They seem to hope still to stave off the subject by treating it with slight regard. But in the following year, it was found advisable and *prudential* to treat other remonstrants more respectfully.

In the Annual Report for 1841, pp. 58 to 61, appears the following Memorial and Report of Committee : —

"MEMORIAL FROM MINISTERS IN NEW HAMPSHIRE.

"The following memorial from ministers in the State of New Hampshire was read to the Board by Mr. Greene : —

AUGUST, 1841.

To the American Board of Commissioners for Foreign Missions :

BELOVED BRETHREN, — The undersigned, ministers in New Hampshire, and most of them honorary members of the Board, address you on a subject in which they feel a deep interest, and which they regard as of the utmost importance to the cause of Missions. We address you as our fellow-laborers, and the especial agents of the church in this cause. And we assure you that we have great confidence in you as such. But we think the circumstances in which you are now placed require a modification of the course you have hitherto pursued. We allude to what has appeared to us a *studied silence* on the subject of American slavery. We know that you have been goaded in unchristian methods, and have been censured for not carrying out plans that were neither wise nor good. But we think you may, and we frankly say *you should, make known your views and feelings on the subject, so that you shall be recognized by all as sympathising with those Christians who deeply abhor that system of abomination.*

And in addition to the consideration that it is *right*, we say also a regard to the pecuniary safety of the Board renders it *expedient*. There is a deep feeling of disapprobation in the community in relation to the *studied silence* above alluded to. Nor is it confined to those who have dealt in denunciation towards all who did not conform to their precise method of opposing slavery. The sober and considerate ministers and members of our churches, who have from the first been the firm and true friends of the Board, are distressed. They love the Board, and have loved it long. They regard it as foremost among the benevolent societies of the day. They have paid more for its support than for the support of any other society. And more than of any other, has its prosperity been the burden of their prayers. But we greatly fear that their contributions must ultimately, and that before long, be suspended, if the Board shall think it their duty to observe such a *studied silence* on this great subject of interest and responsibility to American Christians.

Brethren, do not for a moment think that we are not your friends. We say this in love — love to your cause, and love with assurance of confidence to you. We do think that American slavery is such, and brought in the providence of God so distinctly into the notice of American Christians, that no man or body of men can innocently maintain a doubtful position in relation to it.

JOHN M. WHITON, *Antrim.*
SAMUEL LEE, *New Ipswich.*
WINTHROP FIFIELD, *Epsom.*
RUFUS A. PUTNAM, *Chichester.*
JAMES R. DAVENPORT, *Francestown.*
GILES LYMAN, *Marlborough.*
CYRUS W. WALLACE, *Manchester.*
HORACE WOOD, *Dalton.*
JONATHAN CURTIS, *Pittsfield.*

S. W. CLARK, *Greenland.*
DAVID P. SMITH, *Greenfield.*
JEREMIAH BLAKE, *Wolfborough.*
R. W. FULLER, *Westmoreland.*
JAMES TISDALE, *Dublin.*
SAMUEL NICHOLS, *Barrington.*
J. D. CROSBY, *Jaffrey.*
DAVID SUTHERLAND, *Bath.*

"The foregoing paper was referred to the Rev. Dr. Woods, Chief Justice Williams, Rev. Dr. Hawes, Rev. David Magie, and Rev. J. G. Hammer, who subsequently reported as follows: —

"'The Committee to whom was referred the memorial of several ministers of the Gospel in the State of New Hampshire, beg leave to report.

"'In attending to the subject under consideration, your Committee notice, with heartfelt pleasure, the candid and Christian spirit manifested in the communication from the brethren in New Hampshire. We have entire confidence in their attachment to the cause of foreign missions, and in their disposition to do all in their power to send the blessed Gospel, with all its healing influences, to the ends of the earth. It will ever be our delight to act with such men as they are, in promoting the object of this Missionary Board. And it is our earnest wish that every thing should be removed out of the way, which would be likely, in any measure, to prevent the accomplishment of this object, or to hinder the cordial and uninterrupted coöperation of its friends.

"'This Board was incorporated for the express "purpose of propagating the Gospel in heathen lands, by supporting missionaries and diffusing a knowledge of the Scriptures." In the language of the laws, "the object of the Board is to propagate the Gospel among unevangelized nations." The Board and its missionaries have taken care to confine their efforts to this *one object,* — an object great and excellent enough to engage the labors of angels and men. It appears to your Committee to be a duty of the first importance, — a duty required by a conscientious regard to the sacred trust committed to us, to continue to pursue our *one great object* with undivided zeal, and to guard watchfully against turning aside from it, or mixing any other concern with our appropriate work, as a Board of Commissioners for Foreign Missions. There are indeed many other works of Christian benevolence to be accomplished. But the work of *this Board is one*, namely, *to propagate the Gospel among unevangelized nations.* To *this* we are pledged. There are many forms of evil to be done away. But the evil which it is our object to do away is the evil of idolatry, ignorance and wretchedness among the heathen. And it is doubtless as true in regard to these various objects, as in regard to any others, that *a division of labor is essential to the highest degree of success.* As to the benevolent work in which we are engaged, we have the happiness to be of *one mind*; and we have had the happiness, in all past time, of pursuing this work with remarkable unanimity. And it is exceedingly plain to us, that we are called by Divine Providence to adhere to the plan of operation which has, from the first, been adopted; and that the way, and the only way for us to fulfil our sacred trust, and go forward harmoniously and prosperously in our benevolent enterprise, is, to direct all our proceedings as a Board, and all the labors of our missionaries, to the accomplishment of the *one specific object* of our organization; and that turning aside to any thing else, how important soever in itself, would be a dereliction of duty on our part, and would disappoint and grieve the great body of Christians who patronize the foreign missions.

"'Considering the character of this Board as a Christian institution, and the momentous object which it is pledged to promote, we think it may fairly be presumed, that the funds contributed from time to time to our treasury *are obtained in a proper manner*, and *given from proper motives.* At least, the principle is not to be admitted, that the Board must examine into the motives which influence those who sustain its operations, or into the origin of the funds which are contributed in furtherance of its object. Such a principle would be highly invidious in its character, and altogether impracticable in operation.

"'In regard to the particular object of the memorialists, that of obtaining a formal expression of the views and feelings of the Board respecting slavery, your Committee do not think that such a measure is called for, or that it would be right and expedient. It is indeed perfectly evident, that *this Board of Commissioners for Foreign Missions can sustain no relation to slavery*, which implies *approbation* of the system, and *as a Board* can have no connection or sympathy with it. And on the other hand, it is equally evident that the Board cannot be expected to pass resolutions, or adopt measures against this system, any more than against other specific forms of evil existing in the community. For we are met at once with the question, why we should express and proclaim our opinion in regard to one particular evil, in distinction from others, which are equally obvious and prevalent.

"'We beg leave to say again,—we do entertain a high respect for those ministers of Christ who have addressed us on the subject now under consideration. The spirit which pervades their communication cannot but excite within us feelings of love and esteem towards them. It is our earnest desire and hope that this Board may give them entire satisfaction, and enjoy their entire confidence. And we cannot doubt the continuance of their benevolent efforts and their fervent prayers in behalf of that precious and glorious object, *the conversion of the world*, which they and we are united in seeking. And we will only add an affectionate request to those beloved brethren, and all our other fellow-laborers, that they would keep in mind the great and only object of this Missionary Board, together with the untold labors, the perplexing cares, the burdens, difficulties and anxieties which fall to the share of those who are called to perform the executive business of the Board, and to direct its vast concerns, at home and abroad. Let them join with us in thanking the God of missions for the unexpected and wonderful manner in which he has interposed to prosper our labors. Let them join with us also in endeavoring to avoid whatever would divide the counsels and hinder the success of those who are seeking the enlargement of Christ's kingdom. And as the God of heaven and earth is on his way to have mercy on all nations, let our hearts be cheered and animated with hope ; and let us abound more and more in our labors of love ; waiting in faith and patience and joy for the coming of our Lord.

         " 'In behalf of the Committee,

               LEONARD WOODS, *Chairman.*'

" After a brief debate, with some explanations, and parts of the report having been again read, the report was *unanimously* adopted."

The *italics* in the above are those of the Annual Report. I wish now to call particular attention to one feature in the report of this Reverend and Honorable Committee, some of whom afterwards distinguished themselves as bitter and persistent opponents of all anti-slavery reform.

The Prudential Committee had, for several years, maintained a deceptive *silence* upon this subject. In 1841 began a course, which has been continued to the present time, of deceptive *speech*.

In the last paragraph but one of this report of Dr. Woods, of Andover, after a verbal disclaimer of *approbation* of slavery — a disclaimer certainly not worth much after the persistent suppression, by the Prudential Committee, of testimony from the missionaries against slavery, *as a hindrance to their missionary work* — Dr. Woods says, p. 60 : —

" On the other hand, it is equally evident, that the Board cannot be expected to pass resolutions, or adopt measures against this system, any more than against other specific forms of evil existing in the community. For we are met at once with the question, why we should express and proclaim our opinion in regard to one particular evil, in distinction from others, which are equally obvious and prevalent ? "

The report containing this statement was " unanimously adopted " by the Board (p. 61.) The statement implies (and uses the implication as a main argument against the remonstrants) that no censure " against other specific forms of evil " had been published by the Board. Let us look at the facts.

In the Annual Report for 1840, only one year before, I find censure against the traffic in intoxicating liquors, (pp

37, 167,) against the *use* of intoxicating liquors, (p. 180,) against the use of opium, (pp. 132 and 138, 139,) against *caste* — in Siam, not in Massachusetts or South Carolina — (p. 131,) and against the smoking of tobacco, (p. 161.)

In the Annual Report for 1838, I find censure against the practice of marrying heathen wives, (pp. 91, 95,) against intemperance, (pp. 79, 123,) and against the action of the United States government, in removing the Indians beyond the Mississippi, (p. 136.)

In the Annual Report for 1836, (p. 86,) and in that for 1835, (p. 92,) are complaints of the demoralization produced by gambling; and in the Annual Report for 1830, (pp. 110, 112,) are strong statements respecting the pernicious influence of theatres.

Some of the censures against "specific forms of evil" above referred to were made by the missionaries, and some by the Prudential Committee. And probably every Annual Report yet issued has contained some censure of this sort, from the pen of one or the other (or both) of these two parties, and formally "adopted" by the Board, against one or more forms of vice or evil.

Even in the very Annual Report (for 1841) in which Dr. Woods presents (as an argument against any direct rebuke of slaveholding by the Board) the implication that they did *not* rebuke "other specific forms of evil," I find a statement of church discipline inflicted for "travelling on the Sabbath" and for "playing at cards," (p. 155,) a complaint of the improper food and the want of cleanliness of the Sandwich Islanders, (pp. 168, 169,) a censure of the use of intoxicating liquors, (p. 186,) and on page 156, the following energetic language against the smoking of tobacco: —

"In some villages, not one in a hundred had fallen under church censure, and in others, considerable numbers had indulged in some besetting sin. The direct occasion of the falling of nearly all who had wandered was smoking tobacco. The passion of the natives for this vile narcotic is exceedingly strong and almost universal; and when this intemperate appetite has been indulged for a considerable length of time, it is about as difficult to eradicate it, as to reform the confirmed drunkard. I need not, however, enlarge on this topic, as you are already acquainted with the facts in the case. On visiting the offenders, some appeared truly penitent, others indifferent, and a third class, hard-hearted and determined in sin. However, God wrought, and he is now separating the precious from the vile, and giving us power to 'return and discern between the righteous and the wicked.'"

The Annual Report containing these rebukes of "other specific forms of evil" was already prepared and ready for printing when Dr. Woods read his report containing the utterly erroneous implication above mentioned. The Prudential Committee, who sat on the platform and heard it read, knew not only that that statement was at variance with one of their ordinary customs, but that this variance utterly vitiated Dr. Woods's argument. Nevertheless, they allowed it to be read, voted on, and "adopted," without correction, and they afterwards printed it as sound and true!

The unfair treatment of this Memorial in 1841 was made the subject of remonstrance in other Memorials presented in 1842, which were again referred to a Committee of which Rev. Dr. Woods was chairman. The Prudential Committee avoid giving the language of these Memorials, and the names of the remonstrants. This only is clear, that there were "several memorials and other papers" in regard to slavery. The Report of Dr. Woods replies to the exposure of his former misrepresentations by another misrepresentation, and tries to veil the meagreness and insufficiency of its defence by expanding into irrelevant pious talk, an example which was much followed in subsequent years.

This Report, with the very brief prefatory statement of the Prudential Committee, is as follows — pp. 44–46 of Annual Report for 1842: —

"MEMORIALS ON SLAVERY. Mr. Greene read several memorials and other papers on the subject of the connection of the American Board with slavery. These papers were referred to a committee, consisting of Rev. Dr. Woods, Chief Justice Williams, Rev. D. Brigham, Rev. Drs. Hawes and Parker, Rev. D. Greene, and Rev. Lyman Strong. The following Report was presented by that committee: —

"'The committee to whom were submitted sundry memorials relating to slavery; also, an extract from the will of the late Philander Ware; also, a memorial respecting receiving donations from persons in debt, ask leave to report.

"'Respecting the bequest of Philander Ware, and donations from persons in debt, your committee would not recommend to the Board to take any action.

"'The case of the Rev. John Leighton Wilson, a missionary of the Board to West Africa. It is stated in a letter from Mr. Wilson, that six years ago, and subsequently to his entering on the missionary work, he sustained the legal relation of owner to a number of slaves, who fell to him in consequence of a bequest made before his birth; that he had offered to emancipate them, either in this country or in Liberia, and had done all which he deemed suitable to terminate a relation painful and burdensome to himself, while they had steadfastly refused; and that he was, at the time mentioned, desirous still to emancipate these slaves, if any mode could be pointed out, which should be just and kind to them. Whether Mr. Wilson has emancipated them, or what their situation has been during the last six years, or what it now is, your committee have no information. They understand, however, that the Secretaries of the Board have written to him, making inquiries on these points. With their present want of information, your committee deem it necessary to say nothing more than that Mr. Wilson appears to have intended to act conscientiously and humanely, relative to the slaves under his care. Still, if his relation to them is not already terminated, your committee think it very desirable that it should be with as little delay as circumstances will permit; and they cannot but think that he will ere long be able, with such counsel and aid as the Prudential Committee may give, to accomplish the object in a manner satisfactory to himself, and kind and beneficial to them. More information must be obtained before further action can properly be had.

"'Your committee have no knowledge that any other missionary under the patronage of the Board stands in a similar relation to slavery.

"'This Board, at their last annual meeting, in reply to a memorial from New Hampshire, endeavored very plainly to set forth the principles which have governed their proceedings, and the views they entertain respecting the general object of these memorials; and it was our hope that the course which was pursued would prove satisfactory to all concerned. And here your committee know not what better they can do than to advert very briefly to the leading points contained in the report then adopted.

"'It was stated that this Board was incorporated for the express "purpose of propagating the gospel in heathen lands, by supporting missionaries and diffusing a knowledge of the Scriptures;" that the Board have confined their efforts to this *one great object*; and that a regard to our sacred trust requires us to pursue the object with undivided zeal, and to guard watchfully against turning aside from it or mixing any other concerns with it. We referred to other works of benevolence, but insisted that our appropriate work is to *propagate the gospel among the unevangelized.* It was then, and still is, our deliberate conviction, that we are called by Divine Providence to adhere steadily to the plan of operation which has been adopted, and that the only way for us to prosper in our work is to direct all our proceedings, as a Board, and all the labors of our missionaries, to the one specified object of our organization. We think that our Lord and Master, and the Christian world now and in after ages, will approve this our deliberate course of action, and that we could not be justified in departing from it.

"'In the report adopted last year, we moreover expressed our opinion, that, considering the character of this Board and the nature of its object, it may fairly be presumed that the funds contributed to our treasury are obtained in a proper manner and given from proper motives, and that it is at least manifest that we cannot examine into the motives of those who sustain our operations, or into the origin of the funds which are contributed in furtherance of our object. We think no man, who well considers the subject, can judge differently from us on this point. As to the methods which the Prudential Committee are pursuing to secure funds, we know nothing which any one could think exceptionable.

"'From a hearty desire to satisfy the feelings of the ministers of the Gospel who sent us the memorial from New Hampshire, we also said, with perfect frankness, "*that the Board of Commissioners for Foreign Missions can sustain no relation to slavery which implies approbation of the system, and as a Board,* can have no connection or sympathy with it," plainly intimating, also, that we consider it as one of the obvious evils which exist in the community, but the removal of which, though we regard it as an object of fervent desire and prayer, does not fall within our province as a missionary Board. These are our settled principles.

"'It is alleged by the memorialists that the Board has departed from these principles, and has expressed opinions relative to other prevailing evils. Respecting intemperance, licentiousness, Indian oppression, and some other hindrances to the progress of Christianity, as they prevailed in the countries where the missions of the Board are established, and powerfully counteracted the labors of the missionaries, and in some instances subjected them to great peril, the Board has stated the facts as they occurred, and in various forms, more or less explicit, has uttered the language of condemnation. These evils, existing in the countries where the missions are operating, and standing directly in the way of the Board's accomplishing its object, were, of course, legitimate and proper subjects for its animadversion. If it has at any time gone further than this, and expressed opinions relative to immoralities or evils of any kind, prevailing in this country, and not directly counteracting the labors of the missionaries, your committee regard such action as a departure from the great principles on which the Board was organized, and by which they think its proceedings should always be governed.

"'And now, what more shall we say? Should we undertake to do justice to our own views on all the particular subjects hinted at in these memorials, it would occupy more time than can be afforded on this occasion, and would naturally lead on to discussions in which this Board cannot engage, and which must be left to those who may write and speak on their own individual responsibility.

"'It should be kept in mind, that the work of this Board has not been done in a corner. Its proceedings are open to the scrutiny of the public. Any one who will examine the matter will have no need to inquire of us what are our principles and our modes of action. They are written in our various reports and other printed documents. They are exhibited in noonday light in the extensive fields we occupy, and in the success with which the God of missions has mercifully crowned our feeble efforts.

"'The difficulties which we have found it necessary to encounter have been innumerable, and our hearts have many a time been ready to yield to discouragement. Out of the depths we have often cried unto the Lord; and he hath heard our voice, and hath called forth songs of thanksgiving and praise.

"'And now, feeling ourselves bound for ever to this sacred and momentous cause, and being resolved, in the best use of the powers which God has given us, and with the coöperation of his people and the help of his grace, to go straight forward in our work, we affectionately invite all who love the cause of missions, and who can conscientiously assist us with their prayers and their charities, to join with us in our undertaking, and to share with us in our labors, our trials and our pleasures. But if any are so dissatisfied with our principles or our proceedings, that they deem it their duty to promote the spread of the Gospel through some other channel, we shall indeed be sorry to be deprived of the help they might afford us; but we do not wish to curtail their liberty."'

In this Report, Dr. Woods repeats his statement of the
previous year, that " the Board of Commissioners for Foreign
Missions can sustain no relation to slavery which implies approbation of the system." This disclaimer is not only worth-
less and empty, an offering of barren words when deeds were
needed, but it tries to turn the reader's attention from the
real point at issue. Nobody had charged the Board with
approving slavery! The charge was that they had pursued
such a course of policy, partly by action and partly by silence
and inaction, as to *give countenance and support* to that
wickedness!

But it is the paragraph following this, the one commenc-
ing, "It is alleged," &c., (p. 24,) that contains the chief specimen of dishonest evasion and misrepresentation in this
Report. After referring to the numerous instances presented
by the remonstrants in which the Board *had* condemned
" other specific evils," (thus at once disproving the statement
and annihilating the argument which Dr. Woods had presented in 1841,) the Report takes new ground, as follows : —

" These evils, existing in the countries where the missions are
operating, and standing directly in the way of the Board's accomplishing its object, were of course legitimate and proper subjects for
its animadversion. If it has at any time gone further than this, and
expressed opinions relative to immoralities or evils of any kind,
prevailing in this country, and not directly counteracting the labors
of the missionaries, your Committee regard such action as a departure from the great principles on which the Board was organized,
and by which they think its proceedings should always be governed."

Both sentences in this paragraph show the guilt of the
Board, *if they are examined in connection with its action*,
though, without such examination, the careless and confiding
reader might take them to substantiate Dr. Woods's argument.

If those evils which exist in the countries where the missions are operating, and which stand directly in the way of
the Board's accomplishing its object, are "*of course* legitimate and proper subjects for its animadversion," then the
Board are verily guilty in not having spoken of slavery in
the Sandwich Islands as an obstacle to the Christianization of
that people, and in having suppressed and concealed the testimony of their missionaries there to that effect. If they will

2

bring out from their archives the letter-sheet of resolutions printed on the Sandwich Islands mission press, in 1837,* (immediately after which they voted that the mission presses should no longer† be used to print matter for distribution in the United States,) I doubt not it will be found to repeat the statement made in Mr. Gulick's letter (ante, p. 6,) that the situation of the mass of the Sandwich Islands people keeps the subject of slavery almost constantly before the eyes of the missionaries, and that the condition of the laboring class there *is* that of slavery, though in a milder form than the slavery of our Southern States. Since the missionaries wrote this statement to the editor of an anti-slavery newspaper at that time, no doubt they also wrote it to the Board, hoping that it might receive the much-needed circulation in their Annual Report. But the Prudential Committee not only suppressed the letter-sheet of anti-slavery resolutions, and such further remonstrance upon that subject as the letters and journals of individual missionaries contained, but avoided all spontaneous mention of slavery as a hindrance, in that and the following years, even when, in 1838, they made an express enumeration of "Hindrances to the Work"—p. 117.

Thus the very statement made by Dr. Woods in defence of the Board clearly proves the Board to have been in the wrong.

But, in the second of the two sentences above quoted from this Report, it is implied that the slavery of *this* country, however appropriately regarded as an evil or an immorality, is *not* one "directly counteracting the labors of the missionaries." Let us look a moment at this point.

The following extracts, taken from a subsequent report of a Committee of which Dr. Woods was again chairman, (in 1845,) prove these three things:

---

* In August, 1857, I requested of the senior Secretary permission to see this document, but my request was not granted.

† *Before the Sandwich Islands mission press was used to oppose slavery*, on page 95 of the Annual Report for 1827, is an account of "a circular letter, printed at the mission press, dated Oct. 3d, 1826, and signed by eight missionaries," representing all the stations of that same mission, announcing "to the world" what efforts had been made there against drunkenness, gambling, and other vices, as well as the success of the technical preaching of the Gospel. The prohibition above quoted seems to have been designed solely to stop the mention of slavery, and the annoyance which this would cause to the slaveholding corporate and honorary members of the Board.

1st. That slavery was at the very time in question (1842) existing in two mission stations of the Board within the territory of the United States, namely, in the Cherokee and Choctaw nations, as well as in "all the adjacent white communities."

2d. That the missionaries at these stations not only countenanced slaveholding, but authenticated and honored it by admitting slaveholders to their churches as Christians, indiscriminately with others.

3d. That, when they were compelled by importunate and repeated remonstrances to speak on the subject, both the Committee and the Board (which "unanimously adopted" their Report, see p. 63 of Ann. Rep. for 1845) admitted "the wrongfulness and evil tendencies of slaveholding," even while determining to continue their allowance of it. Here are the extracts : —

"Negro slaves appear to have been introduced among those Indians by white men who removed into their country from sixty to eighty years ago, and to have gradually increased in number till the time when the missions of the Board were established among them, in 1817 and 1818. By a census taken of the Cherokees in 1820, there were found to be 583 slaves. The number among the Choctaws was probably smaller, though neither the missionaries nor the Committee have the means of ascertaining it definitely. Since that time, though the Committee are not aware that there has been any census, the number is believed to have been somewhat increased, almost exclusively, however, by births, as there have been few purchases and little trade of any sort in slaves. The number now owned by both tribes may probably be not far from 2,000 ; while the number of Indians in both is probably about 38,000. These slaves are almost exclusively in the hands of white men or their descendants of mixed blood, very few being possessed by full Indians."— p. 58. * * * * * *

"But slavery had been introduced and was existing there, and in all the adjacent white communities, when the missionaries of the Board entered on their labors among these tribes. They were strangers; no interest was felt in their work as missionaries. They preached the Gospel to all whom they found willing to hear them, whatever their complexion or condition. To the slaves and their masters, both generally understanding the English language, they had, at first, more ready access than to the full Indians; and hence from among these, when the Spirit of God gave effect to the truth, some of the earliest, most intelligent and most stable converts were found, such as the Browns, the Lowreys, the Saunderses, and the Folsoms."— *Ib.*

* * * * · * *

"Strongly as your Committee are convinced of the wrongfulness and evil tendencies of slaveholding, and ardently as they desire its speedy and universal termination, still they cannot think that, in all cases, it involves individual guilt, in such a manner, that every person implicated in it can, on scriptural grounds, be excluded from Christian fellowship."—p. 59.

Thus, by the subsequent admission of the same Dr. Woods, fortified by the *unanimous adoption* of the Board, that is proved to be true which the Board are refusing openly and formally to state, namely, *the injurious influence of American slavery upon their missions.*

Since the Report of Dr. Woods on the Memorials on Slavery presented in 1842 represents that compliance with the prayer of the petitioners would be a turning aside from the " *one great object* " for which the Board was incorporated, namely, "propagating the Gospel in heathen lands," (p. 45,) it may be well to quote some passages from a document further on in the same Annual Report, which provides for just such a turning aside from the " one great object " in matters *other* than slavery, as is here refused on the subject of slavery, and refused *because* it is a turning aside.

These extracts, from a document introduced by Rev. David Greene, one of the Secretaries, entitled—" THE PROMOTION OF INTELLECTUAL CULTIVATION AND THE ARTS OF CIVILIZED LIFE IN CONNECTION WITH CHRISTIAN MISSIONS "—are as follows: —

"The course which a missionary adopts in prosecuting his work must be decided very much by the view which he takes of the great object to be accomplished. If he aims exclusively at being the instrument of immediately converting as many souls as possible to the Christian faith, he will devote himself wholly to what is more strictly termed *preaching the Gospel;* while, if his object is to have the Christian system embraced most intelligently by a people, most fully developed, and most permanently established, he may not confine himself so exclusively to that one kind of labor. Doubtless, both these objects ought to be embraced in the plans of the intelligent missionary. He should take into view both the immediate and the ultimate results of his labors—those which are to be seen principally in the individuals whom he may directly instruct, and those which are to affect the community for which he labors for coming ages."—pp. 68, 69.   *   *   *   *   *   *   *

"3. The missionary may labor to reform what in the habits and condition of a people tends to immorality. Of nearly all the domestic habits of unevangelized nations, it may be said that they are adapted to a corrupt state of morals, and nearly inconsistent with any other."—p. 72.

"4. Those measures which promote the purity and permanent influence of Christianity in a nation, fall within the sphere of a missionary's labors. Converts from paganism are, from the nature of the case, and must for some time continue to be, in a state of pupilage. Their knowledge, even of the Christian doctrines and duties, is very limited and imperfect; and they are so unaccustomed to independent, conscientious moral action, and so incompetent to found and conduct institutions for their own intellectual improvement, that, notwithstanding all the efforts which can be made in their behalf, they must remain, for no short time, morally, in their minority. Still, the aim and effort should be to teach them, as soon as practicable, to bear these responsibilities. The missionary's work is not finished till this point shall be attained." — p. 73.

The document containing these recommendations by a Secretary of the Board was referred to a Committee, who reported that they "heartily concur" in the sentiments it contains, and who "recommend that it be published and circulated under the direction of the Prudential Committee." (p. 75.) But these very considerations demand what the Board refused to give, direct and constant attention to the subject of slavery.

We now come to the Annual Report for 1843. All it contains in regard to slavery is the following brief abstract of a Memorial, and brief Report on it:—

"MEMORIAL ON SLAVERY. Mr. Greene read a memorial from a Committee of the Second Evangelical Congregational Church in Cambridgeport, Mass., requesting the Board to pass resolutions to the following effect: '1. That they will not send agents to solicit funds of slaveholders, nor of churches having slaveholding members. 2. That they will not send slaveholders as missionaries to the heathen, nor employ them as agents or secretaries at home.'

"This memorial was referred to Chancellor Walworth, Dr. Hawes, Rev. David Greene, William Page, Esq., Dr. Hay, Dr. Abeel, and Hon. William Darling. This Committee subsequently made a Report, which was concurred in by the Board, and is as follows:—

"'That they see no reason to depart from the principles sanctioned and adopted by this Board at its two last annual meetings, and which were fully made known to the Christian public through its published proceedings. In the language of the reports of the former Committees on this subject, while we declare, that the Board of Commissioners for Foreign Missions can sustain no relation to slavery which implies approbation of the system, and, as a Board, can have no connection or sympathy with it, we distinctly avow our determination to adhere to the sole purpose for which this Board was organized, the propagation of the Gospel in heathen lands by supporting missionaries and diffusing a knowledge of the Scriptures ; and that we cannot allow ourselves to be turned aside from this most sacred trust by mixing it up with any other concerns ; nor does it belong to us to question the motives of those who think proper to contribute of their substance to aid the operations of the Board in fulfilling the command of our divine Master to preach the Gospel to every creature.

"'In relation to slaveholding agents and missionaries, the Committee are not aware that any are in the employ of the Board.'"—p. 67.

Here the answer to the prayer of the memorialists is the same talk about "turning aside" which had been shown to be disingenuous, inapplicable, and nugatory, by their own admissions (above quoted) in the previous year.

Yet, in this very Annual Report, (in a place where it can be mentioned without interference with slavery in the United States,) the slave trade is spoken of as an "obstacle" to missionary labor. This occurs in the statement respecting the Gaboon mission in West Africa, as follows:—

"Indeed, it seems to be a part of God's wise plan, that his people, in spreading the Gospel over the world, shall not go on without obstacles of some kind, to try their faith and zeal, and compel them to trust his power and grace. Here they are likely to be found in the form of the slave trade, intemperance, and popery. On the south of the Gaboon river is a large Spanish slave factory, of which Mr. Wilson has given an appalling account; and nearly all the towns on that side are engaged in this horrible and suicidal traffic. In conducting it, an indispensable agent is intoxicating liquors. When one of the missionaries lately visited George's town, six slaves had just been sent from that place to the Spanish factory, and six hogsheads of rum received in return, (for that, in African barter, is about the worth of a slave,) and this the people were consuming as common property."—pp. 87, 88.

In the Annual Report for 1844, the Prudential Committee inform us that three memorials on slavery were presented at the Annual Meeting in that year. One of them is quote entire, and all are referred to a Committee of which I Woods is again chairman. The proceedings and the Report are as follows:—

"MEMORIALS ON SLAVERY. Three memorials on the subject of slavery were presented; having been first read, they were referred to Dr. Woods, Dr. Tyler, Chancellor Walworth, Hon. T. W. Williams, Dr. Stowe, Rev. S. L. Pomroy, Rev. D. Sandford, Dr. Tappan, Rev. J. W. M'Lane, and Rev. D. Greene. One of these memorials is in the following language:—

"'Whereas, the Gospel of Jesus Christ recognizes the common brotherhood of all men, and justly regards oppression not only as a grievous wrong to a fellow-man, but as a heinous sin against God; and whereas, the providence of God, in the severe judgments which he has brought upon men and nations, most clearly corroborates his word, and proves that he holds this sin in utter abhorrence ; and whereas, American slavery is a system of oppression, so unjust and so grievous that we have reason to "tremble when we reflect that God is just, and that his justice will not sleep for ever," — a system whose unhappy subjects are as ignorant and degraded as many heathen in foreign lands ; and whereas, Christianity is reproached, and the Gospel hindered, both at home and abroad, because many Christians and Christian institutions appear, by their action or their silence, to approve or tolerate this iniquity without rebuke ; and whereas, your memorialists are informed that slavery is actually tolerated in the churches under the patronage of the Board among the Choctaws and other Indian tribes, by the admission of slaveholding members, and has most evidently interposed an obstacle to the missionary cause ; and whereas, for these and other reasons, many liberal and devoted Christians have withheld their contributions from the Board, and many more have given with great reluctance, and, without a redress of grievances, the funds of the Board will be seriously diminished, or a large increase prevented :

"'We respectfully ask, in view of these facts, that the Board would take this subject into serious and prayerful consideration; that they would declare to the world that the "sole object" of the Board is to carry the whole Gospel to the heathen and benighted of this and other lands, to deliver them not only from the superstition of idolatry, but from the degradation and cruelty of oppression. We ask the Board earnestly to entreat all the missionaries and agents under its patronage to bear a decided testimony against the sin of oppression, wherever and in whatever form it exists ; and most especially to declare, in the name of the Board, of the churches represented by it, and of Jesus Christ whom they preach, that American slavery is a sin against God, and that its existence in a Christian land is in no wise chargeable to the Christian religion which they are commissioned to preach, but is grossly at variance with all its holy doctrines and precepts. And we further pray, that the Board would immediately take measures to ascertain to what extent slavery or oppression exists in the churches under its patronage, and especially among the Choctaws and other Indian tribes ; and take such action at this meeting as shall speedily remove the evil, or exonerate them and their missionaries from all the responsibility and guilt of its continuance or toleration. We also ask that this memorial, and the action upon it, be communicated to all the missionaries and agents of the Board, and to the public generally through the *Missionary Herald;* all which is the prayer of your memorialists, the undersigned, members or patrons of the Board.

" J. C. Lovejoy, Jacob Ide, David Sandford, M. M. Fisher, Charles Packard, Geo. W. Hunt, William N. Haskell, Nathaniel Clark, Samuel Allen, Elijah Stoddard, George Trask, J. C. Webster, R. M. Chipman, M. Blake, William Phipps, Horace D. Walker, C. Simmons, Peter Adams, Israel Trask."

" The above-named Committee made a Report, which was adopted by the Board, and is as follows : —

"'The petitions referred to the Committee are three, and two of them are without date. They have all been received since the commencement of the meeting in this place. One of them is from members of the Trinitarian church in Fitchburg, signed by Rev. Philo C. Pettibone and fifty-two others, making in the whole twenty-four males and twenty-nine females. The next is from ten members of John-street Church, Lowell. The third is from J. C. Lovejoy, Jacob Ide, and ten other highly respectable ministers of the Gospel in this State, and seven laymen. In the first and second petitions above mentioned, this Board are requested and urged to take measures to prevent receiving into their treasury any moneys contributed, in one way or another, by slaveholders, or any of the avails of slave labor. In the one from Fitchburg, we are desired also to pass resolutions declaring that "American slavery is a sin against God and man, and ought to be immediately abolished, and that we will not employ missionaries or agents who are slaveholders."

"'In regard to the above request as to missionaries and agents, this Committee are not able to find what reason the petitioners can have for making such a request, as it is not known that there is at present any complaint, or any ground of complaint, against the doings of the Board in respect to this subject, inasmuch as they have no missionaries or agents who are slaveholders. We did suppose that the particular and full information which has been given of late on this subject, is, and must be, satisfactory to the friends of the cause in which we are engaged.

"'As to the other subjects touched upon in these two petitions, that is, the declaration we are requested to make as to slavery, and the measures we are requested to adopt, the Committee are unable to recommend any thing more, and they think the Board would not be inclined to do any thing more than to refer the petitioners to the reports which have been made and unanimously accepted on the same subjects at previous meetings. In those reports, the Board have set forth, as plainly as possible, the views they entertain on these subjects, and the principles which have governed their proceedings. They have stated, what is never to be forgotten, that the Board was established and incorporated for the express purpose of propagating the Gospel in heathen lands, by supporting missionaries and diffusing a knowledge of the Scriptures; that the Board have confined themselves to *this one great object*, and that a regard to our sacred trust requires us to pursue the object with undivided zeal, and not to turn aside from it, or mix any other concerns with it. And we still think that the Lord of missions and the Savior of the world will approve of this deliberate purpose of ours and this course of action, and would frown upon us if we should depart from it. And we have the comfort to believe, also, that this is the only purpose and course of action which will give permanent satisfaction to the Christian community, who are enlisted in the cause of missions; being fully persuaded that any essential departure from this plan of operation would tend to defeat the great end we are pursuing, the conversion of the heathen.

"'As to the moneys contributed by slaveholders, it is still our opinion that, considering the character of the Board and the nature of its objects, it may fairly be presumed that the funds contributed to our treasury are obtained in a proper manner and contributed from right motives; and that it is very manifest that we cannot properly examine into the motives of those who sustain our operations; and that an attempt to do this would be marked with absurdity, and would plunge us into difficulties from which we could not be easily extricated.

"'It will not, we trust, be overlooked that, in reply to previous petitions, the Board has repeatedly and very frankly declared, that *they can sustain no relation to slavery which implies approbation of the system, and, as a Board, can have no connection or sympathy with it :* — "plainly intimating that we consider it one of the obvious evils which exist in the community, but the removal of which, though we regard it as an object of fervent desire and prayer, does not fall within our province as a missionary Board." We know not how any man, who maturely considers the subject, can desire more than this. And it is quite certain, that without a change of views, the Board can do nothing beyond this.

"'The Prudential Committee, the Secretaries, and the members of this Board, are manifestly enlisted in one of the greatest, most benevolent, and most successful enterprises ever undertaken by man. We glory in the cross of Christ. We glory in that work of the salvation of men, and the approaching conversion of the world, which depends upon that cross, and results from it. We most heartily invite Christians to unite with us, and shall thank and honor all who help to sustain this pious undertaking, and who contribute of their property and their prayers to aid this blessed cause. With any of our brethren who are dissatisfied with our doings, we can have no controversy or contention. We cannot turn aside from our arduous work for the purpose of strife. We have no time for strife, and our Lord forbids us to engage in strife. If any of our dear brethren soberly think that they can do the will of God, and advance his cause in some other way better than by joining their efforts with ours, we will be so far from complaining of them for following their own convictions, that we will pray God to guide them by wisdom from above, and will rejoice in all they do to spread the Gospel of Christ.

"'The last petition above mentioned refers to a new subject, that is, the existence of slavery among some of our missionary churches, particularly among the Choctaws and other Indian tribes, and requests that the Board would take measures to ascertain the facts in the case. In conformity with this request, the Committee have made use of all the means in their power, and some of them of special importance, in order to ascertain these facts. And so far as they are at present informed, they see no reason to charge the missionaries among the Choctaws, or any where else, with either a violation or neglect of duty. But it has been impossible in so short a time to obtain that exact and complete information on the subject which is indispensably necessary to a full and satisfactory report. The Committee must, therefore, for the reason suggested, ask the Board to receive what is now offered, as their report in part on the above mentioned memorials, and request that they may have time to make a thorough inquiry into the state of the churches in our various missionary stations in regard to slavery, and, with the help of the information thus obtained, to prepare a report on this part of the subject committed to them, to be presented to the Board at their next annual meeting. And may the Lord grant that on this, and on every subject relating to the high and holy work of the world's salvation, all who love the name of Jesus may be of the same mind and judgment, and love one another with pure hearts fervently.'" — pp. 66–69.

In this same Annual Report for 1844 is the following incidental information, showing (in a place not affecting slavery in the United States!) that the Prudential Committee recognize the prohibition of slavery, and of distinctions founded upon color, by the governments under which their operations are carried on, as auspicious and highly satisfactory in view of their missionary work:—

"The churches acting through the Board have seen affliction and disappointment in their South African mission, until they generally acquiesced in the idea of its discontinuance. A resolution to that effect was accordingly adopted by the Committee last year, and ap-

2 *

proved by the Board, and the missionaries were instructed accordingly."—p. 81.   *   *   *   *   *   *

"The letter instructing our brethren to close the concerns of the mission was dated Aug. 31, 1848. Previous to this, as it now appears, the native settlements about Umlazi and Umgeni had not only received great accessions of emigrants from the Zulu country, but new light was thrown on the prospects of the native settlers in that region, and their permanent relations to the colony began to assume an auspicious bearing. In creating a new colony at Natal, it was officially announced that no law should be allowed recognizing a distinction founded upon color; that no attack should be made upon any people without the colony by persons not acting under the direction of the colonial government; and that slavery should not be tolerated in any form."—pp. 81, 82.   *   *   *

"This, of course, is a different state of things from that which was known to the Committee and the Board at the last annual meeting, or which they then saw any good reason for anticipating."—pp. 82, 83.   *   *   *   *   *   *   *

"In view of such facts and considerations, the Committee could not hesitate to authorize the missionaries to resume their labors at Natal."- p. 84.

Again, in the same Annual Report for 1844, two pages further on, speaking of the Gaboon nation (again in a place where *American* slavery is not in question!) the Prudential Committee venture to characterize slavery as *a vice*, thus:—

"They are an amiable people; apart from those vices which belong to them as heathen, such as slavery, polygamy, superstition and intemperance."

Slavery among the vices which belong to the Gaboon nation *as heathen!*

Let it be remembered, that at this very time, slaveholders were sitting with the Board as Corporate Members and as Honorary Members, that the missionaries of the Board among the Cherokees and Choctaws were encouraging and protecting slavery by taking slaveholders into their churches, and that Dr. Woods and his Committee were trying to stave off inquiries and remonstrances in opposition to this wickedness!

The Prudential Committee name intemperance and slavery as vices belonging to the Gaboon people as heathen. Intemperance and slavery were also among the vices of the Cherokees. But while their slavery was tolerated and protected by the missionaries, their intemperance was opposed by preaching, and printing, and individual remonstrance, and associated action, in the following vigorous manner :—

"In relation to the cause of temperance, also, it may be proper to remark, that we scarcely know a member of any of our churches in good standing, who does not belong to the Temperance Society. We believe the same is true of professors of religion of other denominations; and that it is now generally considered among the Cherokee people, that the use of intoxicating drinks or the traffic in them is inconsistent with the Christian profession."—p. 219.

This is what the Cherokee missionaries say. On the same page, the Prudential Committee say—

"In addition to what is said above relative to temperance, Mr. Worcester mentions in a letter more recently received, that, during the past year, as near as can be ascertained, about 700 persons have joined the Cherokee Temperance Society, pledging themselves to entire abstinence from all intoxicating drinks. The Society now embraces about 2,300 persons; 300 or 400 of whom are white and black people, and the remainder Cherokees. Temperance is believed to be decidedly advancing in the Cherokee community."—pp. 219, 220.

Among the printing executed this year at Park Hill station, in the Cherokee mission, is—"Evils of Intoxicating Drinks," 2d edition; a tract of 24 pages, of which 5,000 copies were printed.

Such is the difference which the Cherokee missionaries chose to make, and which the Prudential Committee allowed to be made, between the treatment of intemperance and slavery in the Cherokee mission !

There is every reason to think that, had the missionaries chosen to make the attempt, as much ground might have been gained among these Indians against slavery as against intemperance. In the Annual Report for 1824, (p. 70,) it is said of the Cherokee mission —

"The converts generally exhibit a tenderness of conscience, a docility, and a desire for further instruction, which are in the highest degree encouraging."

As an instance of this, it is mentioned that a man came nineteen miles to know when the next Sabbath would arrive, that he and his neighbors might thenceforth regularly observe it.

Neither did the avoidance, by these missionaries, of direct

appeal to their converts against slaveholding, proceed from uncertainty about the proper method of conducting reformatory operations, either on their part, or on the part of the Prudential Committee. For this very Report, under the head "General remarks on the Choctaw mission"—speaking of the fact that intemperate drinking, though diminishing in some places, was increasing in others—said:

"The only way to gain a complete victory over this vice is to exclude spirits altogether. The people cannot receive this enemy into their houses without being overcome by it."—p. 87.

To the same effect we find, in a statement of the Prudential Committee in the Annual Report for 1832—respecting the Choctaws just after their removal to their new territory—

"A Sabbath School and Temperance Society have been organized, and are exerting a good influence.

"A church has been organized, embracing fifty-seven members, all but one of whom were members of churches in the old nation, and all agree to abstain entirely from the use of intoxicating liquors."—p. 109.

In the same Report, (Appendix, p. 162,) among "Instructions of the Prudential Committee" to missionaries then about to depart, are the following:—

"Give no countenance to the use of ardent spirits. Use not the poisoned cup yourselves, nor present it to the lip of foreigner or native."

The missionaries among the Cherokees, finding their labors impeded and their success neutralized by intemperance, took these active measures against it. They preached against it, talked against it, printed tracts against it, adopted church rules against it, formed societies against it, and wrote to the Prudential Committee periodical accounts of these labors, and of the success or want of success attending them; which reports the Prudential Committee printed in their monthly "Missionary Herald," and in their Annual Report.

Of another practice prevailing among the Cherokees, (which the Prudential Committee have admitted to be an evil and a vice,) the missionaries say nothing. They neither preach, print, talk, nor form societies against it. They make no reports against it, and the Prudential Committee acquiesce in their silence! They take members stained with its guilt into their churches, and the Prudential Committee allow it! And when the Sandwich Islands missionaries, finding this same evil and vice of slavery an obstruction to *their* missionary work, make representations and remonstrances against a continuance of it in this country which blocks the wheels of their opposition to it abroad, the Prudential Committee refuse to print their reports!

At the Annual Meeting in 1845, a larger number than ever of memorials against slavery were presented. These were referred to the Committee (Dr. Woods chairman) which made but a partial report the preceding year. As the evasive remarks and suggestions of the reports previously made upon memorials of this class did not satisfy or silence the remonstrants, Dr. Woods seems to have thought it necessary to bestow elaborate attention upon the subject, and his report, and the proceedings in regard to it, occupy nine octavo pages of the Annual Report for 1845, as follows:—

" MEMORIALS ON SLAVERY.

" At the meeting of the Board which was held at Worcester in 1844, three memorials relating to the subject of slavery were committed to Dr. Woods, Dr. Tyler, Chancellor Walworth, Hon. T. W. Williams, Dr. Stowe, Rev. S. L. Pomroy, Rev. D. Sandford, Dr. Tappan, Rev. J. W. McLane, and Rev. D. Greene. The Committee made their report in part; but in respect to 'the existence of slavery among some of our missionary churches, particularly among the Choctaws and other Indian tribes'—one of the topics referred to by the memorialists—they asked leave to submit their report at the meeting to be held in Brooklyn in 1845. To this Committee were also referred, during the recent meeting, certain resolutions of the Worcester Central Association, a memorial of the Worcester North Association, certain resolutions of the Chatauque County Foreign Missionary Society, and a memorial of the Somerset and Franklin Associations. The report of the Committee is as follows:—

" 'The Committee to whom, at the last annual meeting of this Board, were referred certain memorials relating to the Board's alleged connection with slavery, having been instructed to seek further information concerning the admission of slaveholders to churches under the care of the missionaries of the Board, have made the inquiries directed, and now ask leave to report.

" 'The Committee do not deem it necessary to discuss the general subject of slavery, as it exists in these United States, or to enlarge on the wickedness of the system, or on the disastrous moral and social influences which slavery exerts upon the less enlightened and less civilized communities where the missionaries of this Board are laboring. On these points, there is probably, among the members of the Board and its friends, little difference of opinion.

"'The Committee propose to confine themselves mainly to a statement of some of the principles which should govern the Board and its missionaries in prosecuting their work so as to secure the highest measure of the divine approbation, and most effectually and speedily to accomplish the great object in view; together with a statement of the principal facts relating to the connection of persons holding slaves with mission churches under the care of the Board.

"'Among the principles which the Committee would present for the consideration of the Board, and which they regard as fundamental, and to be adhered to in planning and conducting every mission undertaken under the authority of the great Redeemer and Head of the Church, are the following:

"'1. In the manner of preaching the Gospel, judging of the evidences of piety in professed converts, gathering churches, administering the ordinances and exercising discipline, there should be a close conformity to the commission given by Christ to his followers, and to the recorded instructions and acts of his inspired apostles. These are found in the New Testament, and are the models and the laws, which, in all important matters, are to govern those who propagate the Gospel and minister to the churches in Christ's name.

"'2. The primary object aimed at in missions should be to bring men to a saving knowledge of Christ by making known to them the way of salvation through his cross. It has regard to individual character, and is an object simple in itself and purely spiritual. The commission given by Christ evidently contemplates the work to be done as one that is to be wrought in individual men, regarded as rational and immortal beings; all of whom, of every grade and condition, having great interests alike, the more important of which lie in another state of existence. To these interests, primarily and mainly, and to that change of individual character and conduct which is indispensable to secure them, the Christian missionary is to direct his labors. If other objects, less spiritual and important, are connected with the enterprise as predominant objects of interest and pursuit, they impair its efficiency and endanger the great result.

"'3. As the ordinances of baptism and the Lord's Supper are obviously designed by Christ to be means of grace for all who give credible evidence of repentance and faith in him, these ordinances cannot scripturally and rightly be denied to professed converts from among the heathen, after they shall have given such evidence.

"'4. The missionaries, acting under the commission of Christ, and with the instructions of the New Testament before them, are themselves, at first, and subsequently, in connection with the churches they have gathered, the rightful and exclusive judges of what constitutes adequate evidence of piety and fitness for church fellowship in professed converts. They alone can be fully acquainted with all the circumstances affecting the development of piety in individuals, and intelligently form an opinion how far they are aiming to conform their character and conduct to the doctrines and precepts of the Bible.

"'5. Both before and after professed converts are received to church fellowship and the ordinances are administered to them, the missionaries should give them such instructions from the Gospel as they believe to be, in their circumstances, best adapted to nurture and develop all the Christian graces, and lead to the practice of all the Christian duties. The indulgence of any known sin and the neglect of any known duty is to be decidedly discountenanced.

"'Such your Committee deem to be the divinely established principles accordin .o which the missionary work among unevangelized nations should be prosecuted; and in this simple manner only, as it seems to them, can the thoughts and feelings of the heathen and other unevangelized communities be so turned towards God and their relations to him, and be brought into such a spiritual relation to the Lord Jesus Christ, as will at length lead to the correction of all the social wrongs and disorders which now, in various forms, so much afflict the benighted and idolatrous portions of our race.

"' Civil and religious liberty, improvement in civilization and the arts of life, and the introduction of the best social institutions, admitted to be indispensable to the highest well-being of a community, are still secondary to the one primary object of securing holiness in the hearts of individuals. Aiming steadily at this is the way for the missionary most surely and speedily to work out the others; and your Committee believe that it is only by regarding these classes of objects in their proper relations, and keeping them in their proper places, and pursuing them in their proper order, that either can be effectually attained and permanently established on the broad field of the world.

"' In respect to the social and moral evils with which missionaries are to come into contact in prosecuting their work among the benighted nations, and in relation to which the foregoing principles are believed by your Committee to apply, it should be borne in mind that they are by no means few, or of limited territorial extent. The evils of slavery will probably be met in some form, in nearly every part of the great missionary field, and the principles adopted must affect the whole scheme for evangelizing the world; and are, therefore, of the utmost importance, and should be most carefully examined and settled. The unnatural state of society in which these evils originate is one of the consequences of human depravity — of that all-absorbing selfishness — that predominance of the lust of the flesh, the lust of the eye, and the pride of life, which are developed in our fallen nature. This state of society is to be rectified by diminishing the power of that terrible principle in which this, as well as all other wickedness and moral disorders, originate. Involuntary servitude is believed to pervade nearly the whole of the African continent, though with widely different degrees of severity. In some form, it exists in many, if not all parts of India. It pervades Siam, and nearly all Mohammedan communities; and it will probably be found, in some of its modifications, in China and Japan.

"' The unrighteousness of the principles on which the whole system is based, and the violation of the natural rights of man, the debasement, wickedness, and misery it involves, and which are in fact witnessed, to a greater or less extent, wherever it exists, must call forth the hearty condemnation of all possessed of Christian feeling and sense of right, and make its entire and speedy removal an object of earnest and prayerful desire to every true friend of God and man. This object, as your Committee believe, can be effected in no other manner than by the prevalence, in these communities, of that regard for justice and human rights and that humane and philanthropic feeling of which Christian knowledge and piety are the only permanent basis.

"'But slavery is not the only social wrong to be met in the progress of the missionary work, and to which the principles which are adopted in prosecuting that work must probably be applied. There are the castes of India, deeply and inveterately inwrought in the very texture of society, causing to the mass of the people hereditary and deep degradation, leading to the most inhuman and contemptuous feeling and conduct in social life, and presenting most formidable barriers to every species of improvement. There are also the unrestrained exactions, made in the form of revenue, or of military or other services, connected with a species of feudalism, prevailing in many unenlightened communities, which are most unrighteous in their character and paralyzing in their influence, and cause unlimited distress to individuals and families. There are also those various forms and degrees of oppression, whether of law or of usage, prevailing under the arbitrary governments which bear sway over the larger part of the earth's surface. So that the principles which we draw from the word of God for our guidance as a missionary society, are not for use among a few pagan tribes merely, but among nearly all the benighted nations of the earth.

"'Is this Board, then, in propagating the Gospel, to be held responsible for directly working out these reorganizations of the social system, without giving Christian truth time to produce its changes in the hearts of individuals and in public sentiment, and without being allowed to make any practical use of those most effective influences which are involved—in respect to all who have grace in their hearts—in the special ordinances of the Gospel? Or, should it be found, as the result of experience, that souls among the heathen are, in fact, regenerated by the Holy Spirit, before they are freed from all participation in these social and moral evils, and that convincing evidence can be given that they are so regenerated,—then may not the master and the slave, the ruler and the subject, giving such evidence of spiritual renovation, be all gathered into the same fold of Christ? And may they not all there and in this manner, under proper teaching, learn the great lesson, (so difficult for partially sanctified men to learn,) that in Christ Jesus there is neither Jew nor Greek, neither bond nor free; but that all are one in him? And may they not, under these influences, have effectually nurtured in them those feelings of brotherly love, and that regard for each other's rights and welfare, in which alone is found the remedy for all such evils? Under such influences, may not the master be prepared to break the bonds of the slave, and the oppressive ruler

led to dispense justice to the subject, and the proud Brahmin fraternally to embrace the man of low caste, and each to do it cheerfully,
because it is humane and right, and because they are all children of
the great household of God? By such influences, mainly, is not
the great moral transformation to be wrought in the master and the
ruler, in the bondman and the oppressed, all-important to both, and
the only sure guaranty for permanent improvement in the social
character and condition of either?

"'In proceeding on these principles, the missions under the care
of this Board, and the churches gathered by them, are no otherwise
connected with slavery, than they are with every other evidence and
result of imperfect moral renovation in their converts and church
members; and they no more really give their sanction to the one, than
they do to all the others. Wherever the Gospel is brought to bear
upon the community where slavery or any other form of oppression
exists, its spirit is decidedly adverse to such a state of things, tending to mitigate the evils of it while it continues, and ultimately, and
in the most desirable manner, wholly to do it away,—not by con-
straint, nor with violence; but on those principles of Christian love
which this Board and its missionaries are seeking to implant in
every bosom, and to invest with all possible power to govern the
hearts and the conduct of men.

"'Such is the view which your Committee take of the missionary
work, and such are the principles which, it seems to them, should be
adhered to in prosecuting it. How far ecclesiastical bodies in this
country may properly instruct foreign missionaries connected with
them, on these subjects, it is not for this Committee to decide. It is
obvious, however, that the points on which this Board, after having
selected missionaries in whose character and qualifications they confide, should insist, are such as are embraced in the principles already
dwelt upon.

"'These principles, your Committee believe, do not interfere with
that liberty which Christ designed his ministers should possess, or
that responsibility with which he invests them when he sends them
forth to preach his Gospel in heathen lands. If they essentially
depart from these principles, and persevere in so doing, they should
be recalled as incompetent or unfaithful to their trust. How far
holding slaves, or any thing else, involving what is morally wrong,
and which still clings to the heathen convert, affects the evidence
that a principle of grace has been implanted in his heart, the missionary, in view of his commission, the instructions of the New
Testament, and all the circumstances of the case, as they are present before him, must, in connection with his church, and under a
solemn sense of responsibility to Christ, form his judgment, and on
that judgment he must act. Surely, no other persons are in circumstances so favorable as he for deciding and acting correctly. Such
freedom and such responsibility in the missionary, your Committee
believe, cannot be materially abridged, without the most disastrous
consequences to the missionary's own happiness and efficiency, and
to the welfare of the heathen.

"'Having gone so fully into an exposition of the principles on
which, in their opinion, the New Testament requires missionaries to

proceed in preaching the Gospel and administering the Christian ordinances, the Committee would now spread before the Board the proceedings of the missionaries, so far as connected with the subject under consideration.

"'The Committee believe that no established system of involuntary servitude prevails among any tribe of North American Indians, where the missionaries of this Board are laboring, except the Cherokees and Choctaws; nor have they been able to learn that any of the missionaries of the Board, laboring in foreign lands, have been called to act on the question of receiving those who hold slaves to their churches. The following statements will, therefore, relate to the Cherokee and Choctaw missions. From these, full communications have been received in reply to inquiries addressed to the several missionaries.

"'Negro slaves appear to have been introduced among those Indians by white men who removed into their country from sixty to eighty years ago, and to have gradually increased in number till the time when the missions of the Board were established among them, in 1817 and 1818. By a census taken of the Cherokees in 1820, there were found to be 583 slaves. The number among the Choctaws was probably smaller, though neither the missionaries nor the Committee have the means of ascertaining it definitely. Since that time, though the Committee are not aware that there has been any census, the number is believed to have been somewhat increased, almost exclusively, however, by births, as there have been few purchases and little trade of any sort in slaves. The number now owned by both tribes may probably be not far from 2,000; while the number of Indians in both is probably about 38,000. These slaves are almost exclusively in the hands of white men or their descendants of mixed blood, very few being possessed by full Indians.

"'That slavery should exist at all in these tribes, who have suffered so severely from the violation of their own rights by their white neighbors, is deeply to be regretted; and all should earnestly pray, that as social improvement and Christian knowledge are rapidly advancing among them, they may speedily and nobly exemplify the spirit of true philanthropy, as well as the Gospel law of love, by showing that they duly appreciate the rights and welfare of the whole race of man.

"'But slavery had been introduced and was existing there, and in all the adjacent white communities, when the missionaries of the Board entered on their labors among these tribes. They were strangers; no interest was felt in their work as missionaries. They preached the Gospel to all whom they found willing to hear them, whatever their complexion or condition. To the slaves and their masters, both generally understanding the English language, they had, at first, more ready access, than to the full Indians; and hence from among these, when the Spirit of God gave effect to the truth, some of the earliest, most intelligent, and most stable converts were found, such as the Browns, the Lowreys, the Saunderses, and the Folsoms.

"'Relative to the principles on which professed converts were to be received to the churches, all the missionaries of the Board among

the Cherokees and Choctaws seem to have been perfectly unanimous. "Both masters and slaves," says Mr. Butrick, "I received
on the same principle, viz., on the ground of their faith in the Lord
Jesus Christ." Mr. Worcester says, "The general principle on
which I have voted for the reception of members is, that all are to
be received who desire it, and who give evidence of a change of
heart." Mr. Wright says, "When any, whether masters or servants, have given evidence of a saving change of heart, of repentance and faith in the Lord Jesus Christ, they have been received."
Substantially the same is the language of all the missionaries. On
this principle, of receiving to their churches all those, and only
those, who gave satisfactory evidence of repentance and faith in the
Lord Jesus Christ, they all appear to have proceeded.

"'Owing to the changes from one church to another which have
occurred in both these missions, the whole number of slaveholders
received cannot here be stated precisely.

"'The whole number of the Cherokee tribe is probably about
18,000, and the number of slaves owned by them is probably about
1,000. The whole number of members connected with our churches
in this tribe is 240; of whom 15 hold slaves, 21 are themselves
slaves, and four are free negroes.

"'The whole population of the Choctaw tribe, including the
Chickasaws, is about 20,000. The whole number connected with
our churches there is 603; of whom 20 hold slaves, 131 are themselves slaves, and 7 are free negroes. It may also be stated that our
brethren of the Moravian, Baptist and Methodist denominations
have churches in both these tribes, to which many, both of Indian
and African descent, both masters and slaves, have been received;
and of the latter, especially, a much larger proportion have been
gathered into their churches, than into those connected with our
missions. Of the estimated number of slaves in these tribes, it
may, however, be stated, that about one in 18 are connected with the
churches under the care of our missions; while of the Indians and
other classes of persons, less than one in 50 are embraced in the
same churches; showing that the slaves have not, compared with
the Indians, been by any means neglected.

"'In regard to the kind and amount of instruction given by the
missionaries in relation to slavery, and the duties of masters and
slaves, the missionaries seem substantially to agree. Mr. Byington
says, "We give such instructions to masters and servants as are
contained in the epistles, and yet not in a way to give the subject
a peculiar prominence. For then it would seem to be personal, as
there are usually but one or two slaveholders at our meetings. In
private, we converse about all the evils and dangers of slavery."
Of a similar tenor are the remarks of Mr. Wright. "The instructions, public and private, direct and indirect, have been such as are
found in the Bible. As a spiritual watchman, I have wished to
comply with that direction in Ezek. 3 : 17, 'Therefore, hear the word
from my mouth, and give them warning from me.'"

"'In opinion and practice on this subject, there will undoubtedly
be some diversity among those, in different circumstances, who entertain the same views as to the unrighteousness of the system of

slavery itself, and the desirableness of having it abolished. The missionaries of this Board among the Cherokees and Choctaws, and, so far as the Committee are informed, all missionaries, of every denomination, laboring in similar circumstances, among those Indians and in all other places, substantially agree in the views and practice presented in the foregoing extracts.

"'Strongly as your Committee are convinced of the wrongfulness and evil tendencies of slaveholding, and ardently as they desire its speedy and universal termination, still, they cannot think that, in all cases, it involves individual guilt, in such a manner, that every person implicated in it can, on scriptural grounds, be excluded from Christian fellowship. In the language of Dr. Chalmers, when treating on this point in a recent letter, the Committee would say, "Distinction ought to be made between the character of a *system*, and the character of the persons whom circumstances have implicated therewith; nor would it always be just, if all the recoil and horror wherewith the former is contemplated, were visited in the form of condemnation and moral indignancy upon the latter." Dr. Chalmers proceeds to apply this distinction to the subject now under consideration, in the following manner, in which sentiments, substantially, Drs. Candlish and Cunningham, with the whole General Assembly of the Free Church of Scotland, unanimously concur.* Slavery, says he, we hold to be a system chargeable with atrocities and evils often the most hideous and appalling which have either afflicted or deformed our species; yet we must not therefore say of every man born within its territory, who has grown up familiar with its sickening spectacles, and not only by his habits been inured to its transactions and sights, but who by inheritance is himself the owner of slaves, that, unless he make the resolute sacrifice and renounce his property in slaves, he is, therefore, not a Christian, and should be treated as an outcast from all the distinctions and privileges of Christian society.

* The language of the report, presented by Dr. Candlish, chairman of the Committee to whom the subject was referred, and which report the paper containing it says was unanimously adopted by the General Assembly, is as follows :

"Without being prepared to adopt the principle that, in the circumstances in which they are placed, the churches in America ought to consider slaveholding *per se* an insuperable barrier in the way of enjoying Christian privileges, or an offence to be visited with excommunication, all must agree in holding, that whatever rights the civil law of the land may give a master over his slaves, as *chattels personal*, it cannot but be sin of the deepest dye in him to regard and treat them as such : and whosoever commits that sin in any sense, or deals otherwise with his slaves than as a Christian man ought to deal with his fellow-man, whatever power the law may give him over them, ought to be held disqualified for Christian communion. Farther, it must be the opinion of all, that it is the duty of Christians, when they find themselves, unhappily, in the predicament of slaveholders, to aim, as far as it may be practicable, at the manumission of their slaves ; and when that cannot be accomplished, to secure them in the enjoyment of the domestic relations, and of the means of religious training and education."

"'Such, substantially, are the views of your Committee; and the more they study God's method of proceeding in regard to war, slavery, polygamy, and other kindred social wrongs, as it is unfolded in the Bible, the more they are convinced that, in dealing with individuals implicated in these wrongs, of long standing, and intimately interwoven with the relations and movements of the social system, the utmost kindness and forbearance are to be exercised, which are compatible with steady adherence to right principle.

"'The effect of the introduction of Christian knowledge among these Indians, so far as masters and slaves have come under instruction, has, in the opinion of the missionaries, been *highly beneficial*, in respect to the character and conduct of both. The condition of the latter has been, they think, greatly meliorated. So far as the amount of labor required of their slaves, the food, clothing and houses furnished for them, kind social intercourse with them, regard for the domestic and family relations and affections, and for their comfort generally, and opportunities afforded for religious instruction and worship, are concerned, the missionaries think that instances of serious delinquency are very rare among their church members. Should any church member who has servants under him be chargeable with cruelty, injustice, or unkindness towards them; should he neglect what is essential to their present comfort or their eternal welfare; or should he in any manner transgress the particular instructions which the Apostles give concerning the conduct of a master, he would be admonished by the church, and unless he should repent, he would be excommunicated. Such appear, from their communications, to be the views of our missionaries; and such a course they think their churches would sustain.

"'In Christian instruction and care, both of their children and their slaves, the missionaries represent these Indian church members as being generally and often greatly, deficient; but not much more so in respect to the latter, than the former. Converts of the first or even of the second generation, gathered from communities just entering on a course of intellectual, moral and social improvement, will seldom so far rise above their former views and habits, or become so far under the control of the new influences brought to bear upon them, as to compare advantageously, in these respects, with nations on which Christian light has been shining for centuries. Christianity itself, though requiring, and adapted to promote, in those who embrace it, the highest exemplariness in all the duties of life, does not often achieve these great transformations at once. There is to be line upon line — precept upon precept — here a little and there a little — first the blade, then the ear, and after that, the full corn in the ear.

"'Among the Cherokees and Choctaws, the church members are but poorly qualified to give religious instruction; and often the slaves, — owing to their better knowledge of the English language, and consequently their easier intercourse with the missionaries and others, — are more intelligent, on religious subjects, than their masters. Some of the most eminent instances of well-informed, devout and steadfast piety in these mission churches have been among them.

Individuals of them have been much respected, and highly useful in meetings for prayer and exhortation.

"'Some of the slaveholders in these churches have been known to require their slaves to attend meetings and other opportunities for obtaining religious instruction; all are believed to favor their doing so; while none have been known to throw obstacles in their way. Before it was forbidden by law, in 1841, numbers of their slaves were taught to read in Sabbath and some in week-day schools; and such instruction is still, to some extent, given in private. Seven out of fourteen slaves, members of the Fairfield church in the Cherokee country, can read, and one can write. Slaves are sometimes called upon to read the Scriptures and lead in prayer in the families of their masters. One who has been occasionally employed as a helper in the missionary work, highly esteemed for his intelligence and exemplary piety, has been left, by the will of his master, manager of his property and virtually the guardian of his orphan child and heir.

"'The Committee cannot advert to some of the laws enacted by both the Cherokees and Choctaws without pain and regret, especially those which prohibit teaching slaves to read, throw impediments in the way of emancipation, restrict slaves in the possession of property, and embarrass the residence of free negroes among them. Laws of this character, though far less stringent than similar laws existing in most of the adjacent slaveholding States, are disapproved and lamented by the church members generally, it is believed, and by many other intelligent Indians, as unjust and oppressive; and they are not rigorously enforced. For these laws, however, neither the missionaries nor the members of the churches under their care regard themselves as responsible. They could have little or no influence to effect their repeal. Any direct interference of the missionaries would, in their opinion, tend to delay, if not to prevent, rather than to hasten, the accomplishment of the end desired. Changes in these respects are to be brought about by the greater prevalence of humane and Christian feelings throughout these communities; and the agency of the missionary in effecting them is not to be like that which works out a political revolution, but that which results, by the divine blessing, in great moral changes in the hearts of individual men.

"'Slavery was introduced among these Indians, and has been regulated by them, in unhappy imitation of their white neighbors in the adjacent States. Whether the Indians will be the first to abolish it, must depend very much on that power from above which shall attend the prevalence of Christian knowledge among them. This consummation, which justice, humanity, and Christian principle demand should be hastened, none, the Committee believe, more fervently desire and pray for, than do the missionaries themselves; while yet the Committee believe, in agreement with the unanimous opinion of the missionaries, that any express directions from this Board requiring them to adopt a course of proceeding on this subject essentially different from that which they have hitherto pursued, would be fraught with disastrous consequences to the mission, to the Indians, and to the African race among them.

"' That the missionaries among these Indians have been faithful in their work seems evident, not only from their own statements, but also from the fact that the Holy Spirit has most remarkably owned and blessed their labors ; the hopeful converts among the Choctaws being proportionally more numerous than those in any other mission connected with the Board, except that at the Sandwich Islands.

"' In the spirit and with the sentiments of one of our oldest missionaries, who has now spent more than twenty-five years in Christian labors among these Indians — and these are believed to be the sentiments and the spirit of all the missionaries — the Committee would close their report.

"' I have,' he remarks, ' been more in the midst of the slaveholding population, and seen more of the pernicious effects of the system among the Indians, than some of my brethren. Viewed in all its bearings, it is a tremendous evil. Its destructive influence is seen on the morals of the master and the slave. It sweeps away those barriers which every civilized community has erected to protect the purity and chastity of the family relations. We also see its baneful effects on the rising generation. A great proportion of the red people, who own slaves, neglect entirely to train their children to habits of industry, enterprise and economy, so necessary in forming the character of the parent and the citizen. Slavery, so far as it extends, will ever present formidable obstacles to the right training of the rising generation.

"' But what is to be done? Shall we desert our churches and schools, and send back those who compose them to the shades of moral darkness and death, because some among them own slaves? Is not the Choctaw nation a part of that world into which Christ commanded his disciples to go and preach the Gospel to every creature ? Can we expect the half-enlightened, half-civilized Choctaws to proceed on this subject in advance of the white people in the States around them? or in advance of those churches in civilized and enlightened communities where slavery exists ?

"' There can be no prospect of benefitting the slave, in a slave country, without the consent of the owner. The only hope we can have of benefitting either the one or the other, is through the influence of the Gospel; and the Gospel, to be effectual, must be conveyed in the spirit of meekness and love.'

LEONARD WOODS,
BENNET TYLER,
REUBEN H. WALWORTH,
THOMAS W. WILLIAMS,
CALVIN E. STOWE,
BENJAMIN TAPPAN,
DAVID SANFORD,
JAMES W. McLANE,
DAVID GREENE.'

" A motion having been made for the adoption of this report, a deeply interesting discussion ensued, which continued through the afternoon and evening of Wednesday, and the forenoon of Thurs-

day. During the progress of this discussion, several amendments
were proposed, which were finally committed, together with the
report itself, and all the resolutions and memorials relating to the
subject of slavery, presented to the Board during the session, to
Chief Justice Williams, Dr. Bacon, Dr. Stowe, Dr. Tappan, Rev.
David Greene, and Rev. John C. Webster.

"On the following day, this Committee made their report by
recommending the adoption of the report of the previous Committee without amendment. The report last made was accepted, and
the question then arose upon the adoption of the former report.
An amendment having been proposed to this report and rejected,
the question was taken by yeas and nays, when the following persons voted in the affirmative :—

"Theodore Frelinghuysen, Thomas S. Williams, Jeremiah Day, Thomas
DeWitt, Thomas McAuley, John Tappan, Henry Hill, Noah Porter, Rufus
Anderson, David Greene, Charles Stoddard, William J. Armstrong, Levi
Cutter, Nehemiah Adams, Joel Hawes, Elisha Yale, Thomas H. Skinner,
Ambrose White, Samuel Fletcher, David Magie, John W. Ellingwood,
Charles Walker, Pelatiah Perit, Benjamin Tappan, William R. DeWitt,
Isaac Ferris, Thomas W. Williams, William W. Chester, Mark Hopkins,
Reuben H. Walworth, Seth Terry, Daniel Dana, Zedekiah S. Barstow,
William Darling, Edward W. Hooker, David Mack, William Page, Hora-
tio Bardwell, Ebenezer Alden, Albert Barnes, William Jessup, Artemas
Bullard, Anson G. Phelps, Hiram H. Seelye, Aristarchus Champion, Samu-
el H. Cox, Thomas Punderson, Alvan Bond, John W. Adams, William T.
Dwight, Leonard Bacon, Ansel D. Eddy, Joel Parker, J. Marshall Paul,
Benjamin Labaree, Joseph Steele, Henry White, William Adams, Joel H.
Linsley, William Wisner, William Patton, William W. Stone, Edward
Robinson, David L. Ogden, Benjamin C. Taylor, Walter Hubbell, Samuel
H. Perkins, Asa T. Hopkins, Selah B. Treat, Linus Child, Henry B.
Hooker, John Forsyth, Baxter Dickinson, Calvin E. Stowe.

"As no person voted in the negative, the report was unanimously adopted."—pp. 54–63.

The conclusion to which this long report comes is *that
nothing should be done* in regard to the matter in question.
The course of reasoning by which it seeks to establish this
conclusion is worthy of particular attention.

The admissions of Dr. Woods and his Committee respecting the vicious character and pernicious tendencies of slavery
form so striking a contrast with their proposed acquiescence
in its continuance, not only in the nation, *but in the church,*
that I request the reader's especial attention to them.

The Committee say that the slaveholding system is "a tremendous evil ;" that its effects are "pernicious ;" that "its
destructive influence is seen on the morals of the master and
the slave ;" that "it sweeps away those barriers which every

civilized community has erected to protect the purity and chastity of the family relations;" that "we also see its baneful effects on the rising generation;" and that the abolition of it is a consummation "which justice, humanity, and Christian principle demand should be hastened."

Think of the enormity of arguments and exhortations, addressed by a Committee of clergymen to a great missionary association, against interference with a system so bad that, by their own confession, it breaks down the barriers that have been found needful by mere worldly "civilization," to protect the purity and chastity of the family relations!

The Committee confess the extent to which the Cherokee and Choctaw mission churches are implicated in this "baneful," "pernicious" and "destructive" system. The number of slaves held by both tribes is "probably not far from 2,000;" while "fifteen" slaveholders are members of the Cherokee, and "twenty" slaveholders members of the Choctaw, mission churches.

The Committee also admit the systematic deliberation with which the missionaries had chosen to shelter this pernicious and destructive system in the church; they admit that the missionaries are *united* in their policy upon this subject; and they do not shrink from giving, as a specimen of that policy, the astonishing testimony of Mr. Byington, (of the Choctaw mission,) that they "give such instructions to masters and servants as are contained in the epistles, *and yet not in a way to give the subject a peculiar prominence;* FOR THEN IT WOULD SEEM TO BE PERSONAL."

The Committee also admit that there were 500 slaves (more or less) in each of these nations at the time when the missionaries commenced their labors among them. These missionaries might then, if they had chosen, have opposed, from the beginning, this baneful, pernicious and destructive practice. They might have preached against it, and printed tracts against it, and formed associations in opposition to it, *just as they did against intemperance!* They had it perfectly in their power, at the very least, to keep those who practised it out of the church! But they did not choose to do any one of these things! And yet—

The Committee represent, in spite of all these disgraceful

3

facts, that " the missionaries among these Indians have been *faithful in their work* "!

Faithful, in allowing a pernicious and destructive vice to go on without rebuke in the nation, in admitting determined practitioners of it to membership in the church, and in refraining from admonition of these church members on the express ground that "it would seem to be personal"! Are these fair specimens of what the Prudential Committee send out for Christian ministers?

But the evidence assigned by the report in question for considering these pro-slavery missionaries "faithful," is " the hopeful converts among the Choctaws being *proportionally more numerous* than those in any other mission connected with the Board, except that at the Sandwich Islands."

If the standard of church character was so low among the Choctaws that continuance in pernicious and destructive vices did not interfere with membership, if "professors of religion" there might practise without rebuke something that justice, humanity and Christian principle demanded to be abolished, perhaps *this* would more plausibly account for the boasted proportional number of church members!

But another admission of this report is especially worthy of notice, since it directly contradicts ground taken by Dr. Woods, its writer, in his report, made in 1842, against those who complained of the Board's complicity with slavery. He then said —

"These evils, existing in the countries where the missions are operating, and standing directly in the way of the Board's accomplishing its object, were, of course, legitimate and proper subjects for its animadversion. If it has at any time gone further than this, and expressed opinions relative to immoralities or evils of any kind, prevailing in this country, and not directly counteracting the labors of the missionaries, your Committee regard such action as a departure from the great principles on which the Board was organized, and by which they think its proceedings should always be governed." — p. 46, Ann. Rep. of 1842.

The same person now tells us (p. 55, Ann. Rep. of 1845) that — "The evils of slavery will probably be met in some form, *in nearly every part of the great missionary field* "— and that — "Involuntary servitude is believed to pervade nearly the whole of the African continent, though with widely different degrees of severity. In some form, it exists in many, if not all parts of India. It pervades Siam, and nearly all Mohammedan communities; and it will probably be found, in some of its modifications, in China and Japan."

The writer of this report proceeds, from this point, to make the following declaration respecting the moral character of slavery: —

"The unrighteousness of the principles on which the whole system is based, and the violation of the natural rights of man, the debasement, wickedness, and misery it involves, and which are in fact witnessed, to a greater or less extent, wherever it exists, must call forth the hearty condemnation of all possessed of Christian feeling and sense of right, and make its entire and speedy removal an object of earnest and prayerful desire to every true friend of God and man." — p. 56.

Is it not amazing that an acknowledgment like this should be the prelude to a recommendation to leave this "system" unopposed and undisturbed, in the very churches of the American Board? And is it not still more amazing that this recommendation should be made by the same person who formerly sought to silence the protest of the Sandwich Islands missionaries against slavery, on the alleged ground (contradicted by the missionaries themselves) that it was an evil nonexistent in the country where those missions were operating?

But we must not omit to notice that theory of the missionary function, and that asserted distinction between the legitimate province of the missionaries and of their employers, the Board, which Dr. Woods sets forth as the sufficient ground for a continued allowance of slaveholders in the Cherokee and Choctaw mission churches.

The function of the missionaries is described in five specifications, (ante, pp. 38, 39,) assuming that the missionaries are the "*rightful* and *exclusive* judges" of what constitutes fitness for church membership. Whatever force this report has is derived from this statement.

The manifest answer to it is, that when missionaries abuse and desecrate their office so grossly as to use their province of admitting church members in such a manner as to authenticate and uphold a pernicious and destructive system — one that injures the morals of all parties connected with it — one that sweeps away the barriers of purity and chastity in the family relations — one that produces baneful effects upon the

rising generation — one, the abolition of which is demanded
by justice, humanity and Christian principle — then it is the
manifest duty of the employers of those missionaries to discharge them, and to send truly Christian men to supply their
places!

The doctrine of the missionaries, agreed to by Dr. Woods
and his Committee, is that while "a saving change of heart" is
the sufficient reason for admission to church membership, this
" saving change of heart " may exist just as really, and be
manifested just as thoroughly, among persons united in, and
persistently determined to uphold, the system of wickedness
above described, as among any others! If this be so, it will
tend to show — not that slaveholding is right — but that the
influence called " a saving change of heart " is not so good a
thing as it has been assumed to be; that, even if it does, as
alleged, insure salvation in the next world, it does not make
men and women much better in this world!

In this elaborate report by Dr. Woods, as well as in former
reports from the same pen, and in the general *management*
of matters relating to slavery by the Prudential Committee,
many indications are seen, not only of disingenuousness and
sophistry, but of a deliberate attempt to deceive. An instance
of this dishonesty is found in the conclusion of the following
sentence, which the reader may see in its connection, p. 41: —

> "In proceeding on these principles, the missions under the care
> of this Board, and the churches gathered by them, are no otherwise
> connected with slavery, than they are with every other evidence and
> result of imperfect moral renovation in their converts and church
> members; *and they no more really give their sanction to the one than they
> do to all the others.*"

I will take, for example, a single one of the "other" vices
referred to, and, by showing the entirely different treatment
it has received from the missionaries in this same station, and
from the Board, show the utter falseness of this allegation respecting the relation of these parties to slavery.

Suppose it were asserted that the missionaries among the
Cherokees and Choctaws favored *intemperance* among those
nations, receiving habitual drunkards, indiscriminately with
others, as church members; and that the Prudential Committee allowed this, refusing, when requested, to instruct the

missionaries to act differently. What would be said to these assertions?

It would be replied, and very justly, that every Annual Report of the Board proved the falseness of these allegations. It would be shown by these Annual Reports, that the missionaries had spontaneously commenced operations against intemperance very early in their residence among those nations; that they had preached against it, formed societies against it, printed and distributed tracts against it, used special precautions against it in their admission of members to the church, and reported, from time to time, to the Prudential Committee the amount, and the measure of success or failure, of these efforts; and that the Prudential Committee had freely published these reports with the proceedings of the Board.

How monstrous is it, then, to say, when the missionaries have done *no one* of these things against slavery, when they have neither preached, nor printed, nor formed societies, nor distributed tracts, nor made reports to the Prudential Committee against it, but when, on the contrary, they have certified the perpetrators of it to be Christians by freely admitting them to the church, expressing, when inquired of, their determination still to do so—and when the Prudential Committee have not only systematically permitted all this, but have resisted many and strong remonstrances, urging them to interfere with it, and have steadily declared, from beginning to end, that these missionaries have been "faithful," and "exemplary in the discharge of *all* their missionary duties"—how monstrous is it, after all this, to say, as Dr. Woods does, that the missionaries and the Prudential Committee "no more really give their sanction" to slavery than to intemperance! that they "are no otherwise connected with slavery" than they are with intemperance!

The truth is, that while they were connected with intemperance (and some other vices) only so far as diligent and persistent effort on their part had failed to eradicate them, they were connected with slavery by consent, by choice, by system, by fraternal welcome, by deliberate justification, and thus did give their sanction to it, and are to be held responsible for the guilt of it.

Here is one of the questions in Dr. Woods's report, in

which he seeks to defend the position of the Board by misrepresenting the charge against it. He says —

" Is this Board, then, in propagating the Gospel, to be held responsible for *directly* working out these reorganizations of the social system, *without giving Christian truth time to produce its changes in the hearts of individuals and in public sentiment ?* "

Dr. Woods knew very well that nothing like this has been claimed. He knew that the charge was that, from the commencement of the Cherokee and Choctaw missions in 1817, to the year 1845, in which he wrote, the missionaries had systematically refrained from *beginning* the utterance of Christian truth upon the subject of slavery; that they had gone on allowing the practice of slaveholding to continue and increase, even among their church members, without remonstrance; and that the Prudential Committee had gone on permitting this course of conduct, in spite of urgent remonstrances from Christians at home!

The concluding sentence of Dr. Woods's report (I must pass over much other sophistry which needs comment) shows a similar attempt to throw dust in the eyes of his readers. He says—

" There can be no prospect of benefitting the slave, in a slave country, without the consent of the owner. The only hope we can have of benefitting either the one or the other, is through the influence of the Gospel; and the Gospel, to be effectual, must be conveyed in the spirit of meekness and love."

Each of the members of this sentence is suited, and apparently intended, to mislead the unscrutinizing reader.

Nobody had ever asked these missionaries to proceed against slavery in any other than in " the spirit of meekness and love." Nobody had ever intimated that they were to work otherwise than "through the influence of the Gospel." The charge against them was that they refused to apply this influence to the discouragement of slaveholding! that they systematically *refrained* from publishing some parts of the Gospel to their slaveholding hearers! that they refused to " preach deliverance to the captives"! that they purposely omitted to require their candidates for church membership to " set at liberty them that are bruised"!

As to the declaration that—" There can be no prospect of

benefitting the slave, in a slave country, without the consent of the owner "— Dr. Woods might as well say that there can be no prospect of benefitting the drunkard, in an intemperate community, without the consent of the rum-seller. This allegation is not only erroneous in itself — its spirit is not only contradicted by the whole action of the missionaries against intemperance, which proceeded in spite of the bitter opposition of rum-sellers and distillers — but it is im-pertinent, inappropriate to the case in hand; inasmuch as the primary action proposed by the remonstrants in this case was *not* help to the slave, but *purification of the mission churches from the membership of slaveholders!*

It will be observed that the report, containing all this sophistry and misrepresentation in behalf of the continuance of slaveholders in the mission churches, was "unanimously adopted" by the Board.

We now come to the Annual Report for 1846.

Further memorials on slavery were received at the Annual Meeting in this year, and were referred to a Committee which had also in charge certain memorials against polygamy in the mission churches. The report of this Committee upon both subjects, with the prefatory statement in the Annual Report, (pp. 72–4,) are as follows: —

"MEMORIALS ON SLAVERY AND POLYGAMY.

" Resolutions on the subject of slavery were received from the General Association of Congregationalists in Illinois, and from New Haven East Association; also, a memorial and resolutions on the same subject from a missionary convention held in Dexter, Maine. These papers were referred to Chancellor Walworth, Dr. Robinson, Dr. Stowe, Dr. Tappan, Hon. Edmund Parker, Hon. Linus Child, and Rev. David Greene.

" Four memorials were presented to the Board in relation to the subject of polygamy, in its supposed connection, now or heretofore, with some of the mission churches. They were from Rev. George W. Perkins and others; from twenty-four ladies residing in Middletown and Meriden, Connecticut; the Gentlemen's Foreign Missionary Association in Canton, Connecticut; and Rev. William W. Patton and others. These memorials having been read, Mr. Greene made a full statement of the facts in the case, after which the memorials were referred to the Committee on the subject of slavery. This Committee subsequently made their report. During the discussion which arose on its adoption, Rev.

George W. Perkins offered an amendment to the same; after which Dr. Goodrich moved to postpone both the report and the amendment, for the purpose of receiving a substitute for so much of the report as relates to the subject of polygamy. The report, with the proposed amendment and substitute, was finally referred to Chancellor Walworth, Dr. Goodrich and Dr. Humphrey. This Committee subsequently made a report, which is as follows:

" ' The Committee to whom were referred several memorials and resolutions on the subject of slavery, and also the various memorials relative to cases of polygamy which are supposed to exist in some of the churches under the ecclesiastical care of the missionaries of this Board, respectfully report: That in reference to the subject of slavery generally, or in its connection with some of our missionary churches, nothing has occurred during the past year to induce your Committee to suppose this Board should depart from the principles of the elaborate report, sanctioned by two successive Committees; and which report, after being fully discussed, was adopted, with such entire unanimity, by all the members of the Board present, at the annual meeting in 1845. Your Committee, therefore, consider further agitation of the subject here as calculated injuriously to affect the great cause of missions in which this Board is engaged, and for the promotion of which alone the society was instituted.

" ' In reference to the supposed existence of cases of polygamy in our mission churches, and the erroneous supposition that the same has been sanctioned by this Board or its officers, your Committee state that neither the Board nor its Prudential Committee have taken any action, or even expressed an opinion, in favor of receiving a polygamist into a church under the care of any of our missionaries. So far as your Committee have been able to obtain information on the subject, the missionaries of the Board, although many of them are located in countries where polygamy is recognized and sanctioned by law, have had occasion but in four instances to act upon the question of the admission of a polyga. nist to church fellowship; and these were all cases of persons who, previous to their conversion from heathenism, and before they had any knowledge of the doctrines and precepts of the Christian system, had become the legal husbands of a plurality of wives. In one of those cases, it is known that the missionaries at the station where the application was made, refused to admit the applicant to the church. In two others of those cases, your Committee are not informed as to the result of the applications. But as the missionaries who had the pastoral care of the churches to which these requests for admission were made are known to have been opposed to the admission to church fellowship of persons standing in that relation, your Committee have no reason to suppose that either of the applicants was received as a member of the church. The fourth case occurred about twenty years since, and in respect to an individual who has been dead from twelve to fifteen years. The person alluded to was an aged man, who, at the time of his conversion from heathenism to Christianity, was the husband of two wives, both of whom desired to live with him, and, according to the usages of his nation, had equal claims upon him for protection and support. Under those circumstances, the missionaries at that station thought it right to receive him into the church. He was accordingly received by them, and continued in church fellowship until his death. This, as far as your Committee have any definite information, is the only person having more than one wife who has ever been received into our mission churches. And they have no reason to suppose that any person in that situation is now in connection with those churches.

" 'The principles upon which our missionaries are expected to act in dealing with questions of that nature were fully stated in the report of 1845, to which your Committee have before referred. It is unnecessary to say that this Board and its missionaries and patrons unite in the sentiment of all who bear the Christian name, that the practice of polygamy is hostile to the interests of the human race, and diametrically opposed to the spirit of the Christian religion. Nor can there be any difference of opinion among Christians as to the absolute impropriety, under any circumstances, of permitting church members to marry a second wife during the life of the first, except in cases of legal divorce. And in respect to converts from heathenism in a state of polygamy, this Board expect its missionaries, in considering the question of admission to the church, to carry out the principles of the Gospel in their full extent. If any such cases should arise, your Committee think this Board may confide in the piety, learning and sound judgment of its missionaries abroad, and in their general competence to decide, upon scriptural grounds, these questions and others of a similar character which may arise in the course of their labors, without requiring its Prudential Committee to assume the very questionable power of giving more specific directions, which might be considered an infringement of the religious liberty of the ministers and members of our mission churches. Your Committee therefore see nothing in the subject of these memorials requiring the further action of the Board at this time.'

" This report was adopted by the Board.'

It is to be observed, that the paragraph at the commencement of this report, which coolly dismisses the memorialists without either consideration of their requests or action upon them, not only refers to the sophistical and deceptive report of Dr. Woods in 1845, as perfectly satisfactory, but deprecates " further *agitation* of the subject" of slavery as " injurious."

In the Annual Report for 1847, the only direct action respecting slavery is found in a brief statement on p. 59, as follows:—

" RESOLUTION ON SLAVERY.

" President Blanchard offered a resolution, 'that a Committee be appointed to inquire and report to this body whether any fur-

ther action is required of this Board in reference to our relations
to slavery in the Cherokee and Choctaw missions; and, if so, to
propose such action as they may judge best.' This resolution was
referred to the Business Committee, who subsequently reported as
follows: —

" ' The Business Committee, to whom was referred the resolution
for the appointment of a Committee upon the subject of slavery in
the mission churches in the Cherokee and Choctaw nations, report,
that it is inexpedient that the attention of the Board should be
occupied with the discussion of that subject at its present meeting.
Mr. Greene, the Secretary who has charge of the Indian correspondence, and who alone is in possession of the facts to give the
necessary explanations to the Board or to a Committee, is detained
by ill health from attending this meeting; so that, if any further
action on this subject should be deemed proper, it cannot be had at
this time. This Committee are also informed that it is the intention
of the Prudential Committee to allow Mr. Greene to visit these
missions previously to the next annual meeting; and if so, he will
be prepared to give all the necessary explanations which may then
be required in relation to the actual state of those missionary
churches.'

" The report was adopted by the Board."

I have said that the above was the only *direct* action
respecting slavery in the Annual Meeting of 1847. Subsequently, however, to the adoption of this report, the following innocent-looking resolution was passed, which, judging
by the magnitude of its results in the next Annual Report,
seems to have been designed to introduce another elaborate
piece of sophistry, in the hope of staving off the dreaded
" agitation ": —

" *Resolved*, That the Prudential Committee be requested to
present a written report, at the next annual meeting, on the nature
and extent of the control which is to be exercised over the missionaries under the care of the Board, and the moral responsibility of
the Board for the nature of the teaching of the missionaries and
character of the churches."--p. 61.

In that portion of the Annual Report for 1848 which
speaks of the Cherokee and Choctaw missions, the Prudential
Committee seek to help their policy of discouraging "agitation" about slavery among their patrons, by glowing representations of the satisfactory spiritual state of these slaveholding tribes. They say—

" In the history of the efforts of this Board to christianize the
Choctaws and Cherokees, we find much to awaken the liveliest

gratitude to God. The Lord has done great things for us. If the Gospel has n t accomplished all for these people, in their civil and social relations, which the friends of the Redeemer among us could desire, very happy results have been secured. For twenty years past, the spirit of grace has been almost continually descending, especially upon the Choctaws. We find evidence of this, not only in the organization of churches, and frequent additions to them of hopeful converts, but also in the general advance made in the arts and comforts of civilized life."—p. 62.

With still greater hardihood, Mr. Secretary Treat, in the same year, represented the increased number of slaves in the Cherokee and Choctaw nations, and the general preference there felt for investing money in this " species of property," as one of the results of " the doctrines of the Gospel having exerted their appropriate influence." [*Missionary Herald*, the official organ of the A. B. C. F. M., October, 1848, p. 349.]

Immediately following the above-quoted eulogy of the Prudential Committee on the Choctaw and Cherokee slave-holders, in the Annual Report of 1848, comes their special report, ordered the previous year, on the "control of missionaries and mission churches." This document, occupying eighteen closely printed octavo pages, is signed by the three Secretaries. In spite of the *general* aspect appearing in it, and in the resolution calling for it in 1847, the preceding and following circumstances seem clearly to show that the one great object of this document was to persuade the remonstrants against slavery that its continued allowance in the mission churches was both right and unavoidable, and thus to stop the further " agitation" of that subject. Notwithstanding the great length of this report, and of the correspondence with the Cherokee and Choctaw missions immediately following, they are given entire in this volume, like all the other documents quoted from the Annual Reports. Only thus could the reader learn how extensively sophistry and misrepresentation have used the dialect of piety in defence of slavery. The *italics* are those of the report.

The report in question occupies pp. 62–80 of the Annual Report of 1848, as follows : —

"CONTROL OF MISSIONARIES AND MISSION CHURCHES.

" At the meeting of the Board held in Buffalo, 1847, the Prudential Committee were requested to submit a written report, at the next annual meeting, on the nature and extent of the control to be exercised over missionaries, and the responsibility of the Board for their instructions, as also for the character of the churches. This was presented to the Board accordingly, at an early stage of the meeting; but as the members had not time to give the subject that considerate attention which its importance demanded, the final disposition of the same was postponed, after a single amendment had been adopted, to the next annual meeting, the Committee being authorized to print the report as amended, with such modifications as might seem desirable. This document, as thus amended and modified, is as follows:—

" ' The Board adopted the following Resolution at its last Annual Meeting, viz.:—"That the Prudential Committee be requested to present a written report, at the next annual meeting, on the nature and extent of the control which is to be exercised over the missionaries under the care of the Board; and the moral responsibility of the Board for the nature of the teaching of the missionaries, and for the character of the churches." The Prudential Committee have attended to this duty, and present the following Report.

" ' It will be seen that this call upon the Prudential Committee involves a discussion of the whole working of the system of Foreign Missions. We must determine the ecclesiastical standing and liberty of missionaries, and of the churches they gather among the heathen; inquire whether ecclesiastical liberty be not as safe for missionaries abroad as for pastors at home, and whether missionaries and pastors are not in fact controlled by similar means and influences; show in what manner missionaries are obtained, what are the nature and force of their voluntary engagements, what are the powers and responsibilities of the Board, and what is the actual extent of the claims of missionaries upon the Board and upon the churches. This will exhibit the working of the principle of voluntary association in missions, involving, as the main reliance, influences that bear directly on the reason, judgment, and heart; and a brief mention must be made of the more important of these influences. The Prudential Committee will also be expected to show the adaptation of the constitution of the Board to its various trusts and duties. In respect to the native mission churches, the inquiry will arise, how far they ought to be independent of the jurisdiction of all bodies of men in this country; how they are to be trained to self-support and self-government; what expectations it is reasonable to cherish concerning them; and what are the responsibilities of the Board for the teaching of the missionaries, and for the character of the mission churches.

I.
"'THE MISSIONARIES.

"'1. THE ECCLESIASTICAL LIBERTY BELONGING TO MISSIONARIES.

"'The Board affirmed at Brooklyn, in the year 1845, that "the missionaries acting under the commission of Christ, and with the instructions of the New Testament before them, are themselves at first, and subsequently in connection with the churches they have gathered, the rightful and exclusive judges of what constitutes adequate evidence of piety and fitness for church-fellowship in professed converts."

" 'It was doubtless intended, by this declaration, to recognize the missionaries under the care of the Board as entitled to equal liberty, in all ecclesiastical matters, with ministers at home. They certainly are equally the ministers, messengers, and ambassadors of Christ; they equally receive from him their call, commission, office, and work. *As a body*, they sustain to the churches at home a relation equally as close as do the *body* of the pastors. The several Christian denominations acting through the Board have, in all practicable ways, given to the missionaries it has sent forth their countenance, sanction, and adoption. " These missionaries," says a standard work on the Constitution of the Congregational Churches, "may justly be considered as sent abroad by the churches, inasmuch as they are supported by their contributions, attended by their prayers, and protected by their constant solicitude. It is true that the immediate agents, in designing and arranging their departure, are Missionary Societies; but these Societies, when the subject is rightly considered, are only the agents and representatives of the churches." * It should be added, that the missionaries are ordained to their office, as really as pastors, and by the direct representatives of the churches, and with the same formalities, and almost always with the knowledge that they are to be sent forth and directed by the Board. In this manner, the Board itself has been recognized by the churches and accredited as an Agent in the work of foreign missions; as it has been, also, by resolutions and other formal acts of General Associations, Synods, and General Assemblies, and by thousands of collections in aid of its funds made in the house of God on the Sabbath, and at other times and places, with the concurrence of pastors and churches.

" 'The denial that a missionary is an office-bearer until a Christian church has invited him to take the oversight of it in the Lord, is made in utter forgetfulness, as it would seem, of the commission by which a preaching ministry was originally instituted. The primary and preëminent design of that commission was to create the *missionary* office, and to perpetuate it till the Gospel should have been preached to every creature.

" 'It is not claimed for missionaries that they are Apostles, since they have not the "signs of an Apostle," and since the apostolical office was not successive and communicable to others. That office was extraordinary, in the range both of its objects and its powers, and the Apostles can have no proper successors. Missionaries are Evangelists. They do the work of Evangelists; and such they are, as Timothy and Titus were in the primitive missions, and as Eusebius says many were in the second century. "These," says that historian, "having merely laid the foundations of the faith, and ordained other pastors, committed to them the cultivation of the churches newly planted; while they themselves, supported by the grace and coöperation of God, proceeded to other countries and na-

* Upham's Ratio Disciplinæ, p. 128.

tions." The method of conducting missions has, indeed, been considerably modified by the altered condition of the world, rendering it possible to send forth a far greater number of missionaries than in ancient times, and to augment their value as instruments, and to accelerate what may be called national conversions, by sending missionaries forth in the family state, and making their labor less itinerant and transitory than in early times; but the true relation of missionaries to the churches at home, and to the heathen world, appears to be that of Evangelists.

"'Considering the weakness and waywardness so generally found in men just emerging from heathenism, native pastors must, for a time, and in certain respects, be practically subordinate to the missionaries, by whom their churches were formed, and through whom, it may be, they are themselves partially supported. This is true, also, of the mission churches; as will be explained in another part of this report. Should a practical parity, in all respects, be insisted on between the missionaries and the native pastors, in the early periods when every thing is in a forming state, it is not seen how the native ministry can be trained to system and order, and enabled to stand alone, or even to stand at all. As with ungoverned children, self-sufficiency, impatience of restraint, jealousy, and other hurtful passions will be developed. The native pastors themselves are, for a season, but "babes in Christ," children in experience, knowledge and character. And hence missionaries, who entertain the idea that ordination must have the effect to place the native pastors at once on a perfect equality with themselves, are often backward in intrusting the responsibilities of the pastoral office to natives. They fear, and justly, the effects of this sudden comparative exaltation; especially when aggravated by ordination formalities multiplied and magnified beyond the scriptural precedents; involving a convocation of ministers and people, an ordination sermon, a formal charge, perhaps a right-hand of fellowship, and possibly an address setting forth the importance of the occasion, in place of the simple laying on of hands and prayer, as in the apostolical ordinations. All this may be well in old Christian communities; but whatever advantages it is supposed to have among the heathen, these are thought to be overbalanced by its tendency to inflame the self-conceit and ambition remaining in the heart of the heathen convert, however carefully he may have been educated in the doctrines and duties of Christianity. We scarcely need any great amount of experience, indeed, when our thoughts are once turned to the subject, to see that there is wisdom in the apostolical view of the pastoral office in mission churches, and in their mode of bringing forward a native ministry and training it for independent action.

"'It must be obvious, that the view just taken of this subject involves no danger to the future parity of the native ministry, considered in their relations to each other; for, in the nature of things, the missionary office is scarcely more successive and communicable to the native pastors, than was the apostolical office to Evangelists.

"'The point specially insisted on is this,—that ministers of the Gospel lose none of their ecclesiastical standing and liberty by engaging in the work of foreign missions. No plea for abridging their ecclesiastical liberties can be founded on the fact of their support coming from the churches at home; because the obligation of the churches to support missionaries rests on precisely the same basis with the obligation of missionaries to become such. Both the service and the support are to be rendered as a duty owed to Christ. The one is no more voluntary, no more optional, no more a work of supererogation, than the other. Missionaries are no more objects of charity, or beneficiaries, than are pastors at home. Their labors as truly entitle them to a support from some quarter. When the reality of the missionary's call from the Head of the Church to go on a mission has been settled by competent and acknowledged testimony, an obligation arises and exists *somewhere* to send him forth and support him. And after he has gone into the field, he can no more properly be *starved* out of his appropriate liberty by those to whom he looks for support, than he can be *legislated* out of it by those who direct his labors. Nor do missionaries become, in any servile sense, the servants of those who support them; they are not their hired servants, but their fellow-servants. Christ is their common spiritual Head, and he sends his missionaries forth a free ministry. And the Board seeks to accommodate itself to this principle in Christ's kingdom. "With great care, it seeks out competent men as missionaries and worthy of confidence, and then sends them out under the broad commission of the great Head of the Church, to preach the Gospel to every creature; themselves free, to propagate a free Christianity in the field of their labors. With a scrupulous regard for the rights of the missionaries in this particular, it places them among the perishing heathen, to gather as many as possible into the fold of Christ, and there leaves them, in the free and untrammeled exercise of their own judgment, under a due sense of accountability to Christ, to decide on the spot, in each particular case as it occurs, what is sufficient evidence of genuine conversion, and what is the proper and sufficient ground for the admission of the heathen convert to the privileges of the Christian Church." *

"'When the Committee come to treat of the checks and influences under which missionaries operate, it will be seen that this degree of liberty is compatible with as perfect a responsibility as is attainable in the present state of human nature and of the world. But it is important to remark here, that this responsibility can never be perfectly enforced, except by guarding the religious liberties of missionaries with the most scrupulous care. Men must be free, and must feel that they are free, in order to rise to the full capacity and dignity of moral agents, and be subjected to the full control of law, reason, and the moral sense. And, of all Gospel ministers, the missionary among the heathen most needs to have his mind and spirit erect, and to feel that all good men are his brethren. This is necessary to the unity, peace, order and efficiency of every mission. The law of liberty is an all-pervading law in Christ's kingdom.

"'2. HOW THE RE)NSIBILITY OF MISSIONARIES IS SECURED.

"'So far as the Committee can rely on the experience of more than thirty years, they regard it as not less safe to concede ecclesi-

---

* Prof. William Smyth, of Bowdoin College.

astical liberty to missionaries than to pastors. And how eminently safe it has been at home, the last two centuries can testify. In each of the denominations of Christians represented in this Board, the understanding, conscience and heart of ministers is supposed to operate with equal freedom in the performance of their spiritual duties ; and it is the prevalent belief, in each of these denominations, that this liberty could not be advantageously diminished.

"'What the Prudential Committee are to show is this : — *That foreign missionaries are subjected to similar controlling influences with pastors at home.* These influences are exerted in the selection of missionaries; in their voluntary engagements; in the terms of their pecuniary support; in their mutual watchfulness over each other; and in the direct influence of truth upon their minds and hearts.

"'1. Missionaries are, in an important sense, selected for the work, and it thus comes to pass that they have, as a body, a trustworthy character.

"'The Board does not, indeed, extend a "call" to them, as churches do to those whom they would have for their pastors. This has sometimes been recommended, as preferable to the course now pursued. But few missionaries would be obtained in this way. The missionary spirit has not yet strong hold enough upon the churches, or upon the colleges and theological seminaries, for the adoption of such a plan. Were the responsibility to be thus taken from students and candidates for the ministry, and assumed by missionary institutions, the young men in our theological schools would seldom be found in a state of mind or in circumstances to give an affirmative answer to a "call," by the time their characters and qualifications should have been sufficiently developed to warrant one. It is found to be better to lay the case before all, and leave the result to the providence and grace of God. Consecration to the foreign missionary work for life involves a somewhat peculiar experience of its own; and the earlier and more thoroughly that experience is wrought in the soul, the better is the prospect of continuance and usefulness in the work of missions.

"'The Committee have been accustomed, generally, to wait for written *offers* from the candidates to go as missionaries under the direction of the Board. These are usually made some time before the theological course of studies is completed, and are commonly preceded by personal conferences or an informal correspondence with the Secretaries. The offer is accompanied by testimonials from pastors, instructors in colleges and seminaries, and others. If the testimony be decisive and satisfactory, the individual is invited to visit the Missionary House in Boston. This arrangement is found useful and satisfactory to all parties. There is now, if there has not been before, a free conference with him as to his religious principles and experience, his social relations, his motives in choosing the missionary work, his adaptations and preferences with respect to a field of labor, and whatever else is important in determining the question of his appointment and designation Should it now appear to be the candidate's duty not to engage in a foreign mission, it is generally easy to convince him of the fact, and his case does not proceed to any formal action on the part of the Committee. Where the duty to go is clear, an appointment follows. The candidate next seeks ordination, at his discretion, from some ecclesiastical body; which body subjects him to as thorough an examination as if he were to settle as a pastor. He is not taken on trust from the Board, but his call to the missionary work is brought under a renewed investigation.

"'It is believed that the missionaries laboring in connection with this Board are equal, as to ministerial qualifications and character, to the body of pastors in either denomination represented in the Board, in any one of the States of the Union; and this fact is evidently one of great importance, in an inquiry as to the possibility of exerting a reasonable control over their proceedings.

"'2. Missionaries come voluntarily under similar engagements with pastors at home.

"'The pastor's engagements are made to his church and people, to the body that ordains him, and, through that body, to the churches; in addition to his solemn and well-understood vows to his Lord and Master. The missionary's engagements are to the Board, acting in the way of a general superintendence over his proceedings as a missionary, and to the ordaining body, and, through those bodies, to the community from which he is to derive his support; and he also makes explicit vows to his divine Master.

"'The missionary engages, on accepting his appointment, to conform to the rules and regulations of the Board, the nature of which he is supposed distinctly to understand. He thus pledges himself, among other things, to be governed by the majority of votes in his mission, in regard to all questions that arise in their proceedings; the proceedings being subject to the revision of the Prudential Committee. He comes, moreover, under certain other distinct and well-understood pledges: — (1.) As to his *manner of life;* which is to be one of exemplary piety and devotion to his work. (2.) As to his *teaching;* which must be conformed to the evangelical doctrines generally received by the churches, and set forth in their well-known Confessions of Faith. And (3.) As to *ecclesiastical usages;* to which he must conform substantially as they prevail among the churches operating through the Board. He must hold to a parity among the clerical brethren of his mission. He must hold to the validity of infant baptism. He must admit only such to the Lord's Supper as give credible evidence of faith in Christ. So far as his relation to the Board and his standing in the mission are concerned, he is of course not pledged to conform his proceedings to any other book of discipline than the New Testament.

"'3. The missionary's claim for continued support, like that of the pastor, depends upon his fulfilling his engagements.

"'Unless faithful to these engagements, the missionary cannot claim a continuance of his support. And the Board not only may, but it must, insist on his performance of them. It is bound to know that the missionary preaches the Gospel and administers the ordinances according to his expressed and implied pledges; which of course he must do, or retire from his connection.

"'The responsibilities and powers of the Board, in this aspect of the case, are easily defined. While it cannot depose a missionary from the ministry, nor silence him as a preacher, nor cut him off from the church, it can dissolve what it formed, namely, his connection with itself and with the mission. While the Board may not establish new principles in matters purely ecclesiastical, it may enforce the observance of such as are generally acknowledged by the churches, and were understood to be acknowledged by the missionaries when sent to their fields. While the Board may not require that baptism shall always be performed by sprinkling, nor forbid that the Lord's Supper shall be administered to converts after they have given what the missionaries believe to be credible and satisfactory evidence of piety; it may require, (for such are the established and acknowledged usages,) that he receive none into the church, except such as are believed to be truly pious persons; that he baptize in the name of the Father, the Son, and the Holy Ghost; and that he do not refuse baptism to the infant children of the church.

" ' Where the opinions of the great body of its patrons are divided in regard to the *facts* of Scripture, the Board may not undertake to decide, positively, as to the nature of those facts, with a view to binding the conduct of its missionaries. Such a fact, at present, is the admission of slaveholders into the apostolical churches. The Board may not undertake to decide, that this class of persons was certainly admitted to church membership by the Apostles, nor that they were excluded, in such a way as to have the effect on the missionaries of a statute, injunction, or Scripture doctrine, in respect to the admission of such persons into churches now to be gathered in heathen nations where slavery is found. The Board, the Prudential Committee, and the Secretaries may have their opinions on this subject, as well as on all others, and (as will be stated more fully hereafter) may freely express those opinions in their correspondence with the missionaries, and ought to do so, if they see occasion, with such reasonings, persuasions and remonstrances as they may think proper. But they cannot properly go farther. Nor can the Board assume, as the basis of any of its proceedings, or imply in any manner, that the apostolical usages are not the wisest and best for all modern missionaries to follow, who are similarly situated with the Apostles. Nor can it do any thing in direct and manifest contrariety to the great Protestant maxim, on which our own religious liberties depend, that *the Scriptures are the* ONLY *and the* SUFFICIENT *rule of faith and practice.*

" ' On the other hand, if it was an usage of the Apostles to give definite and positive instructions to the holders of slaves as to their treatment of them—instructions which had a tendency to do away the institution—and if such instructions are found in their Epistles, then modern missionaries may be expected to conform to that usage, and to give the same instructions in like circumstances; though the time and manner of doing this must be referred, in great measure, to their own discretion, as with ministers at home, in respect to the direct inculcation of specific duties. The successful inculcation of such duties pre-supposes a certain amount of doctrinal knowledge in those who are to be operated upon, as well as of moral susceptibility, and also a due adaptation in the instructions to time, place, and circumstances.

"'But while the Board may require that the missionaries under its care instruct all classes of men after the manner of the Apostles, it is not at liberty to restrict the missionaries to the identical instructions given by the Apostles; because there is no good reason to suppose that all the instructions are recorded in the New Testament which the Apostles were accustomed to give. Missionaries may go farther, if their convictions of duty require it, and may apply what they regard as the obvious and generally conceded principles of the Gospel to the case. They have the same liberty, in their preaching, with ministers of the Gospel elsewhere. They may instruct their converts, among other things, on the Christian duty of fully conceding the right of marriage to the slaves; of not holding them as property; of sacredly respecting the relation between husbands and wives, and between parents and children; and of securing to all the right of worshipping God, and of reading his Holy Word. And the Committee have no hesitation in urging the duty of such instruction upon their brethren among the heathen; with the plain inculcation, in the prosecution of their ministry, of whatever obligation grows out of the fundamental law of love, as given by the Lord Jesus Christ, "Whatsoever ye would that men should do to you, do ye even so to them;"—it being understood that the missionaries are to have the liberty of exercising their discretion as to time and manner.

"'Nor have the Committee any hesitancy in saying that, since the Gospel was so preached by the Apostles as ultimately to root out the most extensive and terrible system of slavery the world has ever seen, so ought missionaries now, in times and ways within the range of their own discretion, so to hold up the doctrines, duties and spirit of the Gospel, that it shall have the same beneficent tendency on the social condition of the heathen.

"'A writer of unquestioned opposition to slavery, to whose discriminating pen the Board is indebted, has justly remarked, that it would seem to be within the discretion of a missionary in a slaveholding community, whether he will attack slavery directly, and by name, or "whether he will strike at some one or more of the things which enter essentially into it, and the wrong of which can, in the actual circumstances of that community, be set home with convincing power upon the conscience of the slaveholder." *

"'Slavery is, indeed, at variance with the principles of the Christian religion, and must disappear in any community, in proportion as the Gospel gains upon the understandings and the hearts of men. But the Board and its missionaries are restricted to moral means, and these must have time and opportunity to exert their appropriate influence. Missionaries should be employed who *deserve* confidence, and then confidence should be reposed in them; nor should results be required which are beyond the power of their labors to produce. Many things which, at first, it might seem desirable for the Board to do, are found, on a nearer view, to lie entirely beyond its jurisdiction; so that to attempt them would be useless, nay, a ruinous usurpation. Nor is the Board at liberty to withdraw its confidence from mis-

* Prof. Smyth.

sionaries, because of such differences of opinion among them as are generally found and freely tolerated in presbyteries, councils, associations, and other bodies here at home.

" 'Polygamy stands on a somewhat different footing from that of Slavery. Little difficulty is apprehended from it in gathering native churches. The evidence that polygamists were admitted into the church by the Apostles is extensively and increasingly regarded as inconclusive, by the patrons of the Board. We no where find instructions given in the New Testament to persons holding this relation. Nor is there evidence of the practice having existed in any of the churches subsequent to the apostolical age. The Committee believe, that no positive action by the Board in relation to this subject is needed, or expedient. Unsustained as the practice is by any certain precedents in the apostolical churches, and unauthorized by a single inspired injunction, the native convert will rarely be able to prove the reality of his piety, should he persist in clinging to it, or refuse to provide for the education of his children, or for the support of their mothers, (when they need such provision,) if he may not be permitted to regard the mothers as his wives.

" 'Should the missionary violate his compact in respect to the character or amount of his preaching and teaching; or in respect to the administration of the ordinances of the Gospel; or by refusing to conform to the resolutions of his mission, or of the Prudential Committee, or of the Board, or in any other manner, the Prudential Committee, on being certified of the fact, is in duty bound to consider and act on the bearing this ought to have on his relations to the Board, and his claim for a continued support.

" 'This claim for support, so far as it applies to the Board, is understood to be only for an equitable proportion of the sum-total of funds actually placed at the disposal of the Board, for the expenses of the year. The Board can divide only what it receives. The missionary goes forth trusting in God that there will always be enough for his wants. He cheerfully incurs the risk, whatever it may be, and which past experience of God's goodness shows to be small. And he does this the more cheerfully, because his work is so eminently a work of faith. Mere pledges for his support from churches and ecclesiastical bodies are too delusive to be depended on. It is only to a small extent that pledges can be obtained from individual Christians, and even the precise import and obligation of these are apt to be forgotten by those who give them. Nor are the formal pledges of support given to the Board worth any thing, except so far as they represent the deep-seated missionary principles and sentiments of the Christian community. There is, indeed, no firm footing for the missionary, except in the promises of his Lord and Master. Faith in Christ is the basis of his enterprise. It is so in respect to himself, his children, his work, and the desired results of all his sacrifices and labors, — preëminently so, compared with that of the pastor at home. And herein lies the special dignity of his calling. He goes on his mission in the discharge of his own personal duty, because he believes his Lord and Savior requires him to go as his servant and ambassador. If he have a proper view of his mission, he would regard it as lowering the work immeasurably, to bring in the churches, or the Board, as *principals;* as any thing else, indeed, than mere *voluntary helpers,* selected and chosen by himself to carry out the benevolent purpose of his own independent self-consecration. The idea that a mission is a contract between the churches and the missionary in any such sense, that he may cease to perform missionary labor, and claim a pension, (as the servants of the East India Company do,) after a certain number of years, and while he is yet able to labor—should it ever become an effective element in the reasoning of missionaries—would prove destructive to the faith and vitality of the enterprise. If this idea has sometimes been advanced by missionaries, it has been when reasoning under the pressure of parental solicitude, and in great part on the assumption that the work of publishing the Gospel was committed by Christ to the church as a society, or corporate body, to act as a principal in the matter; and as such, in the discharge of its own preëminent duty, to send forth and support preachers in all the world; whereas, the command was given to individual disciples, before an organized Christian church existed; and whatever use was made of social organizations during the apostolical age, the work was always regarded as the discharge of an individual and personal obligation. It is not less an individual and personal duty now, than it was then. The enlisting in the missionary enterprise is wholly voluntary, as well on the part of the missionary who goes abroad, as on the part of his fellow-Christian who remains at home. They are co-workers and mutual helpers; and the coöperation of the donor may be as essential to the prosecution of the work as the labors of the missionary. On the part of all concerned, the consecration, whether of person or property, must be a voluntary offering by individual subjects of Christ's kingdom. Churches, in their organized capacity, have no authority to prescribe to any one of their members what he must do; but each must decide for himself, as the result of his own consciousness of duty and privilege, what he ought to do, and to what part of the work he should devote himself. It is a question of individual responsibility. "As we have many members in one body, and all members have not the same office, so we, being many, are one body in Christ, and every one members one of another;" and whatever any one does, he is to feel that it is in the discharge of his own prescribed duty. Christians at home will no more feel that they are really indebted to the missionary, than that the missionary is indebted to them. They will no more feel that the missionary is doing their work, by going on a mission, than that they are doing his, by giving to support him. Each will regard himself as a fellow-servant of a common Master, engaged in a common service, and performing just that part of the work which the Master has assigned to him. This view of the subject is doubtless the correct one, and the only one that will comport with the successful prosecution of missions, for a prolonged period of time, and on an extended scale. It is necessary for all parties to feel, *that they are discharging only their own personal obligations, that they are performing only their own appropriate work.*

"'The system, as it has been described, is found to work easily and well. The missionary is as free, in every sense, as the pastor. One

is no more really held accountable for the manner of expending his
salary, than is the other. One can no more absent himself from his
field of labor and his work, without the concurrence of the body
that furnishes the means of his support, than the other. The pastor
can no more travel at the expense of his people, whether for health
or business, without their consent, than the missionary can do so at
the expense of the Board, without the consent of the Committee, or,
in certain specified cases, of his mission. The greatest embarrassments experienced in the working of the system are when the
Committee are constrained to interpose their action, in order to relieve a mission from the influence of one of its own members, and
where the questions at issue relate to points in missionary practice
and expediency with which the community at home have not yet
had opportunity to become fully conversant; or to mere matters of
fact, dependent on testimony, and requiring to be heard on both
sides; — giving advantage to a disaffected missionary, should he
choose to address himself to the popular mind. In a case of immorality, if it be flagrant, the compact may be annulled; and every
one is ready to appreciate the reason. So if the missionary, however conscientiously, break fellowship with his brethren, and deny
their baptism, or their ordination, his right to continue in the mission would cease; — it being a well-ascertained fact, that such opinions, in addition to violating the understood engagements, usually
prove destructive to the harmony of a mission, when embraced by
any of its members. The same is true if there be error in respect
to important doctrines of the Gospel. It is not the mere doctrinal
errors that are to be considered, but their distracting, disastrous
effect on the happiness and efficiency of the mission. There is no
need of making out formal charges to prove a case of heresy by a
formal trial, as an ecclesiastical body would do. The question assumes a plain business form, — whether there is an actual departure
from the basis on which the missionary appointment was made, and
what effect it has exerted on the peace and usefulness of the mission,
and on the operations of the Board.

"'That the action of the Prudential Committee, dissolving the
connection of a missionary with his mission and the Board, is not of
the nature of an *ecclesiastical* proceeding, technically speaking, is
evident from the fact that it leaves his ecclesiastical relations undisturbed. His regular standing, both as a minister of the Gospel and
a member of the church, is not directly affected. As his appointment to the mission did not destroy his relations to his association or
presbytery, so neither does his dismission. The Committee of course
leave the ecclesiastical relations of the case for the ecclesiastical body
(if it choose to consider them) with which the missionary may happen, at the time, to be connected.

"'It will often be found, where difficulties between a returned
missionary and the Committee come out to the view of the community, that the original difficulty was not between the missionary and
the Committee, but between the missionary and his brethren of the
mission; and that the Committee interfered and assumed responsibility in the matter only when it became necessary, in order to
relieve the mission from distracting and paralyzing divisions. The

Board has had as few unpleasant relations to its missionaries, it is believed, in proportion to the number of persons, as any other missionary society in the new or old world.

"'It should be stated, that the missionary has his safeguards, as well as the pastor. The latter is not dismissed from his people without the intervention of a council or presbytery. Such a direct ecclesiastical intervention is manifestly impossible, as the case stands between the missionary and his directors. But the Committee do not see that the case would be otherwise, were the Board elected by an ecclesiastical body, a General Assembly, for instance. As it is, the missionary has the right of appeal from the Prudential Committee to the large body of ministers and laymen composing the Board. If the question between him and the Board relate merely to Christian doctrine, or to alleged immoralities, and has sufficient importance to awaken the interest of an ecclesiastical body, he can obtain an opinion on his proper Christian or ministerial standing from his presbytery or classis, or from a council, and have the benefit of such a result. With this right, the Committee have never attempted to interfere.

"'Enough has been said to show, that whatever of salutary influence there is in the connection between a pastor's faithful performance of his engagements and the continuance of his support from his people, there is no less with the missionary.

"'But the grand reliance for the proper conduct of missionaries, is

"'4. On their mutual watchfulness over each other, and the direct influence of truth on their minds and hearts.

"'As soon as a mission contains three or more missionaries, it is expected to organize itself as a self-governing community, under the laws, regulations, and general superintendence of the Board. Mutual watchfulness thus becomes the official duty of each member. It is also in a high sense the interest of each one to exercise a fraternal watchfulness over his brethren, in order to the safety and success of the enterprise in which the common welfare and happiness are embarked. And as brethren in Christ, as members of his church, and as jointly and severally his ambassadors to the heathen, — by the force of each of these relations, they are impelled to the same duty. Nor have the several missions under the care of the Board been a whit behind the ecclesiastical organizations of their native land in mutual and faithful watchfulness.

"'The influence of truth on the reason, judgment and heart of missionaries, is mainly through the intercourse kept up with the Christian world, and especially with their native land, and through their reading and studies, and the reacting effect of the faithful discharge of their missionary duties.

"'The interest which missionaries feel in their native land is not diminished by distance. Their home for Christ's sake, the home of their duty, is among the heathen, and grace makes them more than willing to live and die there. But nature has another home, dear to memory and ever interesting to thought and feeling, and with this they keep up an active correspondence during life. It is striking to observe the number of letters passing between missionaries and their friends. The effect of this correspondence must be great in cherishing the social feelings, and especially in preserving the desire for a good name in their native land. This effect is increased by the reading of religious and other newspapers, and of magazines and books, that are continually going to the missions, and causing the public opinion at home, on all subjects, to bear directly on missionaries, as it does on pastors. The Committee have long deemed it wise to pursue a liberal policy with respect to these matters, since well-informed, active and growing minds, yield most readily to wholesome rules and decisions, and to reason and common sense.

"'The correspondence of the executive officers of the Board with particular missions is more or less extended, at different times, according to circumstances. The free use of reasoning has always been awarded to them on all subjects, upon which they believe it would be useful to correspond with their brethren in the missions. No points are so much in dispute, but the Secretaries feel themselves at liberty to advert freely to them, — always being subject, of course, to have their correspondence revised at pleasure by the Committee, or by the Board. They may write upon caste, polygamy, slavery, creeds, preaching, education, the use of the press, modes of worship, evidence of piety, the Christian life, and numberless other kindred subjects. And they may give all the weight they can to their arguments, by bringing the experience of other missions, and what they know of the state of the public mind at home, to bear on the questions at issue. The religious newspapers and other periodicals furnish the means of performing this latter service in respect to all subjects that interest and excite the community. It is believed to be the duty of the Secretaries, acting under the direction of the Committee, to see that the missions are well furnished with the lights of truth. The Committee have had ample evidence of the value of this method of control. No class of ministers being more select than that which is engaged in the foreign missions, on none does correct reasoning, and especially that which is founded on the word of God, have more influence. In general, nothing more is needed, in the actual relations and responsibilities of missionaries, to control the opinions and operations of a mission, than good scriptural arguments. And in all cases affecting the conscience, the less there is of an appearance of authority, the better the result.

'"Libraries are connected with the several missions, some of which are large and valuable; the *material* for labor, in all the departments, is abundantly supplied; and the missionary, in common with the pastor, has his peculiar inducements to study, and to cultivate his mind and heart, growing out of the exigencies of his position. And the more devoted, laborious and faithful he is in his work, the less need does he commonly stand in of influence and direction from without. Truth, conscience, a sense of duty, regard for unity and peace, deference to public opinion, and concern for God's glory and the good of mankind, — things such as these (not without some thought, it may be, of engagements to the Board and its patrons, and of the inconveniences resulting from their violation) have rarely failed to be sufficient, with the divine blessing, to secure order and efficiency in the working of Christian missions in foreign lands. In other words, it is the blessing of God on the free and vigorous working of the voluntary principle in missions, based on Christian piety and intelligence.

"'The Committee believe it would be found, on a careful examination of the history of missions, that no method of controlling missionaries, differing substantially from the one described in this report, has ever been effectual. Protestant missions, especially, and most of all from this country, can in no other way be long kept in existence.

"'Should it be supposed, that the great distance of the missions from the community which supports them must weaken the controlling influence, two things are to be considered: — (1.) The public attention is more generally and intently fixed on the conduct of the missionaries, than it is upon that of ministers any where at home. (2.) There is no greater probability that all the members of one of the larger missions will go wrong together, or will countenance one of their own number in so doing, than that there will be similar wrong doing in almost any body of ministers, of equal numbers, which can be named in our own country. For they are as intelligent, as pious, have as much principle and sense of character, and as much desire to please God and do good; and they know that they are watched by Christians over the world.

"'It is due to the patrons of the Board, who may entertain doubts whether its constitution is well adapted to secure the safest and most efficient prosecution of missions among the heathen, to advert briefly to the subject; indeed, the discussion would not otherwise be complete.

"'The Prudential Committee have not been able to see that the Board would increase its working power by any considerable changes in its constitution. So far, indeed, as the greater part of New England is concerned, there does not seem to be a possibility of forming what is called an ecclesiastical Board, unless the relations of the Congregational churches to each other are first essentially modified. And were such a Board to be created, it would no more possess authority to perform purely ecclesiastical acts, than has the present Board. The Committee presume that it would not be wise to attempt a change in the present organization, until the details of the change are clearly proposed and understood, and well considered; nor until there is good reason to believe the new or modified organization would work better than the present; that it will command more confidence at home among the churches, and more abroad with the missionaries; and that it will secure the confidence which the present Board has gained in the mercantile world. Our fathers were providentially led to adopt the existing form of organization for conducting foreign missions, as best adapted to their day; and when the existing form is found not to answer the purpose, their children will doubtless change it. It was instituted solely for the spread of the Gospel among the heathen, and in times favorable for taking an unbiassed view of the subject; and hitherto it has actually worked better than any of its founders ventured to expect. It has, indeed, signally enjoyed the blessing of God. The attendance and interest at its annual meetings, the responses to its appeals for funds, the number and character of the men who go as its mis-

4

sionaries, the success of its missions, and the standing it is permitted to hold in the estimation of Christians generally, place it on a
footing with other kindred institutions, whether voluntary or ecclesiastical. Nor does it appear to have less hold than other societies
on the confidence, affection and conduct of its missionaries, nor upon
the community to which it looks for support. Those who suppose
that the leading motive with the community to contribute funds for
the support of a system of missions is in the *origin* of a missionary
society, or in the *form of its constitution*, fall into an error. It is
rather in the number and importance of the missions ; in the tokens
of God's presence in those missions ; in the evidence of judgment,
faithfulness and energy in the administration. The essential thing
doubtless is, that the contributors have the means of obtaining
satisfactory evidence that their money is well employed. This
they have in respect to the Board. Its one hundred and eighty
Corporate Members, and its five or six thousand Honorary Members, invariably secure for it an annual meeting, (continuing three
days,) that forms a *representation* of the individuals and of the Christian community supporting its operations, as real, active and extensive, as any other benevolent society has in this country, or
in the world. There is at that meeting a representation from most
parts of the community ; and the greater portion, if not the whole
of those present, take an intelligent and lively interest in the enterprise. It would seem to be scarcely possible, in the present state
of the churches, that the interests of a system of missions should
be more perfectly represented, or be surrounded with more effectual
safeguards.

"'The Honorary Members have the same right with the Corporate
Members of calling up subjects for inquiry at the meetings, of proposing resolutions, of acting on committees, of declaring their opinions, and of exerting every kind of moral influence ; and there was
never an important subject before the annual meeting for discussion,
when the prevailing opinion of the meeting was not certainly known.
The right of voting is, indeed, restricted by the Charter to members
elected by ballot ; and the value of the charter, in a financial point
of view, forbids its being unnecessarily relinquished, or set aside.
These voting members are the trustees for the funds ; and by accepting the trust, they come individually under special obligation
with regard to the disposal of the funds, the preservation of the
credit of the institution, and the general working of the system.
They are specially bound to attend the annual meetings. Whatever
theoretical importance (and it is not to be undervalued) is attached
to an extension of the privilege of voting, the Committee believe
that, from the beginning, it would not have altered a single result of
any importance in the proceedings of the Board. And greatly must
the religious state of our churches be changed for the worse, before
there can be any real danger in the present organization.

"'The Board is to be viewed as an AGENCY, acting for such as
choose to employ it. It does not profess to be, and it is not, a distinct power with separate interests from the churches ; nor are its
agents sent into parishes as a substitute for the pastor, or as a co-
ordinate power, to advocate a distinct and independent interest, in

which the pastor and people have no concern; but, for the time being, they are mere auxiliaries to the pastors — the *agents of the pastors* — the pastors being the responsible persons. When the present organization is no longer deserving of confidence, it will soon die, as a thing of course. So far as the Board is an active and influential body, it is a mere creature of the public mind. It must go along with the permanent majority. It has no authority. It cannot, except by an abuse of terms, be said to levy taxes. It taxes no one. It can only state the command of Christ, the necessities of the heathen, the facilities for doing the work of missions, its own plans and operations, and God's blessing upon them; and argue, exhort and plead. Men give or not, just as they please; and it is best that it should be so.

"'The corrective power, in respect to the undue multiplication and irregular working of voluntary associations, lies with the pastors and churches. It is for them, individually, to decide what objects shall and what shall not have access to their pulpits by means of agents. Here lies the only corrective power — where it ought to lie — in the primary associations and assemblies of the Christian Church; and here there is such a power, easily applied, and, if applied, adequate to the emergency.

II.
THE MISSION CHURCHES.

1. THE LIBERTY BELONGING TO MISSION CHURCHES.

"'The Mission Churches in foreign lands, connected with the missions under the care of the Board, do not come properly under the jurisdiction of any body of men in this country. This is true of course so far as the Board is concerned, since that is not a body having ecclesiastical authority; and it is believed to be equally true in respect to all ecclesiastical bodies. The influence exerted upon the mission churches by the ecclesiastical bodies of this country must be through the missionaries. We can claim no jurisdiction over them because we planted them.

"'The great object of foreign missions is to persuade men to be reconciled to God, as their rightful and only Sovereign; and the organization of churches is as really a means to this great end, as the preaching of the Gospel, or the printing of the Holy Scriptures. When the time comes for organizing native converts into churches, the missionaries, acting in behalf of these children in knowledge and in the power of self-organization and government, cannot properly be restrained, by foreign interference, from conforming the organization to what *they* regard as the apostolical usage in similar cases; — having respect, of course, to those necessary limitations already mentioned, to which they have voluntarily subjected themselves for the maintenance of their social existence as missions, and for securing a regular and competent support from the Christian community at home. (See pp. 66, 67.) The result may be a much simpler organization for the mission churches, than is found in lands that have long sat under the light and influences of the Gospel.

Indeed, experience has clearly shown, that it is not well to attempt the transfer of the religious denominations of Christendom, full-grown and with all their peculiarities, into heathen lands ; at least, until the new-born churches shall have had time to acquire a good degree of discriminative and self-governing power. The experience acquired in lands long Christian partially fails us when we go into heathen countries. We need to gain a new experience, and to revise many of our principles and usages ; and for this purpose to go prayerfully to the New Testament.

" ' The religious liberty which we ourselves enjoy is equally the birthright of Christian converts in every part of the heathen world, on coming into the spiritual kingdom of Jesus Christ, which they may claim as soon as they are prepared for it ; just as American freedom is the birthright of our own children. The right of our children is not infringed by that dependence and control which they need during their infancy and childhood. It is even their right to claim, that the parent *shall* thus act for them in the early stages of their existence. But the wise parent will always form the principles and habits of his child with reference to the time when the right of self-control must be fully exercised and yielded. In like manner, the missionary must needs give form, at the outset, to the constitution and habits of the mission churches ; and for a time he must virtually govern them. But he will do this with a constant regard to the coming period, when those churches must and will act independently. He will train them, as the Apostles evidently trained the churches under their care, so that they may be early freed from the necessity of missionary supervision. In the infancy of the Christian community that is placed under his care, he will act on such scriptural principles and usages as he deems best fitted to make the most of every individual member of the church. And this he will do at any amount of personal inconvenience to himself ; remembering that the power of carrying burdens is acquired by practice, and that native converts can be inured to responsibilities only by having responsibilities placed upon them, and by a conviction that they are trusted. At the risk of multiplying his most painful cares and disappointments, he will also aim to provide a native pastor for each church, just as early as he can in the period of his own missionary supervision, that the spiritual machinery may be homogeneous and complete in all its parts, and may the sooner be made to work without foreign aid. In no other way, indeed, can he secure the grand result for which he labors — the development of the self-sustaining, self-governing power in the native Christian community.

" ' Nor may we expect or require of the mission churches, as the condition of giving them the Gospel and its institutions, that they shall always think, judge and act just as we do. We ought cheerfully to abide the consequences of the full assertion of our principles ; and have patience, and bear long, and not give over, till it is evident that our moral means are exhausted, and that our enterprise has failed.

" ' The necessity for long-suffering forbearance with churches gathered from among the heathen will be the more obvious, if we consider three things.

"'One is thus stated in the Cambridge Platform.* "The weakest measure of faith is to be accepted in those that desire to be admitted into the church; because weak Christians, if sincere, have the substance of that faith, repentance and holiness, which is required in church members, and such have the most need of ordinances for their confirmation and growth in grace. The Lord Jesus would not quench the smoking flax, nor break the bruised reed, but gathers the lambs in his arms and carries them in his bosom." None will question, that the liberty of mission churches, with respect to the admission of members, goes to this extent. Of all churches, those gathered among the heathen have most reason for asserting this freedom, since nowhere are the lambs of the flock so much exposed while out of the fold, and nowhere, comparatively speaking, are they so many.

"'Another thing is this. There are not several churches existing in one place, as in most of our towns, formed to a great extent on the principle of elective affinity. *All* who give credible evidence of Christian character must come into one and the same church, or be excluded altogether from church membership, and the ordinances of the Gospel.

"'Again, we should consider the extreme moral and social degradation of all heathen communities, in which mission churches are gathered. Read the first chapter of the Epistle to the Romans. Read the journals of modern missionaries. Consider the decline of mind among the masses of the people, under the long reign of paganism; the paralysis of the moral sense and conscience; the grossness of habits, physical and mental, in speech and action, in domestic life and all social intercourse. Consider the absence of almost all those ideas which lie at the foundation of moral elevation in character; the absence of words, even, to serve as pure vehicles of holy thought and sentiment; the absence of a correct public opinion on all things appertaining to manners and morals; and the constant and all-pervading presence of polluting, degrading, soul-destroying temptations.

"'Causes such as these had their effects in the churches gathered by the Apostle Paul, as we see in his Epistles. When the Apostle directed his attention, for instance, to the church at Corinth, on which he had bestowed so great an amount of labor, he found occasion to lament the many who were carried away by false teachers, the disorder of their worship, their irregularities at the Lord's Supper, their neglect to discipline immoral members, their division into parties, their spirit of litigation, their debates, envyings, wraths, strifes, backbitings, whisperings, swellings, tumults. And how soon were a portion of the Galatians seduced from the Gospel, and from their loyalty to the truth, and turned again to their old bondage unto weak and beggarly elements, observing days, and months, and times, and years; so that the Apostle confesses his fears that he had labored in vain among them. He thinks it needful to exhort the Ephesian church to put away lying, and to exhort those who had been dishonest before their conversion to steal

* Ch. XII., § 3.

no more, and those who had been avaricious and impure to have
nothing more to do with fornication and covetousness. Four years
after he had addressed his Epistle to the Ephesians, he informs
Timothy that all his helpers in Lesser Asia were turned away from
him, and even two who had attained to some distinction. Before
the date of his Epistle, he evidently had not full confidence in some
of the native pastors in that province, as appears from his address to
them at Miletus. While at Rome, he writes that some in that city
preached Christ of envy and strife, supposing to add affliction to his
bonds; and at his first arraignment before Cæsar, not a member of
that church had the moral courage to stand by him. Writing to the
Philippians, he declares his belief that many church members were
enemies of the cross of Christ, whose god was their belly, who
gloried in their shame, and minded earthly things. In this same
Epistle, he speaks in desponding terms of his native helpers, among
whom were none like-minded with Timothy, but all sought their
own, and not the things which were Jesus Christ's. He thought it
needful to exhort the Colossians not to lie one to another; and the
Thessalonians to withdraw from such of their number as walked
disorderly. He cautions Timothy against fables, endless genealogies,
and profane and vain babblings, as if such were prevalent in some
of the churches; and speaks of preachers destitute of the truth,
possessing corrupt minds, ignorant, proud, addicted to controversies
which engendered envy, strifes, and perverse disputations and rail-
ings; and of some who had even made shipwreck of the faith, and
added blasphemy to their heresies.

"'And it should be added, that the Apostle John, somewhat later,
declares that many "antichrists" had gone out from the church,
because they did not really belong to it in spirit and character, and,
of course, had been in it, denying, as he says, the Father and the
Son.

"'Yet it is generally supposed, whether correctly or not, that the
apostolical churches possessed as much piety as exists in any portions of the visible church of our country and times, if not more.
Indeed, the Apostle Paul speaks of the Roman Christians, only a
few years before the date of his Epistles to Timothy, as being noted
for their faith throughout the world. At the very time of his censures on the Corinthians, he declares that church to be "enriched
by Jesus Christ, in all utterance and in all knowledge," so that it
came behind in no gift. And while he so seriously cautions the
Ephesians, he ceases not to give thanks for their "faith in the Lord
Jesus, and their love unto all the saints." He thanked God upon
every remembrance of the Philippians; and when he wrote to the
Colossians, he gave thanks for their faith in Christ Jesus, and their
love in the Spirit and to all the saints. And how remarkable his
testimony in behalf of the Thessalonians! He remembered without ceasing, and with constant gratitude, their work of faith, and
labor of love, and patience of hope in the Lord Jesus Christ, wherein
they had become followers of him and of the Lord, having received
the word in much affliction, with joy of the Holy Ghost; so that
they were ensamples to all that believed, in Macedonia and Achaia.

"'The fact undoubtedly is, that visible irregularities and disorders, and even scandalous immoralities, are more to be expected in churches gathered from among the heathen; and are, at the same time, to a certain extent, more consistent with grace in the church, than in countries that have long enjoyed the light and influence of the Gospel. While the primitive converts from paganism were remarkable for the high tone of their religious feelings, and the simplicity and strength of their faith, they were wanting in respect to a clear, practical apprehension of the ethical code of the Gospel. It is obvious, indeed, that Paul found the burden of his "care of all the churches" much increased by the deceptive, impure, and thoroughly wicked character of the age and countries in which he labored as a missionary and apostle. His manner of treating the native pastors and churches, notwithstanding their imperfections, is a model for missionaries and their supporters in our day; who ought to expect greater external manifestations of ignorance on moral subjects, and of weakness and sin, in churches that are gathered in Africa, India, the Sandwich Islands, and among the Indian tribes, than in churches that existed at Ephesus, Colosse, Corinth, and the cities of Galatia, in the palmy days of Roman civilization.

"'In reasoning, however, about mission churches among the heathen, whether ancient or modern, we should take into view the moral imperfections found in all human associations, in every land and every age. How many such imperfections do actually exist now in the churches of which we are members, and how difficult it has been found to apply a remedy. How much time and labor has it cost, in our most favored States, so to affect the public sentiment of professed Christians, as to induce them universally to abandon and avoid the trade in ardent spirits; how hard to restrain multitudes of professors of religion from divers conformities to the world, having no countenance in the Gospel; and how impossible, hitherto, to create a public sentiment in any church, that shall give the sin of *covetousness*, for instance, the place expressly assigned to it in the Word of God.

2. HOW FAR THE BOARD IS RESPONSIBLE FOR THE TEACHING OF THE MISSIONARIES, AND FOR THE CHARACTER OF THE MISSION CHURCHES.

"'The Board is responsible *directly*, in the manner which has been described, for the *teaching of the missionaries*. It cannot guaranty, however, an entire uniformity in their teaching. That diversity in mental habits, opinions, preaching, and social intercourse, which exists without rebuke among ministers of the same denomination at home, must be expected and tolerated among missionaries.

"'The Board can require of missionaries a compliance with their express and implied engagements, and the performance of all duties that are manifestly essential to the success of the enterprise. But in respect even to those fundamental obligations, when the mind of the missionary has swung so far off from the line of his duty as to refuse a compliance, *enforcement* is commonly found to be out of the question; generally, no other course is left but to dissolve his connection. The Board cannot, therefore, be held responsible for the invariable continuance of its missionaries in the path of their duty, even in respect to matters of vital importance. Its responsibility is limited to the proper selection of fields to be cultivated; to the judicious appointment and designation of missionaries; to the constitution and laws by which the several missions are formed into self-governing communities; to the equitable distribution of the funds placed at its disposal; to the just and proper instruction of the missionaries in matters within the province of the Board; to timely and needful suggestions, admonitions, exhortations and appeals, fraternally addressed; and, finally, to a faithful superintendence of the missions, and a decisive intervention when there are manifest departures from duty in the missionaries.

"'But while the Board is directly responsible for the *teaching* of the missionaries, it cannot be held to a full responsibility for the *results* of their labors. Paul may plant, and Apollos water, but God giveth the increase. The Apostle to the Gentiles, as we have seen, had to sorrow much over the imperfect results of his labors. As *he* was not fully responsible for the character of the churches he planted, so *missionaries* cannot now be held to a full responsibility for the character of their mission churches. But the *Board*, as a missionary institution, (and the same would be true were it an ecclesiastical body,) is even less responsible than are its missionaries, for the character of the mission churches. It is not even directly responsible for the character of those churches, but only through the missionaries; and only so far through them, as it is properly held accountable for their character and teaching. If there be stupidity, ignorance, weakness, waywardness, perverseness, and even more scandalous wickedness in the mission churches — as the history of the Apostolical Churches would lead us to expect, even when the churches are gathered by the most able and faithful missionaries — they can be operated upon only through the missionaries. The Board cannot wisely address those churches directly on the subject, nor can any other body of men in this country, however constituted.

"'But when evils exist in the mission churches, the Prudential Committee may and must inquire, whether the *missionaries* are performing their duty. In one instance, some years ago, having reason to apprehend that admissions were made to a church in one of the missions, without a proper attention to the evidences of piety, the Board, at its annual meeting, instructed the Prudential Committee to inquire into the facts, with a view to a correction of the evil; and such inquiries were made by the Committee, and with a satisfactory issue. Inquiries have also been made by the Committee, as to the teaching of missionaries in some of the missions, with respect to alleged irregularities and evils in mission churches, and in the social and domestic state of native Christian communities. So far as a judicious and proper correspondence with the missionaries may properly affect their incipient measures, in the formation of churches, and their subsequent teachings, and so far as those measures determine the character of the churches, the Board is responsible for the character of the native churches.

"'Its responsibility in respect to the *existence of slavery* in several of the Indian churches has some peculiar modifications in the cir-

cumstances of the case. The *incipient* measures for the formation of
churches among the Cherokees and Choctaws were taken thirty
years ago,—long before the subject of slavery came up for discussion among the churches at home. God was soon pleased hopefully
to renew the hearts of a number of slaveholding Indians, and, upon
giving credible evidence of piety, they were received into the church.
What the missionaries *could then* have done, had they perceived all
the bearings of that subject, cannot be known. The Indians are
now partially civilized, and have organized governments. There
are slaveholding whites without, who are supposed to take an interest in continuing slavery among them, and slaveholding whites
within, married to Indian wives, and thus become a part of the
nation; and their churches are organized Congregationally in one
tribe, and Presbyterially in another. So that the missionaries, like
pastors among ourselves, are obliged now to depend wholly on instruction and persuasion for their influence on the churches under
their care. The religious liberty of those churches is to be respected. We should stand firm in support of our principles as to the
rights of churches. Unless the missionaries are able to produce
conviction—however desirable it may be that they should do it—
the *churches* in the one case, and the *sessions* in the other, will vote
in opposition to their views. It is admitted, however, that the missionaries should do all in their power, in the exercise of their best
discretion, to lead those churches and sessions to a right appreciation of their duty in this matter; and that they should use a direct
influence, at their discretion, to eradicate the evil of slavery, as well
as all other evils, from the churches under their care. But it is
obvious that the Board, and the missionaries under its direction,
have not precisely *the same degree* of responsibility for the existence
of slavery in the churches just referred to; that they would have in
respect to churches yet to be formed among the tribes of the African
continent, or were churches now to be formed, for the first time,
among the Indian tribes.

"'How long we should bear with mission churches that do not
come up to our standard of duty, and may even greatly try our
spirits, is what the Committee are not able to decide. But they
cannot doubt that we should imitate the example of Him, who
"maketh his sun to rise on the evil and on the good, and sendeth
rain on the just and on the unjust;" and who "so loved the world
that he gave his only begotten Son, that whosoever believeth in
him should not perish, but have everlasting life:" and who "is long
suffering to us-ward, not willing that any should perish, but that all
should come to repentance." We need an abounding charity, a
most Christ-like feeling, when we come to the question of withdrawing our support from churches we have gathered among the
heathen, because they are slow in rising to our standard of Christian
excellence. Should their deficiency be in any measure owing to
our lack of knowledge on the subject, when we commenced our
labors among them, it will strengthen our motives for forbearance.
Before deciding a question so momentous to the interests of souls,
and to our own future peace of conscience, it would be well to see
whether we do not find in those churches the same spiritual results.
4 *

the same living Christianity, and the same moral defects, that existed in the churches planted and nurtured by the Apostles ; and
whether the Lord Jesus does not bless them with outpourings of his
Holy Spirit, though they cannot yet be persuaded, in all important
respects, to follow us.

" ' We should remember, that none of us are principals in this work
of missions. The work is Christ's, not ours ; and we, are all his
servants, to do his will. And if we look into our own churches, and
consider their manifold imperfections, we shall find abundant cause
for charity and forbearance in respect to all churches gathered
among the heathen ; and if we study the intellectual and moral condition of the pagan world, we shall only wonder that the first generation of converts from heathenism can be so far raised in the scale
of Christian morals and general excellence of character.

" ' By order and in behalf of the Prudential Committee.

RUFUS ANDERSON,   ⎫
DAVID GREENE,   ⎬ *Secretaries.*
SELAH B. TREAT,   ⎭

Missionary House, Boston, Sept., 1848.' "

Under the pretext of maintaining " the ecclesiastical
liberty of the missionaries," this report seeks to make it
appear that those missionaries have a right to admit slaveholders into their churches, and to allow them to continue
there in good standing, *and that there is ample Scriptural
warrant for such a course.* It seeks to make this appear,
in spite of the antagonistic concession, in the same document,
that slavery is " *at variance with the principles of the
Christian religion.*"

It further urges, in maintenance of the right of the
churches to vote in slaveholding candidates for church membership, (amazing as it may seem, after the concession just
mentioned !) that " The religious liberty of those churches is
to be respected. We should stand firm in support of our
principles as to the rights of churches."

What sort of thing is the " right" of a Christian church
to endorse acts " at variance with the principles of the
Christian religion " ?

But, as if to clench and secure the above amazing position
in regard to the missionaries, the report proceeds to say that,
though the Board " *is* responsible, *directly,* for the *teaching*
of the missionaries," it " cannot be held responsible for the
invariable continuance of its missionaries in the path of their
duty, *even in respect to matters of vital importance.*" Then,

it would seem, it may allow the missionaries to apostatize
without discharging them!

It would take too much space to specify and formally
expose even the principal instances of gross sophistry in this
report. The reader who is at once intelligent and careful
will find many such instances for himself. I shall speak particularly of only two of them, both contained in the last
division of the report.

In the second division of the second part, where there is a
pretence of answering the inquiry, "how far the Board is
responsible for the teaching of the missionaries, and for the
character of the mission churches," the two opening paragraphs are doubly self-refuting. This is their course of
argument, in substance, namely : —

1. The Board *is* responsible, *directly*, for the teaching of
the missionaries, and it can require of them compliance with
their engagements, and fulfilment of all duties manifestly
essential. But —

2. If the missionary refuses compliance, enforcement is
commonly impossible, and, generally, no way is left *but to
dissolve his connection.*

3. *Therefore*, the Board can*not* be held responsible for the
continuance of its missionaries, even in duties of vital
importance. For —

4. Its responsibility is limited to . . . . a faithful
superintendence of the missions, *and a decisive intervention
when there are manifest departures from duty in the
missionaries.*

This, as I have said, is doubly self-refuting. For, since
the second statement admits that the Board may *dismiss* the
persistently unfaithful missionary, it is evident that the third
statement should read—"Therefore, the Board *must* be held
responsible for the continuance of its missionaries in their
duty"! It is the obvious duty of the Board to dismiss unfaithful missionaries and substitute faithful ones. And this
fact is recognized in the fourth statement, which, in direct
and unblushing contradiction of its predecessor, admits a
"*decisive intervention*" by the Board, whenever the missionaries shall violate their duty.

The other passage upon which I wish to remark is three
paragraphs further on, where the Secretaries try to excuse

the Board from responsibility for the existence of slavery in the mission churches.

After admitting that the Cherokees and Choctaws were slaveholding nations thirty years before, when missionary labor was first commenced among them, and that slaveholding Indians were soon adjudged to have given " credible evidence of piety," and were thereupon received into the church, the report proceeds —

" What the missionaries could then have done, had they perceived all the bearings of that subject, *cannot be known.*"

This statement is absurdly false. What the missionaries could have done *is* known, and is as plain as daylight. They could have taught their disciples that, slavery being " at variance with the principles of the Christian religion," the persistent slaveholder could not possibly give " credible evidence of piety," and thus could not be admitted to the church! Whether the unconverted Indians were purified from slavery or not, the missionaries were able to keep their *churches* pure, by utterly refusing to admit slaveholders! But they did not choose to do this! And the Board did not choose to require it of them! And the Secretaries do not shrink from the disingenuousness of saying, in the very paragraph treating of the *commencement* of slavery in the Indian churches, (contained in the same Annual Report which admits, p. 89, that " some of the *earliest* converts, in both nations, were the proprietors of slaves,") that the action of the missionaries is limited by the vote of the churches! As if this excused the original formation of a church, by the admission of slaveholders as its earliest members, on the responsibility, and by the action, of the missionaries alone!

Such are some of the disgraceful shifts which were found absolutely necessary to make out a plausible case in vindication of the Board.

Let us see now by what means the report tries to excuse the failure of the missionaries to perform their duty of keeping slaveholders out of the churches, and the failure of the Board to require its performance. It says that these churches were formed, and slaveholders incorporated into them, " long before the subject of slavery came up for discussion among the churches at home." This is true. And it is an unspeakable disgrace to the clergy, the teachers and

guides of those "churches at home," that they not only
slumbered over the complicity of themselves and their people with this awful sin, (neglecting, in the first place, to
recognize or look at it,) but that, when William Lloyd
Garrison brought out the evidence of the oppressions of the
slave and the direct influence of the Northern people in continuing this oppression, and made direct appeal to the
ministers of Boston, and of Massachusetts, to lift up their
voices on that subject, they first utterly refused,* and then
gave their influence on the other side.

It is true, most disgracefully for the churches and their
clerical leaders, that the subject of slavery did not "come
up for discussion in the churches" until a portion of what
those churches opprobriously call "the world" had for years
been actively and heartily engaged in it. But how amazing
is the plea, offered by the recognized teachers of morals and
religion, in excuse for having failed to teach a certain
essential part of morality and religion, that the pupils had
not yet discovered that it was needful to be taught! Yet
the Secretaries *must* say such foolish things as this, unless
they will either confess their great sin, or utterly hold their
peace!

The pious language with which this report is filled—
intended, as it is, to continue the recognition of slaveholding
in the mission churches as right, and to stave off all
remonstrances against it, (in spite of the admission, p. 68, that
slavery is "at variance with the principles of the Christian
religion,")—is a serious aggravation of its guilt.

Immediately following this long report by the Secretaries,
in the Annual Report of 1848, comes a still longer correspondence with the Cherokee and Choctaw missions, making
a practical application of the theory of the Prudential Committee (just rehearsed) for the continued permission of slaveholding in church members, and giving elaborate statements,
from the missionaries of both nations, of *their* theories, their
customs, and their intentions, in regard to that subject.

---

* One of the ministers thus individually appealed to by Mr. Garrison on
this subject was Rev. Dr. Lyman Beecher, then a recognized leader among
the Orthodox Congregational churches. To a statement of the appalling
facts involved in slavery, and an urgent appeal that he would do *something*
in opposition to it, he replied that he "had already too many irons in the
fire to be able to give any attention to it."

This correspondence, covering nearly thirty-three closely printed octavo pages in the Annual Report, (pp. 80 to 113,) is here subjoined.

" CORRESPONDENCE WITH THE CHEROKEE AND CHOCTAW MISSIONS.

" This correspondence was brought before the Board by a special report of the Prudential Committee. Their communication is as follows:—

" 'It has been the wish of the Committee, for more than a year past, that the Secretary having charge of the Indian department might visit the Cherokee and Choctaw missions. Prior, indeed, to the last annual meeting, Mr. Greene was requested to hold himself in readiness to make such a visit in the course of a few weeks. The object of the Committee was twofold:—1. To ascertain, as fully as practicable, the state and prospects of these missions; and, 2. To inquire more particularly into their relations to the subject of slavery.

" 'After the meeting at Buffalo, however, the Committee became satisfied that Mr. Greene ought to be excused from taking this journey, for reasons growing out of the state of his health. Mr. Treat was directed, therefore, to visit the Cherokee and Choctaw missions as soon as he could make the necessary arrangements. He left accordingly on the 30th of November, and returned on the 1st of April, having been absent seventeen weeks and a half. While he was in the Indian territory, he had personal interviews with all the missionaries individually; and he spent several days with each of the missions assembled in their collective capacity. His attention was particularly directed to the subject of slavery in its relations to the labors of these brethren; and much time was given to the acquiring of such information as appeared to be most important for the guidance of the Committee. After a full conference, each mission concluded to address a letter to the Committee, exhibiting their views and principles in detail. The letter from the Cherokee mission was received April 26; that from the Choctaw mission, May 6. Subsequently, and as soon as was practicable, Mr. Treat drew up a report on the general subject, presenting what seemed to be the leading features of the case. This report, together with the letters from the two missions, were taken into consideration on the 20th of June; and the Committee directed a communication to be addressed to the missions in reply, setting forth their views in regard to the different topics which were thought to require notice. The answer of the brethren has not been received. Both missions had previously appointed meetings to be held simultaneously with the annual meeting of the Board; and it is presumed that they have the subject now under consideration.

" 'The Committee regret that they are not able to report a final adjustment of this embarrassing question; but they have found it impossible to bring about this result. Knowing, however, the anxiety of the Board to be informed as to what has actually been done, they now submit for its consideration the documents which have been already mentioned.'

" The report of Mr. Treat, the first of the documents mentioned in the foregoing communication, is in the following language: —

"' To the Prudential Committee of the American Board of Commissioners for Foreign Missions: —

"' The instructions under which I was directed to visit the Cherokee and Choctaw missions will be apparent from the following action of the Prudential Committee, Nov. 23, 1847: —

" Mr. Treat having requested definite information as to the views of the Committee, in directing him to visit the Choctaw and Cherokee missions, it was

" Resolved, 1. That he be instructed to ascertain, as fully and accurately as practicable, the present state and prospects of the missions, for the information of the Committee, and for the assistance of himself in his correspondence hereafter with the missions.

" Resolved, 2. That he be instructed to go into a full and fraternal examination of the relations of the missions, and the churches under their care, to the subject of slavery ; and the missionaries are requested to give him all the information in their power bearing upon the case."

"' I arrived at Dwight, the first station which I visited, on the 4th of January, 1848. The eight following weeks were wholly spent within the limits of the Cherokee and Choctaw nations. During this period, I saw all the missionaries and assistant missionaries under the direction of the Board ; as also the missionaries and educational establishments sustained by other organizations within the boundaries of the two nations. It was my endeavor to acquaint myself, as fully as practicable, with the plans and labors of our brethren ; and in relation to the general interests of the missions, I shall hold myself in readiness to make such communications, and in such form, as the Committee may direct.

"' It seems desirable, however, that the Committee should receive a report on the relation of the two missions to the subject of slavery, without any further delay. Much time and reflection have been given to the examination of those topics which occurred to me as most important ; and it is but simple justice to the missionaries to say, that they have done all that I expected, or wished, to facilitate my inquiries. They were fully aware of the delicacy of their position. Still, they withheld no information which I asked ; but, on the contrary, met the difficulties and trials of the case with a frankness and self-forgetfulness which entitle them to my warmest thanks.

"' As there are many points of resemblance between slavery as it exists among the Cherokees, and the same institution as it is found among their brethren south of the Arkansas ; and as the two missions stand upon ground which, in many respects, is common to both, it will be more convenient, and probably more satisfactory, to consider the subject in its relations to both at the same time. For

88   THE AMERICAN BOARD

the purpose of preventing misapprehension, it may be well to state, in this place, that the Choctaws and Chickasaws who have removed to the Indian territory now live under one government, and constitute one people, known as the "Choctaw Nation." In the following remarks, therefore, I shall be understood as applying the term "Choctaws," "Choctaw Nation," &c., to the whole community, as thus constituted; unless I expressly distinguish one class of Indians from the other.

"'I. SLAVERY AMONG THE CHEROKEES AND CHOCTAWS.

"'1. *Its Origin.*

"'It was hardly to be expected, perhaps, that we should be able to ascertain the early history of slavery, as it exists among these Indian tribes, to our perfect satisfaction. All accounts agree, however, that it was introduced into each of them by white men.

"'Some have supposed that it had its origin among the Cherokees no farther back than the Revolutionary war; when a number of tories, holding slaves, fled from the Southern States, and took refuge among this people. But there is one slave now living, at the age of seventy-five, who was born in a state of servitude in the old Cherokee nation. Hence we may conclude that the institution first took root in this tribe nearly, if not quite, one hundred years ago. And it is not unlikely that the evil began with white men, who settled in the nation, and married Cherokee women. At a later day, slaves were frequently introduced by purchase; and many are now to be found who came originally from the Southern States.

"'It is said that negro slaves were first introduced among the Chickasaws about the middle of the last century, by unprincipled white men, who stole them from Southern planters, and afterwards secreted them within the old nation. Slavery among the Choctaws, it is affirmed, had its origin in the intermarriage of white men with Choctaw women. Subsequently, as they obtained the means, they imitated the example of their civilized neighbors; and those who lived upon the "Natchez Trace," and who were accustomed to entertain travellers in their humble dwellings, seem to have acquired, in process of time, quite a number of slaves. The treaty of 1830 led to a considerable increase of this species of property; and when the Chickasaws sold their lands east of the Mississippi, they made large additions to their slave population.

"'2. *Its Character.*

"'The foregoing statements will suggest all that is necessary to be known in relation to this topic. As the institution was derived from the whites, it has all the general characteristics of negro slavery in the southern portion of our Union. In such a state of society as we find among these Indians, there must of necessity be some modification of the system; but in all its essential features, it remains unchanged.

"'3. *Number of Slaves.*

"'Upon this point, it is impossible to obtain reliable information. No census of the slaves has been taken recently in either nation;

and different individuals have very different opinions as to their present number. Some say that among the Cherokees there are not more than seven hundred ; while others think there are as many as fifteen hundred. The latter is the estimate of the Principal Chief, and it is most likely to be correct. At any rate, we must suppose the proportion of slaves to Cherokees to be nearly, if not quite, as one to ten.

" ' The better opinion seems to be, that the whole number of slaves in the Choctaw nation is at least two thousand. Of these, however, the Chickasaws possess more than their proportionate share. The ratio of the Chickasaws to their slaves is about five or six to one ; while the Choctaws are to their slaves, probably, as ten or twelve to one.

" ' The number of slaves, whether among the Cherokees or Choctaws, does not appear to be materially affected by the introduction of negroes from the adjacent States. But there is undoubtedly a natural increase going on all the while ; an increase, too, which is greater than that of the Indians themselves. A few slaves are sold out of these nations, from time to time ; and occasionally one obtains his freedom by his own efforts or those of his friends, or by the voluntary act of his master.

" '4. Their Treatment.

" ' It is the opinion of almost every missionary, that slavery exists among these tribes in a milder form than that which is generally found in the States ; and this is thought to be the opinion of the slaves themselves who reside in the Indian territory. As a general truth, it is affirmed, they have a comfortable supply of food and clothing ; and they are seldom tasked beyond their strength. It is admitted, however, that there are cases of gross cruelty and oppression.

" ' The conclusion to which my own mind has been brought does not differ materially from that of the missionaries. I do not imagine that the slaves held by Cherokees or Choctaws are generally overtasked. On the contrary, I presume that they frequently have too little labor to perform for their own good. Indolence is one of the besetting sins of all red men ; and hence their ideas of labor, not only as affecting themselves, but others also, are very apt to be erroneous. Nor do I suppose that there is much intentional omission, on the part of the masters, to furnish the necessary food and clothing. And it is quite certain that slaves are much more on a footing of equality with their owners in these tribes, than they are among the whites.

" ' Still, it is hardly possible that persons held in bondage by such a people should be in as favorable circumstances as those who have fallen into the hands of enlightened and humane masters in the States ; especially if those masters are under the influence of Christian principle, and are endeavoring to treat their slaves according to the injunctions of the Gospel. For, while it is true that a few slaveholders in the Cherokee and Choctaw nations manifest a commendable solicitude in regard to the spiritual interests of their slaves, it is also true, that they cannot have that ability to give religious instruction, even if they fully appreciate its importance, which is found in communities further advanced in Christian knowledge and civilization. I should say, therefore, that many slaves in the States are better off than any among the Cherokees; while, at the same time, there are multitudes who are in a much worse condition.

"'5. *Laws relating to Slavery.*

"'The legislation of the Cherokees, so far as it affects free negroes and slaves, appears to be milder than that of most slaveholding communities. For example, the only restriction upon emancipation is contained in the third section of an act, passed Dec. 2, 1842, which is as follows:—

"*Be it further enacted*, That should any citizen or citizens of this Nation free any negro or negroes, the said citizen or citizens shall be responsible for the conduct of the negro or negroes so freed; and in case the citizen or citizens, so freeing any negro or negroes, shall die or remove from the limits of this nation, it shall be required of such negro or negroes that he, she or they give satisfactory security to any one of the Circuit Judges for their conduct; or, herein failing, he, she or they shall be subject to removal as above specified."

"'In the two previous sections of the same act, it is made the duty of the sheriffs to notify all free negroes then in the nation, (excepting those who had been previously freed by Cherokees,) to leave the same by Jan. 1, 1843, or as soon thereafter as practicable. In case of a refusal to comply, the sheriffs were directed to report such free negroes to the United States Agent for the Cherokees, for immediate expulsion. It is by the provisions of these two sections that the "removal as above specified," in the third section, is to be explained.

"'The Committee will be sorry to learn, however, that there is another statute which debars alike the free negro and the slave from all direct access to "the lively oracles." It is as follows: "*Be it enacted by the National Council,* That from and after the passage of this act, it shall not be lawful for any person or persons whatever to teach any free negro or negroes, not of Cherokee blood, or any slave belonging to any citizen or citizens of the Nation, to read or write." The penalty annexed to a violation of this enactment is a fine of $100 to $500, at the discretion of the court trying the offence. This law is the more to be regretted, as it must needs embarrass the mission in its efforts to benefit this injured and neglected portion of the community.

"'The restrictions upon the right of property, as applicable to the colored race, are as follows: 1. No free negro or mulatto, not of Cherokee blood, may hold or own any *improvement* in the nation. 2. Slaves are prohibited from owning horses, cattle, hogs or fire-arms; and it is made the duty of the sheriff to sell, at public auction, all such property when found in his district; the proceeds of the sale, however, are to be paid to the offender, after deducting eight per cent. for the sheriff's fees. The reason assigned for so much of the law as relates to horses, cattle, and hogs, is that the ownership of such property by the slaves had become a nuisance to the master, at the same time that it was a temptation to theft, &c. It is the opinion of one missionary, at least, that this statute is not very rigidly enforced.

"'It is also enacted that patrol companies may take up and bring to punishment any negro not having a legal pass, that may be strolling about, away from the premises of his master. And any negro, not entitled to Cherokee privileges, who may be found carrying guns, pistols, bowie-knives, butcher-knives, or dirks, is liable to the summary infliction, by the patrol companies, of forty stripes save one.

"'The legislation of the Choctaws has been less enlightened and humane than that of the Cherokees. So long ago as October, 1836, the following law was passed: —

"*Be it enacted, &c.*, That from and after the passage of this act, if any citizen of the United States, acting as a missionary, or a preacher, or whatever his occupation may be, is found to take an active part in favoring the principles and notions of the most fatal and destructive doctrines of abolitionism, he shall be compelled to leave the Nation, and for ever stay out of it.

"*And be it further enacted*, That teaching slaves how to read, to write, or to sing in meeting-houses, or schools, or in any open place, without the consent of the owner, or allowing them to sit at table with him, shall be sufficient ground to convict persons of favoring the principles and notions of abolitionism."

"'At the same session, it was provided that no slave should "be in possession of any property or arms." The only penalty, however, was a forfeiture of the prohibited articles, and "any good honest slave" might "carry a gun by showing a written pass from his master or mistress." And it was further provided, that if any slave infringed any Choctaw rights, he should "be driven out of company, to behave himself;" and, in case of his return and further intrusion, he should receive ten lashes.

"'Four years later, it was enacted that all free negroes in the nation, unconnected with the Choctaw or Chickasaw blood, should leave the nation by the first of March, 1841, and for ever keep out of it; and in case of their infringing this law, they were to be seized and sold to the highest bidder for life, the proceeds of the sale to be divided among the districts according to their population. It was also enacted, that if any citizen of the nation hired, concealed, or in any way protected, any free negro, to evade the foregoing provision, he should forfeit from $250 to $500; or, if unable to pay this fine, receive fifty lashes on his bare back. And it was further enacted, that if any white man in the nation should abet, encourage or conceal a free negro, to screen him from the foregoing provision, he should be forthwith ordered out of the nation by the Chief or the Agent.

"'In October, 1846, another law was passed, which prohibited all negroes from the United States or the neighboring tribes of Indians, whether they had "papers" or not, from entering and remaining in the Choctaw nation, under pretence of hiring themselves to work. The offenders were to be taken up by the light-horsemen, and to receive not less than one hundred lashes on the bare back; and all property found in their possession was to be sold publicly, one third of the proceeds to go to the light-horsemen, and the rest to be applied to some beneficial purpose.

"'The most objectionable enactment which I find, having any bearing upon slavery, was approved Oct. 15, 1846. It is as follows:

"*Be it enacted, &c.*, That no negro slave can be emancipated in this Nation, except by application or petition of the owner to the General Council; and *Provided also*, that it shall be made to appear to the Council the owner or owners, at the time of application, shall have no debt or debts outstanding against him or her, either in or out of this Nation. Then, and in that case, the General Council shall have the power to pass an act for the owner to emancipate his or her slave, which negro, after being freed, shall leave this Nation within thirty days after the passage of this act. And in case said free negro or negroes shall return into this Nation afterwards, he, she, or they shall be subject to be taken by the light-horsemen, and exposed to public sale for the term of five years; and the funds arising from such sale shall be used as national funds."

"'6. Effects of Slavery.

"'In relation to this point, there can be but one opinion. The institution is decidedly prejudicial, in a great variety of ways, to the most important interests of both nations; and this is the conviction of some of the slaveholders themselves. Among the Cherokees, slave labor is generally, if not universally, unprofitable; and though it is more valuable in the Choctaw country, in consequence of the greater adaptation of the latter to the raising of cotton, it prevents, to a considerable extent, there as elsewhere, that self-relying industry and enterprise which are so desirable in such a community. It should be stated, however, that labor appears to have less dishonor attached to it in both these nations, than in some other slaveholding communities.

"And if we look at the moral effects of slavery on these tribes of Indians, we find them to be very much as they are found to be in other parts of the world. If there is any difference, it grows out of the fact that the moral condition of the people is lower than that of some other slaveholding communities; and, consequently, the injury inflicted upon them is less palpable. I know of no other qualification which it is necessary to make.

"'As between the tribes themselves, however, I must say, that I had deeper and more depressing emotions as to the moral evils of slavery, while I was among the Choctaws, than I had among the Cherokees; still, there may be, and there probably is, no material difference. I was told by a very intelligent white man, that two thirds of the whiskey brought into the Choctaw nation were introduced by slaves. The retributive influence which they are exerting upon their masters and upon the whole community, in this and in other ways, is truly terrific.

"'It is very clear, moreover, that the influence of the missions is neutralized, to some extent, by the existence of slavery. Whatever affects injuriously the industry or the morals of the Indians, must necessarily operate as a hinderance to missionary success. Besides, this institution among these Indians, as elsewhere, tends to foster and strengthen that selfishness which is the grand obstacle to the reception of the truth as it is in Jesus. And it will be seen more fully hereafter, that the missionaries feel themselves not a little straitened whenever they come in contact with the system; hence the Gospel is not brought to bear with its full power upon all those evils which are peculiar to such a state of society.

"'7. *Influence of Christianity on Slavery.*

"'This topic naturally suggests the following inquiries:—1. What effect has the Gospel exerted upon the condition of the slaves? 2. What effect has it had upon their number?

"'As to the first of these inquiries, it is clear to my own mind, that the influence of Christianity has been highly salutary. As the doctrines of the Bible have obtained, from year to year, a wider diffusion and a stronger hold upon the people, the feelings and conduct of masters towards their slaves have become more and more considerate and humane. One of the brethren among the Choctaws uses the following language, in which all the missionaries in both nations would doubtless unite:—"We have much reason to believe that Christianity has greatly improved the condition and character of the blacks, and the views and feelings of their masters towards them, where religion has been embraced. We have much reason to believe that religion has exerted a general and beneficial influence in this respect. And to persons thus situated, the Gospel has been glad tidings. Indeed, it would be painful to see the slaves thrown back to the condition they were in before the Gospel, with its restraints and warnings and encouragements, had reached them and their masters. We should much dread any event that would lead to such a result." And, what is more important still, it will be seen hereafter that a large number of slaves in these tribes are members of the church. Among the Choctaws, indeed, the proportion of enslaved to free communicants is nearly as one to eight, showing that the Gospel has had greater success among the blacks than the Indians.

"'In regard to the second point, however, the conclusion to which I came was less satisfactory. It seems fair to presume that a few persons have been led by Christian principle to abstain from the purchase of slaves; and such I was told was the case. But, on the other hand, we may not shut our eyes to the fact, that a process has been silently going forward which has tended to a different result.

"'As fast as the doctrines of the Gospel have exerted their appropriate influence, the Indians have advanced in civilization. They have felt new desires, and, consequently, new wants. Having these desires and experiencing these wants, they have looked around for the means of gratifying the former, and removing the latter. They have sought to do this, as others had done before them, by the acquisition of property. But the forms of investment accessible to them were very few. They could not buy land, even had they wished to do so; because their whole country belonged to the nation in common. Indeed, there was hardly any species of property it was so natural for them to desire and seek as this of which we are speaking; for it became not only a mode of investment, but, in their judgment, the means of further acquisition. If we also take into the account the hereditary repugnance of the Indian to labor; if we reflect that the slaves were capable of doing many things better than their masters; we shall see how the number of slaves may have increased, rather than diminished, as the Indians became more and more like the people around them.

" '8. *Prospective Termination of Slavery.*

" ' The mass of the people have no direct interest in slavery; and could the expediency of bringing it to a speedy termination be brought fairly before their minds, they would probably desire its removal. But they have given very little thought or attention to the subject; and it is very uncertain when the question will be extensively agitated among them.

" ' The predominant influence in both nations is mainly in the hands of slaveholders. The intelligence and enterprise which enable them to acquire this species of property, also qualify them for an active and successful participation in public affairs. And many belonging to this class would certainly resist, to the utmost, any proposal tending to the abolition of slavery. A few, indeed, might be glad to see a new order of things; but their voices, should they advocate such a change, would soon be drowned by the louder remonstrances of those who are less considerate and less disinterested.

" ' And, in looking forward to the termination of slavery among the Indians, we must not forget the adverse foreign influences to which they are exposed. The owners of slaves among the Cherokees and Choctaws are mostly whites or mixed bloods. In their feelings, sympathies and interests, therefore, they may be expected to agree, to a very considerable extent, with the same class of persons living without the nation; and hence they will be easily affected by whatever is said or done to obstruct any plans which may be proposed for the melioration of this institution within their own borders. This is particularly true of the Choctaws. Now, we may consider it as a settled point, that slaveholders in the adjacent States will never consent to the adoption of any scheme of emancipation by the Indians, or to any measures manifestly tending to this result. On the contrary, they will make the most strenuous efforts to keep things just as they are; and at the slightest indication of danger, the alarm will be sounded.

" ' The conclusion to which my own mind has been brought is, that the Indians must be expected to follow, and not precede the surrounding communities, in any scheme which contemplates the extinction of slavery.

" ' II. POLICY OF THE MISSIONS.

" ' Before entering upon the various topics which grow out of this general subject, it will be advisable to recur to the circumstances in which missionary operations were commenced among these tribes of Indians.

" ' The Cherokee mission dates from January, 1817; the Choctaw mission was begun in the summer of 1818. The laborers in both nations have generally gone from the North; and they have carried with them the sympathies and the opinions prevailing in the non-slaveholding States at the time of their departure. It is evident from their correspondence, that they were often tried and perplexed by questions of duty, occasioned by the existence of slavery around them, which arose during the progress of their work. But it was not to be expected that they should place themselves far in advance of public sentiment in New England and the Middle States, and act in accordance with views which began to be entertained among us only at a later day.

"'The leading motive of the Indians, in yielding their assent to the commencement of missions among them, was the procurement of certain educational advantages for their children. Few had any desire to have the Gospel preached to them for its own sake. On the other hand, the mass of the people felt a strong repugnance to any change in their established usages and institutions. Hence the missionaries thought themselves called upon, as far as possible, to act with that wisdom which was enjoined upon the first preachers of the Gospel by the Savior himself.

"'It so happened, moreover, that many of the earliest and warmest friends of the missions were slaveholders. "On our arrival among the Choctaws," says one of the missionaries, "these men held a commanding influence in the land. They took us by the hand, lent us aid, showed us kindness, opened their houses for us to preach in, both to themselves and to their servants; to whom we were also able to preach, because they understood English. The great mass of the Choctaws knew but little about us; nor did they feel any interest in the Gospel at that time."

"'One other fact should be kept in mind, as showing more clearly the embarrassments which appertained to the case; namely, that the Indians were dwelling in the midst of slaveholding communities. Their intercourse with whites was confined almost entirely to persons living in these communities. The public men in that part of the United States were all slaveholders. Even their great Fathers, Washington, Jefferson, Madison, &c., belonged to the same class. On the other hand, they had heard but little of the "more excellent way" that prevailed at the North; and it is presumed that they were not at all solicitous to know more. It was more congenial to their feelings to float along with the broad current in which they found themselves, leaving the responsibility, where it mainly belonged, with their white neighbors.

"'Such were the circumstances in which the missionary operations were commenced among the Cherokees and Choctaws. The way is now prepared for an inquiry into the policy which was actually adopted.

"'1. *The Preaching of the Gospel.*

"'At this distance of time, and after so many of the early laborers in the two nations have been removed by death, it would be very difficult, if not impossible, to ascertain the precise impressions of each individual as to the proper mode of exhibiting the Gospel in its bearings upon slavery. But the policy of the missions, as a whole, can be known with sufficient accuracy for all practical purposes.

"'It does not seem to have been the aim of the brethren to exert any *direct* influence, either by their public or their private teachings, upon the system of slavery. And they discovered, as they supposed, a sufficient warrant for this course in the New Testament. On looking to the example of the Savior and his Apostles, they found what they conceived to be an infallible rule to guide them in their labors. They found that nothing was said in direct condemnation of slavery as a system; neither was its sinfulness denounced, nor its continuance prohibited. But they did find that the mutual obligations of masters and servants were repeatedly and freely discussed. "Here then," they seem to have argued, "is our course marked out for us. We must give instruction on the relative duties of the master and his slaves, just as the Bible has enjoined. As for the rest, we must rely on the earnest and faithful preaching of Christ and him crucified. With the blessing of God, and in his own time, we hope to see a great change effected. We hope to see the evils of slavery not only diminished, but actually and finally brought to an end. But in no other way do we regard ourselves as commissioned to labor for the accomplishment of this object."

"'And the same policy has generally prevailed to the present time. There are individuals, perhaps, in both nations, who would refuse their assent to the principles which have just been ascribed to the missions in their early history. Others are well understood by the people around them to be unfriendly to slavery; and all, or nearly all, may have expressed opinions in private adverse to the system. But most of them uniformly avoid this topic in their public ministrations; and in their private intercourse with the Indians, they generally deem it advisable to use great caution. Among the Choctaws, however, there has been one example of a bolder policy; but excitement has been occasioned, and opposition has been stirred up; and the brother who has felt constrained to adopt this course thinks it may be necessary for him to leave the nation.

"'2. *Instruction of Slaveholding Converts.*

"'Some of the earliest converts in both nations were the proprietors of slaves. The question will naturally arise, "What instructions were given them by the missionaries?" I do not find that any distinction was made between this class of persons and others. Probably the attention of these brethren was not particularly called to the subject, any more than was that of the churches at the North. Nor has there been any marked difference to the present time. In some cases, the attention of the convert has been called to the instructions of the New Testament, and he has been told what he should do, as a Christian master, for his slaves; but seldom has the missionary gone further than this.

"'3. *Admission of Slaveholders to the Church.*

"'A few owners of slaves were early received into Christian fellowship. The only inquiry raised by the missionaries seems to have been, 'Does the candidate give reasonable evidence of his being a new creature in Christ Jesus?' They appear to have required the slaveholder to furnish the same amount of evidence that others furnished; but they did not consider the mere fact of his sustaining this relation a barrier to his admission to the Lord's table. And this is their practice at the present time.

"'In defence of their policy in this respect, past and present, they make their appeal, first of all, to the Bible, as showing the only condition of church membership. This, they say, is evidence of a change of heart; and when such evidence is furnished, there is no law for excluding the candidate from the privileges of Christ's house. They also say, that the adoption of a different rule in regard to slaveholders would have been fatal to the prosperity of the mission. And they are confident, should they now determine to subject this portion of the community to a new test, that their usefulness would at once come to an end.

"'In my intercourse with the different missionaries, I endeavored to ascertain the exact number of slaveholders in each church, as also the number of slaves. The first item I found it somewhat difficult to obtain, owing to the fact that the relation of husband and wife among the Indians, in regard to property, is not governed by the rules which prevail in the States. She may, and often does, own slaves; and sometimes, I am told, both own them jointly. In the following table, both the husband and wife are reckoned as slaveholders, in all doubtful cases.

"'CHEROKEE MISSION.'				"'CHOCTAW MISSION.'			
Churches.	No. of mem.	Slave'lders.	Slvs.	Churches.	No. of mem.	Slave'lders.	Slvs.
Park Hill,	36	4	3	Pine Ridge,	63	6*	25
Fairfield,	85	12	20	Wheelock,	238	7	17
Dwight,	50	5		M'tain Fork,	113	4	6
Mount Zion,	22	2		Good Water,	259	5	7
Honey Creek,	44	1*		Mt. Pleasant,	36		
	—	—	—	Mayhew,	36	1	3
	237	24	23	Six Towns,	60	7	13
* Living permanently out of the nation.				Chickasaw,	77	8	33
					872	38	104
				* Four of these are whites.			

"'4. *Treatment of Slaveholders in the Church.*

"'The Committee will have anticipated the course which the mission have pursued in dealing with slaveholding church members It has been the aim of our brethren to act, in the main, in accordance with the general theory already described. The relation of the Christian master to his slaves, either as to its lawfulness or its continuance, they have not disturbed; and little has been said to him, calling in question the fundamental principles of the system. But they have acknowledged their obligation to secure, as far as in them lies, his compliance with the injunctions of the New Testament which are specifically addressed to those sustaining this relation.

"'The views of the Cherokee mission, in regard to the discipline

5

of slaveholding church members, will appear from their letter of March 21st, herewith submitted. Those of the Choctaw mission, as I understand them, are substantially the same. I ought to say in this place, however, that both missions appear to be satisfied that there has been little or nothing in the conduct of this class of persons, as it affects their slaves, which ought to subject them to church censure.

" ' 5.   Employment of Slave Labor.

" ' Both missions have encountered more or less difficulty, from the first, in obtaining suitable aid in their domestic and farming operations. The plans of the brethren, owing to the number of boarding schools which they have sustained, and the quantity of land which they have cultivated, have demanded a large amount of manual labor. At first, the Committee endeavored to meet this demand by sending out laborers in the character of assistant missionaries; but the scheme was successful only in part. In these circumstances, what was to be done? Should the missions employ white laborers, residing among the Indians, or in the adjacent States? But persons of this description, of suitable character and qualifications, were seldom to be found. Should they call in the aid of the Indians themselves? Till within the last few years, they have been but poorly qualified, and but little disposed, to render the needful coöperation; and even now, most of the brethren among the Choctaws deem it unsafe to rely on such assistance. To the employment of males, moreover, at stations where there were female boarding schools, there were objections of a different sort.

" ' In this state of things, it has seemed to many of our brethren that the employment of slave labor, either by hiring or by purchase, was expedient, nay, inevitable; but in the minds of others, doubts and misgivings, as to one or both these modes, arose at an early day. In November, 1825, the attention of the Committee was called to the propriety of hiring slaves by some members of the Choctaw mission, and it was then resolved, "that the Committee do not see cause to prohibit this practice; but, on the contrary, they are of the opinion that it may be expedient, in some circumstances, to employ persons who sustain this relation." It was understood, however, that this hiring should always be with the free consent of the slave.

" ' About the same time, those missionaries among the Choctaws who had conscientious scruples in regard to the hiring of slaves, proposed to buy them with their own consent, with the understanding and agreement that they should be allowed to work out the purchase money, and then be free. To this plan the Committee consented, and in this way some ten or twelve subsequently gained their liberty. The same plan was adopted by the Cherokee mission, and with similar results; but I am not able to say how many slaves, with the assistance thus afforded them, effected their emancipation.

" ' On the 23d of Feb., 1836, the Committee reviewed the last mentioned decision, and came to the conclusion, as "the Board or its missionaries had been regarded by some of the friends of missions as holding slaves," "in consequence of these transactions," to instruct the missionaries among the south-western Indians, "to enter into no more such contracts," and to relinquish all claim to the services of any one with whom there had been a previous agreement of the kind. In the following month, (March 12,) the Committee reconsidered the propriety of permitting the missionaries to *hire* slaves; and they decided that it was expedient for them "to dispense altogether with slave labor," and it was resolved that they be instructed accordingly. In July following, in consequence of a letter from several members of the Dwight station, affirming that they could not perform the secular labors of the mission without the assistance of hired slaves, the Committee instructed the Secretary for the Indian department to inform those brethren, that the resolution of March 12 was adopted in the belief that the brethren could dispense with slave labor; but that if it were otherwise, the matter was left to their Christian discretion. I do not find that any action has since been taken by the Committee, either in respect to the buying or hiring of slaves.

"'When I was at Dwight, I found one slave laboring upon the farm connected with that station, hired at his own urgent request, but without any absolute necessity for his employment. No other slave is in the service of the Cherokee mission. And I am happy to say, that probably no embarrassment will arise to the Board from this mission, on account of any such question, in future. All the members of the mission are opposed to the hiring of slaves, with one exception, unless in extreme cases; and the excepted individual will conform to the wishes of his brethren and the Committee. And these brethren are also unanimous in the opinion, that slaves ought not to be purchased by them, even with a view to their prospective emancipation.

"'In the Choctaw mission, however, this question is one of a much more serious character. Since the arrangement which was made with the Choctaw government, in 1843, in relation to the four female boarding schools, the amount of secular labor at Pine Ridge, Good Water, Wheelock, and Stockbridge, has very greatly increased. The boys' boarding school at Norwalk has had the same effect at that station. The brethren at these stations have seen no way of meeting the wants of the mission, in this respect, but by hiring slaves. Accordingly, at the time of my visit, they had ten laborers of this description, male and female, in their employment. And they give us no reason to hope for any material change in future.

"'I did not learn that any slaves had been purchased by the mission, with the funds of the Board, since the vote of Feb. 23, 1836. Individuals have made such purchases on their own responsibility and with their own funds; and one of the brethren, and only one, now sustains the legal relation of master to two slaves, one of whom has earned her price by laboring in his employment, the other (her husband) having furnished the sum at which he was valued at the time of the sale. This legal interest in these two persons is understood, by them and by others, to be solely for their protection and benefit. They receive wages as if they were free, and they know that they can be free at any moment, by their own volition. Provision has also been made for the contingency of the missionary's death. But the mission expressed the opinion, during my interviews with them, that it was not expedient for them, either as a mission or as individuals, to purchase any more slaves, even with a view to their future emancipation.

"'CONCLUSION.

" 'I have now presented to the Committee, as briefly as seemed desirable, a general view of the relations of our brethren among the Cherokees and Choctaws to the system of slavery in those two nations. I have not felt called upon to express any opinion in regard to the various questions which naturally grow out of this subject; but I have preferred rather, and have endeavored accordingly, to submit the facts just as they would appear to an impartial observer, having no theory of his own to support, and having no wish to make out a case for or against the missions. Upon many of the points, however, which will claim the attention of the Committee, I have opinions; and I shall hold myself in readiness to state them, with all frankness, whenever they shall be required.

"And I may be allowed to say, that I have had more or less discussion with the missionaries themselves, in respect to their policy, and have freely pointed out certain differences between their sentiments and my own. I would hope, however, that this has been done in the spirit of Christian charity, and that we parted with feelings of mutual attachment and esteem, deepened only by the trials through which we together passed. In the integrity and faithfulness of these servants of Christ, I have entire confidence; and whatever errors they may have committed in their difficult position, the Master has evidently been with them and blessed them.

" 'All which is respectfully submitted.

" 'S. B. TREAT.

" '*Missionary House, June 15th,* 1848.'

" 'The letter of the Cherokee mission, already referred to, is here subjoined.

" 'DWIGHT, March 21, 1848.

" 'REV. S. B. TREAT :

" '*Dear Sir :* — Our conference with you when at this place, respecting the attitude in which we stand in relation to slavery, led to a conviction of the propriety and expediency of expressing to you in writing, and through you to the Prudential Committee, some of our united views in relation to that difficult and delicate subject. We are aware that we stand between two fires; in danger of displeasing, by what we may write, on the one hand, the people for whose good we labor, and on whose esteem and confidence our success must depend, and, on the other, the Christian community by whom we are sustained in our work. We do not say, in danger of displeasing the one *or* the other, but both at the same time, for opposite reasons. But we must ask the candor of all, and endeavor, frankly and kindly and meekly, to tell the truth.

" ' I. The first part of the subject before us relates to the holding or employment of slaves by missionaries. On this we remark : —

" ' 1. That no slave has ever been purchased by any missionary of the Board in this nation, except with a view to emancipation ; none who has not actually been emancipated ; consequently, that none of us now holds a slave on any terms whatever. And no apprehension need be entertained that any slave will be held by any member of the mission hereafter.

" ' 2. On the subject of the hiring of slaves from their masters, we have to acknowledge a difference of opinion among ourselves. Some of us suppose that when it is done with the free consent, and especially at the earnest desire, of the slave himself, and when his condition is improved by it, and his privileges increased, and he is brought into the way of religious instruction, and so, perhaps, of salvation, to hire him is no violation of the law of love, but rather an act of kindness. Others, while they admit, — as, indeed, we see not how any person can fail to admit,— that a kindness instead of an injury is done to the individual slave, yet believe that the practice tends to uphold and encourage the system of slavery, and is, therefore, an evil to be avoided as far as possible. None of us, however, whatever may be our individual opinions, have any intention of employing slaves, unless in such peculiar circumstances as, from our conference with you, we understand would constitute a sufficient justification in the view of the Prudential Committee and of the Board.

" ' Thus far, therefore, we see no ground of difficulty between ourselves and the patrons of the Board.

" ' II. But when we come to the question, how far it is right or expedient for us to attempt to enforce our own views of Christian duty by the discipline of the church, we must remark, (1.) That our churches are Congregational churches, and are not subject to our dictation, but govern themselves. (2.) That we ourselves are bound by our own consciences, and cannot submit to dictation as to what we shall do, or attempt to do, in the discipline of the church. Yet (3.) that we cheerfully acknowledge the right of the Board to know the principles on which we act, and the course which we pursue ; and to withdraw from us their patronage and support, if those principles or that course render us unworthy to be sustained.

" ' Premising, therefore, that in what further we have to say in relation to the discipline of the churches, we mean to be understood as speaking only of the influence which we ourselves should exert, and not as having power to lord it over God's heritage, we proceed to state more particularly our views in relation to several points to which you, dear Sir, have directed our attention.

" ' 1. We mourn the existence of slavery, and long for the coming of the day when neither in our churches nor in the world shall a slaveholder or a slave be found. At the same time, we cannot doubt that the course which many would urge us to pursue in relation to our churches would only tend to retard, and not to hasten, the coming of that happy day.

"'2. We regard it as essential to evidence of piety, that a man profess and appear to adopt, as his own practical guide, the rule of our blessed Savior, "Whatsoever ye would that men should do to you, do ye even so to them." And we deem it our duty to inculcate this rule of action on church members and candidates for church fellowship, in relation to slaves and slavery, as well as to every other subject. But we suppose it would be highly unreasonable to expect that we should be able to bring all true Christians to see always as we see, in regard to what are the actual requirements of the law of love; or to demand of us that we reject such from our communion, because they cannot see with our eyes, or with the eyes of Northern Christians, brought up in so different circumstances, and under so different influences.

"3. It is a comparatively easy task to apply the discipline of the church to evils which are *explicitly* condemned in the word of God; but a far more difficult and delicate task to apply it to such as are only *impliedly* condemned by the general law of love.

"'4. The laws of the Nation, sustaining the system of slavery, prevailing jealousy of missionary interference with what is generally regarded as simply a political institution, and the views of church members themselves, all are difficulties in the way of any church discipline which has a direct bearing on the subject of slavery.

"'5. It is not always wise to attempt what is manifestly impracticable to be accomplished, though in itself desirable. In our answers to questions, we must have reference sometimes to what we suppose practicable to be done, rather than to what we might be glad to do.

"'6. In regard to the question of rejecting any person from the church *simply* because he is a slaveholder, we cannot for a moment hesitate. For (1) we regard it as *certain* that the Apostles, who are our patterns, did receive slaveholders to the communion of the church; and we have not yet been able to perceive any such difference between their circumstances and ours, as to justify us in departing from their practice in this respect. And (2) our general rule is to receive all to our communion who give evidence that they love the Lord Jesus Christ in sincerity; and we cannot doubt that many slaveholders do give such evidence.

"'7. Nor can we even make it a test of piety, or a condition of admission to the privileges of the church, that a candidate should express a determination not to live and die a slaveholder. For while, on the one hand, a determination to hold on to the possession of slaves, from motives manifestly selfish, would indeed constitute, in our minds, an evidence that the heart was not under the influence of the law of love: yet, on the other hand, we cannot doubt the sincerity of many Christians, who, while they lament the existence of slavery, are yet fully persuaded that the emancipation of all their slaves, and suffering them to remain in the country, would only be doing an injury to the slaves themselves, as well as to the community at large. And such, not seeing a near prospect of a change of circumstances, can ordinarily have no definite purpose of emancipating their slaves. The propriety of receiving such persons to Christian communion depends not upon the correctness of the opinion referred to. It is enough that the entertaining of such an opinion is shown by clear examples to be compatible with sincere piety; for if this be so, it does not constitute a sufficient ground of exclusion from the privileges of the church of Christ.

"'8. You asked, among other things, whether we would undertake to discipline a church member for buying or selling slaves as merchandise, for gain.

"'Before giving a direct answer to this inquiry, we must remark that there are two extremes in relation to the traffic in slaves. One extreme is where a man purchases slaves for the mere purpose of traffic, transporting them to where they command a higher price, and there selling them again. Such a man, even in a slaveholding community, is generally looked upon with abhorrence. And though such may be tolerated in many churches, they are not generally regarded as worthy of the name of Christian. *Our* churches have never yet furnished such an example. We trust they never will.

"'The other extreme is where a slave is purchased under an agreement between himself and the purchaser, that he shall be set free, so soon as the value of his labor shall equal the price of his purchase. Of this we *have* examples. And this the members of our churches would commend, as a praiseworthy deed.

"'But take another case, which, at least in its principal features, is not uncommon. A slave is about to be sold to a slave-trader, but has leave, if he can, to find a neighbor who will purchase him. He applies to A., who replies, that he would gladly *set him free*, if he had the means, but is not able; and to hold him as a slave his principles forbid. He cannot buy him. With tears and entreaties, the slave tells of a wife and children whom he loves, and from whom he must be separated for ever; but A. remains unmoved. He goes to B., and receives the same answer. But by long pleading, with crying and tears, B. is at length prevailed upon to make the purchase. Now, however true it may be that a more expanded and far-reaching view of the case would justify A. in his decision, yet we suppose it would be hard to persuade that poor slave that A. was not hard-hearted; and that B. had not at least come nearer than A. to the fulfilment of the law of love. Hard, we should probably find it, to convince most of the members of our churches.

"'Between the two extremes of purchasing for the slave's sake, and buying and selling with a total disregard of the interest of the slave, there are many cases of mixed motive, where the buyer or seller might allow that he had regard to his own interest; but yet, as he makes the condition of the slave no worse, but perhaps much better, by the transfer, neither he, nor most of his brethren in the church, could be led to see that he had been guilty of any violation of the law of love. Occasional exchanges of masters are so inseparable from the existence of slavery, that the churches could not consistently receive slaveholders to their communion at all, and at the same time forbid all such exchanges. We regard it, therefore, as impossible to exercise discipline for the buying or selling of slaves, except in flagrant cases of manifest disregard to the welfare of the slave.

"'9. Again, you inquired whether we would discipline a member who, by sale or purchase, should separate husband and wife, or parents and children.

"'In relation to the separation of parents and children, we must first remark, that it is one of those things which are not forbidden by any *express* injunction of Scripture ; so that, where wrong exists, it can be shown to be such only by exhibiting its inconsistency with the general law of love. Very young children, we believe, are seldom separated from their mothers. In our churches, we do not remember to have known an instance. In regard to older children, many cases may arise, where neither the condition of the parent nor that of the child will be rendered worse, but that of one of them may be greatly improved by the proposed separation ; and where it cannot be readily shown to be any more a violation of the law of love, than any other transfer of a slave from one master to another. It is impossible, in our circumstances, to make it a general rule that the separation of parents and children, by sale or purchase, shall be regarded as a disciplinable offence.

"'The separation of husband and wife is a different case, being a violation of the express injunction, "What God hath joined together, let not man put asunder." The current of public sentiment, too, is against the parting of husband and wife, unless in cases where the parties are known to be so unfaithful to each other as not to deserve that appellation, or in cases of aggravated crime on the part of the slave sold ; such, for example, as in New England would separate a free man from his family by consigning him to a protracted residence in the penitentiary. With exceptions like these, we should hope to be sustained by our churches in the exercise of discipline for the separation of husband and wife, if occasion should require ; but we hope rather that no such occasion may ever arise.

"'10. Cruelty and injustice on the part of masters towards servants we should regard in substantially the same light with injuries of parents to their children, of a mechanic to an indented apprentice, or of an employer to a hired servant ; always, with the Apostle Paul, enjoining upon servants to be obedient to their masters, and upon masters to render unto their servants that which is just and equal ; and holding it as our duty, in cases of delinquency, to instruct, exhort, rebuke, or tell it to the church, according to the circumstances and the measure of aggravation in each particular case.

"'11. In regard to the religious instruction of slaves, we inculcate on all our members the duty of teaching the way of salvation to all under their care and influence, and especially their children and servants. The covenants of our churches require it. That we perform our whole duty in this or any other respect, we dare not claim. That we attain all we wish is far from the truth. How far the neglect of this duty should be made a matter of discipline, we suppose, must be left to the discretion of each pastor and each church. And while we have to confess that we painfully witness sad deficiencies in members of our churches, in regard to the instruction of their servants not only, but of their children also, for which we have not attempted to procure the exercise of church discipline, we think we may safely appeal to the pastors of churches in the most highly favored portions of our country, whether they also do not feel the same pain in regard to the same neglect, on the part of some of their members, towards their children, apprentices and hired servants, and yet make no attempt to procure the exclusion of such delinquents from the privileges of the church.

" ' These, dear Sir, are our views; this the position in which we stand. And this statement we wish you to present to the Prudential Committee, and have no objection that it be published to the world. Whatever the consequence may be, we have nothing to conceal.

" ' We trust that we shall not, for this, be looked upon as advocates of slavery. We are not so. We lament and deplore the existence of such a system. Our feelings, our example, our influence, are against it. But to make the adoption of all our views respecting it, and a corresponding course of action, a test of piety and a condition of fellowship in our churches, is what we cannot in conscience do. Nor do we believe that our Northern brethren and friends could desire it, if they could see, as we think we see, what must be the inevitable result.

" ' And now, dear Sir, if on account of this the Committee or the Board can no longer sustain us ; if they must withdraw from us their support, as we are aware that a portion of the Christian community would urge them to do, and, so far as they are concerned, leave the Cherokee people without the preaching of the word of God, then wherever the responsibility belongs, there let it rest. As to ourselves, we must act according to the dictates of our consciences, and be making known the Gospel to the Cherokee people while we may, and only then cease, when it is no longer in our power to continue.

" ' But we pray the Committee to remember, that if the patronage of the Board be withdrawn from us, it will not be for the violation, on our part, of any condition on which we were sent into the field ; but in consequence of new conditions, with which we cannot in conscience comply.

" ' Again, if support be withdrawn from us on account of views which we have expressed in this communication, it will of necessity be, so far as the Board is concerned, an entire withholding of the word of God from the Cherokee people. For to recall us on this ground, and send others who would pursue an opposite course, would be manifestly preposterous and vain. Such an idea, we suppose, the Board could not for a moment entertain.

" ' It is truly painful for us to think of a dissolution of our connection with the Board, which dwells always in our hearts, and whose prosperity our thoughts always identify with the prosperity of the Zion of our God, and of which each of us is ready to say, "If I forget thee, let my right hand forget her cunning ; if I do not remember thee, let my tongue cleave to the roof of my mouth." At the same time, and for the same reason, we know not how to endure the thought that our connection with the Board should be an incumbrance, clogging its wheels, and diminishing its means of spreading

5 *

the Gospel in the earth. But if our voice could reach that portion of the Christian community who disapprove our course, and would have the Board require us to do otherwise, or withdraw from us their patronage and support, we would respectfully ask whether they are quite *sure* that the course, which they require us to pursue, would do more to promote the object they desire than that which we *do* pursue. We would humbly confess our liability to error. But we would ask whether they are not liable to error too. We make no pretensions to superior wisdom. Yet we suppose we may, consistently with Christian modesty and humility, refer to our superior advantages for observing the circumstances in which we and the churches under our care are placed. *They* see very obscurely, in the dimness of the distance, what we see clearly, immediately before our eyes. It is impossible, we suppose, for them to appreciate the difficulties which lie in the way of such a course of church discipline as they would recommend; impossible to appreciate the palliations which frequently exist, in relation to many evils incidental to the system of slavery; impossible to see, at such a distance, the complication of difficulties by which the whole subject of slavery is embarrassed and perplexed. We have scarcely a doubt, that by far the greatest part of those ministers of the Gospel who are ready to censure or condemn our course would themselves, in the same circumstances, pursue the same course.

"'We would not claim a confidence to which we are not entitled; but we ask for candor. And if it should be found, on inquiry, as we believe it would, that among all who, with principles opposed to slavery, become pastors of churches in communities where slavery prevails, there are none, or next to none, who pursue a course materially differing from our own, we think that that single fact should lead distant Christians at least to *suspect* that there may be better reasons for it than they are able to perceive, but which a closer and clearer view of facts and circumstances and characters would enable them to discover. And we would further ask whether, if we are in other respects worthy of support, it is not at least better to continue our care of the churches, than to leave them either as sheep without a shepherd, or to the care of men whose influence would tend still less than ours to hasten the day, to which we all rejoice to look forward, when every bond shall be broken, and every slave go free.

"'We have endeavored distinctly, though briefly, to make known our views. We earnestly hope that what we have written, instead of leading to any protracted discussion, will rather be taken as a final exposition of our sentiments, a defining of our position. Not that we are immutable, or dare pledge ourselves to see always exactly as we now see; but at present, certainly, we can perceive no reason to change our course. So we do; and in so doing, we must stand or fall.

"'In behalf of the brethren of the Cherokee mission,

"'Very respectfully and truly yours,

"'ELIZUR BUTLER, *Moderator.*

"'S. A. WORCESTER, *Clerk.'*

"The Choctaw mission sent the following letter to the Prudential Committee, as expressing their views: —

"'NORWALK, CHOCTAW NATION, March 31, 1848.
"'*To the Prudential Committee of the A. B. C. F. M., Missionary House, Boston:*

"'DEAR BRETHREN AND FATHERS: —The letter which was prepared and written you by us, while our highly esteemed counsellor and friend, Mr. Treat, one of the Secretaries of the Board, was with us, was not forwarded, as was expected when he left us. It was soon ascertained that it did not satisfactorily express the views and wishes of all the members of the mission. It was accordingly retained. It was written in circumstances that required more haste, and admitted of less mutual consultation, than was desirable, considering the importance of the subject. There was something wanting to produce in our own hearts the conviction, that it contained a full and faithful expression of the sentiments of the mission. And for the same reason, it was not adapted to convey to your minds the right impression. More time was needed to examine and discuss so great a subject. The letter was retained, that it might be laid once more before the members of the mission, who would assemble at the meeting of the Indian Presbytery, on the last Thursday of March, at Norwalk.

"'The letter having been read and considered, the mission are not willing to have it forwarded according to its form when Mr. Treat left us. We now wish to submit to the consideration of the Committee the following statements and remarks.

"'First, respecting our *neutrality*.

"'For many years, it has been deemed by us important to our usefulness in *our own sphere of labor*, not to agitate our own minds, nor those of our people, with any of the great and exciting topics of the day, in church or state, such as cause debate and division, and the ranging of men into parties against each other. We had our principles once tried in this respect, when the Presbyterian Church was divided into two schools. The subject was once introduced into our Presbytery, for action thereon. A few words were spoken, enough to show that division might be near us. We then resolved to remain neutral. We deemed it of vital importance among our people to act as a band of brothers, and not have them suppose that Christ is divided. We endeavored to attend to our own work, and we were prospered in it. Since then, about one hundred persons yearly have been added to our churches.

"'In regard to one feature of the subject of slavery, we feel that our principles in favor of neutrality are also to be tried. We have been aware of the approach of this subject. And we thought our situation was described by the prophet Isaiah, when he said, "Their strength is to sit still." We have endeavored as a mission to keep aloof from the abolition movement, from some of the same reasons that forbade us to join our own Presbyterian brethren in either of their schools, so long as it would endanger our own unity.

"'And we wish you, and all our friends here and elsewhere, to be assured that we feel much more pleasure and satisfaction in the hope of doing masters and servants good, by preaching the Lord Jesus directly to them, than we can in explaining and enforcing the prominent principles of *equal rights*, merely *as such;* especially so far as they imply that they contain something of importance, which has become so only within a few years. We feel that the Bible contains all that we have need to know or teach. And we prefer to use the plain language of the Bible, just as it is, upon the subject of slavery, to any other code of principles or plans of operation. We have had trials on the subject of slavery ever since we came here. But we have endeavored to bear with each other and our fellow-Christians. And we have, until recently, succeeded as a mission in maintaining neutrality. You are aware that there is now, upon this subject, a division among us. And we do not wish for its growth. In our neutrality, we supposed that we had enjoyed your approbation. For we have noticed that at the annual meetings of the Board, when memorials have been presented on the subject of slavery, it was apparently with reluctance that they were considered, because they did not pertain to the great object of the organization of the Board. And yet we are now so involved in the matter that we can be silent no longer.

"'We wish to touch briefly on the *history* of our connection with slavery. We have been and are concerned with it in two ways; by employing slaves as laborers, and by admitting them and their masters to the church, as we do other persons who give evidence of personal piety. We are not *slaveholders*, nor have we been, save for the single purpose of emancipation, while laboring in our families.

"'In the year 1818, at the commencement of this mission, African slavery was in existence in this nation. The early missionaries were called to make it a subject of inquiry and prayer. There was no avoiding all contact with it. The large boarding-school establishments, and other multiplied and constant labors, in a hot and sickly climate, *then* as well as *now*, made the employment of considerable slave labor indispensable. For the plain reason, that the man who devotes his time and energies to the welfare of others, must himself have help in the performance of all such labors as he is not able to perform. Our brethren not having received instructions from the Prudential Committee, adopted that course which they deemed proper, and not inconsistent with the Bible.

"'In the spring of 1824, when we were favored with our first visit from Mr. Evarts, of blessed memory, the matter of employing slave labor underwent an examination. Written views against such labor were laid before the Secretary. His own were clearly expressed at a large meeting of missionaries. The early course of the mission was continued with his approbation. And we are not aware that his views upon the points submitted to him were afterwards changed.

"'We need not here spread out before you in detail the correspondence and resolutions of the Prudential Committee in regard to the purchasing of slaves, with a reference to their working out their own redemption. We trust you have noticed in us an ordinary willingness, at least, to comply with your instructions. Yet we have been painfully tried at the necessity of employing this kind of help.

We did once hope that assistant missionaries could be found, and sent out in sufficient numbers, to avoid this difficulty. In this we have been disappointed. We have made expensive efforts to hire free people, and again have we failed. In our situation, we need help that can be relied on. And thus it will be while we remain here as missionaries. Good free help for us, in our situation, is very rare in this land.

"'We have felt it to be a peculiar privilege in a matter of so much importance to communicate freely with the Prudential Committee, and to receive their instructions. Of late years, the subject of slavery has awakened a deep and growing interest in the minds of a large number of our best friends and patrons in our father land. Such an interest had not manifested itself when the older members of this mission were sent forth from New England to their work. The various measures adopted within a few years to present the slavery question, *as connected with us*, to the American Board at several of its annual meetings, we have not failed to notice. And we read with peculiar interest and satisfaction the proceedings of the Board, especially the great and good result to which, in the autumn of 1845, that venerable body of men arrived, when assembled at Brooklyn. We thought it was not in our power to express, in so clear a manner, our own leading principles on that whole subject, as were then given to the world. We thought that we occupied *ground in common* with our brethren and fathers. And some of us promised ourselves a time of rest, and of going forward in our work, without any further agitation, or necessity of having the slavery question introduced at our ecclesiastical and missionary meetings, as well as at the annual meetings of the Board. But the public mind did not find rest. Many publications indicated this. Letters also from the Missionary House have been of a kind since to awaken in us an apprehension, that we were not proceeding altogether right.

"'Public conventions held since 1845 in Ohio and Illinois, especially in Chicago last summer, have expressed formal opinions which strongly indicate that all was not right among us. And we speak it with pain, we have strong reasons to fear, in reference to this one subject in our missionary labors, that full and fraternal confidence has not been exercised toward us by some who are the benefactors of the mission. And that we may regain and share their confidence, and sustain the character of good missionaries in their estimation, we apprehend that something more than we have ever done is now called for, something that is in advance of all that has been purposed and effected by us, which shall be *positive and tangible*, and which shall go directly to check a pro-slavery spirit, and to bring the system itself to an end. The above historical sketch shows also our *position*.

"'For the first twenty-five years of the mission, our course was generally in accordance with the views of the Prudential Committee. Since that time, it has appeared, in some respects, to be otherwise.

"'It may be proper to state some of our own views, that neither ourselves nor the Board be spoken of as "the propagators of a slaveholding Christianity." And yet it will be difficult to present rightly all the considerations which have had an influence in the formation of our opinions, during the long period of our stay here, upon the subject of slavery.

"'When we came here, the question with us had ceased to be a *speculative* one. It was a *practical* one. Necessity was laid upon us to learn the *divine mode* of treating it. For slavery was among the Choctaws. It was not our work to inquire for its author, or into its history, but for our *duties* in regard to it. We thought that we need not grope our way in the dark, and that the Lord had given his church a revelation of his will. We are clearly of this impression now. The wrongs and evils of the system, in all their bearings and influences, are known to him. He alone can devise rules to remedy them all. We judge that he did take this subject under his own guidance, and has given his Church a knowledge of his will. Plain instructions are given to masters and servants, and to their *teachers*.

"'Under the application and influence of these instructions, we are to look for those results, whatever they may be, which will be most pleasing to God, in their nature, time, and manner and measure. It is our peculiar and appropriate work, as ministers of the Lord Jesus, to communicate the truths God has given, and as he gave them, hoping in this way to bring about that state of things which he holds dearer than all others. And it becomes us to go forward in the exercise of a full and living faith in these counsels of the Lord, and to trust the work and the issue in his hands. To man it might seem wise to take hold of the work, in some respects, in some other way. But we must remember that we are not to be wise above what is written; that "the word of God is quick and powerful, and sharper than any two-edged sword." He says by the mouth of the prophet, "It shall not return unto me void, but it shall accomplish that which I please." The Apostle Paul also says, "For the weapons of our warfare are not *carnal,* but mighty through God to the pulling down of strong holds, casting down imaginations and every thing that exalteth itself against the knowledge of God, and bringing into captivity every thought to the obedience of Christ." Here is the ground of our confident hope of doing any good to masters and servants; and yet, who is sufficient for these things? And, oh! that we could add, "Now thanks be unto God, which always causes us to triumph in Christ, and maketh manifest the savor of his knowledge by us in every place"! We have much reason to be grateful that several masters have given evidence of piety, and were received into the church, because the Apostles have set us plain examples. More than two hundred of their servants, we have been allowed, at different times, to feed as members of the Savior's flock in these woods. These are some of our views of what we think we ought to do, and which we hope will also be pleasing to God, if performed as he directs.

"'There are some things connected with slavery as a *civil institution,* with which we have not yet considered it our duty to meddle.

"'As a civil relation, it exists by virtue of the constitution and laws of the land. We are taught in the Bible our duties as citizens. It may be deemed our duty by some to adopt a train of measures which shall aim in their object directly to countervail the whole system, and in the end undermine the entire fabric which human legislation has framed in regard to slavery. We do not feel that we are required to adopt such a course. Nor do we regard this as our work. We are not citizens of the nation. We are missionaries, residing here by the permission of our national Government, and we can be removed at their pleasure. We are, in a civil respect, *foreigners and tenants at will* under the officers of our Government. The civil interests of this people are not committed to us. Other interests are, and such as are of more value than all civil and political interests combined. The Savior and his Apostles have not left any recorded example of their devoting themselves to the reformation of systematic civil wrongs, although many such existed where they lived and labored. Their practice and instructions have weight with us. Other members of the Church may be raised up to accomplish good to their country as legislators, rulers, and reformers.

"'We would remark that, in our opinion, this is not the most eligible part of the United States for attempting, at this time, a change in the civil relations of masters and servants. If all the region, far and near, and on every side, were another New England in its glory, then another sun would shed down light. But it is far otherwise.

"'There is another remark which should be made. This nation, in its improvements, schools, churches, and public spirit pertaining to the great cause of benevolence, is but an *infant*. This must be remembered by us all, especially if we would try to manage their civil matters. Thirty years here cannot be equal, in their religious influence on slavery, to two hundred years in the Carolinas. The past experience of missionaries among the Indian tribes, who have meddled much with the civil and political concerns of their red brethren, has not been encouraging, either in its influence on their own minds or those of the people. Such a course may lead to the formation of worldly, instead of heavenly attachments; or, on the other hand, worldly and wicked animosities and jealousies may arise.

"'Besides, the good results to individuals of a temporal nature which we might look for, if successful, when we have done our utmost, appear to be of minor value, and of a doubtful tenure, when compared with those of a spiritual kind, offered in the Gospel, and which we are bound to promote at all times. Shall we not then attend to this great work, which was made ours by the Head of the Church?

"'We feel safe because we are sure that we are right, when we can make the Apostles our guide and example. They were often in a situation so nearly akin to ours, in this very respect, that all human wisdom would have failed them. They needed the aid of inspiration, which they received, and under its influence they wrote as they did for the common benefit of others, wherever slavery might prevail. Their instructions and examples we feel bound to regard.

"'We should be careful how we risk the spiritual interests committed to us, by attempting to manage worldly ones, which are not given us by the Savior.

"'These are some of our views and thoughts which we wished to submit to your consideration. The inquiry may now be made, Wherein do we, as a mission, differ from our Patrons and Counsellors? We apprehend that the difference may relate chiefly to slavery as a civil institution. But whether it be so or not, we suppose that a difference does somewhere exist; and yet it has been formed honestly, and with the exercise of a good conscience. It seems to us to be an instance of an honest and real difference of opinion, among men who have a common and a good object in view; men, too, who love the kingdom of the Savior more than any earthly object, and who retain full confidence in each other's motives, piety and religious faith, and who are united in their views of the greatness and extent of the evils of slavery and the desirableness of having them all done away. But they do not agree as to the mode of operation in all respects.

"'The question which now arises is, whether this difference of sentiment is of that kind and nature which calls for mutual forbearance, patience, study of the Bible and prayer, or for something else? It appears to us very desirable, if practicable, to continue our labors as heretofore, and rely on God for his continued blessing. This is not the first instance in which the people of God have found themselves thus situated, and especially those who dwell amidst slavery, as thousands of them do this day, and may for ages to come. As slavery with various modifications has, for a long time, had an existence in the Church of God, it is proper for us to inquire how the servants of the Lord in "old time" were taught by him, as well as how they conducted in regard to it. May it not be agreeable to the Head of the Church that his people labor for him in the exercise of mutual forbearance and love, while proclaiming steadfastly his own word and his rules for all our relative and social duties, trusting in God for the safe and best result?

"'There are interests here dear to us as life itself, and there are responsibilities of great weight. Many of them are connected with the subject matter of this communication, which reach far beyond ourselves and our families, and the present generation of Choctaws and their friends. We feel them keenly, whenever our thoughts turn upon the churches and schools God has gathered in this land through our feeble instrumentality. These interests we have not the power to sustain, nor the wisdom to guide. Nor can we understand every thing connected with this subject, and especially those which are at a distance, and which press with most weight on the Prudential Committee. We cannot know and feel them as you do. And we entreat you, if you find that we do not sufficiently identify ourselves with your plans, views and counsels, not to think it strange, or as indicating a loss of confidence, or a rebellious temper. It is a long and weary time, and one too of many changes, during which we have been absent. We have been often told that a great change has taken place at the North, and that we have not kept pace with this change. It may be that we have not; yet, whenever we lay our hands on our hearts, we feel the pulsations of brotherhood as strong as ever.

"'This people is a dependent one. Our mission is still so. We have made but a promising commencement in our work. Help, in missionaries, teachers and supplies, will be needed for years to come, to continue what is already commenced, as well as to occupy new portions of our field. The Lord's hand is to be acknowledged with humility and reverence in all our ways. He may wish to effect some great change. But will he not go before us in a pillar of cloud by day, and of fire by night? May we not look for some plain indication of his will, before we determine upon a change that shall greatly affect this mission? If it should be his blessed will that we cast all our cares on him, cease all our anxieties, and engage and continue with still more love and zeal and with greater success in our labors, we shall greatly rejoice. And if he will so order the events of his providence, that we shall never fail hereafter to welcome, as formerly, new fellow-laborers from the North; and so that the streams of charity which have flowed so long and with such rich blessings from that good land, shall never dry up; and so that the name of the mission, as well as our own names and those of our sisters here, shall not be stricken from the list where they have long stood with those of other dear brethren and sisters gone to other heathen lands, and with the Fathers and Brethren of the Board, who meet in council yearly for our good and the world's salvation, then our joy will be full. We need not write more.

" ' After reviewing what we have written upon the several topics, viz : *neutrality, our position, history of slave labor, scriptural instruction, civil relation, differences in sentiment,* and *future course,* and after calling to mind our prayers and labors, our obligations to the Savior, our relations to you and to this people, we wish, so far as practicable, to lay the whole over upon your arms, and we do refer the great question, as to what must be done, to you, with entire confidence in your wisdom, the uprightness of your purpose, and your wish to act in the matter as will, in your judgment, best secure the great and important interests at stake.

" ' And that wisdom from the great Head of the Church may ever guide you and the executive officers of the Board, will be the prayer of your brethren in our glorious Lord and Savior Jesus Christ,

C. KINGSBURY,	C. C. COPELAND,
ALFRED WRIGHT,	DAVID BREED, JR.,
CYRUS BYINGTON,	H. K. COPELAND,
E. HOTCHKIN,	D. H. WINSHIP.

" ' I would cheerfully unite with my brethren in the last paragraph, in referring what is to be done to the wisdom of the Prudential Committee.

J. C. STRONG.'

" To this communication, the following answer was made, by the direction of the Prudential Committee : —

" ' MISSIONARY HOUSE, BOSTON, June 22, 1848.
" ' TO THE MEMBERS OF THE CHOCTAW MISSION :

" ' *Dear Brethren :* — Your letter of March 31 was received on the 5th of May. It was my wish to lay it before the Prudential Com-

mittee, together with my own report on the relations of the Cherokee and Choctaw missions to the subject of slavery, at the earliest
opportunity ; but my ordinary duties have been so urgent, since I
returned from the Indian country, and my health has been so poor,
that I could not complete the necessary preparation till within the
past four or five days. At our last Committee meeting, however,
held on the 20th instant, the matter was taken into consideration ;
and I now sit down to give you the result.

" ' Your kind expressions of attachment and confidence we most
cordially and fully reciprocate. We love the Choctaw mission.
Towards the older members, especially, those who have toiled faithfully and successfully for twenty-five or thirty years, we entertain
feelings such as few missionaries even have awakened in our hearts.
It has given me the highest pleasure, as a humble individual, to
bear testimony to the integrity and devotedness with which you
have labored, and the signal success with which God has crowned
your efforts ; and while life lasts, I shall cherish the remembrance
of my brief sojourn among you.

" ' But none will be more ready than yourselves to admit that
errors of judgment may have occurred in the history of your mission. And in regard to the particular subject discussed in ; our
letter, you will concede, we doubt not, a peculiar liability to such
errors. Your circumstances have been difficult and embarrassing
from the first ; and it was not to be expected that you should avoid
mistakes in every instance. You will not be surprised, therefore,
when we say (what, indeed, you seem to anticipate) that there are
principles involved in your mode of procedure from which we are
constrained to dissent. With that frankness which belongs to the
relation we sustain to you, and in a spirit which we hope our
gracious Master will not disapprove, we present our own views ;
from which you will be able to infer the nature and extent of the
difference between us. We take this course, without particularly
noticing all the points in your letter, because in so doing we hope to
exhibit our sentiments in a more orderly and intelligible manner.

" ' But here let us guard your minds against a possible misapprehension of our principles.

" ' 1. We do not claim any *direct* control over the churches which
you have gathered ; nor shall we ever approach them with the language of authority or dictation. Most happy are we to acknowledge
them as churches of our Lord Jesus Christ. We can suppose a
case, indeed, in which we should feel it our duty to address them as
brethren, beloved in the Lord, calling to our aid whatever power
there is in argument, or appeal, or expostulation, as circumstances
might demand. And we can suppose still another case, in which
we might be constrained, by the sacredness of the trust committed
to us, to withhold that pecuniary aid it has given us, in past years,
so much pleasure to afford. But in all this we should recognize
them as having all the privileges and immunities which appertain
to any body of Christians in any part of the world.

" ' 2. We do not wish *you*, either individually or collectively, to
bring any influence to bear upon those churches, or the community
in which you dwell, except such as belongs to the ministerial office.

Your churches, as well as yourselves, being in connection with the General Assembly of the Presbyterian church, (meeting annually,) we expect you to claim only those prerogatives which are conceded to pastors under the jurisdiction of that body, so far as they are suited to your circumstances.' The rights of your sessions and your churches must be duly regarded; for no apparent good can compensate for the injury done to a fundamental principle. You may argue with these brethren whom you have begotten in the Gospel, making your appeal to reason and to Scripture; but when you have exhausted your powers of persuasion, they must be left to act according to their own views of duty, being answerable only to the higher judicatories of your church, and to their Lord and Master. In what circumstances, and for what reasons, you may be allowed or required to withdraw from them, is a question which we have no occasion to consider at the present time.

"'3. We do not design to infringe in the least, by what we shall say in this letter, upon *your* rights as ministers of the Lord Jesus Christ. From him, primarily and mainly, you hold your commission; to him, primarily and mainly, you are responsible for the manner in which you discharge the duties of your office. We speak to you as brethren, engaged in a common work, under the eye of a common Master. Upon one point, which will come up in this discussion, we might address you in the language of authority; but even in regard to this question, as well as others, we choose to approach you with suggestions and arguments. We ask you to give them, as we doubt not you will, a candid and prayerful consideration. Perhaps we shall yet see eye to eye. And if this may not be, we will then raise the inquiry, "What further shall be done?"

"'Before proceeding to speak of the course which it is proper for missionaries to follow in a slaveholding community, it will be expedient to advert, for a moment, to the character of the system which has given rise to this discussion. And here, we presume, your views are in substantial accordance with our own. In your letter, indeed, you refer to the report adopted by the Board at its meeting in Brooklyn (1845) in terms of decided approbation. "We thought it was not in our power," you say, "to express in so clear a manner our own leading principles on that whole subject." But that document speaks of "the wickedness of the system" of slavery, "the unrighteousness of the principles on which the whole system is based, and the violation of the natural rights of man, the debasement, wickedness and misery it involves, and which are in fact witnessed, to a greater or less extent, wherever it exists;" and it quotes with approval the following declaration of one whom we all love and honor: "Viewed in all its bearings, it is a tremendous evil; its destructive influence is seen on the morals of the master and the slave; it sweeps away those barriers which every civilized community has erected to protect the purity and chastity of the family relation." Thus far, then, we are perfectly agreed. Domestic slavery is at war with the rights of man, and opposed to the principles of the Gospel.

"'But you will say, perhaps, that a distinction should be made between the system itself and the persons implicated therein, between slavery and slaveholding. We acknowledge the justice of this distinction; and, because of its importance in this discussion, we will briefly state our views in relation to it.

"'A *system* of slavery, like that which we are now considering, we believe to be always and every where sinful; but we do not believe that every act of *slaveholding* is sinful. A person may come into this relation, and may continue in it for a time, involuntarily. He may wish to put an end to it, and may actually put an end to it, as soon as he can. Such an one incurs no guilt whatever. His purpose was always right; and the first act which he had the power to put forth, bearing upon the continuance of the relation, was also right.

"'But a man may have the power to free his slaves, and yet not do it, out of regard to their highest good. He honestly hopes, we will suppose, that their day of freedom will soon come; he is doing, as he thinks, all that he can to hasten that day; in the mean time, he omits nothing that a considerate and humane master can devise for their temporal and spiritual advantage. Now, it is possible that he has misjudged in deferring emancipation. Perhaps it would have been better for the slaves to receive their liberty at once; perhaps there were other considerations that should have been decisive. If so, what is his position? The answer would seem to be two-fold. 1. The continuance of the relation is wrong; but, 2, the master may stand acquitted in the sight of God, because he was influenced solely by benevolent motives. Just as the selling of ardent spirits, in the days of our common ignorance on the subject of temperance, was clearly wrong; and yet many good men, never imagining that they were acting contrary to the law of love, engaged in the traffic. The *external* character of an act is one thing; its *internal* character is quite another thing. A man may conscientiously do that which is injurious in its tendency; as, on the other hand, he may, with a bad motive and purpose, do that which is innocent or beneficial in its tendency.

"'As we pass from such slaveholding as we have just considered to that which is manifestly selfish, we find a tract of debateable ground, on which we have no occasion to tarry. Sooner or later, we shall come to that mournfully large class of cases, in respect to which no distinction or qualification can be made. We would not speak too confidently; still we fear that the owners of slaves generally regard and treat them as property, making their own advantage, and not the good of those who are in bonds, the grand objects which they keep in view. And we cannot suppress the apprehension, that this is true even in that community which has shared so largely, through your labors, in the benefits conferred by Christian missions.

"'I have already said, that we regard domestic slavery as at war with the rights of man, and opposed to the principles of the Gospel. We do not claim that either Christ or his Apostles expressly condemned this system in the New Testament. But we do claim that they said and did much that, by fair implication, bears strongly against it; while, on the other hand, they said and did nothing that,

by fair implication, gives it the least sanction. Suppose, for example, that brief but comprehensive injunction of our Savior,
"Whatsoever ye would that men should do to you, do ye even so
to them," to be carried out to its legitimate results. What would
become of slavery? In all its essential features, it would cease at
once. Whatever might be the result as to the legal relation, its
spirit would die. And then the Scriptures invest every man with
privileges and responsibilities, which are utterly inconsistent with
his remaining in a state of servitude. The slave cannot receive the
fruit of his toil, according to the divine arrangement. He can
neither enjoy all the rights nor perform all the duties of a husband
or parent, as set forth in the Bible. He cannot develop those intellectual powers which, as seen in the light of revelation, are a trea-
sure beyond all price. Above all, he cannot, in most cases, have
that untrammeled access to God and his Holy Word, which is worth
more to him, as a lost yet immortal and accountable being, than any
thing else.

"'It is not our design to go into any extended argument on this
point; and still it may be well to make a passing allusion to the
inference which is often drawn from the injunctions in the New
Testament, addressed to masters and servants. The question is,—
"Do these injunctions concede or recognize the right of property in
a human being?" Now, it does seem to us, that every thing which
is said to masters and servants is consistent with the hypothesis,
that the Apostles regarded the general relation as unnatural and
sinful. Any one at the present day who believes the system to be
wrong, and labors, however diligently, for its termination, may with
perfect propriety use the very same language. Besides, if these
directions of which we are speaking prove that slavery is right
now, they prove that this institution, as it then existed in the Roman
empire, giving the master the power of life and death even, was
also right; a proposition, we presume, that no one will undertake to
defend.

"'But why did not the Apostles directly and unequivocally
affirm the sinfulness of slavery? Why did they not insist upon the
duty of emancipation? Simply because (if we may venture to give
an opinion) they saw that such a course, in their circumstances,
would not soonest and best extirpate the evil. And for this policy
they found the amplest authority in the dealings of God with his
covenant people, and in the life of Christ.

"'To us, then, it seems very clear, that slavery is opposed to the
principles of the Gospel. What line of conduct, then, shall the missionary pursue, when he is brought into contact with it? The
answer, to be complete and satisfactory, must embrace the following
topics; namely, *the preaching of the Gospel, the instruction given to
slaveholding converts, the admission of this class of persons to the church,
and the treatment they receive in the church.*

"' *The Preaching of the Gospel.*

"'It is the duty of the missionary, we suppose, to declare "all
the counsel of God." He may not, in his expositions of the divine
will, restrict himself to those forms of transgression which are

specifically denounced in the Scriptures. What pastor thinks of
placing himself on this narrow basis? No. The man who carries
the Gospel to the heathen must keep his eye always open; and
whatever he sees around him that is contrary to this Gospel, he
must consider as falling within the purview of his high commission.
We do not say *when*, or *where*, or *how* he shall bring the truth to bear
upon any sin. Whether he shall declare his testimony against it
to-day or to-morrow, next week or next year; whether he shall do
it in the sanctuary, by the way side, or in the home of the wrong-
doer; whether he shall do it in the spirit of John the Baptist, or
with the unseen approaches of Nathan the prophet, or with the
melting earnestness of Paul, or in the gentler tones of John;
whether he shall do it by marching directly on the citadel of error,
or proceeding first against the outworks; all these are questions for
the missionary. He has been sent forth because he is thought to
possess the wisdom, integrity and zeal which are needful for this
very work; and far be it from us to encroach upon his lawful pre-
rogative. But that the work must be done, in some way, and at
some time and place; that it must be done in the name and the fear
of the God of missions, is to us very clear.

"'From this general law for the conduct of missions, we think
that slavery can claim no exemption. You may say, indeed, that
the Apostles did not directly assail it in their writings, because, according to our own showing, there was a better way. But it does
not follow, by any means, that they *never* opened their lips in
denunciation of the monstrous iniquity of Roman servitude. Still
less does it follow that the ministers of Christ are never to be at
liberty, in any state of society, or in any age of the world, to raise
their voice against the enslaving of their fellow men. The example
of the Apostles, as we believe, goes to the extent of constituting
the missionary the judge of the *time* and *mode* of exhibiting the
truths of the Gospel in their relation to this system; but it cannot
justify him, as we think, in closing his mouth for ever.

"'In the commencement of a mission, as also in the commencement of the pastoral relation, it may be proper to say little or
nothing respecting certain evils which are found to exist. A different course, indeed, might shut every door of usefulness for a
long series of years. But when the servants of the Lord Jesus
Christ have obtained an acknowledged standing in the community;
when their character and their aims have begun to be appreciated;
and when their influence, as teachers of a new religion, has become
an established fact, they may cast aside something of their reserve.
And if the great Head of the Church gives them tokens of his
favor, manifest and marked, if churches are gathered, and converts
are multiplied; if all the departments of missionary labor are
carried forward with success, they may venture upon a still bolder
course of action.

"'Now, we will not say at what stage in your history it became
expedient to exhibit, with that wisdom which is profitable to direct,
the legitimate bearing of the Gospel upon slavery. Nor does it
seem at all important to go into that inquiry. But when we consider the age of your mission, its remarkable success, the strong

hold it has gained upon the Choctaw Nation, it does appear to us, that if the time has not yet come to hold up, in some way, the great law of love in its obvious relation to the subject, we may well ask, " When will that time come ? "

" ' What you have said respecting " slavery as a civil institution," has been duly considered. We are fully aware that, being " in a civil respect foreigners and tenants at will under the officers of our government," you have neither political rights nor political responsibilities. But it so happens that this institution has its moral relations. Go where you may, and do what you will, in your own appropriate work, it lies directly across your path. It is an anti-Christian system, and hence you have a right to deal with it accordingly. True, it is regulated by law ; but it does not, for this reason, lose its moral relations. Suppose polygamy or intemperance were hedged in by legal enactments. Could you not speak against them as crying evils ? We are grieved to hear that the Choctaws have a law, which practically debars the slave from all direct access to the Word of God, without the consent of the owner. Did you never bear your testimony against the wrongfulness of shutting out this class of persons from the " lively oracles " ?

" ' *Instruction of Slaveholding Converts.*

" ' This topic might be considered as embraced in " the preaching of the Gospel ; " but I prefer to give it a separate notice. In the instruction imparted to new converts, the teachings of Christianity are presented in circumstances peculiarly interesting and favorable, and may, on that account, take a wider range and extend to a greater variety of subjects than is customary on other occasions.

" ' It would seem that the aim of the missionary, in his intercourse with a recent convert, should be two-fold. 1. To ascertain the actual state of his affections ; whether they are renewed or unrenewed. 2. To give him clear and explicit information on all the great questions of Christian duty. The latter is important, not only because his life should be conformed, as perfectly as may be, to the only true standard of action, but because the spirit with which he receives the principles of the Gospel will show how much reason he has to call himself a new creature in Christ Jesus.

" ' And if this recent convert be connected with the system of slavery, what can be more natural and proper than a discreet and friendly inquiry into the nature of his views in regard to this institution ? The missionary may and should, unquestionably, watch his time ; he may and should leave the impression that he is governed, in what he says, by considerations that will commend themselves to any man's conscience ; but in all ordinary cases, as we suppose, he may give utterance, at some time and in some way, to the opinions which he himself has derived from God's Holy Word. The mind of this new learner of Christian truth, if a genuine disciple, or a sincere inquirer, is peculiarly open and susceptible to the teachings of his spiritual guide. At what other moment, indeed, during his whole life, can he be approached on this theme with so much promise of good ? And if he cannot bear the gentle and skillful probing of his honored father in the Gospel, how little of the spirit of Christ must there be in his heart !

" ' *Admission of Slaveholders to the Church.*

" ' The Board, at its annual meeting at Brooklyn, adopted two general principles, which are applicable to all its missions. 1. The ordinances of baptism and the Lord's Supper cannot be scripturally and rightfully denied to those converts who give credible evidence of piety. 2. The missionaries, in connection with the churches (if any) which they have gathered, are the sole judges of the sufficiency of this evidence. In the application of these principles to the case before them, they say that slaveholding does not always, in their opinion, involve individual guilt in such a manner as to exclude every person implicated therein from Christian fellowship. This conclusion seems to flow irresistibly from the distinctions already made in this letter, in regard to the character of slaveholding. If a person may be the legal owner of slaves, and yet be free from all blame in the sight of God, then it is clearly wrong to say that no slaveholder shall be admitted to the Church of Christ.

" ' But the Board could never have intended that all belonging to this class, and yet applying for this high privilege, should be received without inquiry as to their views and feelings in regard to slavery. Indeed, it seems to us that such an inquiry is, in all cases, fundamental. Here is a man involved in a system that is unchristian and sinful, and yet requesting admission to the table of our blessed Lord. Must he not prove himself free from the guilt of that system, before he can make good his title to a place among the followers of Christ?

" ' Perhaps he can show that his being the owner of slaves is involuntary on his part; perhaps he can show that he retains the legal relation at their request and for their advantage; perhaps he can show that he utterly rejects and repudiates the idea of holding property in his fellow-men. If so, let the facts be disclosed, and let him have the benefit of them. But, on the other hand, it may appear that, while professing to have the love of Christ in his heart, he holds and treats those for whom Christ died with a selfish spirit and for selfish purposes, thus showing that he has not compassed the length and breadth of the law of love, and, therefore, showing that he needs to be more perfectly taught in the right way of the Lord. For admitting such an one to the privileges of the people of God, especially in the advanced stage at which your mission has arrived, we know of no warrant whatever.

" ' In what particular mode or form the missionary shall proceed to elicit the facts to which we have just alluded, we do not say. That he may feel himself greatly embarrassed, at times, by the question, we can readily see, especially if there has been none of the preliminary instruction imparted which has been already mentioned. But, if he "lack wisdom, let him ask of God, who giveth to all men liberally, and upbraideth not; and it shall be given him." It is not the design of our great Leader to carry forward the missionary work without the trying of our faith. We must expect to encounter caste, polygamy, oppression, and the opposition of the powers that be. We must look for a contest with the brahmin and the moollah; with gigantic forms of superstition and error; with spiritual wickedness in high places. But if we go to Him who is faithful to his promises, and take shelter under his wings, we shall be safe.

"'In all that we have now said, you will understand that we have kept constantly in mind the circumstances in which you are placed. The power of admitting or rejecting candidates for the ordinances of the Gospel does not rest exclusively with you; and, as we have heretofore remarked, the prerogatives of your sessions must be duly regarded. But there are certain things which you may do; there are certain rights which you may exercise; there are certain responsibilities which are inseparable from your office. It is to the extent of these rights and responsibilities only that we desire you to go.

"' *Treatment of Slaveholding Church Members.*

"'The principles which we have already submitted to your consideration suggest the general course which seems to be proper in dealing with this class of communicants. If there are any in your churches at the present time whose views on the subject of slavery are inconsistent with the law of love, it would appear to be your office to bring them, so far as in you lies, to entertain sentiments which are scriptural and correct. Your attention, you will remember, was called to this point in Mr. Greene's letter to your mission, dated November 19, 1845. In that communication, he said:—"It seems specially important to train your church members to act out, in an exemplary manner, the spirit of the Gospel toward the enslaved, emancipating them where duty to them admits of that; and where it does not, taking special pains to promote their social and religious welfare, and prepare them as moral and accountable beings, hastening forward to the retributions of the eternal world, for the holiness and blessedness of heaven."

"'In the application of discipline to this class of persons, we conceive it to be your duty to set your faces against all overt acts which are manifestly unchristian and sinful in their character. Denying, as we do, that there can be, morally and scripturally, any right of property in any human being, unless it be in consequence of crime, and holding that the slave is always to be treated as a man, we suppose that whatever is done in plain and obvious contravention of these doctrines, may properly receive the notice of yourselves and your sessions. Hence, if the master treat his slaves with inhumanity and oppression; if he keep from them the knowledge of God's holy will; if he sell them as articles of merchandise; if he disregard the sanctity of the marriage relation; if he trifle with the affections of parents, and set at nought the claims of children on their natural protectors; and in all analogous cases, he fairly brings himself within the reach of that power which is given to the Church for the edifying of the body of Christ.

"'But we will not enlarge upon this topic. We have said enough to indicate the general direction of our views and wishes in relation to it. And still we cannot forbear an allusion to the exceeding desirableness of your pursuing such a course as shall deliver the Choctaw churches from all connection with slavery. For a whole

6

generation, the Gospel has been preached to this tribe of Indians; and during the greater part of this period, the work of the Lord has greatly prospered. You have a large and increasing body of communicants. You have schools of great interest and promise. Civilization and general intelligence are making steady advances. With these facts before us, is it too much to ask, "May not these churches soon be freed from all participation in a system that is so contrary to the spirit of the Gospel, and so regardless of the rights of man ? " We wish, indeed, that a much more desirable end were attainable. Most ardently do we pray that the whole nation may be delivered from this "tremendous evil." And we reiterate the language of Mr. Greene, as contained in the letter above referred to, in which he stated it to be the desire of the Board and of the Committee that "you should do whatever you can, as discreet Christian men and missionaries of the Lord Jesus, to give the Indians correct views on this subject, and to induce them to take measures, as speedily as possible, to bring this system of wrong and oppression to an end."

"'Employment of Slaves by the Mission.

" ' As the views of the Committee on this subject have been heretofore communicated to you, it will not be necessary to go into any discussion at the present time. In February, 1836, the expediency of *buying* slaves, with their consent, and with the understanding and agreement that they should be allowed to work out their purchase money, according to the practice of the mission at that time, was fully considered ; and it was resolved "to instruct the missionaries among the South-Western Indians" "to enter into no more such contracts," and to relinquish all claim to the benefit of any previous arrangement of the kind. In the following month, the expediency of permitting the missionaries to *hire* slaves was taken into consideration ; and it was resolved to be expedient for them "to dispense altogether with slave labor." Of the action of the Committee in both cases, you were duly apprised. Now, it was not the design of the Committee to affirm that in no possible state of things should you be allowed to hire slaves ; for we can conceive of circumstances where it may be proper, just as we are at liberty to perform "works of necessity and mercy" on the Sabbath. But except in cases of manifest necessity, we deem it altogether inexpedient to resort to this species of labor. And it also enters into our ideas of this necessity, that it is only temporary.

" ' It is with profound regret, therefore, that we have learned how many hired slaves are now in the service of the Choctaw mission. We readily acquit you of any plan or purpose to disregard our known wishes. We cheerfully accept the excuse you offer, namely, that the boarding-school established in 1843, in consequence of the arrangement made with the Choctaw government, in your view made such assistance necessary ; and that for this reason you supposed the Committee must have assented to its employment. Still, we must frankly say, that we never intended, by agreeing to the plan proposed on the part of the Choctaws, to sanction or authorize the practice which we now find so prevalent among you. And had the Committee known, when the subject was under consideration, that the hiring of slaves must follow the adoption of this plan, as a necessary and permanent result, they would not have engaged in the present boarding-school system.

"'We feel ourselves not a little embarrassed by our position. The engagement with the Choctaw government has some fifteen years to run, and yet we do not feel willing to be a party to the hiring of slaves for this long period. By so doing, as it seems to us, we countenance and encourage the system. We make this species of labor more profitable to the owner; at the same time that we put it in his power, if he will, to plead our example to justify or excuse the relation. In this state of things, it appears to be our duty to ask you, first of all, to inquire once more into the supposed necessity of this practice, and to see if slave labor cannot in some way be dispensed with. And if you can discover no method by which a change can be effected, we submit for your consideration, whether it be not desirable to request the Choctaw government to release us from our engagement in respect to the boarding-schools. It is with pain that we present this alternative; but such are our views of duty in the case, that we cannot suggest a different course.

"'The sentiments of the Committee have now been frankly and fully expressed, on the different topics which it has seemed important to discuss at the present time. We doubt not you will receive them in the spirit which has characterized our intercourse in past years, and will take them into consideration at as early a day as practicable. You are already aware that much interest is felt in this question by the friends of the Board; and there is a general desire that the relations of your mission to the subject of slavery may be put upon a broad scriptural basis as soon as possible. If you can reply to this communication before the next annual meeting, and especially if you can declare your acquiescence in the views herein presented, and your readiness to act in accordance with them, so that we can announce the fact to those who shall have come together on that occasion, you will give us much pleasure by so doing.

"'Praying that God may be with you at all times, and give you wisdom and grace as you shall need,

"'I remain, dear brethren, very affectionately and truly yours,

"'S. B. TREAT,

"'Sec'y of the A. B. C. F. M.'

"The reply to the letter of the Cherokee mission was as follows:—

"'MISSIONARY HOUSE, BOSTON, June 30, 1848.

"'To THE MEMBERS OF THE CHEROKEE MISSION:

"'Dear Brethren:—Your letter of March 21 was duly received. You have doubtless expected a reply before this, and I regret that there has been any necessity for delay. As the brethren among the Choctaws, however, adopted a course similar to yours, and drew up a letter, after I left them on my return, expressive of their sentiments in regard to the subject which you have discussed so fully, it seemed desirable that the relations of both missions to slavery should be considered at the same time. But it so happened that I was not able to bring the whole subject before the Prudential Committee till the 20th instant; on which occasion I was directed to communicate the views entertained by them, both to the Choctaw brethren and yourselves.

"'In replying to the former, it has been found necessary to discuss all the topics which are brought before us by your letter; and though we do not regard the two missions as occupying precisely the same ground (your opinions being obviously more in accordance with those of the Committee), it has seemed unnecessary at this time to address a distinct and independent answer to you. I am authorized by the Committee, therefore, to send you a copy of the letter which has been written to the Choctaw mission, as containing a full expression of their views on all the questions which appear to grow out of the relations of the two missions to the subject of slavery at the present time. You are requested to examine the principles set forth in this communication, so far as they are applicable to your circumstances, and to forward your reply with us little delay as practicable.

"'In expressing your warm attachment to the Board, you have only given utterance to sentiments which we have uniformly believed to exist in your hearts. And permit us to say in return, that we have always taken a strong interest in your mission. Its history, so full of hope and disappointment, of success and disaster, we can never forget. For the members of the mission, those in particular who have long shared in the joys and sorrows of the Cherokees, we feel the highest respect; and in them, as honest and conscientious laborers in the vineyard of our common Master, we have entire confidence.

"'That God may make your way plain before you, and may keep you to the end, is the prayer of

"'Your affectionate brother and fellow-laborer in the Gospel,

"'S. B. TREAT,

"'Sec'y of the A. B. C. F. M.'

"After these documents had been read to the Board, they were referred to a Committee, consisting of Dr. Beman, Rev. Albert Barnes, Dr. DeWitt, Dr. Hawes, Judge Darling, Dr. Magie, and Henry White, Esq. This Committee subsequently presented their report; which, having been discussed at some length and amended, was adopted by the Board. The amended report is as follows: —

"'The Committee to whom were referred the papers relating to the subject of slavery in connection with the Cherokee and Choctaw missions, have carefully deliberated on the same, and beg leave to submit the following report.

"'The documents put into the hands of the Committee, and which they have examined, are the following: The "report on the relation of the Cherokee and Choctaw missions to slavery," being an account of a visit made by the Rev. S. B. Treat to these stations; a letter from the Cherokee mission, on the same subject; a letter from the Choctaw mission, on the same; a letter to the Choctaw mission, by Rev. S. B. Treat, one of the Secretaries, communicating to the missionaries the views of the Prudential Committee on this whole subject; a brief letter from the same Secretary to the Cherokee mission, referring the brethren of that mission to the last-named letter, as containing the views of the Prudential Committee, on the subject of inquiry; together with the report of the Prudential Committee, submitting the above-named documents to this meeting of the Board.

"'The subject to which these papers relate is one of intense interest in our day, and is becoming more and more so, in all its relations. The Board has not been unmindful of its own relations to this matter, in times past; nor will it probably be, in its careful deliberations and circumspect action, in time to come. It is one of those great questions which seem destined to awaken the interests and sympathies of a world. Christians and others are beginning to feel this.

"'Your Committee express their cordial approbation of the fidelity with which the Prudential Committee have discharged this part of their trust. The report of the Rev. Mr. Treat of his visit to the Cherokee and Choctaw missions, embodies a vast fund of information, which we have all needed, and which cannot fail, as it shall be diffused, of doing great good. This paper should be extensively known and read. No agent could have executed this mission more wisely, or more kindly, than your Secretary has done it; and it may be hoped that practical and permanent good will grow out of it in many ways. It has brought to the Prudential Committee, and to the Board, information which we needed; and, especially, of the practical working of the system of missions, in some of the relations of life, on which we have not been very well informed. This whole report, your Committee believe, will bear scrutiny and analysis.

"'Of the two letters from the missions in question, your Committee need not give an opinion, for the following reasons. They have been particularly examined in the communication written by order of the Prudential Committee; these letters are only a part of a correspondence which has not yet closed; and some things therein stated may be modified by the views since expressed by the Prudential Committee. These letters, your Committee take pleasure in saying, breathe an excellent Christian spirit.

"'Nor do your Committee feel themselves called upon to give an opinion on every position and every sentiment to be found in the last letter addressed to these two missions. We refrain from a critical examination of it in this report, because it is a part of an unfinished correspondence; and no final action, as your Committee apprehend, can, with any propriety, be had upon it at the present time. If it were to be examined in all its statements, and fully discussed by the Board, it is probable that some might think that it goes too far; and others, that it does not go far enough, in relation to the evil of which it treats. But your Committee are unanimous in the opinion, that this is not the time for a discussion of its subject-matter. It is now pending in the deliberations of those missions. Speaking of this document, the Prudential Committee say, "The answer of the brethren has not yet arrived. Both missions had previously appointed meetings to be held simultaneously with the annual meeting of the Board; and it is presumed that they have the subject now under consideration."

"'It is the judgment of your Committee, that the whole subject should be left for the present, where it now is, in the hands of the Prudential Committee.'

"Before the question was taken on the acceptance of this report, Dr. Blanchard proposed, as an amendment to the same, the following resolutions:—

"'*Resolved*, That this Board distinctly admits and affirms the principle, that slaveholding is a practice which is not to be allowed in the Christian Church.

"'*Resolved*, That it is, in the judgment of the Board, the duty of our missionaries in the Cherokee and Choctaw nations to discontinue the practice of hiring slaves of their owners to do the work of the missions; and, in the reception of members, to act on the principle laid down by Mr. Treat and the Prudential Committee, that slaveholding is *prima facie* evidence against the piety of the candidates applying for admission to the church.'

"Dr. Blanchard having been requested to withdraw these resolutions, consented to do so; and the Board permitted them to be inserted in the minutes of the meeting."

The careful reader will have noticed that this elaborate correspondence is unfinished; the last letters of Mr. Secretary Treat to the Cherokee and Choctaw missionaries having requested further replies on their part, which replies did not arrive until the following year. The record of the correspondence, therefore, is continued in the Annual Report of 1849, preceded by some *explanations* which the Prudential Committee found it needful to make, and these again preceded by an addition to the special report, presented by the Secretaries in 1848, on the "Control of Missionaries and Mission Churches."

These additions occupy more than nine closely printed pages in the Annual Report of 1849, (pp. 69 to 79,) and are as follows:—

"CONTROL OF MISSIONARIES AND MISSION CHURCHES.

"Dr. Anderson read as follows, in relation to the 'Special Report' which was laid before the Board last year by the Prudential Committee:—

"'The "Special Report of the Prudential Committee on the Control to be exercised over Missionaries and Mission Churches" was presented to the Board, at its last meeting, in a printed form; but as the members had not time to give it that attention which the importance of the subject demanded, the consideration of it, after a single amendment, was deferred to the present meeting. Meanwhile, the Prudential Committee were authorized to print the report as amended, and to make such modifications as, on further reflection, they should deem proper.

"' They lay this report again before the Board, with an addition to be introduced on page 39, immediately following the article designed to show that the Board is responsible for the *teaching* of missionaries. The addition which is now made to the report is intended to show, that *this responsibility of the Board for the teaching of the missionaries does not interfere with that of Ecclesiastical Bodies in respect to the same thing.* It reads as follows : —

"It may be important, however, to remark, that the responsibility of the Board for the *teaching* of the missionaries does in no degree interfere with the responsibilities of ecclesiastical bodies in respect to the same thing. Such has been the result of an experience in this country continued through forty years. Within this period, the Board has had about two hundred and seventy-five ordained missionaries laboring under its direction in heathen lands, and has extended its supervision to every department of their duty as missionaries; and there has never been the least sign of interference in the working of its own responsibilities and of those of the ecclesiastical bodies with which the missionaries were connected. But one case is recollected, in which an ecclesiastical body in this country has thought itself called upon to discipline a missionary, and then it deposed him from the ministry, and for the *same cause* that had *previously* led the Prudential Committee to dismiss him from the missionary service. The fact is, the missions, when fully organized, may easily constitute themselves ecclesiastical bodies; and the whole influence of the Prudential Committee is and has been to sustain them in their freedom and efficiency for missionary purposes. It is also true, that there has been no case, where the Prudential Committee has been called to act, in which doctrinal error was the only element of difficulty; nor has there been a case, involving doctrinal error as an obvious element, where it would have been convenient, or even practicable, for a mere ecclesiastical body to adjust it, *as a whole.* The cases were of a mixed and complicated nature; and they can hardly fail to be otherwise in distant organized missions among the heathen, and so must of necessity be regarded and treated as appertaining rather to the missionary than to the minister. The elements of character, which constitute a man an efficient and faithful minister, are almost identical with those which are essential to the character of a good and faithful missionary. It can hardly be questioned that the body, which is accountable for the proper application of the funds contributed for the support of missionaries, is under solemn obligation to see that those funds are not wasted upon an unworthy or unfaithful missionary. Indeed, it is impossible effectually to transfer this responsibility to another body, which is not only remote from the missions, but not in correspondence with them. And when the Board dismisses from the missionary work for a reason (as in the case above mentioned) that would make it the duty of an ecclesiastical body to depose from the ministry, there is no interference with the rightful authority of any ecclesiastical body. The Board does not assume to decide upon the fitness of an indi-

vidual to be a minister of the Gospel; but it is their duty to decide, and
that intelligently, on his original and continued fitness to be sustained, by
the funds committed to their disposal, as a missionary to the heathen.
Nor is there more practical difficulty in adjusting his missionary, ministerial, and church relations in foreign missions, than there is in home
missions; and no more in respect to those Congregational missionaries,
whose ordaining councils ceased to exist immediately after their induction
into the ministerial office, than in respect to missionaries connected with
presbyteries or classes in their native land. The contributors to the funds
for foreign missions demand more evidence of faithfulness in the preaching of the Gospel, than can possibly be in the possession even of the
permanent ecclesiastical bodies scattered over our country. And they
will hold the Prudential Committee and the Board responsible for seeing
that no part of their contributions go for the propagation of error, either
in doctrine or practice; nor will they have any serious doubt, in case
radical or serious mistakes are committed or abuses occur in the discharge
of this trust, that the fact will soon be known, and the evil be in some
way corrected. The Board claims to be only an *agency* for those, whether
individuals or associated missionary bodies, who commit funds to its disposal for the support of foreign missions; and to see that the funds thus
committed are appropriated according to the known wishes and expectations of the donors. Such is a simple, practical view of this subject, as it
has existed ever since the Board was formed.

"Experience has shown, that the responsibilities of missionaries to missionary societies are entirely consistent with the unimpaired existence
and operation of their responsibilities in their distinct and separate relations as ministers. The churches and other ecclesiastical bodies at home,
or in the missions, or the missions themselves regarded as ecclesiastical
bodies, can take their own time and method of looking after alleged
heresies or immoralities in individual missionaries. The Board need not
wait for the ecclesiastical body, nor the ecclesiastical body for the Board.
And the Board, conducted as it has been from the beginning, will be a
help to the ecclesiastical bodies, whether church, council, presbytery,
classis, or mission, in the discharge of their supervisory duties towards
the ministers of the Gospel laboring as missionaries in foreign lands. Nor
can it cease to be thus helpful, except by a change in its course of proceedings, which would speedily prove destructive alike to its influence and
its existence."

"'The Prudential Committee having had under consideration the
subject of this special report another year, deem it proper to suggest, that there seem to them to be reasons which render it inexpedient that a formal vote of adoption should be passed; but that
the report should rather be received as a record of the results of the
experience of the Prudential Committee in conducting foreign
missions,—as information which may properly go into the official
publications of the B.   It is not to be supposed that the
measure of our experie   is yet full, in any one of the great departments or modes of   iting in the work of missions. Doubtless we have much yet t   earn, both through our failures and suc-
cesses, connected wi... . prayerful contemplation of the word and
providence of God. The Prudential Committee see not indeed, at
present, any reason to doubt the correctness of the principles and
views embodied in this report; but the report covers much ground,

and embraces a great number of points in missionary practice; and the Committee *might* hereafter experience embarrassment, in case the report is now taken out of their hands by a vote of adoption, should further experience demand a change in any of the principles, opinions and usages set forth in the report. The ends aimed at, in ordering and preparing it, appear to be sufficiently attained by its embodiment and publication, so as not to require any formal adoption of the report, at least for the present.'

" After the reading of the foregoing statement, the Board resolved, that the 'Special Report' of the Prudential Committee 'on the Control to be exercised over Missionaries and Mission Churches,' as now presented by the Committee, be received as a record of the results of their experience in the long period of their official duty; but, in view of reasons suggested by them, the Board do not at this time act upon the question of its adoption, leaving the subject with the Committee, however, to make such use of their report in the publications of the Board, and in all other ways, as they shall deem proper.

"CORRESPONDENCE WITH THE CHEROKEE AND CHOCTAW MISSIONS.

" The following statement was submitted by the Prudential Committee, in regard to their correspondence with the Cherokee and Choctaw missions:—

" 'It will be remembered, that the Prudential Committee submitted to the Board, at its last annual meeting, an unfinished correspondence with the Cherokee and Choctaw missions, on their relation to the subject of slavery. As a part of the history of the case, the Committee deem it proper to say that, on the 20th of February last, perceiving that the Christian community had extensively misunderstood their letter to the last-named mission, dated June 22, 1848, they published the following brief statement:—viz.

" The letter sent by Mr. Trent to the mission had not that authoritative character which some have attributed to it. It expressed *opinions* then and still entertained by the Committee; but not in a form which made those opinions *decisions*, or *instructions*. The Committee have given no *instructions* to the missionaries in relation to slavery; they say expressly that they address their brethren ' *with suggestions and arguments.*' The distinction between suggestions, opinions and arguments, on the one hand, and decisions, rules and instructions, on the other, though necessarily familiar to the conductors of missions, seems to have been overlooked by some who have written on this subject. The missions reply to suggestions, if they see cause, by suggestions, to opinions by opinions, and to arguments by arguments. On some subjects, this interchange of views has extended through several years, before the opinions of the Committee and their brethren have become perfectly consentaneous; and not unfrequently, as the result of this free correspondence, the sentiments at first entertained on both sides have been modified.

6 *

"This distinction is vital to the proper understanding of Mr. Treat's letter to the Choctaw mission; and for want of attention to it, very erroneous constructions have been put upon that letter. With this practical distinction in view, moreover, it will be seen that the Committee and the Secretaries have done nothing inconsistent with the letter or spirit of the two fundamental principles recognized by the Board at Brooklyn; namely, that credible evidence of piety is the only thing to be required for admission into the churches gathered among the heathen; and that missionaries and their churches are the rightful and exclusive judges as to the sufficiency of this evidence. It is believed that foreign missions cannot be successfully prosecuted in disregard of these principles, at least by the Congregationalists and Presbyterians of this country, and that such missions are and must be controlled mainly by the free use of suggestions, opinions and arguments; and those who have the direction of the missions must have truth and reason on their side, in order to be successful. Time must also be allowed for the requisite interchanges, and for necessary reflection on both sides.

"We merely add, that the Committee have never had any intention of 'cutting off' the Choctaw mission from its connection with the Board. Indeed, the last two paragraphs in the 'Special Report of the Prudential Committee on the Control to be exercised over Missionaries,' laid before the Board in a printed form, and published in the Minutes of the last Annual Meeting, show that nothing of the kind was contemplated. Nor have the Committee preferred any 'charges' against the mission. On the contrary, they would repeat the sentiment in the letter of Mr. Treat, expressing their undiminished confidence 'in the integrity and faithfulness of these servants of Christ.'"

"'In submitting to the last annual meeting the unfinished correspondence which has already been mentioned, the Committee departed from the established usage of the Board. It was their wish, (1.) to gratify the desire which so many have felt to ascertain the precise relation which the Cherokee and Choctaw mission sustain to slavery, and what opinions those brethren entertain on the general subject; and (2.) to give the Board and its patrons an opportunity to understand the sentiments of the Prudential Committee, in respect to slavery as affecting the missionary enterprise among the heathen; and also the manner in which the Secretaries, under the supervision of the Committee, might be expected to interchange views and impressions with their fellow-laborers in the Gospel of Christ. It was neither the purpose nor the desire of the Committee to obtain any formal action of the Board on the correspondence; as they did not suppose that such action was necessary.

"'And perhaps the Committee may be allowed to say, that a vote adopting their letter to the Choctaw mission seems to them, not only unnecessary, but of doubtful expediency. It was not written with any such object in view. And in the very nature of the case, there can be no opportunity for amending or improving such a letter when it comes before the Board for its sanction. It is not a report, presented by a Committee in the ordinary routine of business, to be curtailed, or amplified, or changed in whatever way may seem best, but a statement of the views of the body from which it emanated, and already sent to those for whom it was intended.

"'It was the wish and hope of the Committee last year, that the correspondence with both missions might be brought to a close before the present meeting. In this, however, their expectations have been disappointed. Letters have been interchanged with the brethren among the Cherokees; and the points of difference have been gradually disappearing. For reasons which are deemed entirely satisfactory, the Choctaw mission did not reply to the letter of the Committee dated June 22, 1848, until April last. Although the delay on some accounts is to be regretted, still it is manifest that nothing has been lost; on the contrary, time has thus far been a kind and helpful coadjutor.

" ' The conclusion to which the Committee have come in regard to the correspondence of the past year is as follows :—

" ' 1. They submit to the Board the letter from the Choctaw mission already referred to, dated April 14, 1849. Indeed, they deem it an act of simple justice to those brethren, that the patrons of the mission should at once be made acquainted with the views therein expressed.

" ' 2. The Committee do not think it expedient, at present, that the correspondence with the Cherokee mission should be laid before the Board. In expressing this opinion, however, they distinctly and fully admit the right of the Board to call for this or any other correspondence, and indeed to institute inquiries into any of the proceedings of the Committee, in such manner and form as shall seem best.

" ' As already intimated, it was thought that the peculiarities of the case were such, last year, that an exception should be made to the usage of the Board ; and when the second letter of the Choctaw mission shall have been read, it will be seen to have a special relation to what has gone before ; and, consequently, to fall within the exception.

" ' But as regards the letters which have passed between the Missionary House and the brethren among the Cherokees, within the past twelve months, there does not appear to be any sufficient reason for deviating from the ordinary course.

" ' Upon one other point it may be well for the Committee to say a few words. The members of the Choctaw mission have directed their attention very particularly, during the past year, to the substitution of free labor for that of slaves. They are anxious to make a change as soon as practicable, not only to gratify a large portion of their friends and patrons, but that they may increase the economy, comfort and efficiency of their own labors. The Committee have been cordially coöperating with the mission in this matter; but they are sorry to say, that they have not succeeded, as yet, in relieving their brethren according to their earnest request. The subject will continue to receive attention, however, and it is hoped and believed that, in some way, free labor will be successfully introduced at an early day. Indeed, a reduction has already been made in the number of slaves hired from year to year, at the different stations. And the Committee will say in conclusion, that, as it seems to them, the mission are willing to do all that can properly be required of them, in existing circumstances, to place this question on the desired basis.

" The letter of the Choctaw mission, referred to in the preceding statement, is here subjoined.

" ' STOCKBRIDGE, CHOCTAW NATION, April 14th, 1849.
" ' REV. S. B. TREAT, Cor. Sec. of the A. B. C. F. M., Boston :

" ' *Rev. and Dear Sir :* — Your letter of June 22d, 1848, was duly received, and has been the subject of our prayerful deliberations. We reciprocate the feelings of kindness and confidence expressed in your letter, and shall ever retain a grateful remembrance of your visit among us.

" ' When we first entered on our missionary labors, we were young and inexperienced. There were no examples of schools or churches among the South-Western Indians, save those of the Moravian brethren at Spring Place. The counsel and example of the devoted Gambold were instructive and encouraging. The visit of the beloved Mr. Cornelius at Brainerd, when one of our number was there, and when our first mission church was organized, was timely and welcome. The visit of the venerable Dr. Worcester at Mayhew, in the spring of 1821, was very refreshing. While he was with us, the Mayhew church was formed ; and there he offered the consecrating prayer at the communion table, and administered the bread to the communicants. " This was the last time he assisted in public worship on earth." It is to us cause of devout gratitude that we were favored with the counsels and prayers of these beloved men, while laying the corner-stones of the first Indian churches.

" ' We came to the Choctaws to labor for their conversion, and to make our graves with them, expecting to fall in our field of labor as your missionaries. We have ever had attachments to the American Board, its officers and members, especially the Secretaries, Treasurers, and Prudential Committee, such as we have felt towards no other persons. Their oft-repeated expressions of approbation, relative to our labors, have greatly encouraged and strengthened us. We earnestly desire to retain a hold on their affectionate confidence, and on the confidence of the religious community, who still dwell in the land which gave us birth, and who sent us to the Choctaws as the messengers of the churches.

" ' But at this late period, we, with the Committee, are pressed with peculiar and complicated difficulties on the subject of slavery. We wish you to feel assured that we have no personal attachments to this institution, and that we have ever been deeply impressed with the great evils which mark its character, and of our duty to do all in our power, as servants of the Lord Jesus, to mitigate and remove them. It is a trial of no small magnitude to reside more than a quarter of a century in the midst of such things, and here to train up families of children, from the cradle, not knowing how soon we may die, and leave them in the midst of all these evils.

" ' For more than five and twenty years, the evils and the wrongs of slavery have been the subjects of our anxious and prayerful deliberations. With Mr. Evarts, one of the early Secretaries of the Board, we had repeated personal conversations, at different times, on this subject ; and also an extended correspondence, through him, with the Prudential Committee. Long before the p. :sent agitation, the subject of slavery, as it related to our mission, had been discussed and settled, as we then thought, on a scriptural basis. Nor did we receive an intimation from either of the early Secretaries, or from any member of the Prudential Committee, that it had been settled on a wrong basis.

"'Amid all our cares and labors, the condition of the colored population has not been forgotten; and while our hands have been full of other work, we suppose the Choctaw missionaries have done as much as any other missionaries of the Board to promote practical emancipation, and to produce an impression favorable to that object. So well and so favorably were our principles understood, that, before leaving Mississippi, the agency of one of the brethren of this mission was solicited by a highly respectable planter of that State, to aid in securing the emancipation of more than twenty slaves, who, in compliance with their own wishes, were liberated and sent to Liberia. We have ever felt it our duty to seek the spiritual good of both masters and servants, and not to interfere with the legal relations they sustain to each other. When, with the consent of the master, we have seen an opportunity of extending a helping hand to the slave, we have ever been ready to embrace it. Since the commencement of our mission, we have by our own direct agency, and in part by the use of our own funds, secured liberty to eight slaves. In common with thousands in the slave country, we regard slavery as a tremendous evil; one which casts a dark and ominous shadow over the future prospects of this people. Had we consulted our feelings rather than our duty, long ere this we should have fled from it to a land where we could have breathed a freer and more congenial atmosphere. But when we look around on those for whom we are laboring, most of whom are not involved in this evil, and remember that the Savior hath said, "Go ye into all the world, and preach the Gospel to every creature," we dare not leave them; and when we look on those whom we trust the Lord has given us as the seals of our ministry, how can we forsake them? These considerations have kept us at our post. We have not one particle of sympathy for slavery, except that we may be instrumental of mitigating and removing its evils.

"'Since receiving your letter, we have endeavored to review this whole subject, and to inquire what more can be done by us to advance the cause of truth and righteousness in this land, and to meet the views expressed in that letter.

"'We have supposed that we accorded with the sentiments advanced in the several Reports of the Board, on the subject of slavery. The one of 1845 so ably and so fully defined and settled the principles on which we were to proceed, that we apprehended no serious embarrassments to our future labors. We entirely accorded with the sentiments expressed in that Report, and especially with the two fundamental principles there laid down: 1. "The ordinances of baptism and the Lord's supper cannot be scripturally and rightfully denied to those who give credible evidence of piety." 2. "The missionaries, in connection with the churches which they have gathered, are to be the sole judges of the sufficiency of this evidence." These have been our principles from the commencement of the mission.

"'The employment of slave labor is one ground of objection to our mode of procedure. By this, it is thought, "we countenance and encourage the system"; that "we make this species of labor more profitable to the owner, at the same time that we put it in his power, if he will, to plead our example to justify or excuse the relation." We have wished, as far as possible, to avoid every thing which might seem to sanction this system. Gladly would we have avoided the hiring of slaves, could we have obtained other suitable help. With us it has been a matter of necessity. We apprehend the difficulties with which we have had to struggle in relation to this subject are not generally understood. It is but justice to ourselves that some of them, at least, should be known.

"'1. In the first place, the Committee at Boston find it much more difficult to send us helpers to perform the *manual labor* at our mission stations than formerly. Twenty years ago, we were supplied, to a considerable extent, with kind, faithful, industrious mechanics and farmers from the Eastern States, who took off the great burden of secular cares and labors from those whose duty it was to preach the Gospel. Now, it is rare that such a man is sent to our assistance. A few we have had, and they have been highly esteemed for their work's sake.

"'2. It is much more difficult, in our present location, than it was on the other side of the Mississippi, to obtain such *free* help as will at all answer our purpose. Since the great openings for laborers and mechanics in the free States and territories of the West, and especially since the commencement of the Mexican war, there have been few free laborers to be obtained; and those have generally been of a character very unsuitable to be employed at a mission station. In order, as far as possible, to comply with the instructions of the Committee, we have sought for the best free help to be obtained in the country. Some who came to us with fair appearances and professions have on trial proved profane, intemperate, dishonest and licentious.

"'3. Another thing which has greatly increased our embarrassment, in relation to this subject, has been the peculiar character of our families. Our schools, with one exception, are schools of females. Our families consist mostly of females. This renders it extremely difficult, and in some instances altogether inexpedient, to employ native help for our out-of-door work. We have come near having two of our schools broken up, by the improper conduct of our free hired help. We cannot express the deep anxiety which has pressed upon us from this source.

"'In connection with these facts, we ask the Committee to consider for a moment, that some of us have to be absent on preaching tours to distant congregations two weeks at a time, leaving our families dependent on such help, with none to oversee or control them but females. We presume those to whom we now appeal would not be willing to leave their own families, if they consisted of from thirty to fifty females, under such protectors; and that they would not wish us to do it, if it could be avoided. Our circumstances at different stations, of course, differ very considerably. At some, we have suffered much more than at others. Oppressed as we have been by these troubles, we have felt compelled, in sundry instances, to resort to slave labor. And here it may be asked, " Can we procure slave labor of a better character ? " We not unfrequently have an opportunity to hire slaves, both male and female, of established characters, in whom the community, as well as ourselves, have confidence. Some of these persons feel it a great privilege to live with us ; and several, in consequence of such residence, have been brought to a saving knowledge of the truth. When we can leave our families with such helpers, we can be absent on tours to preach the Gospel, without that distressing solicitude which, under other circumstances, has so often oppressed us. But we should greatly prefer good free help ; it would be much more efficient, and more desirable in every respect. We have repeatedly and most earnestly solicited a supply of such help. That we have not had it, we believe is not the fault of the Committee at Boston. They would have granted our request, had it been in their power. We are grateful to the Committee for the efforts now making to supply us, at least in part, with such free help as our necessities require. We shall most gladly second every effort that may be made in this direction.

" ' At the same time, we wish the difficulties relating to this subject to be understood and appreciated. There must always be much uncertainty attending help, brought a distance of from one to two thousand miles. They may soon become dissatisfied, and either wish to return, or to proceed onward to Texas or to the golden regions of California. True, they may be bound by contract ; but if disposed, as has sometimes been the case, they may annoy us, until we are more than willing to release them. And when they leave, months and sometimes a whole year may pass away, before other free help can be obtained. We hope the efforts now making to secure such help as our necessities require may be more successful than those heretofore made have been.

" ' In this place, permit us to state some of our thoughts as to the *amount* of encouragement given to slavery by the hiring of slaves in the mission. This may be considered in relation to two particulars ; the pecuniary gain resulting to the owners, and the moral influence arising from our example.

" ' As respects the first of these, *the pecuniary gain to the slaveholder*, there is undoubtedly some encouragement and support given to slavery by what we pay for hired slave labor. So far as it goes, it tends to make slavery profitable. This we would avoid, if we could. But we think the encouragement, in this way, given by us to slavery, is very inconsiderable, compared with what is done in other quarters. The small amount paid by us annually for slave labor will bear no comparison with the immense sums paid every year by the free States, by England, and by the rest of the world, for the products of slave labor. Now, so far as profit to the holder is concerned, there can be little difference between the hiring of slaves, and the purchasing of what is raised by them of their owners. We think it must be obvious, that should the market for slave products be closed in the free States, and in other parts of the world, the system could not long survive the measure.

"'We are aware that those living in the free States consider it impracticable to dispense with the products of slave labor. If it be so, — if it is found impracticable where slavery does not exist, and where free help is easily obtained, to dispense with the products raised by slaves, how much more impracticable must it be for those living in the midst of slavery, and where free help is not to be obtained!

"'With us, the employment of slave labor, and the use of slave products, are not a mere matter of convenience, or a calculation of profit and loss. It is a matter of necessity. We have often no other alternative. If we want a horse shod, a slave must do it. If we stop for the night at a public house, a slave must take care of our horse and cook our food. If we want repairs made, or a house built, or land cleared and cultivated, there is often no other one but a slave to do it. To say the least, there is as much *necessity* for the use of slave labor, and of what is produced by the slave, where slavery exists, as where it does not exist. And we think it will not be contended that, so far as mere profit to the slave owner is concerned, there is any essential difference between the hiring of slaves, and the purchasing of the master of what is raised by them.

"'The thought has occurred to our minds why we, in our necessities, should be expected to abstain from every thing which may in a small degree add to the profit of slavery, while the rest of the world, with ample funds, are sustaining it on a vastly larger scale, without fearing rebuke, or seeming to apprehend that they are doing wrong.

"'With the intense interest prevailing in the free States, in England, and we may say, throughout the civilized world, in relation to the wrongs of slavery, we see no prevailing disposition to lay an embargo on the products of slave labor. The cotton, sugar, rice and tobacco of the slave States are purchased as freely now, as before the present movement existed. All the materials and means, necessary to make slave labor productive and profitable, are furnished now as readily by the free States to slaveholders, for the use of the slave, and for the benefit of the master, as they were twenty years ago. We see no tendency, in any quarter, to operate to any considerable extent against slavery, by dispensing with the products of slave labor.

"'This fact has led us to suppose that God has another way of bringing this grievous and oppressive system to an end. We believe the power of the Gospel, and of an enlightened public sentiment, will be brought to bear upon it, until it shall disappear from our otherwise happy land. An evil so enormous cannot long withstand the combined influence which is now brought to bear upon it from every part of the civilized world. We look for this great work to be accomplished ultimately by those who are most deeply affected by it, and who can do it more effectually and more safely than it can be done in any other quarter. The great duty devolving on the *Church*, as we think, is to bring the Gospel, with all its kind and heavenly influences, to bear upon those sections of our country where this evil exists. The law of love, if faithfully and affectionately applied both to masters and servants, must overcome and eradicate all opposing interests.

" ' As relates to the other particular referred to, *the moral influence of our example*, we think it is not what many have supposed it to be. We are not regarded by the people among whom we reside as the advocates and abettors of slavery. They understand that what we do, in the way of employing slaves, is done reluctantly and from necessity. We are regarded as opposed to slavery, and by many are called "abolitionists."

" ' About a year since, one of the brethren of the mission received a letter from a leading man of the nation, in which he says, "You are a Northern man, and meddle yourself too much about the abolition doctrine, which we condemn. With this doctrine, you will divide us up among the Choctaws, and stop the good work of God, by chilling the hearts of the Choctaw Christians." The brother to whom this was addressed has probably employed as much slave labor as any one in the mission. We think the above ought to be received as conclusive testimony, that our general influence and example are not regarded by the people among whom we live as sustaining slavery.

" ' At the same time that we give these as our deliberate convictions, we are desirous of avoiding even the appearance of evil. We wish, if possible, to give no offence to those whose judgment may differ from our own. We shall most cheerfully employ none but free help, provided it can be obtained. But in cases where free help cannot be obtained, we trust the privilege will be granted us of employing such help as our necessities require, without its being considered a dereliction of duty.

" ' We could say more in relation to other topics embraced in your letter, but do not wish unnecessarily to prolong this communication. We have attentively read and considered the letter of the Cherokee brethren of March 21, 1848, relating to this subject, and do adopt it, as expressing, in a clear and condensed manner, our main views and principles.

" ' In closing, permit us to request the Committee, our patrons and friends, to bear us on their hearts at a throne of grace, remembering the great responsibility still resting on us as the missionaries of the Lord Jesus Christ to this tribe of red men, and to every class of people residing among them. "Out of the depths have we cried unto thee, O Lord." And we hope he has heard us. We wish to repeat our cordial approbation of the Reports of the Board, and our grateful remembrance of the visits we have received from the Secretaries. And we wish ever to bear in mind our obligations to the Committee under whose patronage we labor; and also to that church to whose communion we belong, whose standards are based, as we believe, on the Holy Scriptures, and whose discipline we have ever wished faithfully to exercise in our churches.

" ' We are going to the judgment with responsibilities resting on us in regard to this mission, and all connected with it, which can be felt in no heart as in ours; and which can be sustained only by a humble reliance on him who has said, "Lo, I am with you alway."

Wherein we have erred, or been unfaithful, may we find mercy, and receive guidance from the Savior, as to all that is to come.

" ' We do not cease to search the word of God, that we may know what is his good and acceptable and perfect will concerning us in all things; feeling a peculiar obligation to inculcate the great relative duties which pertain to the subject of this letter.

" ' In behalf of the brethren of the Choctaw mission, affectionately and truly yours,

" ' C. KINGSBURY, *Chairman.*

" ' C. C. COPELAND, *Clerk.*'

" A motion was made to refer the foregoing statement of the Prudential Committee, and the letter of the Choctaw mission, to a special committee; which motion, together with the documents, was referred to the Business Committee. The last-named committee subsequently reported that, in their judgment, there was no occasion for a reference of the statement and letter to a special committee; and they recommended that the papers be left with the Prudential Committee, for publication with the other documents of the Board; which was done accordingly."

I will now rehearse, as briefly as possible, the admissions, and the practical conclusions, of this remarkable correspondence, and its result, the order of time of whose several parts is as follows, namely:

1. The report of Mr. Secretary Treat, after his visit to the Cherokee and Choctaw mission stations.

2. The letter of the Cherokee mission in regard to that visit and report.

3. The letter of the Choctaw mission on the same subject.

4. The reply of the Prudential Committee, through Mr. Treat, to the Choctaw missionaries.

5. Their reply, through the same functionary, to the Cherokee missionaries.

6. The report of a Committee, to which all the foregoing had been referred.

7. The amendment moved by Dr. Blanchard, but ultimately withdrawn by the mover, at the request of members.

8. The adoption of the Committee's report, "that the whole subject should be left for the present [1848] where it now is."

9. The addition, in 1849, to the Prudential Committee's "Special Report" of 1848, respecting the "control of missionaries and mission churches."

10. The very important and significant "statement" of

the Prudential Committee in 1849, respecting their correspondence with the missionaries in 1848.

11. The reply of the Choctaw mission to the Prudential Committee's letter of the previous year.

12. The conclusion of the whole matter, being a report of the Business Committee, " that the papers be left with the Prudential Committee for publication,"—and *nothing else!*

I.

TESTIMONY OF MR. TREAT IN REGARD TO SLAVERY AMONG THE CHEROKEES AND CHOCTAWS.

Slavery began among these people long before the missionaries came to them, and it has all the general characteristics of negro slavery in the Southern portion of our Union.

The Cherokees hold probably 1,500 slaves, the Choctaws at least 2,000, and in both nations they are increasing.

The laws of the Cherokees discourage individual emancipation, expel free negroes (except a certain class) from the Nation, forbid the teaching of reading and writing to both slaves and free negroes, and forbid to both these classes the ownership of certain kinds of property.

The laws of the Choctaws expel from the Nation any person favoring abolitionism, and declare that teaching slaves to read, write, or sing, or sitting at table with them, shall be sufficient proof of favoring abolitionism ; they forbid to slaves the possession of property ; they expel from the Nation free negroes, and all who encourage, abet, or conceal them ; and they very strongly discourage individual emancipation.

Slavery is decidedly prejudicial, in many ways, to the most important interests of both nations ; the evils proceeding from it are truly terrific ; its existence neutralizes the influence of the missions, and necessarily hinders missionary success ; the power, in both nations, is mainly in the hands of slaveholders, and there is no present prospect of emancipation. And yet [strange to say] the Indians have increased their investments in *this species of property* in proportion as " the doctrines of the Gospel have exerted their appropriate influence "!

Slaveholders were among the earliest converts and warmest friends of the missionaries in both nations. And the course of the missionaries was, in regard to slavery, uniformly to avoid the mention of it in preaching; to use great caution, even in speaking of it in private; but, if they were obliged to speak of it, to declare that nothing was said in Scripture, either directly condemning it as a system, denouncing it as sinful, or forbidding its continuance. They therefore received slaveholders "early," and without representing this relation as in any manner objectionable, into their churches, and continued to do so.

In the Cherokee mission churches, there were 24 slaveholders, in the Choctaw, 38. And the missionaries did not attempt to disturb the relation of these persons to their slaves, either at first or subsequently.

Mr. Treat closes his report by asserting his entire confidence in "the integrity and faithfulness" of these missionaries. His idea of what constitutes "faithfulness" in a minister of the Gospel may be inferred from his previous assertion, (under the head "Policy of the Missions,") that "it was not to be expected that they [the missionaries] should place themselves far in advance of *public sentiment in New England and the Middle States.*"

II.

TESTIMONY OF THE CHEROKEE MISSIONARIES.

Since the laws of the Cherokees sustain slavery, and the members of the mission churches favor it, church discipline directed against it would be difficult, even if the missionaries wished such a proceeding. But,

On the contrary, regarding it as *certain* that the Apostles did receive slaveholders to the communion of their churches, and being unable to see any material difference between their circumstances and those of the present time, and finding that *many slaveholders* give evidence that they love the Lord Jesus Christ in sincerity, (complying thus with the general rule of church membership,) the missionaries cannot think of rejecting any person from the church *simply* because he is a slaveholder.

Nor can they make it a test of piety, or a *condition of admission* to the church, that a candidate should express a determination not to live and die a slaveholder.

They also regard it as impossible to exercise discipline for the mere buying or selling of slaves, because "occasional exchanges of masters are inseparable from the existence of slavery."

They also refuse "to make it a general rule that the separation of parents and children, by sale and purchase, shall be regarded as a disciplinable offence." And they mention, as an important point in regard to such separation, that "it is one of those things which are not forbidden by any *express* injunction of Scripture."

III.

TESTIMONY OF THE CHOCTAW MISSIONARIES.

They have endeavored, as a mission, "to keep aloof from the abolition movement."

They have been connected with slavery in two ways; by employing slaves as laborers, and by admitting them *and their masters* to the church.

They assume that slavery has long existed "in the Church of God," and that they have plain apostolic warrant for the admission of slaveholders to the church.

They decline even to adopt measures which shall aim at, or tend towards, an *ultimate* removal of slavery from the Choctaw people.

They admit that slavery was among the Choctaws at the commencement of the mission, (showing that it was by the *choice* of the missionaries that it gained a footing in their churches.)

They refer to the full acquiescence of the Prudential Committee in their early policy, and mention, "with peculiar interest and satisfaction," the result to which the Board came in 1845, (namely, the unanimous adoption of Dr. Woods's report in justification of their course.)

IV.

REPLY OF THE PRUDENTIAL COMMITTEE TO THE CHOCTAW MISSION.

The substance of this elaborate letter may be expressed in very small space. It consists, first, of certain expressions, showing the theoretical estimate which the Prudential Committee find it desirable to announce in regard to slavery; next, of certain concessions, showing the practical allowance which they are willing to give to it; and lastly, of certain suggestions (emphatically declared, in the Annual Report of the following year, to be *only* suggestions, *not* decisions or instructions) of a future policy in regard to it.

They declare that "Domestic slavery is at war with the rights of man and opposed to the principles of the Gospel," and that a *system* of slavery is always and everywhere sinful. This is the theoretical view.

Treating the subject *practically*, they agree that, nevertheless, every act of slaveholding is not to be regarded as sinful, nor yet as properly excluding the slaveholder from "Christian fellowship": that the slaveholder's duty *may* be to keep his slaves, and *not* to emancipate them: and that the missionary and his church must judge for themselves, in each case, whether a slaveholding candidate should be received.

Finally, they suggest, for the candid and prayerful consideration of the missionaries, (whose faithfulness, integrity, and devotedness, hitherto, they cheerfully certify,) the inquiry whether they cannot dispense with the hiring of slave labor, and whether they cannot take more stringent precautions that none but truly Christian slaveholders gain admission to their churches.

V.

REPLY OF THE PRUDENTIAL COMMITTEE TO THE CHEROKEE MISSION.

The Committee do not regard these brethren as occupying precisely the same ground with the Choctaw missionaries. Nevertheless, as their letter (foregoing) to the Choctaw mission covered the topics belonging to both, they desire the Cherokee missionaries to consider that letter addressed to them also.

VI.

THE REPORT OF A COMMITTEE TO WHICH ALL THE FOREGOING HAD BEEN REFERRED.

This Committee declare their cordial approbation of the fidelity of the Prudential Committee; of the wisdom and kindness of the Secretary who conducted the correspondence; and of the excellent Christian spirit of the letters from the two missions; they refrain from critical examination of a correspondence as yet unfinished; and recommend that the whole subject be left in the hands of the Prudential Committee.

VII.

THE AMENDMENT MOVED BY DR. BLANCHARD.

Before any vote was taken in regard to the report last mentioned, Dr. Blanchard offered two resolutions by way of amendment to it, requesting the Board to declare these three things: that slaveholding ought not to be allowed in the Christian church; that the missionaries ought to stop hiring slaves; and that they should consider slaveholding as *prima facie* evidence against the piety of a candidate for church membership.

If these resolutions had been acted on, it is plain that they would have been rejected by a nearly unanimous vote. But the policy of the Prudential Committee has always been to try evasion first; " to win, like Fabius, by delay;" and to make as little affirmation, in regard to these troublesome subjects, as possible. These allies of the slaveholder therefore asked the advocate of the slave to oblige them by *withdrawing* his advocacy! And he, most unjustifiably, at once consented.

VIII.

THE ADOPTION OF THE REPORT.

The report of the special Committee was then adopted, (p. 111 of Ann. Rep. of 1848,) leaving the whole matter in the hands of the Prudential Committee until the next year.

IX.

THE CONTROL OF MISSIONARIES AND MISSION CHURCHES; AN ADDITION, IN 1849, TO THE PRUDENTIAL COMMITTEE'S SPECIAL REPORT OF 1848.

This document, admitting that the Board are only agents of the contributors for missionary purposes, and that these contributors may hold the Board responsible for seeing that no part of their contributions goes for the propagation of error, either in doctrine or practice, further concedes that, though the Board do not assume to decide upon the fitness of an individual to be a minister of the Gospel, it *is* their duty to decide on his original and continued fitness to be sustained, by the funds entrusted to them, as a missionary to the heathen.

It is a significant circumstance that, at the close of a paper making this very important concession — a concession which brands the Prudential Committee with inexcusable guilt for every one of the forty-two years during which they have left these stations under the guidance of pro-slavery mission-aries — this Committee should suggest as expedient that the Board "receive" their report, but *not* "adopt" it. The Board, of course, very readily complied with this suggestion.

X.

THE "STATEMENT" OF THE PRUDENTIAL COMMITTEE, IN 1849, RESPECTING THEIR CORRESPONDENCE WITH THE CHEROKEE AND CHOCTAW MISSIONS IN 1848.

The Prudential Committee allege that the Christian commu-nity have extensively misunderstood the purport of their letter of June 22d, of the previous year, to the Choctaw mission, and that the following explanation of the meaning of that letter has become needful. They say, therefore, that that letter had not the *authoritative* character which some have attributed to it; that it brought *no charges* against the mis-sion; that, though it expressed opinions, then and still enter-tained by the Committee, these were *only opinions,* and *not decisions or instructions;* that this distinction is *vital* to the proper understanding of. Mr. Treat's letter; that, for want of it, very erroneous constructions have been put upon that letter; that the Committee and the Secretaries have done nothing inconsistent with the doings of the Board at Brook-lyn in 1845 [which were designated by the missionaries as so perfectly satisfactory to them]; and that they feel undi-minished confidence in the integrity and faithfulness of the missionaries.

The meaning of this seems to be, that sundry pro-slavery members or patrons of the Board, disturbed by the strength of their theoretical statement of the previous year against slavery, had jumped to the conclusion that their practice was to be conformed to it, and had not read the sophistical report and correspondence in question with sufficient care to see that the practical difficulty was provided for, and that slaveholders were to be rated as Christians just as before.

The Prudential Committee repeat the artful suggestion that their letter to these missions had better not be "adopted" by the Board, and annou___e the reception of —

XI.

THE REPLY OF THE CHOCTAW MISSION TO THE PRUDENTIAL COMMITTEE'S LETTER OF 1818.

The missionaries repeat, that they feel it their duty not to interfere with the legal relations which slaveholders and slaves hold to each other; they refer to the silent acquiescence practised by the Board, from the beginning, in their custom of admitting slaveholders to the church, and mention again, with hearty approval, the Board's deliberate allowance of that custom in their Annual Report of 1845, at Brooklyn; they express a willingness to comply (as soon as circumstances shall permit) with the Committee's request that they will discontinue the hiring of slave labor; they intimate that it is God's business, and not theirs, to bring the system of slavery to an end; they slily suggest that the people of the free States generally (of course including the Board) are quite as much implicated in the tolerance and support of slavery as they (the missionaries) are; they declare that, far from being regarded by their parishioners as advocates of slavery, they are stigmatized, by some of them, as "abolitionists;" * and they assume that now, as heretofore, the preaching of the

---

* No doubt the allegation is true, that some of the Choctaws call these missionaries "abolitionists." The extensive scope with which this word is vituperatively used, all over the South, by extremists in the maintenance of slavery, may be judged by the following definition of an abolitionist, taken from *The Southern Literary Messenger*, a magazine published at Richmond, Virginia : —

"An abolitionist is any man who does not love slavery for its own sake, as a divine institution; who does not worship it as the corner-stone of civil liberty; who does not adore it as the only possible social condition on which a permanent republican government can be erected; and who does not, in his inmost soul, desire to see it extended and perpetuated over the whole earth, as a means of human reformation second in dignity, importance and sacredness alone to the Christian religion. He who does not love African slavery with this love is an abolitionist."

7

Gospel [so managed as not to displease or interfere with slaveholders] fills up the measure of their duty.

XII.

THE CONCLUSION.

The foregoing proceedings and documents were referred to the Business Committee, consisting of Chief Justice Williams, Dr. Hopkins, Dr. Thomas De Witt, Dr. Bacon, Samuel H. Perkins, Esq., Dr. Bond, and Rev. Eli Thurston. This body reported that, in their judgment, no further action respecting these matters is needed; and they recommended that the papers be left with the Prudential Committee, for publication with the other documents of the Board. This was done. And the connection of the missions with slavery was thus left to continue entirely undisturbed.

As if to clench the position thus practically taken, (however directly opposed to the theoretical statement accompanying it,) that piety can flourish just as well among slaveholders as elsewhere, the Prudential Committee say of one of these missions in the same year, 1849 —

"No other tribe of Indians has shared so largely in the favor of Zion's King as the Choctaws; and few Christians, in any part of the world, have beheld such displays of the converting and sanctifying power of the Holy Spirit, for the last nine years, as have the Choctaw churches." — p. 204.

The result thus reached — after movements so elaborate as the long Report of Dr. Woods in 1845, the journey of Mr. Treat to the Indian country, and his Report concerning it, in 1848, and the subsequent correspondence between the Prudential Committee and the Cherokee and Choctaw missionaries in 1848-9 — deserves especial notice, both on account of its intrinsic importance, and for the sake of fixing a point from which to survey future operations. After feeling the influence of such diverse breezes and currents, and after such numerous, various and long-continued movements on the part of officers, crew, and passengers, we need to assure ourselves of the true latitude and longitude; to note the exact position of the Board in 1849.

The missionaries had now been for more than a quarter of a century protecting and cherishing slavery in their Cherokee and Choctaw churches, and favoring the practice of slave-holding in various other ways. For twelve years, at least, (how many more we know not,) urgent remonstrances had been addressed to the Board, from time to time, against their complicity, direct and indirect, with slavery. When these remonstrances could no longer be ignored and neglected, they were referred to committees; the committees made reports that nothing was to be done, the Board voted to accept and adopt these reports; and thus it went on until 1845, when it seems to have been judged necessary to make a show of *reasons why* nothing was to be done. I say, to *make a show* of reasons! And I use this expression because, although the reasons given were self-contradictory and manifestly deceitful, as well as insufficient, the same course of policy as before was recommended, showing a foregone conclusion that it should still be adhered to, independently of reason and right.

The *self-contradictory* character of the positions thus taken is so veiled in a profusion of pious words, that I will rehearse a few of the principal points of this sort.

In Dr. Woods's elaborate report in 1845, which not only permits, but pleads for, the continued allowance of slaveholders in the church, it is yet admitted that

"The unrighteousness of the principles on which the whole system is based, and the violations of the natural rights of man, the debasement, wickedness, and misery it involves, and which are in fact witnessed, to a greater or less extent, wherever it exists, must call forth the hearty condemnation of all possessed of Christian feeling and sense of right, and make its entire and speedy removal an object of earnest and prayerful desire to every true friend of God and man."

In the Prudential Committee's statement of their principles in 1848, through the three Secretaries, it is admitted, that slavery is at variance with the principles of the Christian religion ; that the Board are directly responsible for the teaching of the missionaries, and also for the character of the churches, *as far as this results from the character and teaching of the missionaries;* that the Board are bound to employ missionaries who *deserve* confidence; and to *dismiss* those who shall be found undeserving.

From these premises it necessarily follows, that it was the

duty of the Board to dismiss the Cherokee and Choctaw missionaries as soon as it appeared that they were determined to
receive and retain slaveholders in the mission churches, and
to substitute others who would not insist on baptizing with
the Christian name something " at variance with the principles of the Christian religion." It was their duty spontaneously to do this; and this duty became more manifestly
urgent with every year that this wickedness was practised,
and with every remonstrance against it addressed to them by
their employers, the Christian public.

Nevertheless, even in the very document which admits
that the Board are responsible for the teaching of the
missionaries, and for the *dismissal* of such as shall be found
unfaithful, the three Secretaries pass by this last consideration as if they had not mentioned it, and seek to represent,
in their conclusion, that the missionaries have been right,
and the Board right, and their course of policy such as
should still be continued!

Mr. Treat's report of his visit to the Indian country in the
same year, (1848,) assuming throughout that the slaveholding members of the mission churches are genuine Christians,
admits the existence of the following atrocious laws, voted
by the two nations to which these church members belong,
without even the pretence that they opposed such laws, or
that the missionaries called them to account for voting for
them !

The laws of the Cherokees expel free negroes (except a
certain specified class) from the nation; forbid the teaching
of reading and writing alike to free negroes and slaves; and
authorize the seizure and sale, at public auction, of the kinds
of property most easily acquired by slaves, and most beneficial to them.

The laws of the Choctaws expel from the nation all who
actively favor " abolitionism," and provide that the teaching
of slaves to read, write or sing, or the sitting at table with
them, shall suffice to convict of this offence; they provide
that no slave shall " be in possession of any property;" that
free negroes (except a specified class) shall leave the nation
or be sold as slaves; that a heavy fine, or a public scourging,
should be the penalty of hiring, concealing, or in any way
protecting such free negroes; and that no slave shall be

emancipated except by formal permission of the General Council.

The Cherokee missionaries, in their letter of the same year, (1848,) not denying the existence of the above atrocious laws, not denying that their church members voted for them, and not pretending the exercise of any pastoral influence on their part against such voting, declare that they will not reject slaveholders from the church, *simply* because they are slaveholders; that they will not require a pledge against slaveholding from a candidate for church membership; and that they will not inflict church discipline for the buying and selling of slaves, even when it separates children from their parents.

The Choctaw missionaries—not denying the existence of the above atrocious laws, not denying that their church members voted for them, and not pretending the exercise of any pastoral influence on their part against such voting—declare that they have endeavored as a mission to keep aloof from the abolition movement; that they choose not to adopt measures which shall aim *even ultimately* to undermine slavery; that slavery has long existed *in the church of God*, and that, being quite satisfied with the evidence of piety given by the Choctaw slaveholders, they propose still to admit them to the mission churches.

The reply of the Prudential Committee to these two letters (1848) declares *their opinion* that " slavery is opposed to the principles of the Gospel;" it however allows the continuance of slaveholders in the churches, and the admission of more, conceding that such may give ample evidence of piety; it strongly urges a discontinuance of the *hiring* of slave labor by the missionaries; it gently suggests to them the inquiry whether they cannot, in their private teaching and their examination of slaveholding candidates for church membership, exercise *some* influence adverse to the worst features of the slaveholding system; and it compliments the integrity and devotedness, the faithfulness and success, of their missionary labors.

After all this had been read, in the Annual Meeting of 1848, the Board added its authentication to the result thus reached, by declining to affirm the proposition of Dr. Blanchard—" that slaveholding is a practice which is not to be

allowed in the Christian church;" and, in the following
year, to meet a misapprehension which had gained ground
among their pro-slavery members and patrons, the Prudential
Committee took pains to volunteer the declaration, (p. 72,
Annual Report of 1849,) that the expressions in their letters
adverse to slavery were only "*opinions*" entertained by them,
and in no wise "*decisions*, or *instructions*," binding upon the
missionaries. This distinction, they said, was *vital* to the
proper understanding of their letter.

The whole of the foregoing matter was then (September,
1849) formally "left with the Prudential Committee."

It thus appears that, up to that time, *nothing whatever*
had been accomplished against the persistent and manifold
complicity of the Board with slavery, except an urgent
recommendation, by the Prudential Committee, that the
Cherokee and Choctaw missionaries should discontinue the
hiring of slave labor! And this result seems, for a time, to
have accomplished its purpose of discouraging the remonstrants from further effort.

In the Annual Meeting of 1850, no further remonstrances
seem to have been offered against the continuance of slaveholders in the mission churches, or against any other form
of the Board's complicity with slavery. No mention of any
action on this subject is made in the Annual Report, which
states that "nothing occurred to disturb the delightful
harmony" of the meeting. Reports of Committees declare
that the Cherokee missionaries appear to have labored faithfully, and that the Choctaw mission appears to be in a satisfactory and encouraging condition.

A similar silence prevailed in the Annual Meeting, and
also in the Annual Report, for 1851.

In the Annual Meeting of 1852, Mr. Secretary Treat
read a paper, prepared under the direction of the Prudential
Committee, on "The Success of the Indian Missions." It
occupies nine pages (pp. 26–35) of the Annual Report for
that year, unblushingly making the following assertions, in
spite of the antagonistic evidence given in 1848–9, and without even the pretence that the shameful laws and customs of
the Cherokees and Choctaws had changed since that time.

This paper speaks first of the Choctaws, (the *italics* are
those of the Report,) as follows:

"1. *A large number of the Choctaws are the followers of the Lord Jesus Christ.*"

"2. *Intemperance among the Choctaws has been greatly curtailed.*"

"3. *The Choctaws are an agricultural people.*"

"4. *Education is highly prized by the Choctaws.*"

"5. *The Choctaws have a good government.*"

Under this last head, the Prudential Committee say —

"Of the laws which relate to slavery, the Committee have no occasion to speak, as they were laid before the Board four years ago."

This shows that those unspeakably wicked laws still remained the same; and yet, the Committee declare, "*The Choctaws have a good government!*"

They speak next of the Cherokees.

"1. Of the *Churches.*" Satisfactory evidence of piety is afforded by the professors of religion, including the slaveholders.

"2. *The Cherokees are struggling manfully against the evils of intemperance.*"

"3. *The Cherokees have made great improvement in agriculture.*"

"4. *The Cherokees are advancing in knowledge.*"

"5. *The Cherokees have an excellent government.*"

Under this head, the Prudential Committee say —

"The usual safeguards for person and property, the rights of conscience, &c., are provided. The printed laws of the Cherokee nation are more clearly and technically expressed than those of the Choctaws. They are simple and brief, however, and adapted to the wants of the people. Many of the friends of the Cherokees could well spare the provisions which relate to slavery; but it is believed that correct opinions on this subject are to be found among all classes; more that is encouraging and hopeful the Committee do not feel at liberty to say in this public manner."

Is not the hardihood amazing which can speak in this manner of laws which expel free negroes from the Cherokee nation? which forbid the teaching of reading and writing alike to free negroes and slaves? and which allow slaves to be robbed, by public functionaries, of even the little property which they can acquire by over-work? Yet, not only do the Prudential Committee call this system of laws, and the Excentive which puts them in force, "*an excellent government,*" but the Board, in view of this deceitful representation of "the success of the Indian Missions," adopted the following series of resolutions, presented by Dr. Bacon, of New Haven:

"*Resolved,* That this Board acknowledges, with gratitude to Him who giveth the increase, the success which, in circumstances most unfavorable to success, has attended the missions of this Board among the American Indians, and particularly the missions to the Cherokees and the Choctaws, and accepts that success as conclusive evidence that the tribes of the wilderness may be civilized by being Christianized.

"*Resolved,* That as the advancing civilization of the Cherokee and Choctaw nations is to be referred, primarily and chiefly, to the introduction of Christianity among them by missionary labors, so its permanence and progress must depend upon the further prosecution of those labors; and it is, therefore, the desire of this Board that the Prudential Committee take measures, as early as possible, to strengthen the Cherokee and Choctaw missions.

"*Resolved,* That the great wrongs which the Indians, and particularly the South-Western tribes, have suffered in their connection with the American people, should incite all who fear God, and all who love justice, to renewed efforts for the temporal and eternal welfare of that injured race; so that whether in the form of separate political communities, or incorporated as equal fellow-citizens in the great American Union, they and their posterity, from age to age, may be a living monument to the praise of Christ and to the honor of his Gospel." — Ann. Rep. of 1852, pp. 35, 6.

Neither in this year, nor in 1853, does it appear that any further remonstrances were presented against the complicity of the Board with slavery.

On page 48 of the Annual Report of 1853, however, appears the following record of the faithfulness with which a missionary in Africa opposed slavery there. Mr. Lewis Grout, a missionary among the Zulus, mentions the following incident. Meeting a company of natives, one of them thus addressed him: —

"'Teacher, white man! We black people do not like the news which you bring us. We are black, and we like to live in darkness and sin. You trouble us; you oppose our customs; you induce our children to abandon our practices; you break up our kraals, and eat up our cattle; you will be the ruin of our tribe. And now we tell you to-day, if you do not cease, we will leave you and all this region, and go where the Gospel is not known or heard.' 'But,' said I, 'how is this? I oppose your customs, of course, because the word of God is opposed to them, and because they are all wrong, and will be your certain and endless ruin, if you do not forsake them. Your children I teach, as I do you, to become wise and good and happy. But how do I eat up your cattle, and break up your kraals and your tribes? All that I obtain from you I pay for. Do I not? And I sometimes try to do you a good turn besides.' 'Yes. But you teach repentance and faith; and a penitent believing man is to us as good as dead. He no longer takes any pleasure in our pursuits, and no longer labors to build up his father's kraal; but he leaves it, and joins the church; and then he tries to lead others away to the station after him. And as to our cattle, our girls and our women are our cattle; but you teach that they are not cattle, and ought not to be sold for cattle, but to be taught and clothed, and made the servants of God, and not the slaves of men. That is the way you eat up our cattle. Many have left us, and been engulphed at the station; and more wish to leave us. And now, if you continue these labors and instructions, we shall just leave you, and go to another country.'"

What an amazing contrast is here presented to the conduct of the missionaries among the Cherokees and Choctaws! The African missionary makes such a faithful presentation of the utter incompatibility between a Christian life on one hand, and the treating of human beings like cattle on the other, that those who are determined to buy and sell women, to treat them like cattle, and to prevent their learning to read and write, *recognize* this incompatibility, and do not *pretend* to be Christians, or ask the missionary to certify them as such by admission to the church. And thus the African missionary at once preserves his own integrity, and secures the purity of his church, in this particular.

How different the conduct of the Cherokee and Choctaw missionaries! They too were sent among a heathen people, who were accustomed to treat a class of human beings as cattle; to buy and sell them. They made no objection to this. They received the buyers and sellers of human beings as worthy members of the churches they established, and among the earliest members of those churches. When, afterwards, a movement was made by other persons against the treating of human beings like cattle, these missionaries carefully *held themselves aloof* from it, declining even to favor measures which should *"in the end"* undermine this wicked system. When, still later, the human cattle-dealers whom they called Christians had copied the forms of civilization sufficiently to frame their iniquity into a system of laws, enacting that certain men and women *might* be bought and

7*

sold, but *should not* be taught to read, the missionaries still acquiesced; still ranked the buyers and sellers as Christians; and still held themselves aloof from vindication of the rights of the unfortunates who were bought and sold!

The disgraceful picture is not complete until we look at the time-serving course of the *employers* of both these classes of missionaries, the Prudential Committee of the American Board, who have used these diametrically opposite measures in their treatment of slaveholding and slave-trading in two different countries.

When their missionary away off in Africa denounces slaveholding as sin, teaching that human beings "are not cattle, and ought not to be sold for cattle, but ought to be taught," they approvingly echo his statement, printing it in their Annual Report.

On the other hand, when their missionaries in this country silently acquiesce in the human-cattle system, receive its traders into their churches as Christians, hold themselves aloof from the opposers of it, quote the Bible in support of it, and declare all this to be their settled purpose for the future, the Prudential Committee give, first silent acquiescence, and then extenuation and defence, even at the expense of truth as well as of justice!

Still further: when their missionaries in a third quarter of the globe, feeling the disastrous influence of the American human-cattle system upon their own labors, used their only effective means of operation (the Sandwich Islands mission press) to make appeal to their American brethren against this sin, the Prudential Committee suppressed and smothered this appeal, and immediately caused a law to be passed, forbidding such action of their missionaries in future!

What is the occasion of this opposite treatment, by the Prudential Committee, of two precisely similar cases? Is it any thing else but the fact that some of the clerical brethren of these Reverend gentlemen, some of the pillars of the several religious denominations to which they belong, and some of the Corporate and Honorary members of the Board who employ them, are personally interested in the human-flesh market, living on its wages of sin, and pledged to its support?

If this be not the reason, what is?

In the very Annual Report for 1853, from which I have last been quoting, appears another evidence that the Prudential Committee are willing to speak against slavery, and to maintain the right of freedom, *except where American slavery is concerned!*

In their report for this year on the Sandwich Islands, (pp. 136–153,) the Prudential Committee announce that "*the people of the Sandwich Islands are a* CHRISTIAN NATION"; and that the ministry and churches of those islands, having become "an independent Christian community," will be no longer under the direction of the Board, or responsible to it. The Prudential Committee congratulate themselves on their success among this people, and thankfully recognize their appropriate work as a Foreign Missionary Society as completed. Part of this statement is a contrast between the former and present condition of this people.

Among the specifications of its heathen condition, they say (p. 142): "The land was owned by the king and his chiefs, *and the people were slaves.*"

Among the details of their converted state are the following, expressing their attainment of the rights of freedom and of education. They are said (pp. 143, 4) to be "united under one balanced government; rallied to the fold of civilization by a written language and constitution, *providing security for the rights of persons, property and mind,* and invested with all the elements of right and power which can entitle them to be acknowledged by their brethren of the human race as a separate and independent community."

Such is the difference between the Board's treatment of slavery in America and slavery in Africa.

Let it be noted, that up to this time, 1853, there is no evidence that the Cherokee and Choctaw missionaries exercised the slightest influence against slaveholding, either in their churches, or among the other people of those nations, or that the Board required them to attempt such a policy. While, on the other hand, abundant evidence has been shown that those missionaries, with the allowance of the Board, did exert an efficient influence towards making slavery reputable among those nations, and thus towards its continuance and perpetuity.

In the years 1854 and 1855 there was much movement,

by the Prudential Committee and the Secretaries, respecting a matter connected with slavery, giving rise to elaborate reports, hereafter to be quoted. But it was movement without progress, precisely resembling the execution, by a military body, of the following orders,—"Advance two paces!" —"Mark time!"—"Retreat to your former position!"

The reason for the making of this movement (which was unmade the next year) seems to have been the *appearance* of an interference by the Choctaw Council with the professional action of the missionaries. Examination showed (as Mr. Secretary Wood formally testifies) that the missionaries had not done, and did not propose to do, the things forbidden by the Council, and then (1855) it was decided to proceed as before, without regard to the disrespectful *form* of the Choctaw edict.

The proceedings above referred to commence on page 23 of the Annual Report for 1854, and are as follows:—

" The Committee on the missions among the Choctaws, Cherokees and Dakotas made a report, which, after having been recommitted and amended, was adopted by the Board, and is in the following words:—

"' The Committee on the missions to the Choctaws, the Cherokees and the Dakotas would report, that they have seen with much satisfaction the statements of the Prudential Committee respecting the progress of religion among the Choctaws during the past year. The faithful labors of the missionaries have been abundantly blessed ; while labors, no doubt as faithful, among the Cherokees, have not been attended with similar blessings. Among the Dakotas, whose migratory habits render the constant preaching of the Word a far more difficult matter, but little comparative success was to be expected; while yet among one branch, the Wahpetons, some cheering facts are reported.

"' The relations of the Board to the schools connected with the Choctaw mission have been essentially changed during the past year. In November last, the Choctaw Council enacted certain laws, one of which forbids that any "slave, or the children of slaves, shall be taught to read or write, in or at any school or academy in the nation, by any person whomsoever, or connected in any manner whatever, either a superintendent, missionary, teacher, farmer, matron, pupil or otherwise, with any school or academy in the nation, under pain of dismissal from such school and removal out of the nation, in case the person offending is not a citizen of the Choctaw nation." Another provision of the same law is as follows : "It shall be the duty of the General Superintendent and Trustees of schools to be vigilant in the performance of their functions, and promptly remove, or report to the Commissioner of Indian Affairs for removal, according to the nature of the contract between the Choctaw nation and the different boards of missions having charge of public schools and academies, any and all persons who may be connected therewith, who is or are known to be abolitionists, or who disseminate, or attempt to disseminate, directly or indirectly, abolition doctrines, or any other fanatical sentiments, which in their opinion are dangerous to the peace and safety of the Choctaw people.''

" ' The same body also passed a joint resolution, authorizing the Trustees to propose to the various boards of missions, having charge of Choctaw academies or schools, to insert in their contracts with the Choctaw nation a clause providing for the termination of such contracts by either party on giving six months' notice.

" ' When the Prudential Committee heard of the enactment of these laws, they decided at once that they could not carry on the schools on this new and unequal basis; and with them in their decision the missionaries concur. We doubt not that the unanimous concurrence of the Board will sanction this decision. The Choctaw Council are supreme in their jurisdiction over their national schools; neither our missionaries nor the Board can control them. But provisions so anti-Christian and unjust we are required to disapprove and condemn without any qualification, so far as our refusal to act in accordance with them is such a condemnation.

" ' These provisions, it should be remarked, do not restrict the missionaries in their preaching. They are still permitted to declare the whole counsel of God, on all subjects, and to all individuals, without any interference by legislation or otherwise; neither are we authorized to affirm that any such interference is contemplated. Should any such restrictions, unhappily, be hereafter imposed, we cannot doubt that the Board will determine at once, through the Prudential Committee, to withdraw their missionaries from the Choctaws.

" ' The other provision, requiring the removal from the nation of "abolitionists," and of all persons disseminating fanatical sentiments, if we are to interpret it by the common meaning given to such language, is only to be deplored, as indicating hostility to freedom and to the Gospel, which augurs disastrous results among that people.

" ' We would remark on one other topic. The murderous contests between detached parties of the Dakotas and the Ojibwas are so frequent as to threaten the speedy extinction of the two tribes. We concur in the suggestion of the Prudential Committee, that it is exceedingly desirable that the United States should pass a law, punishing every such case of homicide with death. In no other manner, as we apprehend, can this evil be arrested.'

" The same Committee reported certain resolutions, which were discussed, and finally adopted in the following form:—

" ' Resolved, That the Board acknowledge with gratitude to God the wisdom and fidelity with which, so far as appears from the documents submitted to them, the Prudential Committee are advising and directing the missionaries among the Choctaws, in conformity with the principles asserted by them in their correspondence with those missions, reported to the Board in 1848.

" ' *Resolved*, That the decision of the Prudential Committee, with the concurrence of the missionaries, not to conduct the boarding-schools in the Choctaw nation, in conformity with the principles prescribed by the recent legislation of the Choctaw Council, meets the cordial approbation of the Board.

" ' *Resolved*, That the commission given by Christ to his disciples to go and teach all nations, and to preach the Gospel to every creature, which is the warrant of Christian missions, is to be respected and obeyed in all the operations and by all the missionaries of this Board ; and that while our missionaries among the Choctaws are allowed, in fact, to preach the Gospel to all persons, of whatever complexion or condition, as they have opportunity, and to preach it in all its applications to human character and duty, they are to continue patiently in their work.'

" While the discussion on the foregoing report and resolutions was in progress, the following preamble and resolution were offered for the consideration of the Board:—

" ' Whereas, several of the matters pertaining to this case are in an inchoate state, being yet matters of unfinished correspondence between our executive officers and the authorities and missionaries in the Choctaw nation ; and whereas differences of opinion exist among the officers and members of this Board as to the true construction and import of the recent legislation of the Choctaw nation ; and whereas this Board cherishes the utmost confidence both in its Prudential Committee and the Choctaw missionaries, therefore be it

" ' *Resolved*, That the several documents pertaining to this subject be referred to the same Committee, to consider and report at the next annual meeting, in the hope that the authenticated and completed facts pertaining to this case will at the same time lead this Board to perfect unanimity of sentiment and action.'

" The vote was taken by yeas and nays, with the following result:—

" *Yeas*—Aaron Warner, Bennet Tyler, David L. Ogden, Thos. H. Skinner, Reuben H. Walworth, Horace Holden, William Adams, Joel Parker, Robert W. Condit, William F. Allen, Theodore Frelinghuysen, David Magie, Richard T. Haines, Ansel D. Eddy, Benjamin C. Taylor, David H. Riddle, John H. Cocke, Chauncey Eddy, William H. Brown.

" *Nays*—Enoch Pond, Levi Cutter, Benjamin Tappan, John W. Ellingwood, William T. Dwight, Asa Cummings, Zedekiah S. Barstow, John Woods, John K. Young, David Greene, Charles Walker, Silas Aiken, Joseph Steele, William Allen, Lyman

Beecher, Heman Humphrey, John Tappan, Henry Hill, Charles Stoddard, Nehemiah Adams, Horatio Bardwell, Ebenezer Alden, Richard S. Storrs, Swan L. Pomroy, Selah B. Treat, William J. Hubbard, Linus Child, Henry B. Hooker, Baxter Dickinson, Samuel M. Worcester, Daniel Safford, John Todd, John Kingsbury, Noah Porter, Joel Hawes, Thomas W. Williams, Edward W. Hooker, Alvan Bond, Leonard Bacon, Henry White, Joel H. Linsley, Andrew W. Porter, Pelatiah Perit, Hiram H. Seelye, Charles Mills, William Patton, Henry W. Taylor, Charles J. Stedman, Henry A. Nelson, George W. Wood, Asa D. Smith, Oliver E. Wood, Samuel H. Perkins, Julian M. Sturtevant, John C. Holbrook, John W. Chickering, Seth Sweetser, James M. Gordon, Samuel W. S. Dutton."

The adoption of the above report, and of the three resolutions which follow it, (which ascribe faithfulness in labor to the missionaries, and wisdom and fidelity to the Prudential Committee,) and the rejection, by a very large vote, after an excited discussion, of a subsequent preamble and resolution, (expressing. the existence of " differences of opinion among the officers and members of the Board,") show not only a general approval by the Board of the position of the Prudential Committee and of the missionaries, but a determination to maintain the independence of the missionaries, and to repel even the appearance of disrespect to them in the action of the Choctaw Council.

The Prudential Committee, at the close of their account of the Annual Meeting of 1854, refer to this report, and the debate upon it, as follows : —

" The debate which grew out of the report on the Choctaw mission awakened a general and absorbing interest. The question was ultimately narrowed to a single point, namely, ' Shall the general principles of the letter addressed by the Prudential Committee to the Choctaw mission, in 1848, receive the *express* sanction of the Board ?' It was admitted that these principles had received an *implied* sanction. In fact, there could have been no controversy on this point. A Committee on this letter and other documents recommended to the meeting of 1848, ' that the whole subject should be left for the present' ' in the hands of the Prudential Committee ;' which recommendation was adopted by the Board. Nor was this all. The Prudential Committee were all re-elected at that meeting ; and they have been re-chosen annually, except in case of death or removal, from that time to this. They have felt, therefore, that their views must be considered as having the *implied* sanction of the Board ; and they have acted accordingly. In no particular would their course have been different, had a vote of approbation been passed in any previous year. 'Is it expedient then for the Board to say in words what it has been saying for six years by its acts?' That was the question. And it is not strange that there should have been some diversity of sentiment in reference to it. The surprise is rather, that there should have been so much unanimity in the final vote.

"Seldom has an exciting discussion been followed by such exhibitions of a kind and fraternal spirit. It was worth passing through the storm, to enjoy such a sweet and hallowed calm."—pp. 45, 6.

In the Annual Report for 1855, the action of the Prudential Committee—reversing their last year's decision, and authorizing the *continuance* of the boarding-schools, in spite of the objectionable new laws of the Choctaw Council— appears in the following paragraph, p. 129:—

"EDUCATIONAL LABORS.

"The last Report apprised the Board of certain changes which the Choctaw Council had made in their school laws. The Committee stated their reluctance 'to believe that such legislation truly and faithfully' expressed 'the sentiments of the Choctaw nation;' but they did not deem it safe to predict any formal modification thereof. The enactments to which exception was taken remain unrepealed; but, on the other hand, there has been no attempt to enforce them. Nor do the missionaries see any reason for supposing that they will be enforced hereafter. In these circumstances, the Committee have authorized the continuance of the boarding-schools at Stockbridge, Wheelock and Pine Ridge for the present. A special communication will be made to the Board, however, which will explain this matter more fully; to that the Committee beg leave to refer."

The reason for this sudden change is concealed in such a voluminous mass of subsequent matter, that, though it will be quoted hereafter in its proper connection, in Mr. Secretary Wood's report, its use in *explaining* the action of the Prudential Committee will be best served by giving the purport of it here also.

However disrespectful *in form* were the new laws of the Choctaw Council, (providing that any missionary found to be an abolitionist, or found teaching reading or writing to slaves, or the children of slaves, in the schools, should be expelled from the Nation,) it was found that these laws would not at all affect the missionaries *in fact*. For, first, these missionaries *were not* abolitionists, as has manifestly appeared from their whole course of language* and action; and next, in regard to the teaching of slaves, Mr. Wood positively testifies (p. 23 of Ann. Rep. for 1855):—

"The teaching of slaves in these schools *has never been practised* OR CONTEMPLATED"!

The policy of the missionaries had spontaneously gone side by side with the pro-slavery legislation of the Choctaw Council.

The full action of the Prudential Committee and of the Board in regard to the Cherokee and Choctaw missions, including the famous "Good-water Statement," by which the continued allowance of slaveholders in the mission churches was confirmed, is herewith subjoined. It covers eleven closely printed pages. In connection with the "Good-water Statement," Mr. Wood quotes, adopting it as a part of his report, the famous "Act of the General Assembly of the Presbyterian Church in 1818," by the allowance of which Presbyterians in this country have ever since been accustomed to hold, breed, buy and sell slaves. These proceedings of the Board commence on page 19 of the Annual Report for 1855, as follows:—

"THE CHOCTAW AND CHEROKEE MISSIONS.

"The Prudential Committee, at an early stage of the meeting, submitted a special communication in reference to the Choctaw and Cherokee missions, in which they say:—'Since the last meeting of the Board, it has seemed desirable that one of the Secretaries should visit the Indian missions in the South-West, for the purpose of conferring fully and freely with them in reference to certain questions which have an important bearing upon their work. Mr. Wood, therefore, was directed to perform this service, which he did in the spring of the present year. After his return

---

* For instance: on p. 511 of the Public Documents of the U. S. Senate (2d session, 1858, 9) may be seen, at the close of a letter written by one of the Choctaw missionaries to "Douglass Cooper, United States Agent"— dated "Goodland, Choctaw Nation, Oct. 4, 1858"— the following designation of the charge of abolitionism against them as preposterous as well as false:—

"We have been accused, too, of being abolitionists, and the emissaries of abolition societies. Public men ought not to betray so much ignorance of missionaries and missionary operations so near home, and with so many sources of information within their reach. The position of the Choctaw missionaries on this subject is so WELL UNDERSTOOD IN THE RELIGIOUS COMMUNITY, that we cannot believe those who make these charges to be honest in doing so.

"O. P. STARK."

to New York, he drew up a report of this visit, and presented the
same to the Prudential Committee. It is deemed proper that this
document should be laid before the Board at the earliest opportunity; and it is herewith submitted. The results obtained by this
conference are highly satisfactory to the Committee.'

"The report of Mr. Wood is in the following language : —

" ' *To the Prudential Committee of the American Board of Commissioners
for Foreign Missions : —*

" ' I have to report a visit made by me to the Choctaw and Cherokee missions, in obedience to instructions contained in the following
resolutions adopted by you, March 6, 1855 : —

"*Resolved*, 1. That Mr. Wood be requested to repair to the Choctaw
Nation, at his earliest convenience, with a view to a fraternal conference
with the brethren in that field, in respect to the difficulties and embarrassments which have grown out of the action of the Choctaw Council in the
matter of the boarding-schools, and also in respect to any other question
which may seem to require his attention.

"2. That, in case the spring meeting of the Choctaw mission shall not
occur at a convenient time, he be authorized to call a meeting at such
time and place as he shall designate.

"3. That on his return from the Choctaw mission, he be requested to
confer with the brethren of the Cherokee mission, in regard to any matter
that may appear to call for his consideration, and that he be authorized to
call a meeting for this purpose.

"4. That on arriving in New York, he be instructed to prepare a
report, suggesting such plans and measures for the adoption of the Committee in reference to either of these missions as he may be able to recommend."

" ' Leaving New York, March 19, and proceeding by the way of
the Ohio and Mississippi rivers to Napoleon, thence up the White
river, across to Little Rock, and through Arkansas to the Choctaw
country, I arrived at Stockbridge, April 11. Including the portions
of the days occupied in passing from one station to another, I devoted three days to Stockbridge, three to Wheelock, six to Pine
Ridge, three to Good-water, and three to Spencer ; the latter a station of the mission of the General Assembly's Board. Five days,
with a call of a night and half a day at Lenox, were occupied in the
journey to the Cherokee country, in which I spent two days at
Dwight, and three at Park Hill ; my departure from which was on
the 11th of May, just one month from my arrival at Stockbridge.
My return to New York was on May 31, ten and a half weeks from
the time of leaving it.

" ' I should do injustice to my own feelings, and to the members
of the two missions, not to state that my reception was every where
one of the utmost cordiality. The Choctaw mission, when my
coming was announced, agreed to observe a daily concert of prayer,
that it might be blessed to them and the end for which they were
informed it was designed. They met me in the spirit of prayer ;
our intercourse was much a fellowship in prayer ; and, through the

favor of Him who heareth prayer, its issue was one of mutual congratulation and thanksgiving.

"'The visit, although a short one, afforded considerable opportunity (which was diligently improved) for acquainting myself with the views, feelings, plans and labors of the brethren of the missions. Their attachment to their work and to the Board with which they are connected is unwavering. With fidelity they prosecute the great object of their high calling; and in view of the spiritual and temporal transformation taking place around them, as the result of the faithful proclamation of the Gospel, we are compelled to exclaim, "What hath God wrought!" It was pleasant to meet them, as with frankness and fraternal affection they did me, in consultation for the removal of difficulties and the adoption of measures for the advancement of the one end desired equally by them and by the Prudential Committee.

"'Several topics became subjects of conference, on some of which action was taken by the missions; and on others recommendations will be made by the Deputation, that need not be embraced in this report. In respect to them all, there was entire harmony between the Deputation and the missions.

"'In their first resolution, the Committee requested me to repair to the Choctaw Nation, with special reference to the embarrassments and difficulties which have grown out of the action of the Choctaw Council in the matter of the boarding-schools. A condensed statement of the action of the Council, and of the missionaries and Prudential Committee, previous to the sending of the Deputation, seems to be here called for.

"'In the year 1842, the Choctaw Council, by law, placed four female seminaries "under the direction and management of the American Board of Commissioners for Foreign Missions," subject only to "the conditions, limitations and restrictions rendered in the act." In accordance with the act, a contract was entered into, by which the schools were taken for a period of twenty years. The "conditions, limitations and restrictions" specified in the act and contract, so far as they bind the Board, are the following: 1. The superintendents and teachers, with their families, shall board at the same table with the pupils. 2. In addition to letters, the pupils shall be taught housewifery and sewing. 3. One-tenth of the pupils are to be orphans, should so many apply for admission. 4. The Board shall appropriate to the schools a sum equal to one-sixth of the monies appropriated by the Choctaw Council. With these exceptions, the "direction and management" of the schools were to be as exclusively with the Board, as of any schools supported by the funds of the Board.

"'Thus the schools were carried forward until 1853. At the meeting of the Council in that year, a new school law, containing several provisions, (and sometimes spoken of in the plural as "laws,") was enacted, bringing the Board, through its agents, under new "conditions, restrictions, and limitations." A Board of Trustees was established, and a General Superintendent of schools provided for, to discharge various specified duties, for the faithful performance of which they are to give bonds in the sum of $5,000.

The enactments of this law, affecting the agents of the Board under the existing contract, are the following : —

" ' 1. The Board of Trustees, convened by the General Superintendent, are to hear and determine difficulties between a Trustee and any one connected with the schools; to judge of the fitness of teachers, &c., and request the Missionary Boards to remove any whose removal they may think called for; and, in case of neglect to comply with their wishes, to report the same to the Commissioner of Indian Affairs through the United States Agent. Section 5.

' " 2. The Trustees are to select the scholars from their several districts. Section 7.

' " 3. No slave or child of a slave is to be taught to read or write " *in or at any school*," etc., by any one connected in any capacity therewith, on pain of dismissal and expulsion from the nation. Section 8.

" ' 4. Annual examinations are to take place at times designated by the General Superintendent. Section 10.

" ' 5. The Trustees are empowered to suspend any school in case of sickness or epidemics. Section 11.

" ' 6. It is made the duty of the General Superintendent and Trustees promptly to remove, or report for removal, any and all persons connected with the public schools or academies known to be abolitionists, or who disseminate, or attempt to disseminate, directly or indirectly, abolition doctrines, or any other fanatical sentiments, which, in their opinion, are dangerous to the peace and safety of the Choctaw people. Section 13.

" ' By a separate act, the Board of Trustees was authorized to propose to the Missionary Boards, having schools under contract with the Nation, the insertion of a clause providing for a termination of the contract by either party, on giving six months' notice.

" ' With respect to the question, "Shall we submit to the provisions and restrictions imposed by this new legislation, as a condition of continued connection with the national schools?" the views of the Prudential Committee and the brethren of the mission have been entirely in declared agreement. As stated in the last Annual Report to the Board, (p. 166,) "the Committee decided at once that they could not carry on the schools upon the new basis; and in the propriety of this action the missionaries concur." The concurrence of the missionaries in this view, viz., that they could not carry on the schools with a change from the original basis to that of the new law, may be seen clearly expressed in their correspondence with the Secretary having charge of the Indian missions, particularly in the following communications : From Messrs. Kingsbury and Byington, as the committee of the mission, under dates of December 14 and 27, 1853 ; Mr. Kingsbury, January 4 and April 25, 1854 ; Mr. C. C. Copeland, March 1, 1854 ; Mr. Stark, August 22, 1854 ; Mr. Edwards, July 13, 1854 ; Mr. H. K. Copeland, May 16, 1854. See also letters from Mr. Chamberlain, January 7 and June 20, 1854. In some of these, the declaration is made, that, in the apprehension of the writers, the schools must be relinquished, *if the law should not be repealed*; one specifying, as justificatory reasons, the breach of contract made, and the increased difficulty of obtaining teachers — reasons also assigned by others ; another stating that he " never could consent to take charge of a school under such regulations;" a third testifying, not only for himself, but for every other member of the mission, an unwillingness to continue connection with the schools with subjection to the new requirements ; a fourth affirming his "feeling" to be "that a strong remonstrance should be presented to the Council, and on the strength of it, let the mission lay down these schools;" which, he states, would not involve "giving up the instruction of these children, but would be simply changing the plan," inasmuch as, according to his and others' understanding of the case, the new law not having application to other than the national schools, "at every station it will be found an easy matter to have as large, and in some cases even larger, than our present boarding-schools."

" ' In certain other communications, the view which the Committee adopted is exhibited, together with the opinion that it would be better to wait for a movement on the part of the Choctaw authorities, before giving up the schools. See letters from Mr. Byington, December 26, 1853 ; January 3 and 12, April 15, 1854; Mr. Kingsbury, February 1 and 21, 1854; Mr. Chamberlain, January 13, 1854; Mr. Stark, February 6, 1854. This view was also formally announced, as understood by the Committee, in resolutions of the mission at its meeting in May, 1854, embracing a recommendation of a course of procedure with the hope of securing the repeal, by the next Council, of the obnoxious law. See Minutes, and letters of Mr. C. C. Copeland, May 19 and June 9, 1854. The Prudential Committee, in the exercise of their discretion, as a principal party to the contract, preferred another method, viz., to address the Council directly, and sent a letter, under date of August 1, 1854, to one of the missionaries for presentation. The missionary, with the advice of his brethren, given at their meeting in September, (intelligence of which was received at the Missionary House, October 20, thirty-five days subsequent to the meeting of the Board at Hartford,) withheld the letter, on the ground that, in their judgment, its presentation would defeat the object at which it aimed, and be "disastrous to the churches, to the Choctaws, and to the best interests of the colored race." In respect to this action for obtaining the repeal of the school law, there was a difference between the mission and the Committee. The missionaries desired delay, and the leaving of the matter to their management. The decision of the Committee, approved by the Board, "not to conduct the boarding-schools in the Choctaw nation in conformity with the principles prescribed by the recent legislation of the Choctaw Council,"* was in agreement with the previously and subsequently expressed sentiments of all the missionaries ; the objection felt by some of them to this resolution being, not to the position which it assumes, but to the declaration of it at that time by the Board. This being a determined question, its settlement formed no part of the object for which the Deputation was sent.

" ' Two other questions, however, required careful examination ; and on these, free conference was had with the brethren at their

---

* Resolution of the Board adopted at Hartford.

stations, and in a meeting of the mission held at Good-water, April
25 and 26, Mr. Edwards, who was absent from the mission, and Dr.
Hobbs, not being present: 1. The law remaining unrepealed, is it
practicable to carry on the schools while refusing conformity to the
new "conditions, limitations and restrictions" imposed by it?
2. If so, is it expedient to do it?

"'On the first of these questions, the opinion of the missionaries
was in the affirmative. No attempt has been made to carry out
these new provisions. The Trustees and General Superintendent
have not given the required bond. One of the Trustees informed
me that he should not give it, and that, in his belief, the law would
remain a dead letter, if not repealed, as it was his hope that it would
be. The course of the missionaries has been in no degree changed
by it. The teaching of slaves in these schools has never been
practised or contemplated. The law was aimed at such teaching in
their families and Sabbath schools. So the missionaries and the
people understand it. It is generally known among the latter that
the former are ready to give up these schools, rather than retain
them on condition of subjection to this law. Our brethren are now
carrying on the schools, and doing, in all other respects, just as they
were before the new law was enacted; and they have confidence
that they may continue to do so.

"'The second question was one of more uncertainty to my own
mind, and in the minds of some of the mission. The maintenance
of these schools is a work of great difficulty. In the opinion of
several of the missionaries, it was at least doubtful whether the cost
in health, perplexity, trouble in obtaining teachers, time which
might be devoted to preaching, and money, was not too great for
the results; and it was suggested that an opportunity, afforded by
divine Providence for relieving us from a burden too heavy to sustain for nine years longer, should be embraced. See letters from
Mr. Hotchkin, March 21, 1854; Mr. H. K. Copeland, January 23
and July 27, 1854; Mr. Lansing, December 22, 1853, and May 13,
1854. The fact and manner of the suspension of the school at
Good-water, in 1853, were portentous of increasing embarrassment
from other causes than the new school law; and grave objections
exist to the connection with civil government of any department of
missionary operations.

"'My observation of the schools, however, interested me much
in their behalf. They are doing a good work for the nation. Many
of the pupils become Christian wives, mothers and teachers. The
people appreciate them highly; and I was assured of a general
desire that they should remain in the hands of the mission, unsub-
jected to the inadmissible new conditions of the recent legislation.
In view of all the relations, which after full consideration the subject seemed to have, the following resolution, expressing the sentiment of the Deputation and the mission, was cheerfully and
unanimously adopted by the mission; one of the older members,
however, avowing some difficulty in giving his assent to the latter
part of it, viz:

"Resolved, That while we should esteem it our duty to relinquish the
female boarding-schools at Pine Ridge, Wheelock and Stockbridge, rather

than to carry them on under the provisions and restrictions of the late school law, yet, regarding it as improbable that the requirement so to do will be enforced, we deem it important, in the present circumstances of the Choctaw Nation and mission, to continue our connection with them *on the original basis*, and carry them forward with new hope and energy."

"'Our hope of being allowed to maintain these schools as heretofore, and make them increasingly useful, may be disappointed. Neither the Prudential Committee nor the mission wish to retain them, if they for whose benefit alone they have been taken prefer that we should give them up. The relinquishment of them would be a release from a weight of labor, anxiety and care, that nothing but our love for the Choctaws could induce us longer to bear. Our desire is only to do them good.

"'A second subject of conference, but the one first considered, was the principles, particularly in relation to slavery, on which the Prudential Committee, with the formally expressed approbation of the Board, aim to conduct its missions. I found certain misapprehensions existing in the minds of a portion of the mission in regard to the origin and circumstances of the action of the Board at the last annual meeting, which I was happy to correct. Several of the members, including one of the two not present at this meeting of the mission, have ever cordially approved the correspondence in which the views of principles entertained by the Committee were stated. Others, being with those just referred to a decided majority of the whole body as at present constituted, have expressed their agreement with those views as freely explained in personal intercourse, with an exhibition of the intended meaning of his own written language, by the Secretary who was the organ of the Committee in communicating them. Others have supposed themselves to differ, in some degree, from these principles, when correctly apprehended. A full comparison of views, to their mutual great satisfaction, showed much less difference than was thought to exist between the members of the mission themselves, and between a part of the mission and what the Deputation understands to be the views of the Prudential Committee. A statement of principles drawn up at Good-water, as being, in the estimation of the Deputation, (distinctly and repeatedly so declared,) those which the Committee had set forth in their correspondence, particularly that had with the mission in 1848, was unanimously adopted, as the brethren say, "for the better and more harmonious prosecution of the great objects of the Choctaw mission on the part of the Prudential Committee and the members of the mission, and for the removal of any and all existing difficulties which have grown out of public discussions and action on the subject of slavery; it being understood that the sentiments now approved are not, in the estimation of the brethren of the mission, new, but such as for a long series of years have really been held by them."

"'The statement is given, with the appended resolution, in the following words:

"'1. Slavery, as a system, and in its own proper nature, is what it is described to be, in the General Assembly's Act of 1818, and the Report of the American Board adopted at Brooklyn in 1845.

"'2. Privation of liberty in holding slaves is, therefore, not to be ranked with things indifferent, but with those which, if not made right by special justificatory circumstances and the intention of the doer, are morally wrong.

"'3. Those are to be admitted to the communion of the church of whom the missionary and (in Presbyterian churches) his session have satisfactory evidence that they are in fellowship with Christ.

"'4. The evidence, in one view of it, of fellowship with Christ, is a manifested desire and aim to be conformed, in all things, to the spirit and requirements of the word of God.

"'5. Such desire and aim are to be looked for in reference to slavery, slaveholding, and dealing with slaves, as in regard to other matters; not less, not more.

"'6. The missionary must, under a solemn sense of responsibility to Christ, act on his own judgment of that evidence when obtained, and on the manner of obtaining it. He is at liberty to pursue that course which he may deem most discreet in eliciting views and feelings as to slavery, as with respect to other things, right views and feelings concerning which he seeks as evidence of Christian character.

"'7. The missionary is responsible, not for correct views and action on the part of his session and church members, but only for an honest and proper endeavor to secure correctness of views and action under the same obligations and limitations on this subject as on others. He is to go only to the extent of his rights and responsibilities as a minister of Christ.

"'8. The missionary, in the exercise of a wise discretion as to time, place, manner and amount of instruction, is decidedly to discountenance indulgence in known sin and the neglect of known duty, and so to instruct his hearers that they may understand all Christian duty. With that wisdom which is profitable to direct, he is to exhibit the legitimate bearing of the Gospel upon every moral evil, in order to its removal in the most desirable way; and upon slavery, as upon other moral evils. As a missionary, he has nothing to do with political questions and agitations. He is to deal alone, and as a Christian instructor and pastor, with what is morally wrong, that the people of God may separate themselves therefrom, and a right standard of moral action be held up before the world.

"'9. While, as in war, there can be no shedding of blood without sin somewhere attached, and yet the individual soldier may not be guilty of it; so, while slavery is always sinful, we cannot esteem every one who is legally a slaveholder a wrong-doer for sustaining the legal relation. When it is made unavoidable by the laws of the State, the obligations of guardianship, or the demands of humanity, it is not to be deemed an offence against the rule of Christian right. Yet missionaries are carefully to guard, and in the proper way to warn others to guard, against unduly extending this plea of necessity or the good of the slave; against making it a cover for the love and practice of slavery, or a pretence for not using efforts that are lawful and practicable to extinguish this evil.

"'10. Missionaries are to enjoin upon all masters and servants obedience to the directions specially addressed to them in the Holy

Scriptures, and to explain and illustrate the precepts containing them.

"'11. In the exercise of discipline in the churches, under the same obligations and limitations as in regard to other acts of wrong-doing, and which are recognized in the action of ministers with reference to other matters in evangelical churches where slavery does not exist, missionaries are to set their faces against all overt acts in relation to this subject, which are manifestly unchristian and sinful; such as the treatment of slaves with inhumanity and oppression; keeping from them the knowledge of God's holy will; disregarding the sanctity of the marriage relation; trifling with the affections of parents, and setting at nought the claims of children on their natural protectors; and regarding and treating human beings as articles of merchandise.

"'12. For various reasons, we agree in the inexpediency of our employing slave labor in other cases than those of manifest necessity; it being understood that the objection of the Prudential Committee to the employment of such labor is to that extent only.

"'13. Agreeing thus in essential principles, missionaries associated in the same field should exercise charity towards each other, and have confidence in one another, in respect to differences which, from diversity of judgment, temperament, or other individual peculiarities, and from difference of circumstances in which they are placed, may arise among them in the practical carrying out of these principles; and we think that this should be done by others towards us as a missionary body.

"'*Resolved,* That we agree in the foregoing as an expression of our views concerning our relations and duties as missionaries in regard to the subject treated of; and are happy to believe that, having this agreement with what we now understand to be the views of the Prudential Committee, we may have their confidence, as they have ours, in the continued prosecution together of the great work to which the great Head of the church has called us among this people.

"'The statement thus approved was read throughout, and was afterwards considered in detail, each member of the mission expressing his views upon it as fully, and keeping it under consideration as long, as he desired to do. After the assent given to it, article by article, on the day following it was again read, and the question was taken upon it as a whole, with the appended resolution, each of the eight members giving his vote in favor of its adoption. It is perhaps proper also to mention, that no change by way of emendation, addition or omission of phraseology was found necessary to make it such as any member of the mission would be willing to accept. It should further be stated, that while the first article was under consideration, the act of the General Assembly of the Presbyterian Church, adopted in 1818, was read, and its strongest expressions duly weighed. The document thus considered and referred to is herewith submitted as a part of this report.*

* "The General Assembly of the Presbyterian Church, having taken into consideration the subject of slavery, think proper to make known

8

" 'So also was adduced the abundant testimony contained in the Report of the American Board adopted in 1845, as to what, in its view, slavery, without qualification of place or time, and as it exists in the United States and among the Indians, is : such as its classification of slavery with war, polygamy, the castes of India, and other things which it speaks of as "social and moral evils;" and such language as the following : "The Committee do not deem it necessary to discuss the general subject of slavery as it exists in these United States, or to enlarge on the wickedness of the system, or on the disastrous moral and social influences which slavery exerts upon the less enlightened and less civilized communities where the missionaries of this Board are laboring:" "The unrighteousness of the principles on which the whole system is based, and the violation of the natural rights of man, the debasement, wickedness and misery it involves, and which are in fact witnessed to a greater

their sentiments upon it to the churches and people under their care. We consider the voluntary enslaving of one part of the human race by another as a gross violation of the most precious and sacred rights of human nature; as utterly inconsistent with the law of God, which requires us to love our neighbor as ourselves; and as totally irreconcilable with the spirit and principles of the Gospel of Christ, which enjoins that 'all things whatsoever ye would that men should do to you, do ye even so to them.' Slavery creates a paradox in the moral system; it exhibits rational, accountable and immortal beings in such circumstances as scarcely to leave them the power of moral action. It exhibits them as dependent on the will of others, whether they shall receive religious instruction; whether they shall know and worship the true God; whether they shall enjoy the ordinances of the Gospel; whether they shall perform the duties and cherish the endearments of husbands and wives, parents and children, neighbors and friends; whether they shall preserve their chastity and purity, or regard the dictates of justice and humanity. Such are some of the consequences of slavery — consequences not imaginary, but which connect themselves with its very existence. The evils to which the slave is always exposed often take place in fact, and in their very worst degree and form; and where all of them do not take place, as we rejoice to say, in many instances, through the influence of the principles of humanity and religion on the mind of masters, they do not, still, the slave is deprived of his natural right, degraded as a human being, and exposed to the danger of passing into the hands of a master who may inflict upon him all the hardships and injuries which inhumanity and avarice may suggest.

"From this view of the consequences resulting from the practice into which Christian people have most inconsistently fallen of enslaving a portion of their brethren of mankind — for 'God hath made of one blood all nations of men to dwell on the face of the earth'— it is manifestly the duty of all Christians who enjoy the light of the present day, when the inconsistency of slavery, both with the dictates of humanity and religion, has been demonstrated, and is generally seen and acknowledged, to use their honest, earnest and unwearied endeavors to correct the errors of former times, and as speedily as possible to efface this blot on our holy religion, and to obtain the complete abolition of slavery throughout Christendom, and if possible throughout the world.

" We rejoice that the Church to which we belong commenced, as early as any other in this country, the good work of endeavoring to put an end to or less extent wherever it exists, must call forth the hearty condemnation of all possessed of Christian feeling and sense of right, and make its removal an object of earnest and prayerful desire to every friend to God and man:" "Strongly as your Committee are convinced of the wrongfulness and evil tendencies of slaveholding, and ardently as they desire its speedy and universal termination, still they cannot think that in all cases it involves individual guilt in such a manner that every person implicated in it can, on Scriptural grounds, be excluded from Christian fellowship. In the language of Dr. Chalmers, 'Distinction ought to be made between the character of a *system*, and the character of the persons whom circumstances have implicated therewith; nor would it always be just, if all the recoil and horror wherewith the former is contemplated, were visited in the form of condemnation and moral indignancy upon the latter. Slavery we hold to be a system chargeable with

slavery, and that in the same work many of its members have ever since been, and now are, among the most active, vigorous and efficient laborers. We do, indeed, tenderly sympathize with those portions of our Church and our country where the evil of slavery has been entailed upon them; where a great and the most virtuous part of the community abhor slavery, and wish its extermination as sincerely as any others — but where the number of slaves, their ignorance, and their vicious habits generally, render an immediate and universal emancipation inconsistent alike with the safety and happiness of the master and the slave. With those who are thus circumstanced, we repeat that we tenderly sympathize. At the same time, we earnestly exhort them to continue, and if possible to increase their exertions to effect a total abolition of slavery. We exhort them to suffer no greater delay to take place in this most interesting concern, than a regard to the public welfare truly and indispensably demands.

"As our country has inflicted a most grievous injury on the unhappy Africans, by bringing them into slavery, we cannot indeed urge that we should add a second injury to the first, by emancipating them in such manner as that they will be likely to destroy themselves or others. But we do think, that our country ought to be governed in this matter by no other consideration than an honest and impartial regard to the happiness of the injured party, uninfluenced by the expense or inconvenience which such a regard may involve. We, therefore, warn all who belong to our denomination of Christians against unduly extending this plea of necessity; against making it a cover for the love and practice of slavery, or a pretence for not using efforts that are lawful and practicable to extinguish this evil.

"And we, at the same time, exhort others to forbear harsh censures and uncharitable reflections on their brethren, who unhappily live among slaves whom they cannot immediately set free; but who, at the same time, are really using all their influence, and all their endeavors, to bring them into a state of freedom, as soon as a door for it can be safely opened.

"Having thus expressed our views of slavery, and of the duty indispensably incumbent on all Christians to labor for its complete extinction, we proceed to recommend — and we do it with all the earnestness and solemnity which this momentous subject demands — a particular attention to the following points.

"We recommend to all our people to patronize and encourage the Society lately formed for colonizing in Africa, the land of their ancestors, the free atrocities and evils, often the most hideous and appalling which have either afflicted or deformed our species; yet we must not, therefore, say of every man born within its territory, who has grown up familiar with its sickening spectacles, and not only by his habits been inured to its transactions and sights, but who by inheritance is himself the owner of slaves, that unless he make the resolute sacrifice, and renounce his property in slaves, he is, therefore, not a Christian, and should be treated as an outcast from all the distinctions and privileges of Christian society.' " And the language (quoted approvingly) unanimously uttered by the General Assembly of the Free Church of Scotland: "Without being prepared to adopt the principle that, in the circumstances in which they are placed, the churches in America ought to consider slaveholding *per se* an insuperable barrier in the way of enjoying Christian privileges, or an offence to be visited with excommunication, all

people of color in our country. We hope that much good may result from the plans and efforts of this Society. And while we exceedingly rejoice to have witnessed its origin and organization among the holders of slaves, as giving an unequivocal pledge of their desires to deliver themselves and their country from the calamity of slavery, we hope that those portions of the American Union, whose inhabitants are by a gracious Providence more favorably circumstanced, will cordially, and liberally, and earnestly coöperate with their brethren in bringing about the great end contemplated.

"We recommend to all the members of our religious denomination, not only to permit, but to facilitate and encourage the instruction of their slaves in the principles and duties of the Christian religion; by granting them liberty to attend on the preaching of the Gospel, when they have opportunity; by favoring the instruction of them in the Sabbath school, wherever those schools can be formed; and by giving them all other proper advantages for acquiring a knowledge of their duty both to God and to man. We are perfectly satisfied that it is incumbent on all Christians to communicate religious instruction to those who are under their authority; so that the doing of this in the case before us, so far from operating, as some have apprehended that it might, as an incitement to insubordination and insurrection, would, on the contrary, operate as the most powerful means for the prevention of those evils.

"We enjoin it on all church sessions and presbyteries, under the care of this Assembly, to discountenance, and as far as possible to prevent, all cruelty, of whatever kind, in the treatment of slaves; especially the cruelty of separating husband and wife, parents and children, and that which consists in selling slaves to those who will either themselves deprive these unhappy people of the blessings of the Gospel, or who will transport them to places where the Gospel is not proclaimed, or where it is forbidden to slaves to attend upon its institutions. And if it shall ever happen that a Christian professor in our communion shall sell a slave who is also in communion and good standing with our church, contrary to his or her will and inclination, it ought immediately to claim the particular attention of the proper church judicature; and unless there be such peculiar circumstances attending the case as can but seldom happen, it ought to be followed, without delay, by a suspension of the offender from all the privileges of the church, till he repent, and make all the reparation in his power to the injured party." — See Assembly's Digest, pp. 274-8.

must agree in holding, that whatever rights the civil law of the land may give a master over his slaves as *chattels personal*, it cannot be but sin of the deepest dye to regard and treat them as such; and whosoever commits that sin in any sense, or deals otherwise than as a Christian man ought to deal with his fellow-man, whatever power the law may give him over them, ought to be held disqualified for Christian communion. Further, it must be the opinion of all, that it is the duty of Christians, when they find themselves unhappily in the predicament of slaveholders, to aim, as far as it may be practicable, at the manumission of their slaves; and when that cannot be accomplished, to secure them in the enjoyment of the domestic relations, and of the means of religious training and education.'

"'All this, and more, was immediately before the minds of the members of the mission, and with so much of the connection as to give the true sense, when they declared that slavery is what, in the documents referred to, it is described to be, and made their own the statement of principles above given, as those on which, as missionaries, they should deal with this subject in the circumstances of their field of labor, and when it is to them a practical missionary question.

"'The Cherokee mission in session at Park Hill, May 9, adopted a resolution of concurrence with the Choctaw mission in approving this statement.

"'Excluding two churches then connected with the mission of the Board, and since transferred to another mission, there were in 1848, under the care of the American Board, in the Choctaw nation, six churches, with a total membership of 536 persons, of whom 25 were slaveholders, and 64 were slaves. The churches are now 11 in number, containing 1094 members; of whom, as nearly as I could ascertain, 20 are slaveholders, (some of them being husband and wife, and generally having but one or two slaves each,) and 60 are slaves. Six of the churches have no slaveholder in them; two have but one each. Of the slaveholders in these churches, four have been admitted since 1848; one by transfer from another denomination, and three on profession of their faith; none of the latter having been received since 1850. Statements were made to me respecting each of these latter cases, which show that the principles assented to by the mission at Good-water, as above presented, were practically carried out in regard to them.

"'In the Cherokee mission, in 1848, there were five churches, having 237 members, of whom 24 were slaveholders, and 23 were slaves. In the five churches now in that mission, there are 207 members, of whom 17 (there is uncertainty in regard to one of this number) are reported as slaveholders. Three have been admitted since 1848 on profession of their faith, and two by letter; one of the latter from a church in New Hampshire. Of these, the same remark may be made as above in respect to similar cases among the Choctaws.

"'The Choctaw mission embraces eleven families and three large boarding-schools. Five slaves, hired at their own desire, are in the employment of the missionaries. A less number are employed in the Cherokee mission. Gladly would the missionaries dispense with these, could the necessary amount of free labor domestic service be obtained. Those who employ this labor allege that it is to them a matter of painful necessity known to resort to it unwillingly, and are not regarded. They are giving their sanction to slavery. Some thus employed have been brought to a saving knowledge of divine truth.

"The sentiments of these two missions as to the moral character of slavery, and the principles on which they should act with regard to it, are frankly and unequivocally avowed. We are bound to believe them honest in the expression of these sentiments. It is their expectation that the principles thus acknowledged as their own will be those on which the missions will be conducted. The adjudication of particular cases must be left to the missionary. That it be so left, is both right; it is also unavoidable. The position of the missionary is one of great difficulty, and should be appreciated. That there is such a diversity of judgment among them as men of independent thought and differing mental characteristics, who agree in essential principles, every where evince, and that they have, through a use of phraseology, leading sometimes to a mutual misunderstanding of each other's views, supposed themselves to differ more widely than, in our conferences, they found themselves really to do, has been intimated. That none of them have sympathy with slavery; that, on the other hand, their influence is directly and strongly adverse to its continuance, while they are doing much in mitigation of its evils, and to bless both master and slave, in the judgment of the Deputation, is beyond a doubt. By many, they are denounced as abolitionists. Some of their slaveholding church members have left their churches for another connection on this account. Others have disconnected themselves from a system which they have learned to dislike and disapprove. Strong in the confidence and affection of many for whose salvation they have toiled and suffered, by the supporters of slavery, in and out of the Nations, they undoubtedly are looked upon with growing suspicion. Surely we should not be willing needlessly to embarrass them in their blessed work. They are worthy of the confidence and warmest sympathy of every friend of the red man and of the black man. God is with them. In the Cherokee mission, the dispensation of his grace is not, indeed, now as in times past; and we have some seriousness of apprehension in regard to the progress of the Gospel among that people. Still, the divine presence is not wanting. Among the Choctaws, rapid advance is making. Converts are multiplying; the fruits of the Gospel abound. Both missions need reinforcement. Men filled with the spirit of Christ, able to endure hardness, of practical wisdom, which knows how to do good, and not to do only harm when good is meant, men of faith, energy, meekness and prayer, who will commend themselves to every man's conscience in the sight of God as his servants, are required. It gave me pleasure to assure the missions of the strong desire of the Prudential Committee, and of my future personal endeavors, to obtain such men for them. No philanthropist can behold the change which has been wrought for these lately pagan, savage tribes, now orderly Christianized communities, advancing in civilization, to take ere long, if they go on in their course, their place with those whose Christian civilization is the growth of many centuries, without admiration and delight. But there is much yet to be done for them. "This nation," says the Choctaw mission, in a published letter, "in its improvements, schools, churches, and public spirit pertaining to the great cause of benevolence, is but an *infant*." We must not expect too much from these churches in which we glory. Much fostering and training do they yet need ; and there are many souls yet to be enlightened and saved. Wonderful as are the renovation and elevation which the Gospel, taught in its simplicity by faithful men, has already given to these communities, our only hope for them, and for the colored race in the midst of them, is in the continued application of the same power through the same instrumentality.

"'It was the privilege of the Deputation to spend a part of three days, including a Sabbath, at Spencer Academy, an institution containing one hundred male pupils, excellently managed under the charge of the Board of the General Assembly; and to attend there a "big meeting," or a camp-meeting, at which several hundreds were present. My intercourse with brethren at that station, and the scenes in which I there mingled, — the fellowship in Christ with the heralds of his cross, some of them bowed with the weight of many years of wearing toil and affliction, and hastening to their glorious crown already won by honored names, no longer with them, of our own mission ; and the interchange of sympathy with the disciples of Christ, whom God has given them as the fruit of their labor, will ever live among the pleasantest recollections of my life. I am constrained to repeat my testimony to the fraternal and Christian spirit with which the brethren met my endeavors to remove difficulties, strengthen the ties that bind them and the Board together, and clear the way for harmonious and more energetic prosecution of the great work in which we are associated. To a good degree this object, we may hope, has been gained. To Him, whose is their work and ours, and to whom the interests involved are infinitely more precious than to any of us who are connected with them, we commit the future keeping of this great trust.

"'It is due to the Choctaw mission that I communicate to the Committee the following resolution, presented by the Rev. Mr. Byington, and adopted by the mission at the close of its meeting at Good-water : —

"*Resolved*, That the cordial thanks of the members of the mission be presented to the Rev. George W. Wood, the Secretary of the A. B. C. F. M., who is with us as a Deputation from the Prudential Committee, for his kind, wise and successful efforts in our mission to remove the weight of anxiety which has long pressed down our hearts in connection with the subject of slavery. We now rejoice much in this mutual and kind interchange of thoughts and affections. We would pray for grace ever to walk in the path of life, and that blessings may attend him, while with us and on his way home, his family and brethren during his absence, as well as our mission and the American Board and all its officers. With peculiar sincerity of heart and gratitude to our Savior, we present to him this token of regard for our dear brother, and make this record of divine mercy toward our mission."

"'All which is respectfully submitted,

"'GEO. W. WOOD.

"'*Rooms of the A. B. C. F. M., New York, June 13, 1855.*'

"This communication of the Prudential Committee was referred to a special committee, consisting of Dr. Beman, Dr. Thos. De Witt, Dr. Hawes, Chief Justice Williams, Doct. L. A. Smith, Dr. J. A. Stearns, and Hon. Linus Child, who subsequently made the following report:—

"'Your Committee have endeavored to look at this paper in its intrinsic character and practical bearings, and they are happy to state their unanimous conviction, that this visit will mark an auspicious era in the history of these missions. The report of Mr. Wood is characterized by great clearness and precision; and it presents the whole matters pending between the Prudential Committee and these missions fully before us. The conferences of the Deputation with the missionaries appear to have been conducted in a truly Christian spirit; and the results which are set forth in the resolutions, adopted with much deliberation and after full discussion, are such as we may all hail with Christian gratitude.

"'It is the opinion of your Committee, that the great end which has been aimed at by the Prudential Committee in their correspondence with these missions, for several years past, and by the Board in their resolutions adopted at the last annual meeting, has been substantially accomplished. While your Committee admit that there may be some incidental points on which an honest diversity of opinion may exist, yet they fully believe that this adjustment should be deemed satisfactory, and that further agitation is not called for. While your Committee cannot take it upon themselves to predict what new developments, calling for new action hereafter, *may* take place, they are unanimously of the opinion, that the Prudential Committee, and these laborious and efficient missionaries on this field of Christian effort, may go forward, on the basis adopted, in perfect harmony in the prosecution of their future work.

"'Your Committee feel that the thanks of this Board are due to Mr. Wood and our missionary brethren, for the manner in which they have met, considered and adjusted these difficult matters which have long been in debate; and at the same time, they would not forget that God is the source of all true light in our deepest darkness, and that to him *all the glory is ever due.*'

"The foregoing report of the select Committee was adopted by the Board."

It has been seen that the visit of Mr. Wood to the Cherokee and Choctaw missionaries embraced two subjects; the difficulties growing out of the action of the Choctaw Council in regard to boarding-schools, and the policy to be pursued by both missions in regard to slavery. Upon both these subjects, Mr. Wood testifies, (p. 21,) "there was entire harmony between the Deputation and the missions."

In regard to the first of these subjects, Mr. Wood had strong assurances, from one of the Trustees of the boarding-schools, that the objectionable law would probably remain a dead letter, even if not spontaneously repealed. But this still stronger reason is stated (p. 23) for making no formal objection to the law:—

"The course of the missionaries has been in no degree changed by it. The teaching of slaves in these schools *has never been practised* OR CONTEMPLATED."

Every thing shows that the missionaries had acquiesced, from the beginning, in that system of *caste* which is one of the concomitants of American slavery.

The second and more important subject, settled between the Deputation and the two missions at this time, respected " the principles, particularly in relation to slavery, on which the Prudential Committee, with the formally expressed approbation of the Board, aim to conduct its missions."

The most formal and important part of this action is " a statement of principles drawn up at Good-water," which received the unanimous assent of the Choctaw and Cherokee missionaries, and of Mr. Wood, on the part of the Prudential Committee. The missionaries deemed it important to say, that they agreed to these sentiments *not as being new*, either in theory or practice, "but such as for a long series of years have really been held by them."

It must be admitted, that the claim thus made by the missionaries, of having pursued a uniform and consistent course in regard to slavery, is perfectly just. They have never practised the disingenuousness, tergiversation and direct deceit which have characterized the action of the Prudential Committee and the Board on this subject. They had favored slaveholding from the beginning, passively, by silence respecting the practice of it in the Indian nations at large, and actively, by receiving those who practised it into their churches as Christians; and their difficulties sprang entirely from the time-serving policy of the Prudential Committee,

8 *

who were constantly trying to reconcile this course of conduct, on the part of their pro-slavery missionaries, with
assent to the anti-slavery truths urged upon them by the
remonstrants at their Annual Meetings. Thus the formal
allowance now given, by the adoption of the "Good-water
Statement," to a continuance of slaveholders in the Cherokee
and Choctaw churches, was in truth only a renewed assent,
on the part of the Prudential Committee, to that which had
always been alike the theory and practice of the missionaries.

We have now to consider the meaning and scope of the
"Good-water Statement," which consists of thirteen propositions, followed by a Resolution declaring the concurrence of
the missionaries with the Prudential Committee in all therein
contained.

The first of these propositions seems to intend to define
slavery; but instead of telling us what slavery is, it adopts
the descriptions of it, and the conclusions in regard to it,
contained in two documents —*The Act of 1818, passed by the
General Assembly of the Presbyterian Church*, and *The
Report to the American Board, written by Dr. Woods, and
adopted at Brooklyn in 1845*.

The latter of these documents has already been quoted at
length, and its substance shown to be as follows :

*Although much may be truly said against the system of
slavery in general, we must not undertake to exclude every
slaveholder from Christian fellowship; every person who
manifests "a saving change of heart" is entitled to church
membership; this saving change of heart may exist just as
really, and be manifested just as thoroughly, among slaveholders as others; the missionaries are the proper persons to
decide in what cases this change is manifested; and, since
they have constantly made this decision in favor of slaveholders, with the allowance and consent of the Prudential Committee, the best course for this Board is to do nothing in the
premises, and to let these faithful and devoted missionaries
continue to treat slaveholders as Christians —as heretofore.*

To show that this condensation of the scope and purport of
Dr. Woods's Report (adopted by the American Board at
Brooklyn in 1845) understates rather than overstates its
pro-slavery character, I subjoin the following extracts from
it, prefixing appropriate headings : —

HOW THE PRO-SLAVERY MISSIONARIES ARE AUTHORIZED STILL TO ADMIT SLAVEHOLDERS!

"How far *holding slaves*, or any thing else involving what is morally wrong, and which still clings to the heathen convert, affects the evidence that a principle of grace has been implanted in his heart, the *missionary*, in view of his commission, the instructions of the New Testament, and all the circumstances of the case, as they are present before him, must, in connection with his Church, and under a solemn sense of responsibility to Christ, form his judgment, and on that judgment he must *act*. Surely, no other persons are in circumstances so favorable as he for deciding and acting correctly. Such freedom and such responsibility in the missionary, your Committee believe, *cannot be materially abridged*, without the most disastrous consequences to the missionary's own happiness and efficiency, and to the welfare of the heathen."

HOW THE PRO-SLAVERY MISSIONARIES HAVE BEEN "FAITHFUL," AND THEIR CONVERTS "HOPEFUL" AND "NUMEROUS"!

"That the missionaries among these Indians have been faithful in their work seems evident, not only from their own statements, but also from the fact that the Holy Spirit has most remarkably owned and blessed their labors; the hopeful converts among the Choctaws being proportionally more numerous than those in any other mission connected with the Board, except that at the Sandwich Islands."

HOW THESE "FAITHFUL" MISSIONARIES AVOID PERSONALITY IN THE REBUKE OF SIN!

"In regard to the kind and amount of instruction given by the missionaries in relation to slavery, and the duties of masters and slaves, the missionaries seem substantially to agree. Mr. Byington says — 'We give such instructions to masters and servants as are contained in the Epistles, *and yet not in a way to give the subject a peculiar prominence; FOR THEN IT WOULD SEEM TO BE PERSONAL!*'"

HOW THESE "HOPEFUL" CONVERTS ILL-TREAT THEIR CHILDREN AS WELL AS THEIR SLAVES!

"In Christian instruction and care, both of their children and their slaves, the missionaries represent these Indian church members as being *generally*, and *often greatly*, deficient; but not much more so in respect to the latter than the former. . . . . . *A great proportion* of the red people, who own slaves, *neglect entirely* to train their children to habits of industry."

WHAT THE COMMITTEE THINK OF THE ADMISSION OF THESE "HOPEFUL," SLAVEHOLDING, "HEATHEN CONVERTS" TO THE CHURCH!

"Strongly as your Committee are convinced of the wrongfulness and evil tendencies of slaveholding, and ardently as they desire its speedy and universal termination, still, they cannot think that, in all cases, it involves individual guilt in such a manner that every person implicated in it can, on Scriptural grounds, be excluded from Christian fellowship."

WHO THE COMMITTEE THINK IS RESPONSIBLE FOR THE CONTINUANCE OF SLAVERY AMONG THE INDIANS !

"Slavery was introduced among these Indians, and has been regulated by them, in unhappy imitation of their white neighbors in the adjacent States. Whether the Indians will be the first to abolish it, must depend very much on *that power from above* which shall attend the prevalence of Christian knowledge among them."

WHAT PIOUS CONCLUSION THE COMMITTEE, THE MISSIONARIES AND THE BOARD UNANIMOUSLY ADOPT !

"The Committee believe, in agreement with the unanimous opinion of the missionaries, that any express directions from this Board requiring them to adopt a course of proceeding on this subject essentially different from *that which they have hitherto pursued*, would be fraught with disastrous consequences to the mission, to the Indians, and to the African race among them."

Our next subject of inquiry is the meaning and scope of the Presbyterian General Assembly's Act of 1818, above quoted.

Mr. Wood tells us that while the first article of the "Good-water Statement" was under consideration, this Presbyterian document was read, "and its strongest expressions duly weighed." It is important for the reader to note that it contains two classes of "strongest expressions," having a purport and bearing directly opposite to one another; and that, while it admits (theoretically) many things to the discredit of slavery, it decides (practically) that members of the Presbyterian Church may indefinitely continue to buy, sell, and hold slaves. I select the following passages in proof of this last statement, which the reader may see in their proper connection, *ante*, pp. 169–172.

HOW THE SLAVEHOLDING OF PRESBYTERIAN MINISTERS AND CHURCH MEMBERS IS NOT A SIN, BUT ONLY AN "EVIL," AND NOT VOLUNTARY, BUT "ENTAILED UPON THEM" !

"We do, indeed, tenderly sympathize with those portions of our Church and our country where the evil of slavery has been entailed upon them."

HOW THE GENERAL ASSEMBLY DISCOURAGE IMMEDIATE EMANCIPATION !

"The number of slaves, their ignorance, and their vicious habits generally, render an immediate and universal emancipation inconsistent alike with the safety and happiness of the master and the slave.'

HOW THE GENERAL ASSEMBLY DISCOURAGE AGITATION AGAINST
SLAVEHOLDING IN THE CHURCH!

"And we, at the same time, exhort others to forbear harsh censures and uncharitable reflections on their brethren, who unhappily live among slaves whom they cannot immediately set free."

HOW THEY PROPOSE THE EXPATRIATION OF COLORED AMERICANS,
AND TRY TO WHITEWASH THE SLAVEHOLDING FOUNDERS OF THE
COLONIZATION SOCIETY!

"We recommend to all our people to patronize and encourage the Society lately formed for colonizing in Africa, the land of their ancestors, the free people of color in our country. . . . . . And we exceedingly rejoice to have witnessed its origin and organization among the holders of slaves, as giving an *unequivocal* pledge of their desires to deliver themselves and their country from the calamity of slavery."

HOW THEY NOT ONLY EXPRESSLY LICENSE A CONTINUANCE OF
SLAVEHOLDING, BUT SUGGEST THE TEACHING OF THE SLAVES
THAT GOD AUTHORIZES THEIR ENSLAVEMENT!

"We recommend to all the members of our religious denomination not only to permit, but to facilitate and encourage, the instruction of *their slaves* in the principles and duties of the Christian religion ; by granting them liberty to attend on the preaching of the Gospel, *when they have opportunity;* by favoring the instruction of them in the Sabbath School, *wherever those schools can be formed ;* and by giving them all other *proper* advantages for acquiring a knowledge of their duty both to God and man. We are perfectly satisfied that it is incumbent on all *Christians* to communicate religious instruction to *those who are under their authority;* so that the doing of this, in the case before us, *so far from operating, as some have apprehended that it might, as an incitement to insubordination and insurrection,* would, on the contrary, operate as THE MOST POWERFUL MEANS FOR THE PREVENTION OF THOSE EVILS."

HOW THEY LICENSE SLAVERY, AND FORBID ONLY " CRUELTY "
TO SLAVES.

"We enjoin it on all Church Sessions and Presbyteries, under the care of this Assembly, to discountenance, and, *as far as possible,* to prevent, all cruelty, of whatever kind, in the treatment of slaves."

HOW THEY LICENSE THE SALE OF SLAVES WITHOUT EVEN INQUIRY
ON THE PART OF THE CHURCH, UNLESS THE SLAVE AS WELL AS
THE MASTER IS A CHURCH MEMBER!

"And if it shall ever happen that a Christian professor in our communion shall sell a slave who is also in communion and good standing with our Church, contrary to his or her will and inclination, it ought immediately to claim the particular attention of the proper church judicature." — See Assembly's Digest, pp. 274–8.

To show that the allowance thus given by the General Assembly of 1818 to slaveholding in the Presbyterian Church was *practical*, and not theoretical merely, I need but refer to the following facts.

The Presbyterian ministers and church members were slaveholders, to a very great extent, at the time of the adoption of this document in 1818!

They have continued to be slaveholders ever since!

Since that time, the Presbyterian Church has separated into two divisions, called Old School and New School; and both these bodies retain slaveholding ministers and church members without objection. They now hold 77,000 slaves. And among these slaveholding Presbyterian church members is Deacon Netherland, of Tennessee, who killed his aged slave with a handsaw, on a charge which afterwards was proved a false one, and who, *after this act,* sat without obstruction as a member of a " New School " Presbyterian Convention, at Richmond, Va., in the year of our Lord 1857, while his minister, Rev. Samuel Sawyer, *for having tried to bring Church discipline to bear upon this murderer, was driven out of the Convention!*

The practical bearing, therefore, of this first article of the " Good-water Statement," is to license a continuance of slaveholding in the mission churches, even while admitting the absolute inconsistency of the slave system with the law of God and the Gospel of Christ.

The allowance of a recognition of slaveholding as justifiable, and thus of the admission of people to the church irrespective of their slaveholding (which we have seen to be implied in the first article of the "Good-water Statement") is plainly expressed in its ninth article. This article not only declares that slaveholding may be innocent, but spontaneously suggests three conditions, either of which is assumed to make it " *unavoidable.*"

The sixth article authorizes the missionary (referring, be it remembered, to those very Cherokee and Choctaw missionaries who have constantly admitted slaveholders to their churches, and expressed their determination still to do so) to make, in his examination of candidates for church membership, just as much, *and just as little,* inquiry about slaveholding as he pleases!

The seventh article (seemingly intended to provide against censure to the missionary in case one of his slaveholding church members should turn out a Netherland, or a Legree) declares that the missionary who has thus endorsed the slaveholding of a candidate as right, at the time of his admission, is *not responsible* for the correct *views*, or the correct *action*, of that person afterwards!

The eighth article allows the missionary to ignore and disregard the commission of any sin, however great, by one of his church members, if that sin be connected with a subject classed as *"political"!*

The tenth article (deceitfully using the equivocal word " servants " when speaking of *slaves*) implies that the Scriptural injunction— " Servants, obey your masters "!—means — *Slaves*, obey your masters ! — thus pretending a Scriptural authority for American slavery !

The eleventh article (speaking of cases needing church discipline) excepts the *holding* of slaves from such discipline, and restricts the jurisdiction of the church to certain special *methods* of slaveholding, or particular acts of a master against those whom the whole document recognizes as properly *his* slaves. The extent to which this provision operates as an " indulgence " for the most enormous sins will not be appreciated, until we recognize the fact, that slaveholding churches conform to the custom of the civil community in which they exist, and refuse to receive the testimony of colored persons, slave or free, against the privileged class; so that in the church, just as in the civil courts, the person who is accused *only by slaves* of cruelly bruising or maiming his slave-man, or of ravishing his slave-girl, is not only not tried for this act, but is not considered to be accused at all ! The declaration of the victim, even if a member of the same church with the master, goes for nothing ! The laws and customs of Church as well as State are so contrived, that the master may secure perfect impunity for acts like these, by letting none but slaves witness them !

The testimony in regard to crimes committed by slaveholders against slaves is not only restricted, as above-mentioned, by law in the State and by custom in the Church, but it is further, and yet more effectually restricted, by the habit of slaveholders to stand by each other in the defence of their wicked "institution," and to leave unmentioned and disregarded the facts that would most injure it in public estimation. I will merely allude here to an illustrative fact of later occurrence, which was brought out by the diligent scrutiny of Prof. S. C. Bartlett, of Chicago, and which will be given in full in its proper place ; namely, the burning alive of a slave-woman, the mother of eight children, and a member of the mission-church at Stockbridge, in the Choctaw nation, under the pastoral care of Rev. Cyrus Byington, then a missionary of the American Board. This act was done at the instigation of her mistress, *a member of the same church*, and was done by Choctaw slaveholders, in the presence of many persons who were competent to testify, had they been disposed. The victim asserted her innocence to the last. The Stockbridge church soon after held "a big meeting" *for the communion of the Lord's supper*, but no notice appears to have been taken of this crime, either by the minister or the church members ; and Rev. Mr. Byington, who has always been praised by the Board as a *faithful* and devoted missionary, thought fit to make no report of this fact to his employers.

The thirteenth article of the "Good-water Statement," and the Resolution which closes it, declare an agreement in "essential principles" to be thus established between the missionaries and the Prudential Committee. Mr. Wood, in his subsequent remarks, (p. 26 of the Annual Report,) speaks of the entire and hearty unanimity with which every missionary assented to it, article by article, and then voted for it as a whole. Of course they did so, since this document is an authentication, by the Prudential Committee, of the previous policy of the missionaries, and a license for its continuance ; and, especially, since nothing is here intimated of the right and duty of the Prudential Committee to *dismiss* any missionary who shall prove unfaithful in his ministerial office.

It will be remembered that in the elaborate paper * drawn up by the three Secretaries, "On the Control to be exercised

---

* This paper, *in view of reasons suggested by the Prudential Committee,* was "received" from them by the Board, *without any action on the question of its adoption.* See p. 62 of Ann. Rep. for 1848, and p. 71 of Ann. Rep. for 1849.

over Missionaries and Mission Churches," it was very briefly
noticed — (in the section " How far the Board is responsible
for the teaching of the Missionaries, and for the character of
the Mission Churches," p. 78, Ann. Rep. for 1848,) — that,
if a missionary proved persistently unfaithful, the Board
might " *dissolve his connection.*" This paper, however, proceeded, after such brief mention of the proper key with
which to unlock the whole difficulty — and all the voluminous
subsequent action of the Prudential Committee has proceeded — without the slightest further notice of the possibility of exercising this power of dismissal !

This power should have been exercised by the Prudential
Committee as soon as the missionaries declared their determination to persist in the admission of slaveholders to their
churches. Prompt and consistent action in this direction
would have prevented the necessity of offering those remonstrances against the Board's complicity with slavery, the
attempts to evade which have brought so much labor, expense and guilt upon the Board. The remedy was in the
hands of the Prudential Committee from the beginning. But
so far were they from choosing to use it, that their acknowledgment of its existence is restricted to one little sentence,
while the rest of the elaborate document of which that sentence forms a part, and the whole of their subsequent proceedings, including the " Good-water Statement," utterly
ignore this right and duty, and try to produce the impression that the Board is powerless to oppose the allowance of
slaveholding practised in the mission churches !

In the course of Mr. Secretary Wood's report, (of which
the " Good-water Statement," just considered, forms a part,)
he admits that there were, at that time, (1855,) twenty slaveholders in the Choctaw, and seventeen in the Cherokee mission churches, and that both missions continue the hiring of
slaves ; he further makes the absurd assumption that slaveholding is, in some cases, " unavoidable," and the *false*
assumption, that the Prudential Committee's allowance of
the admission of slaveholders to the mission churches is also
" unavoidable ; " he tries to rebut the abundant evidence of
willing complicity with slavery on the part of the missionaries, by the statement that many denounce them as aboli-

tionists,* and that "some of their slaveholding church members have left them for another connection on this account;" and he quotes a resolution presented by Rev. Mr. Byington, and adopted by the Choctaw missionaries at the close of their meeting at Good-water, acknowledging his (Mr. Wood's) *successful* efforts to set their minds at ease on the subject of slavery.

The special Committee to whom Mr. Wood's report, including the "Good-water Statement," was referred, make the following significant suggestions. They thank the Secretary and the missionaries for the skill with which they have "adjusted these difficult matters"; they believe that "the great end which has been aimed at by the Prudential Committee . . . . has been substantially accomplished"; "they fully believe that this adjustment should be deemed satisfactory, *and that further agitation is not called for"*; and they report their unanimous opinion, that the Prudential Committee and the missionaries may go forward in future, *on the basis adopted*, in perfect harmony.

This report was at once adopted by the Board. What we have to notice in regard to it is, that since the basis for future operations thus agreed upon — the "Good-water Statement" — manifestly provides for a continuance of slaveholders in the mission churches, and is declared by the missionaries to be "not new," but perfectly in accordance with the policy previously pursued by them, *nothing whatever had*

---

* This statement, no doubt a true one, has just as much and just as little significance as the corresponding facts, that subscribers to the *New York Herald*, the *New York Observer*, *Harper's Magazine*, and *Harper's Weekly*, have occasionally stopped those papers, declaring them to have become "abolitionized." There are always fanatical extremists among slaveholders, who stigmatize as abolitionism every thing which does not join the open praise of slavery to the practical support of it. The Cherokee and Choctaw missionaries, always taking the latter of these grounds, have *never* taken the former. But the fact that slaveholders of this worst sort have gone out *voluntarily* from the mission churches, instead of by excommunication, (of course, taking with them certificates of "good and regular standing," which would enable them to join any of the more actively pro-slavery churches of that region,) — and the additional fact, that all the slaveholders who wished to stay in the mission churches were allowed to do so — stamp the charge of abolitionism against the missionaries as not only false, but absurd; and thus show the extreme disingenuousness of Mr. Wood in offering these statements *as evidence that the missionaries were practically opposed to slavery!*

been accomplished, up to this time, (the end of the year 1855,) *in either terminating or diminishing the complicity of the Board with slavery!*

In the interval from 1855 to the present time, no further memorials against the pro-slavery policy of the Indian missions are *mentioned* in the Annual Reports of the Prudential Committee. Perhaps the remonstrating members and patrons of the Board had been so thoroughly discouraged by the utter defeat of their efforts hitherto, as really to have discontinued those efforts. But, at any rate, the Prudential Committee did not attain their expected relief from "agitation"; for, in the very next year after Mr. Wood's "successful efforts" to set the minds of the missionaries at ease, a new trouble appears. In their account of the Choctaw mission, in the Annual Report for 1856, the Prudential Committee give us a glimpse of this trouble, and then immediately cover it up, as follows: —

"CORRESPONDENCE.

"In the month of November, four brethren of this mission forwarded a letter to the Missionary House, expressing their wish to be released from their connection with the Board. The Prudential Committee, conceiving that these brethren had misapprehended the true state of the relations existing between them and the Board, directed an answer to this letter to be prepared and forwarded by the Secretary having charge of the correspondence with the Indian missions. A reply to this communication has recently been received, in which the missionaries intimated a willingness to continue their relations to the Board, awaiting the issue of further correspondence. Under these circumstances, the Committee have informed them that, upon receiving their estimates, which they propose forwarding, for the current year, the customary appropriations will be made. The Committee apprehend, that a publication of the correspondence pending at the present time would be detrimental to the interests of the mission; experience having shown, that, while negotiations are in progress between the Committee and missionaries, a public discussion of the subject tends to hinder the parties from coming to a harmonious result." — p. 195.

It thus appears, that the Prudential Committee wished the pro-slavery Choctaw missionaries to remain, even after they had made an overture towards removal. The result shows that they did remain. And the record of the next year renews the praise of "faithfulness" in these men and their Cherokee associates, as I will proceed to show.

The portion of the Prudential Committee's Annual Report for 1857, relating to the Cherokee and Choctaw missions, was referred to the following Committee: Dr. Todd, Rev. J. J. Blaisdell, D. A. Shepard, Esq., Rev. F. T. Gray, Rev. N. Beach, Rev. E. J. Boyd, and F. W. Tappan, Esq. Their report says: —

"Your Committee are forcibly struck by the fact, that in our Indian missions we have to meet one obstacle, peculiarly great among this people, viz., a natural and transmitted dislike to submit to the great law of Providence, that man must work or perish. Perhaps no people to whom we have offered the Gospel find it so hard to submit to this law as the aborigines of this country. The long and untiring labors of our missionaries have so far conquered this difficulty, that progress in civilization is evident, and constantly growing more marked and distinct. The last year has been one of hope and joy. The people have made advancement in Christian character, in intelligence, civilization, and benevolence; and it seems to your Committee that several tribes have nearly or quite turned the point between civilization and annihilation. We cannot too highly appreciate the perseverance, the faithfulness, and the cheerful and self-denying labors of our missionaries. The Committee see dangers threatening; but they are of such a nature as can be warded off only by Divine interposition. They see no change to recommend, unless it be to suggest to our brethren the inquiry, whether there may not be more attention directed to the training up of natives for teachers and pastors; looking to the time — the first goal in all missions — when there shall be fully developed the self-educating power of the people." — pp. 18, 19.

Thus, not only is the " faithfulness" praised of missionaries who continue to admit slaveholders as Christians to their churches, and to see, without opposing, an *increase* of slavery in the nation they were sent to Christianize, but the special Committee " see no change to recommend," either in this policy, or in the renewed authentication of it by the Prudential Committee; and, although they " see dangers threatening," they recommend the leaving of these to some possible " Divine interposition," instead of demanding a breaking off from the sin which bred these dangers, and is breeding more.

In the Annual Meeting of 1858, the portion of the Prudential Committee's Report relating to the missions among the Cherokees and Choctaws was referred to the following Committee: Dr. Leonard Bacon, Hon. L. Child, Rev. Wm. Hogarth, Rev. James P. Fisher, Rev. Joseph

Emerson, Rev. J. G. D. Stearns, and Rev. C. E. Babb, who made the following Report : —

"The Committee to whom was referred that part of the Annual Report entitled 'North American Indians, No. 1,' have had the same under consideration, and respectfully report:

"That the missions included in the document which was referred to this Committee, are the mission to the Dakotas, and those to the partially civilized nations in the Indian territory.

"At Hartford, in 1854, the views of the Board were clearly and definitely expressed in regard to certain laws and acts of the Choctaw government, which were designed to restrain the liberty of the missionaries as teachers of God's word. All the action of the Board since that date, and so far as we are informed, the action of the Prudential Committee also, has been in conformity with the principles then put upon record.

"Your Committee have reason to believe that the position of our missionaries among the Choctaws is one of much difficulty and peril. Among the various religious bodies in the States nearest to the Choctaw nation, there has been, as is well known, within the last twenty-five years, a lamentable defection from some of the first and most elementary ideas of Christian morality, insomuch that Christianity has been represented as the warrant for a system of slavery which offends the moral sense of the Christian world, and Christ has thereby been represented as the minister of sin. Our brethren among the Choctaws are in ecclesiastical relations with religious bodies in the adjoining States, the States from which the leading Choctaws are deriving their notions of civilization and of government. In those neighboring States, and in the Choctaw nation, the missionaries are watched by the upholders of slavery, who are ready to seize upon the first opportunity of expelling them from the field in which they have so long been laboring. By the enemies of the Board and of the missionaries, our brethren are charged with what are called, in those regions, the dangerous doctrines of abolitionism. At the same time, they are charged, in other quarters, with the guilt of silence in the presence of a great and hideous wickedness.

"It seems to your Committee desirable, that the Board should be relieved, as early as possible, from the unceasing embarrassments and perplexities connected with the missions in the Indian territory. Surely, the time is not far distant, when the Choctaw and Cherokee Indians and half-breeds will stand in precisely the same relations to the missionary work with the white people of the adjacent States; and when the churches there will be the subjects of home missionary more properly than of foreign missionary patronage.

"On the whole, your Committee, with these suggestions, recommend that the Report of the Prudential Committee, as referred to them, be accepted and approved." — pp. 16, 17.

This Report repeats the recommendation of a course of policy which Dr. Bacon had long urged upon the attention of the Board, and suggests also a new method of evading the dreaded agitation, namely, a discontinuance, not of the pro-slavery policy of the missions, but of the missions themselves. The whole document is worthy of careful consideration, showing that evasive and deceptive treatment of the subject of slavery which has already so often appeared in the proceedings of the Board and its functionaries.

The Report refers first to the ideas of the Board expressed at Hartford, in 1854, *as being correct and satisfactory*, and to the action of the Board since that time, as having been " *in conformity with the principles then put upon record.*"

I have fully shown (*ante*, p. 159) that the statements of the Board in 1854 did not interfere in the least degree with the pro-slavery policy of the missionaries, but only took the part of those missionaries in opposition to certain laws, disrespectful to them, just enacted by the Choctaw Council; threatening a relinquishment of certain boarding-schools unless those laws were repealed.

I showed, also, (*ante*, p. 160,) that the very next year, instead of fulfilling this threat, the Prudential Committee decided to continue the boarding-schools, though the unfriendly legislation remained unchanged; and that they made this decision expressly on the ground that the missionaries *had not* committed, and did not *design* to commit, the offence ascribed to them, namely, *the teaching of slaves to read and write* in the schools in question.

Thus both implications in this paragraph of the Special Committee's Report are shown to be incorrect. The subsequent action of the Board has *not* been conformed to their declaration respecting the Choctaw boarding-schools in 1854, and their *clear and definite* expression of views was a clear and definite allowance of continued complicity with slavery.

The next paragraph in the Report, admitting the existence of "a lamentable defection" in regard to slavery, refers this defection to "religious bodies in the States nearest to the Choctaw nation," instead of to that nation itself, and to its missionaries, although those missionaries are admitted to be in ecclesiastical relations with the "religious bodies in the adjoining States" thus pointed at; and it proceeds to quote two directly opposing allegations against the missionaries, as if the charge made by unnamed fanatical extremists in defence of slavery neutralized the opposite charge made (and proved) by abolitionists, and as if the missionaries stood, blameless, between these, perfect illustrators of the golden mean!

The Report, concluding with a hope that the Board may be relieved, as early as possible, from "the unceasing embarrassments and perplexities connected with the missions in the Indian Territory," suggests, as the means of accomplishing this, a relinquishment of the missions, leaving these embarrassments and perplexities to be encountered by the *Home* Missionary Society.

This Report of the Special Committee ends with the suggestion (a policy frequently urged before by Dr. Bacon) that, in agreeing to the Report of the Prudential Committee, the Board "accept and approve" rather than *adopt* it. The Board, however, voted to "accept and adopt" it; and, the next year, the Prudential Committee acted upon the hint they had received, cut the knot which they would not take the trouble to untie, and discontinued the Choctaw mission, instead of discontinuing the allowance of slaveholding in its churches.

Accordingly, at the Annual Meeting in 1859, it appeared that the Prudential Committee, immediately after the close of the previous Annual Meeting, had commenced a correspondence with the Choctaw mission preliminary to its formal relinquishment, which was voted in July, 1859. In the Annual Report, presented in the October next following, this correspondence with the Choctaw missionaries, and the final relinquishment of the mission, are set forth as follows:

"DISCONTINUANCE OF THE MISSION.

"The Committee appointed by the Board at its meeting in Detroit, on so much of the Annual Report as related to its operations in the Indian Territory, thought it desirable that this body should be relieved, as early as possible, from the embarrassments and perplexities growing out of its efforts in that part of the world. This report having been adopted in the usual form, the Prudential Committee addressed a letter to the Choctaw mission, which is as follows:—

"'MISSIONARY HOUSE, BOSTON, Oct. 5, 1858.
"'TO THE CHOCTAW MISSION:

"'DEAR BRETHREN,—The proceedings of the Board at its recent meeting are already in your hands. You will have read, with special attention, the report of the Committee on that part of the Annual Report which relates to your mission. This paper, you will remember, has the following sentence: "It seems to your Committee desirable, that the Board should be relieved, as early as possible, from the unceasing embarrassments and perplexities connected with the missions in the Indian Territory." The Prudential Committee, concurring in this opinion for various reasons, respectfully submit for your consideration, whether, in existing circumstances, it be not wise and expedient that your connection with us should be terminated.

" 'You will readily believe that this suggestion is made with unfeigned regret. We have always felt a deep interest in your labors. For the churches which you have gathered, we entertain the most cordial and friendly sentiments. For yourselves, we have a strong fraternal feeling. For the older brethren, especially, we must ever cherish the tenderest affection. It is with emotions of sadness, therefore, that we contemplate a separation from you.

" 'We are not able, however, to call in question the facts on which the Committee at Detroit founded their opinion. We find in our churches an increasing desire that the Board may be freed from the "embarrassments" above referred to. By reason thereof, it is said, the donations to the treasury are less than they would otherwise be, to the manifest injury of our churches, on the one hand, and of our missions, on the other. It is said, too, that the political agitations, which are likely to take place in coming years, must of necessity aggravate the evil.

" 'The report to which your attention is now called refers to difficulties which you have encountered, because of your present relation. This consideration you will at once appreciate; the Committee have no occasion, therefore, to enlarge upon it. They will only add, that these difficulties will be likely to increase hereafter.

" 'But there is another obstacle to our future coöperation, which the report, already mentioned, did not notice. The Prudential Committee question their ability to keep your ranks adequately filled. When tidings came to us, a few weeks ago, that our excellent friend and brother, Mr. Byington, was dangerously sick, an inquiry of painful interest arose, "Who can take his place?" We had no person ready to occupy such a post; and, in view of our past experience, we could hardly expect to find one.

" 'The Committee do not propose to raise any question as to the agreement of your opinions with those of the Board. In any view of the case, which they have been able to take, the result would be the same. The measure is proposed as one of Christian expediency; and it is on this ground that we present it for your consideration.

" 'We have said that this communication is made with unfeigned regret. But our sorrow is lessened by the hope, that the interests of the people among whom you dwell will not suffer. We have thought it probable that you would come into connection with that Missionary Board under which two of your number formerly labored,—a Board which has your cordial sympathy and your entire confidence. Its missionaries are your "fellow workers unto the kingdom of God," in a common field. This would facilitate a transfer of your relation. Ecclesiastically you would make no change.

"'Praying that the God of missions may keep you henceforth, and direct all your labors, so that the comfort and joy which you have hitherto received therein shall be forgotten by reason of the more abundant coming of the Spirit of promise. I am,

"'Very respectfully yours, in behalf of the Prudential Committee,

"'S. B. TREAT, Secretary of the A. B. C. F. M.'

"To this communication, the following reply was received:—

"'YAKNI OKCHAYA, CHOCTAW NATION, Dec. 24, 1858.

"'TO THE REV. S. B. TREAT, Secretary of the A. B. C. F. M.:

"'DEAR BROTHER,—We have received your kind letter in behalf of the Prudential Committee, under date of Oct. 5. We cordially reciprocate to yourself and the Committee the fraternal feelings which you have expressed towards us.

"'You refer us to the report in relation to our mission, adopted by the Board at Detroit, and especially to the following sentence: "It seems to your Committee desirable that the Board should be relieved, as early as possible, from the unceasing embarrassments and perplexities connected with the missions in the Indian Territory." And you add: "The Prudential Committee, concurring in this opinion for various reasons, respectfully submit for your consideration, whether, in existing circumstances, it be not wise and expedient that your connection with us should be terminated."

"'You do not mention the source of these "embarrassments and perplexities;" but we presume they arise from our relation to slavery. Such have been the peace and quiet among us on this subject, for the past two years, that we fondly hoped the agitation had ceased, not to be renewed in such a way as seriously to affect us. Hence the action of the Board at Detroit took us by surprise.

"'We have taken into prayerful consideration the question submitted to us by the Prudential Committee. We have sought for light on the subject. As for ourselves, through the favor of a kind Providence, we see nothing in our present circumstances requiring a separation. Our position and course in reference to slavery are defined in our letter from Lenox, dated Sept. 6, 1856. These, so far as they are known to our people, meet with their cordial approbation; we are, therefore, going forward without disturbance in our appropriate work as missionaries. Whether circumstances may not hereafter arise, which will render a separation necessary, we are of course unable to say; but we apprehend no such difficulty from the Choctaw people, or from others in this region.

"'In regard to our course above mentioned, we would remark, that it is the same as has been uniformly practised by the mission from its commencement, more than forty years ago. It had the full approbation of the Secretaries and the Prudential Committee for more than five-and-twenty years, and was finally approved, with perfect unanimity, by the Board at Brooklyn, in 1845. However great may have been our shortcomings in duty, we believe this our course to be right and scriptural; and we cannot believe that it is unwise and inexpedient for the Board to sustain us in what is scriptural and right.

"'In your letter you say, "We have thought it probable you would come into connection with that Missionary Board under which two of your number formerly labored." That Board, as you have said, "has our cordial sympathy and entire confidence." But that Board is the organ of the "religious bodies in the adjoining States," with which we "are in ecclesiastical relations;" and "the various religious bodies" in these States are charged, in the report adopted by the Board at Detroit, with "a lamentable defection from some of the first and most elementary ideas of Christian morality." Is not this an implied censure upon us? If not, is there not an inconsistency in the above suggestion of the Prudential Committee? We have no assurance that, under these circumstances, that Board would consent to a transfer of the mission to their care.

"'We, therefore, refer the question back to the Prudential Committee, to be disposed of as they shall deem best. We regret that either the Board or the churches should sustain injury on our account. We, however, do not think that, in our labors as missionaries, we have done that which, by the Gospel standard, can be regarded as just cause of offence.

"'Be assured, that it is not a light matter with us to differ with the Prudential Committee and the Board, as respects the question which you have submitted to us. In our opinion, important principles are involved.

"'We trust and pray that the great Head of the Church may give wisdom from above, that wisdom which is profitable to direct.

"'Most respectfully yours, in behalf of the Choctaw Mission,

"'C. KINGSBURY, *Chairman.*

"'C. C. COPELAND, *Clerk.*'

"Since the receipt of this letter, the Prudential Committee have bestowed the most anxious and careful attention upon the topic discussed in this correspondence. They have felt themselves greatly embarrassed by facts and considerations which they cannot properly submit to the public eye. There are interests involved which ought not to be endangered, if it is possible to preserve them unharmed. The history of the red man puts in a plea, just at this point, which is too tender and too sacred to be disregarded.

"In presenting to the Board, therefore, a letter which has closed its responsibilities in a part of the great missionary field, the Prudential Committee wish it to be understood that the whole case is not here. Knowing that such a document may be widely circulated, they have said only so much as the highest interests of the Choctaws will justify them in saying.

"'Missionary House, Boston, July 27, 1859.

"'To the Choctaw Mission:

"'Dear Brethren,—Your favor of December 24 would have received an earlier answer, but for the desire of the Committee to give it their most careful attention. Seldom have they felt more deeply their need of that wisdom which cometh from above, than during the deliberations which this letter has occasioned. It is their prayer and their hope, that the divine approval will rest upon the result to which they have been brought.

"'The suggestion which was submitted to your consideration, in regard to the discontinuance of the efforts of the Board among the Choctaws, you have referred back to the Committee, "to be disposed of as they shall deem best." In doing this, however, you have made the following statement: "Our position and course, in respect to slavery, are defined in our letter from Lenox, dated September 6, 1856. These, so far as they are known to our people, meet with their cordial approbation; we are, therefore, going forward without disturbance in our appropriate work as missionaries." Had this extract been received in September last, it might have given a different direction to our correspondence.

"'It is proper that we should review, in the fewest possible words, the history of a question which has received so much attention within the last few years. You remark that your policy had "the full approbation of the Secretaries and the Prudential Committee for more than five-and-twenty years, and was finally approved with perfect unanimity by the Board at Brooklyn." For much of the time *since* the meeting at Brooklyn, we have supposed that there was no material difference between your mission and ourselves. In the year 1848, indeed, there seemed to be some divergency; but in the following year, you declared your assent to the letter of the Cherokee mission, dated March 21, 1848, "as expressing, in a clear and condensed manner," your "main views and principles;" and verbal statements, subsequently made by some of your number, gave the Committee very great satisfaction. Whatever doubts may have arisen in 1854, they were effectually removed by the report which Mr. Wood presented to the Committee in June, 1855. The statement of principles which received your assent at Good-water, fully confirmed our previous impressions. When, therefore, we received from four of your number the letter of November 13, 1855, asking that their connection with the Board might be dissolved, we were slow to believe that there was any substantial disagreement, and immediately requested them to take the subject into consideration a second time. We could harmonize the facts which had come to our knowledge, only by supposing that these brethren had written under very serious misapprehensions. Hence, too, the Committee did not regard the letter of September 6, 1856, signed by six of your number, as final. The view which they entertained of the case was embodied in their minute of December 8, 1857, in which they affirmed their belief that the sentiments of the brethren who signed the Good-water document were in substantial accordance with those of the Committee, and that their difficulties were the result of misapprehensions, which could not be easily removed without a personal conference.

"'In looking back from their present position, the Committee are constrained to admit that their action, after receiving the letter of September 6, 1856, was of doubtful expediency. The brethren who signed it declined to withdraw their "letter of resignation," and, at the same time, embodied their main difficulties in the following propositions, viz.: "1. The objections which we have had to endorsing the letter of June 22, 1848, still remain. Nor can we acquiesce in the suggestions and arguments of that letter, or declare our readiness to act in accordance with them. 2. We were much grieved by the action of the Board at Hartford; and we still deeply regret it. 3. The construction put upon the Good-water document, by the Board at Utica, makes it impracticable for us to regard that as an exponent of our views."

"'The event has proved that an acceptance of the "resignation," just at this point, would have been the simplest and easiest solution of a problem which has occasioned so much perplexity. The friends of the Board would have felt that the Committee were justified in taking this step; indeed, it would have been generally supposed that no other course could have been safely pursued. It would have been better for your work, also, so far as the Committee can judge, if they had assented to the proposal at once. Still, in view of all the circumstances, the appropriations for 1857 were made as usual. With the previous history of the question distinctly in mind, the Committee might reasonably hope that your position, sooner or later, would materially change; and they were then, as they always have been, extremely reluctant to entertain the idea of closing their labors among the Choctaws.

"'In 1849, as we have already remarked, your mission accepted the letter of the Cherokee brethren, dated March 21, 1848, "as expressing, in a clear and condensed manner," its "main views and principles." In 1855, the members of that mission accepted the declaration of principles which received your assent at Good-water. By these they still abide. Your late communication, however, refers to the letter of September 6, 1856, as defining your position; and you also say that its sentiments, so far as they are known, have the cordial approbation of your people, and therefore you are going forward without disturbance in your appropriate work. A recent letter from the Superintendent and Trustees of the Choctaw schools, in this connection, has a special significance. It requests the Committee to "authorize some person to meet" them, and "make a final separation from the American Board." "We have no apology to make," it continues, "or argument to offer." "We only hope it might be effected in peace and friendship."

"'The result, therefore, to which we are obliged to come is briefly this: 1. The position which the Board, with the Committee, on the one hand, and you, with the Cherokee mission, on the other, occupied at the annual meeting in 1855, six of your number, after the maturest reflection, and with entire conscientiousness, we doubt not, have relinquished. 2. In doing this, they dissent from the opinions, not only of the Board and the Committee, but, as we be-

lieve, of the great majority of our constituents. We are thus taken
back to the circumstances in which we found ourselves in October,
1856, when these brethren declined to withdraw their resignation;
with this difference, however, that no additional delay can be expected to issue in a favorable change. The letter of November 13,
1855, had said, " We are fully convinced that we cannot go with the
Committee and the Board as to the manner in which, as ministers
of the Gospel and missionaries, we are to deal with slavery;" and
it had also said, " We have no wish to give the Committee and the
Board further trouble on the subject; and as there is no prospect
that our views can be brought to harmonize, we must request that
our relation to the American Board of Commissioners for Foreign
Missions may be dissolved, in a way that will do the least harm to
the Board and our mission." The Committee find themselves
compelled at length to act in substantial accordance with the desire
which was then expressed. It has been our cherished and earnest
hope, as the long delay will have shown, to escape the necessity of
this result. Now, however, we are persuaded that the greatest
efficiency of the Board, as also the highest success of your efforts,
require that a connection which awakens so many pleasant remi-
niscences, should in its present form come to a close. A wide-spread
dissatisfaction has arisen among the churches, which, as the case
now stands, is almost certain to increase. Aside from the injury
that will accrue to the spiritual interests of our constituency from a
prolonged agitation, the income of the Board must inevitably suffer;
while the claims of nearly all the great missionary fields are so
urgent, that any diminution of our receipts would prove a serious
calamity. On the other hand, continued discussion can hardly
fail, as it seems to the Committee, to embarrass your labors.

" ' We do not forget what you say in regard to the peace and quiet
which have prevailed among your people for the last two years.
The fact is easily explained. The Board has been free from agitation during this period, and so you have felt no disturbing force.
But if your relation to the Board continues on its present footing,
neither you nor we can rely on this exemption hereafter. The letter from the Superintendent and Trustees of the Choctaw schools,
already referred to, shows us what we had reason to expect.

" ' The inquiry may possibly occur to you, " Why did the Committee send us the letter of October 5, 1858 ?" The answer is to be
found in the peculiarities of the case. They said in that letter, you
will remember, that they did not raise any question as to the agreement of your opinions with those of the Board. They could not
assume that you accepted the Good-water statement; nor, on the
other hand, could they assume your final rejection of it. Hence
they pursued a line of argument, suggested by the action of the
Board at Detroit, which rendered any discussion of this topic unnecessary.

" ' All that was said in that letter to express our sorrow in view
of the contemplated change, and our affection for you and your people, we would repeat with additional emphasis. The thought that
this letter brings your mission to a close is exceedingly painful !
There is no other course, however, which we can properly pursue.

It is the recorded judgment of the Board that it should be relieved, as early as possible, from the difficulties which have grown out of its operations in the Indian Territory. In this opinion, for the reasons already set forth, the Committee are obliged to concur.

"'It only remains that I apprise you of the formal action of the Committee, on the 26th of July; which is as follows:—

"'*Resolved*, 1. That in view of the embarrassments connected with the missionary work among the Choctaws, which affect injuriously, as well the labors of the brethren in that field, as the relations sustained by the Board to its friends and patrons, it is incumbent on the Prudential Committee to discontinue the Choctaw mission; and the same is hereby discontinued.

"'*Resolved*, 2. That the members of this mission be informed that the preceding resolution does not at once terminate their *personal* relations to the Board; that they are, nevertheless, at liberty to make such arrangements for the future as they shall severally judge proper, and that the Committee fully recognize their claim to such pecuniary aid, whenever they shall retire from their connection with the Board, as, in accordance with its rules and usages, it is able to afford.

"'I am also authorized to say, (1) that the Committee propose to give you, as a retiring allowance, in whole or in part, the property now in your possession and occupancy, (except so much as may be in the boarding-schools); and (2) that they regard Messrs. Kingsbury and Byington, in consideration of their advanced age and long-continued service, as having special claims upon the Board; and, therefore, unless they shall elect to become united with some other missionary organization, these brethren will be at liberty to look to the Board for such annual assistance as shall be needful for their comfort and support, during the residue of their lives.

"'I remain, Dear Brethren, very respectfully and affectionately yours, in behalf of the Prudential Committee,

"'S. B. TREAT, *Secretary of the A. B. C. F. M.*'

"It gives the Committee great pleasure, in closing this report, to believe that a work has been accomplished among the Choctaws of high and permanent value. Whatever may be said of Indian missions, in the general, this is no failure. The efforts of the Board have demonstrated, beyond all controversy, that the red man, in favorable circumstances, may attain to all the blessings of a Christian civilization. For the honor of our aboriginal tribes, and, still more, for the honor of the Gospel of Christ, this truth should live for ever."—pp. 140–146.

The following particulars in the correspondence and action, detailed above, are worthy of special notice.

The real reasons alleged for the discontinuance of the Choctaw mission, in Mr. Treat's first letter, in behalf of the Prudential Committee, (Oct. 5th,) are these two, which, it is intimated, are likely to increase, instead of diminishing, in the future: — 1. More and more objection, among the churches, to the position of the Board; and, as a consequence of this — 2. Less receipts than would otherwise be paid into the treasury.

Not only are these stated as *the* reasons of the proposed arrangement, but the Prudential Committee expressly declare that it is *not* made on account of any difference of opinion between themselves and the missionaries!

The reply of the missionaries corroborates this statement, that no contumacy on their part has produced the discontinuance of the mission. They are surprised at such a movement! They had fondly hoped that the agitation had ceased! They see nothing in the present, and apprehend nothing in the future, to require a separation! Moreover, they find, in the suggestion volunteered by the Prudential Committee as to their future course, something that implies unreasonable censure upon them; and they ask, with great justice, what the Board mean by saying that the missionaries, after this separation, will probably come into connection with a missionary Board, the organ of various "religious bodies in the adjoining States," which bodies are charged (in the Report adopted by the Board in 1858, at Detroit) with "*a lamentable defection from some of the first and most elementary ideas of Christian morality.*"

The missionaries, then, maintaining the perfect rectitude of their position, "*refer the question back to the Prudential Committee.*"

The reply of the Prudential Committee to this letter (dated July 27th, 1859) is one of the most disingenuous towards the missionaries, and deceptive towards the public, that even *they* have ever written. I am aware that this is a very strong expression.

No wonder the Prudential Committee felt themselves "greatly embarrassed" in the composition of this reply, in which the missionaries were to be treated with double injustice, for the sake of avoiding the confession of inconsistency and manifold guilt in their employers!

They pass by, entirely without remark, the inquiry of the missionaries why it is assumed that they will connect themselves with a Board [the Presbyterian] which has shown "a lamentable defection from some of the first and most elementary ideas of Christian morality" — probably considering that, upon that subject, ' least said is soonest mended.'"

To entangle the matter sufficiently to make out an appearance of justification for themselves, the Prudential Committee propose to "review the history" of the correspondence between themselves and the missionaries.

In the course of this *review*, they introduce a portion of a letter which they had never published before, written by six of the Choctaw missionaries, Sept. 6th, 1856, and containing the following statement:—"The construction put upon the Good-water document, by the Board at Utica, makes it impracticable for us to regard that as an exponent of our views."

The Prudential Committee present this *old* statement as the sufficient ground of their present action, saying—

"The result, *therefore*, to which we are obliged to come, is briefly this : 1. The position which the Board, with the Committee, on the one hand, and you, with the Cherokee mission, on the other, occupied at the annual meeting in 1855, six of your number, after the maturest reflection, and with entire conscientiousness, we doubt not, have relinquished. 2. In doing this, they dissent from the opinions, not only of the Board and the Committee, but, as we believe, of the great majority of our constituents. We are thus taken back to the circumstances in which we found ourselves in October, 1856, when these brethren declined to withdraw their resignation ; with this difference, however, that no additional delay can be expected to issue in a favorable change." — p. 144.

I have *italicised* the word "therefore." The use of this word by the Prudential Committee, and their presentation of the letter of the Choctaw missionaries of Sept. 6th, 1856, as furnishing the ground of their present action, are shown to be dishonest by the following facts.

In their Annual Report for 1856, presented at the end of October, the Prudential Committee not only did not quote this passage, or the letter of Sept. 6th containing it, but they represented the purport of this letter to be, that "the missionaries intimated a *willingness to continue their relations to the Board*, awaiting the issue of further correspondence." And the purport of this further correspondence is immediately stated, thus : — "Under these circumstances, the Committee have informed them that, upon receiving their estimates, which they propose forwarding, the customary appropriations will be made." — p. 195.

That the appropriations were forwarded, and that the difficulty was considered to be thoroughly overcome, is shown by the fact that the missionaries continued at their post, and also by the Annual Report of the succeeding year (1857); in which the Prudential Committee make no mention of any further trouble, and the special committee, who had in charge the matters relating to the Choctaw mission, say — "We cannot too highly appreciate the perseverance, the faithfulness, and the cheerful and self-denying labors of our missionaries." — p. 18.

Since, moreover, in the very letter from the Choctaw mission, (Dec. 24th, 1858,) which is followed by the reply now under consideration, (July 27th, 1859,) the missionaries express their surprise at the proposed action of the Board, declare the absence of all dissent and objection on their part, and refer the question *back* to the Prudential Committee, to be decided at *their* pleasure, the bringing up of those old questions as sufficient ground for separation, seems a violation of honor and courtesy, not less than of justice and truth, on the part of the Prudential Committee.

After this attempt to represent a discordance of views between themselves and the missionaries as the principal reason for a discontinuance of the Choctaw mission, the Prudential Committee proceed to mention other reasons, which we may safely consider the actual ones. These are, a dissatisfaction among the churches, already widely spread, and almost certain to increase; the prospect that prolonged agitation, disclosing more and more the real position of the Board, would inevitably diminish the contributions of those churches; and the equally certain prospect, that a continued discussion, showing more and more the complicity of the missionaries with slavery, would *embarrass their labors*.

These were, no doubt, real difficulties in the way of the Prudential Committee. The Anti-Slavery movement, however much discouraged by the clergy, was from year to year taking hold of increased numbers in the churches; more and more people were coming to see that a religion which cherished slavery was not the religion of Christ; those who, from this point of view, scrutinized the conduct of the missionaries, could not fail to see that, in their administration, Christ was not only betrayed anew, and crucified afresh, but made *the minister of sin;* and those who scrutinized the

9 *

policy of the Prudential Committee, marking the discrepancy between their own words, spoken at different times and to different parties — between their language against slavery and their action in allowance of it — and between their general policy on this subject and the dictates of truth and righteousness — could hardly fail to lose confidence *in the men*, and thus in their administration of other branches of the great work entrusted to them.

The Prudential Committee, of course unwilling to expose themselves to another letter so damaging to their cause as Mr. Kingsbury's, (a Damascus blade in keenness as well as in polish,) hurried the matter to a conclusion, and, without further preliminary correspondence, voted the discontinuance of the Choctaw mission.

In the Annual Report for 1859, immediately after the letter communicating this vote to the missionaries, the Prudential Committee made a final statement, which they intend shall sum up the whole matter, and for ever relieve them from the "embarrassments and perplexities" which for so many years had hung around the Choctaw mission. Here are their words : —

"It gives the Committee pleasure, in closing this report, to believe that a work has been accomplished among the Choctaws of high and permanent value. Whatever may be said of Indian missions, in the general, *this is no failure.*"

I wish particular attention to be paid to this declaration, in connection with some evidence next to be given, respecting the character and action of one of the Choctaw churches in that year ; evidence *not* found in the Annual Report.

In *The Independent* of Dec. 6th, 1860, appeared the following editorial notice : —

"A HORRID REVELATION.

" No one can read without horror the shocking disclosures brought out through the correspondence of Prof. Bartlett, of Chicago, which appears in another column. That a slave-woman was burned alive in the Choctaw Nation in January, 1859, appears to be established by the letters of Secretaries Treat and Lowrie. It is evident that neither the Prudential Committee of the American Board, nor the Assembly's Board of Missions, had any knowledge of the transaction at a time when they could have taken responsible action with regard to it. But there is grave reason to apprehend, that Mr. Byington knew the whole transaction at or about the time of its occurrence; that members of his church were in some way implicated in it; and that he and other missionaries have designedly withheld the facts from the Boards to which they are or were responsible. This aspect of the affair is serious and painful.

"The public will ask with astonishment, has such a crime been connived at, or even ignored, by a Christian church, and by the missionary teachers of the nation? Has no testimony been uttered against it?—no inquiry been instituted?—no discipline inflicted upon the accomplices of the crime, if such were in the church?

"These questions must be answered. Mr. Byington cannot longer remain silent. The Assembly's Board, under whose care the Mission now is, cannot longer refrain from investigating the action of the missionaries in the premises. The case is before the public, and the public will not let it rest.

"As to Mr. Byington and his church, judgment must be suspended until further light is gained. But the whole transaction is a fearful comment upon the bloody code of slavery, and the brutalizing influence of the system, wherever it exists."

The correspondence referred to, appearing in the same paper, is as follows:—

"CHICAGO, Nov. 23, 1860.

"To THE EDITORS OF THE INDEPENDENT:

"GENTLEMEN:—It is the right of the Christian public to know the extraordinary transaction which is the subject of the following correspondence, and to investigate it more fully. It will be seen that the American Board never received any intelligent hint of it till the Choctaw mission had passed from their hands; and that the General Assembly's Board has hitherto had no *adequate* report.

"To THE SECRETARIES OF THE A. B. C. F. M.:

"DEAR BRETHREN,—Will you permit me to make a few inquiries respecting an occurrence at the Choctaw mission?

"I have been recently informed, on good and direct authority, that while that mission remained nominally under the care of the American Board, viz., on the first Sabbath in January, 1859, a slave-woman was burned alive at a public meeting in the Choctaw Nation, after having been previously tortured in the vain attempt to extract from her a confession of guilt. I am informed that she was a reputable member of a mission church. If I am not mistaken, her master and mistress were members of the same church. I am told that, at the same time, the dead body of a slave man was also burned; he having been put to the torture, and having committed suicide to escape the doom that awaited him. This transaction took place within ten miles of a missionary station, and it has been intimated to me that church members were not clear of participation in the crime.

"It seems to me due to the cause of our Master that such a transaction should receive from a Christian community that attention which its remarkable character demands. And in order to elicit all the facts of the case, permit me respectfully to ask you the following questions :

"1. While the Choctaw mission was in connection with the A. B. C. F. M., did you receive any information respecting the burning of slaves in the Choctaw nation ? If so, can you state the circumstances ? What were the charges ? Did the parties plead guilty ? What parties took part in the burning ? Were there any church members who gave their assent to the burning, or were in any way implicated in the procedure ? What action was taken in the church or the mission upon the subject ?

"2. Had the Prudential Committee any reference to facts of this description, when they said, in the Annual Report for 1859, that they were ' embarrassed by facts and considerations ' which they could not ' properly submit to the public eye ' ?

"3. Have you, since the Choctaw mission ceased to be under the care of the American Board, received from any responsible party, personally acquainted with the affairs of the mission, any intimation of the transaction above referred to ? If so, when ? and what was the nature of that information ?

" You will oblige me by giving an early reply to these questions, with permission to make known the answer to the public. I have made similar inquiries of the Assembly's Board, and of Rev. Cyrus Byington, missionary to the Choctaws.

"Yours, respectfully,   SAMUEL C. BARTLETT.
" Chicago, Oct. 22, 1860."

"MISSION HOUSE, BOSTON, Oct. 27, 1860.

"Rev. S. C. BARTLETT, CHICAGO, ILL. :

" DEAR BROTHER,— It devolves upon me to reply to your favor of October 22d, addressed to the Secretaries of the A. B. C. F. M., as I have all the information bearing upon your question which has been received at the Missionary House.

" My answer to your first inquiry is, that we received no information respecting the burning of slaves in the Choctaw Nation while the Choctaw mission was connected with the Board. I will add, moreover, that none of us had any suspicion that such a tragedy as you describe could possibly occur.

" My answer to your second inquiry you will have anticipated. The statement in the Annual Report for 1859, to which you have alluded, had no reference whatever to any facts of this description.

" My answer to the third inquiry is, that in August, 1860, I received a letter from Mr. Chamberlain, late of the Choctaw mission, in which he intimated that he might, at some future time, make a statement ' in connection with the burning of slaves on the first Sabbath in January, 1859.' This was the first intimation which I received from any one ' personally acquainted with the affairs of that mission,' that such an event had occurred.

" I ought to say, however, that I had received letters from Mr. Chamberlain, (the earliest dated Dec. 7, 1859,) which were unintelligible to me at the time, but which, as I now suppose, referred to this transaction. From a still earlier letter, (written May 2, 1859, after the Committee had decided to discontinue the mission, but before the formal resolution was passed,) I inferred that Mr. C. felt somewhat embarrassed in his position; but I had no suspicion that his embarrassment grew out of any such matter.

"Very respectfully yours,

"S. B. Treat, *Sec. of the A. B. C. F. M.*"

"The letter of inquiry sent to the Secretary of the General Assembly's Board of Missions is, for brevity's sake, omitted. It covered substantially the points of question No. 1 in the letter to the American Board, and contained the additional inquiry, 'Was the missionary, having under his care the church to which this woman belonged, the Commissioner from the Indian Presbytery to the last General Assembly? And has he made any report of the transaction?' The letter was dated October 18th, and elicited the following reply: —

"Mission House, New York, Oct. 30, 1860.

"Rev. Samuel C. Bartlett:

"Dear Sir,— Your letter of the 22d inst. has been received. The painful transaction to which you refer took place a year before the missionaries of the American Board were received by us, and of course no report in relation to it was made to us. The only information we have on the subject is contained in a letter from one of our original missionaries, dated the 12th of January last, and is the following: 'About a year ago, a black man killed his master without any provocation. The master was a worthy man, and a member of Mr. Byington's church. Afterwards, the man made confession, and accused one of the black women of having instigated him to do the deed. Having made this confession, and discovered the body of his master, he got away from those in charge of him, jumped into the little river, and drowned himself. Lucy, the one charged as the instigator of the murder, was taken by the enraged relatives and burned. The poor woman was also a member of Mr. Byington's church, and protested to the last her innocence. The murdered man was a Mr. Haskins, a brother of Mr. George Haskins, one of the first men in the Nation. His wife is a daughter of Col. P. P. Pitchlynn. It was a terrible affair, but the mission and the church here are not responsible for it.'

"I am, yours respectfully,   Walter Lowrie."

"It will be seen that the communication of Secretary Lowrie fully confirms this tale of woe, in all its essential particulars, and also makes known the fact that the poor victim, her deceased master, and surviving mistress, were all members of a church under the care of Rev. C. Byington, Commissioner in the last General Assembly. The concluding comment of the missionary, that 'neither the mission nor the church here are responsible for it,' will not satisfy

Christian men. They have a responsibility in regard to it, which they do not appear to have met.

"Five weeks have now elapsed since I wrote to Mr. Byington, respectfully asking for such information as he might be willing to give the public concerning this public transaction, the relation of the various parties to the church, and the course which the church have taken. As yet, no reply has been received. I would now earnestly call upon him to break the portentous silence which he has kept for two years, concerning this fearful slaughter of one of the 'little ones' of his flock, and to show us that his church and *all its members* not only are clear of all complicity in the affair, but have discharged their whole duty in the case.

"I would also request that Mr. J. D. Chamberlain would complete the information at which he has hinted in his letters to Secretary Treat, and tell the Christian public what he knows concerning this extraordinary tragedy — a Christian woman, the mother of eight children, 'owned' by another Christian woman, persisting in her innocence, though three times hung up to extort confession of guilt, and burned alive with the words of prayer and praise upon her lips!

"Yours, truly,   S. C. BARTLETT."

It is well said by Mr. Bartlett, that both the mission and the church *have* a responsibility for this awful crime, which they do not appear to have met.

On the 24th of January, 1861, seven weeks after the foregoing, another editorial notice appeared in *The Independent*, as follows : —

"THE BURNT SLAVE. — We have additional authentic evidence touching the burning of the slave-woman in the Choctaw nation, to which Rev. Mr. Bartlett, of Chicago, has called the attention of the public. A person who was in the Choctaw nation at the time, testifies that the woman was burnt on the first Sabbath of 1859; that she was a member of the Stockbridge church; that her mistress, who instigated the crime, was a member of the same church; and that soon after this crime was perpetrated, a 'big meeting' of the mission church was held for the communion, but no notice was taken of this horrible transaction.

"Secretary Treat has already stated that this affair did not come to the knowledge of the Board till after the connection of the Choctaw mission with the Board had ceased. But we believe that Rev. Mr. Byington is still a *pensioner* of the Board, — his subsistence being pledged to him for life. If this is so, the Prudential Committee are fairly called upon to investigate the facts of this case, and if Mr. Byington was guilty of silence and inaction toward such a crime, he is unworthy of any countenance from the Christian community."

In the succeeding week, January 31st, another item appeared in the same paper, as follows: —

"REV. MR. BYINGTON. — We are assured that Rev. Mr. Byington, of the Choctaw Mission, declined a pension from the American Board, as he entered at once into the service of another Board. That body, therefore, have no responsibility whatever for Mr. Byington or his acts, and no censure can rest upon them for the horrible affair of slave-burning, of which they knew nothing till after the mission had passed from their hands."

This statement of *The Independent*, that the American Board "have no responsibility whatever for Mr. Byington or his acts," is an insult to the common sense of this community! Shall "no censure" rest upon them for the horrible affair of slave-burning? Let us see.

The Prudential Committee, to whom the Board entrusted the management of its affairs, allowed their missionary servants to live among the slaveholding Choctaws for more than forty years, pretending to preach the Gospel to them, yet not opposing slavery; they allowed them to honor that infamous system by admitting slaveholders as the first members of their churches; they allowed them, when this course was called in question by Christians in New England, to make excuses for slaveholding; to declare it not only justifiable, but sometimes indispensable; to maintain, when specifications of gross wickedness, inherent in it, were brought up — the buying and selling of men and women as property, and the separation by such sales of husbands and wives, parents and children — that they would make no rule forbidding those things to church members; and to acquiesce in the wicked custom prevailing among those slaveholders, of preventing their victims from learning to read the Bible!

The Prudential Committee had evidence, from time to time, through all those forty years, that the custom of buying and selling human beings as property, and of holding and using them as such, tends to the commission of frightful excesses of cruelty against these unfortunate victims, often on mere suspicion of fault, and sometimes when that suspicion is entirely groundless. They knew that fugitive slaves were hunted with bloodhounds; that slaves resisting even cruel and unreasonable punishment were killed, sometimes quickly, by a pistol-shot, sometimes slowly, by the scourge;

and that there were many well-authenticated instances of these poor unfortunates having been *burned alive!* Having let the practice go on which is accustomed to lead to these excesses of wickedness, is their advocate entitled, in the very act of condemning the last and worst one, to declare *them* GUILTLESS of it? Having allowed, and argued for, their systematic teaching of the alphabet, through a course of forty years, is their advocate authorized to declare, when the letter Z is reached, that the utterance of that letter is a horrible crime, and to declare, in the same breath, that the teachers have "no responsibility whatever" for its utterance by the pupils?

Such an allegation is not only false, but absurd. But *The Independent* has been accustomed to defend the Board through all its shameful complicity with slavery, revealed in the foregoing pages; and now, adhering to that policy, though it yields to Prof. Bartlett's request for the publication of the foregoing correspondence, and admits the appearance of guilt in a missionary who allowed one of his church members to burn another alive, with neither remonstrance at the time nor church discipline afterwards — yet it declares the Board to have "no responsibility whatever" for this act, *and it says not a word about any responsibility of the Prudential Committee!*

It may be well now to inquire who were the pastors and teachers of the Stockbridge mission church at the time of the immolation of this "whole burnt-offering"; and what is the recent history of a church, purporting to be Christian, which did not think the burning alive of one of its members by another sufficient cause for church discipline, or inquiry, or any measures whatever!

In the Annual Report for the year of the burning, 1859, the Stockbridge church stands first in the list of stations of the Choctaw mission. The missionary force belonging to it is as follows: —

"STOCKBRIDGE. — Cyrus Byington, *Missionary;* Jason D. Chamberlain, *Steward of the Boarding School;* Mrs. Sophia N. Byington, Mrs. Elsey G. Chamberlain, Miss Charity A. Gaston, Miss Harriet A. Dada, *Teachers.*" — p. 137.

No remarks are made respecting this particular church,

except the following details, in a statistical table, of its numbers and action during the previous year (p. 139) : —

"Received on profession, ... 19
    "   by letter, ... 3
Present number, ... 149
Contributions to missions, ... $0
    "   for other objects, ... $47."

Of the mission in general it is said, in this Report, "there is reason to believe that the churches, on the whole, were never in a better condition than they are now." — p. 139.

No particular remarks are made respecting this Stockbridge church, either for praise or censure, in the years preceding this, even going back to the commencement of it. Actually, nothing is said of this station, for twenty-five years, of more significance than the bare statistical information that in 1837 it had 116 church members, in 1842, 70, and in 1843, the church and congregation together, "on the Sabbath," numbered "60 or 70" only, though 69 were still rated as church members upon Mr. Byington's list. Perhaps, in like manner, in 1858, the congregation actually attending worship there "on the Sabbath," pious and impious together, proved less in number than the 149 who had "a name to live" on the church record.

Before leaving the record of the shocking transaction above referred to, I wish to call attention to two very remarkable expressions in the Prudential Committee's Annual Report for 1859, treating of the discontinuance of the Choctaw Mission, and presented to the Board eight months after this burning alive of one of its church members by another, in that mission.

They say, p. 143 of the Ann. Rep. for 1859, quoted *ante*, p. 194, (in their remarks immediately preceding their vote recording the discontinuance of the Choctaw Mission,) — "They have felt themselves *greatly embarrassed* BY FACTS and considerations which they *cannot properly submit to the public eye*." And again they say — "The Prudential Committee wish it to be understood that *the whole case is not here*." What is the meaning of these expressions? What are these suppressed *facts?*

In the correspondence above detailed, Prof. Bartlett has made reference to one of these expressions, asking Dr. Treat whether the suppressed "facts" in question were of this horrible class; and Dr. Treat returns, as above, a negative answer; but the assertions of Dr. Treat in this country, as well as of Dr. Pomroy in England, respecting the relation of the Board to slavery, have not been such as to justify entire confidence in the veracity of the Secretaries of the Board, when its reputation is in question. It may be that other discreditable fruits of slavery among the Choctaws, rendering immediate separation from them desirable for the Board, have been more effectually hushed up than the slave-burning in January, 1859. It may be that the "plea" for this suppression (intimated in the Report to be "the history of the red man"!!) is rather the credit of the Board with the Northern churches. And the community can hardly feel well assured on this point, until they know what *is* "the whole case"; what *are* the embarrassing "facts and considerations."

Having placed the record of the slave-burning at a mission-station in the year of its occurrence, and having shown, as I think, that the Prudential Committee, however ignorant of this act at the time, are to be held responsible for it, *because they allowed their missionaries, from the beginning, to pursue a policy naturally leading to it*, I come next to the action of the Board, in the Annual Meeting of the same year, on the Prudential Committee's discontinuance of the Choctaw mission.

Although this abrupt movement of the Prudential Committee had been foreshadowed by Dr. Bacon's hint, in the previous year, of the chance of escaping by this back-door from their "unceasing embarrassments and perplexities" in the Choctaw mission, their sudden action upon this matter seems to have taken the Board by surprise. The special Committee to whom it was referred made two varying reports, and the Board held an animated debate upon them for more than four hours. The statement in the Annual Report respecting the whole matter is as follows: —

"THE CHOCTAW MISSION.

"The report of the Committee on the missions among the Choctaws and Cherokees was introduced by a verbal statement of the chairman, to the effect that their attention had been specially directed to the Choctaw mission, and they had noticed nothing calling for remark in the Report respecting that among the Cherokees. The report was as follows:—

"'The Committee to whom the Report on the Choctaw mission was referred would respectfully submit the following statement and resolutions, as expressive of their views:

"'This mission, as it was one of the earliest, so it has been one of the most cherished under the care of this Board. For more than forty years it has been in existence, occupying, during all this period, a large place in the interest and affection of the churches here represented. It has passed through trials, but in spite of them, it has flourished and prospered.

"'Repeated revivals of religion, the ingathering of many, from time to time, into the church, the holy lives of those brought out of pagan darkness into the light of the Gospel, have been the divine attestation to the faithfulness of the Apostolic men who, for so many years, have labored in this field. The wild Indian reclaimed from barbarism, and the savage brought into a state of civilization, has refuted the oft-repeated assertion, that in his case, to civilize was to destroy.

"'Were these churches fully prepared to sustain the institutions of religion without further aid, their separation from this Board would be the natural and necessary result of their growth — a result full of joy to those who had so long contributed to secure it. But when such a separation is contemplated before this time has arrived; when it is proposed to discontinue the mission, and dismiss the laborers from the field, solely on the ground of a difference of opinion between the missionaries and this Board in respect to the manner of preaching the Gospel, or the application of its principles to the evil of slavery, then it is fit that such a step should be taken only after a thorough investigation of the real difficulties of the case has satisfied the members of this Board of its necessity.

"'It may be, that the best interests of the mission and the usefulness of the Board will be greatly promoted by the separation. But in this case, it should be brought about deliberately, and after the whole subject has been fairly presented to the churches. Your Committee feel, that for this Board to confirm, at this meeting, the action of the Prudential Committee in discontinuing this mission, would be regarded by many of the churches contributing largely to its resources as at least premature.

"'In order, therefore, to secure deliberate and intelligent action on this question, your Committee recommend:

"''That this whole subject be committed to a committee of ——, (members of this Board,) with instructions to examine it; and if in their opinion it is expedient to discontinue the Choctaw mission, to consider what arrangements are necessary to render such discontinuance least perilous to the interests of religion in that nation, and just to the members of the mission, and report thereon at the next meeting of the Board.

"''Your Committee also recommend, that, for this year, the Prudential Committee should grant the mission the usual supplies.'

" Hon. Linus Child, from the same Committee, offered the following resolutions as a substitute for the report of the Committee : —

" ' 1. *Resolved*, That, in consideration of the facts involved in the intercourse between the Prudential Committee and the missionaries in the Choctaw mission, since the year 1847, the happiness of the missionaries, and their prosperity in their work, will be promoted by their separation from this Board, while, at the same time, the termination of their connection will greatly relieve the Board of the serious and painful embarrassments to which it has been subjected.

" ' 2. *Resolved*, That this Board entertain feelings of the highest respect, confidence and affection for the devoted men connected with this mission, and cordially and gratefully appreciate their self-denying and faithful labors, which have been signally blessed of God to the temporal and spiritual welfare of the Choctaw nation, and most earnestly desire that larger fruits of these years of toil may cheer them in the future prosecution of their benevolent and Christian enterprise.

" ' 3. *Resolved*, That while we cannot withhold an expression of deep regret at the withdrawal of this Board from a field which has been cultivated for so long a period, with so much prayer and Christian zeal on the part of the churches, and with so many severe hardships and struggles on the part of the missionaries, we are constrained to recommend, that the action of the Prudential Committee, terminating the connection of the Choctaw mission with the Board, be concurred in, with this distinct modification, that the usual appropriations for a year be made, and placed at the disposal of the missionaries, in order that, with comfort to themselves, they may go on with their work until they shall have fully matured their plans for the future.'

" A prolonged discussion followed the reading of these papers. The question being on the adoption of the resolutions presented by Mr. Child, as a substitute for the report of the Committee, Dr. Cheever moved the following, as an amendment to these resolutions, and to be added to the report of the Committee: —

" ' Your Committee add, that in the opinion of this Board, the holding of slaves be pronounced [is ?] an immorality, inconsistent with membership in any Christian church ; and that it ought to be required, that these missionary churches should immediately put away from themselves this sin, and should cease to sanction it even in appearance.'

" This amendment was, by unanimous vote, laid upon the table.

" The Board also voted, that both the report of the Committee and the resolutions offered by Mr. Child be laid upon the table.

" Dr. Stearns then moved, that the whole subject be referred to a committee of nine, to report at the next annual meeting of the Board. Upon a motion to lay this motion of Dr. Stearns on the table, the yeas and nays being called for, were taken, with the following result:—

" ' YEAS —Benjamin Tappan, Willard Child, Erastus Fairbanks, Joseph Steele, Heman Humphrey, Henry Hill, Rufus Anderson, Charles Stoddard, Ebenezer Alden, S. L. Pomroy, S. B. Treat, H. B. Hooker, Linus Child, S. M. Worcester, A. W. Porter, A. C. Thompson, W. T. Eustis, John Aiken, Seth Sweetser, Jas. M. Gordon, Amos Blanchard, Joel Hawes, Thomas W. Williams, Henry White, S. W. S. Dutton, George Kellogg, Charles Mills, William Patton, C. T. Hulburd, Simeon Benjamin, Geo. W. Wood, William Strong, L. H. Delano—33.

" ' NAYS —John W. Chickering, Sylvester Holmes, Nehemiah Adams, Leonard Bacon, David L. Ogden, William Adams, Samuel W. Fisher, Oliver E. Wood, George B. Cheever, Thornton A. Mills, David H. Riddle, Jonathan F. Stearns, Lyndon A. Smith, William R. DeWitt, Ambrose White, William Jessup, Samuel H. Perkins, Joel Parker, William A. Buckingham, Thomas Brainerd—20.

" Hon. Linus Child then moved, that the Report of the Prudential Committee respecting the Choctaw mission be adopted, and published with other portions of the Annual Report. While this motion was pending, Rev. H. T. Cheever offered the following as an amendment:—

" ' *Resolved*, That the Prudential Committee be instructed to carry on the Choctaw mission, by the appointment and substitution of other missionaries than the present incumbents, who will carry on the mission upon the principles which the Board shall at any time adopt for the government of its missionaries.'

" This was laid upon the table, and the motion of Mr. Child was adopted ; the consideration of the subject having occupied the attention of the Board for more than four hours."

Of the various matters contained in this extract from the proceedings of the Annual Meeting of 1859, the first in order is the two reports of the Special Committee upon the discontinuance of the Choctaw mission by the Prudential Committee.

The majority report finds no sufficient reason for this summary procedure, and recommends investigation of the grounds of it.

The minority report recommends concurrence in the action of the Prudential Committee, thinking this the most prudent course for all parties concerned.

" A prolonged discussion " followed, showing a nearly equal division in the Board between those who thought it most important to vindicate the policy of the missionaries, and those who thought it most important to relieve the Prudential Committee from "embarrassments and perplexities."

Both these parties, however, joined in an "unanimous vote" to lay upon the table the amendment offered by Dr. Cheever, declaring the holding of slaves an immorality, *inconsistent with membership in any Christian church*, and requiring that the Choctaw mission churches should cleanse themselves from this sin.

The Board, after hours of discussion, found themselves unable to agree upon either of the reports, and both were laid upon the table.

Dr. Stearns then made a motion proposing substantially the *action* recommended in the majority report, but omitting the reasons there urged for it, and avoiding all implication against the Prudential Committee. A decided majority voted to lay this motion also on the table.

The writer of the minority report then made a new motion, embodying the essential feature of that report, (concurrence in the action of the Prudential Committee,) without its form, and this was declared adopted, without a count.

While this was pending, however, a resolution offered by Rev. Henry T. Cheever — recommending that the Choctaw *missionaries be changed*, instead of the mission discontinued — was promptly laid on the table.

The prolonged debates and the emphatic votes of this meeting having shown the Board determined not to interfere with the complicity maintained by their Prudential Committee and their missionaries with slavery, Dr. Cheever next tried this body with a less stringent test of principle and duty.

There had been, during that year and the year previous, many indications of a purpose, among the most Southern States of the American Union, to revive the foreign slave-trade in fact, and to seek to legitimate it by legislative and Congressional action, for the purpose of effecting a very great enlargement of its operations.

However careful the Prudential Committee had been to say nothing against the *internal* slave-trade, as practised around and within the territory occupied by their Indian missions, they had frequently and strongly declared the pre-judicial influence of the *foreign* slave-trade upon their *African* missions. Of the influence of slavery itself, *in Africa*, they speak freely, in this very Annual Report, (1859,) as follows. Speaking of the people on and near the Gaboon river, on the West coast of Africa, they say—

"SOCIAL CONDITION.—Domestic slavery is extensive and in-creasing. Slaves outnumber the freemen. Polygamy is universal, and in its loosest form. Marriage can hardly be said to exist. Much of the property is in the form of slaves and wives. The children of slaves, however, are not often sold, and Mr. Walker thinks the French slave trade cannot long continue. The social disorganization is so complete, that all the young men fall early into the licentious habits of their countrymen; and it is almost impossible to obtain and educate virtuous females. It is found next to impos-sible to furnish wives for native helpers."—p. 40.

Of the direct injury wrought by the slave-trade in Africa upon their missionary work, the Prudential Committee say, in their Annual Report for 1858:—

"The mission has found greater difficulties than was expected above the navigable waters of the Gaboon. The slave-trade has demoralized the social life of the country. Tribe lies behind tribe, each with a different language, and each seeking to be the exclusive factors of all the trade that passes to and from the coast."—p. 31.

Of the fact that this desolating trade continues to exist, even where it is claimed to have been suppressed by treaty, they say, in their Annual Report for 1855:—

"The slave-trade is still carried on between that place [Sanga-tanga] and St. Thomas; although the king showed our brethren a very rigid treaty, which he and his chiefs had entered into with the British government, for the entire suppression of the traffic in his dominions."—p. 47.

Since the Prudential Committee had already spoken thus strongly and repeatedly on the pernicious influence of the foreign slave-trade, *in its relation to Africa*, it was not un-reasonable in Dr. Cheever to ask such aid as might be given by a protest of the Board against a reëstablishment of that atrocious traffic by this country, involving, as it necessarily would, a great increase of the evil complained of in Africa. The Board, however, evaded compliance with this request, by their usual method of indirection, and the Prudential

Committee, taking care not to quote Dr. Cheever's memorial in their Annual Report, thus refer to the presentation and final disposition of it:—

" THE SLAVE TRADE.

" Dr. Cheever presented, for adoption by the Board, a memorial addressed to the Senate and House of Representatives of the United States, on the subject of the African slave-trade. After discussion, this memorial was referred to the Business Committee, who subsequently reported, recommending the adoption of the following preamble and resolution, which were adopted:—

" ' While the Board regard with sentiments of unqualified condemnation the African slave-trade, and cannot but feel the liveliest regret and alarm at the disposition manifested in this and other countries to revive it in one form or another, especially in view of the fact that it is interfering, and is likely to interfere, in the most serious manner, with the proper missionary work of the Board, yet, inasmuch as there is not sufficient time, at this advanced stage of the meeting, properly to deliberate and determine upon the course proper to be pursued in so grave a matter:

" ' *Resolved*, That the whole subject, with the memorial that brings it before the Board, be referred to the Prudential Committee, to take such action as in their judgment its relations to their work, as a Board of Missions, shall seem to demand.' "

Thus, at the very time when urgent and speedy action was demanded by the very nature of the case, this important subject was buried for another year.

In the list, given in the Annual Report, (1859,) of persons present at this meeting, is the name of Rev. Justin Perkins, D.D., for many years a missionary of the Board among the Nestorians. As Dr. Perkins had formerly, on two different occasions, taken a decided and active part in opposition to slavery, once in 1853, when he ineffectually tried to unite the more distant missionaries of the American Board in a public protest against American slavery, and again in 1854, when he preached and published a sermon called "Our Country's Sin," it was doubtless hoped, by those who were taking that side in this Annual Meeting, that the weight of his influence would be thrown in their favor. He, however, remained silent. [To avoid recurrence to Dr. Perkins, it may be mentioned here, that he preserved a like shameful silence, though present, when the yet worse transactions of *the next* Annual Meeting were going on.]

The Prudential Committee, in some "remarks" at the close of their account of the Annual Meeting of 1859, express their regret (tempered by resignation) at the fact that some members of the Board chose to occupy its time with debates on slavery, as follows : —

"REMARKS.

"It was, doubtless, deeply regretted by many members, and others in attendance on this meeting of the Board, that so much time should have been occupied by discussions, interesting indeed, and to some extent exciting, but not calculated to awaken the best Christian feeling, or to enlist the deepest sympathies of the followers of Christ, and call forth their most earnest efforts, in connection with the missionary work. Yet, under the circumstances of the case, considering not only the action in regard to the Choctaw mission which was reported by the Prudential Committee, but remembering that the fearful evils and sins of slavery and of the slave-trade were actually witnessed in some of the fields occupied by missions of this Board, seriously affecting the interests of the missions, it was hardly to be expected that a meeting calling together so many persons, from different sections of our widely extended country, would be exempt from such discussions." — p. 30.

The Prudential Committee had now freed themselves from the "embarrassments and perplexities" of further remonstrance against their complicity with slavery in the Choctaw mission, by summarily "discontinuing" that mission. They left its slaveholding church members, "in good and regular standing," with "a name to live" as Christians. They left its pro-slavery missionaries with hearty commendation of their conscientiousness, faithfulness and devotedness, and with the manifestation of especial interest in their "excellent friend and brother, Mr. Byington," of the Stockbridge station. All these were now free, if they chose, to connect themselves with those "religious bodies in the adjoining States," which had been charged by the Board, in September, 1858, with "a lamentable defection from some of the first and most elementary ideas of Christian morality," yet suggested by the Prudential Committee, in their subsequent letter of October 5th, in the same year, as the body with which it was "probable" that their dismissed missionaries would "come into connection."

In the Annual Report for 1860, the Prudential Committee's statement relating to the Cherokee mission is as follows : —

10

"THE BOARD CLOSES ITS WORK AMONG THE CHEROKEES.

" The Committee have arrived at the conclusion, that it is time for the Board to discontinue its expenditures among the Cherokees. To prevent all misapprehensions, it should be stated at the outset; — *First,* that this is not owing to the relations of our work among these Indians to the system of slavery; the mission having formerly assented to the principles embodied in what is generally known as the ' Good-water Settlement,' which was approved by the Board at Utica, and the Committee having no evidence that the brethren now constituting the mission have departed, in theory or practice, from those principles. And, *secondly,* it is due to the missionaries to say further, that the prevailing opinion among them is adverse to the Board's retiring from the Cherokee Nation. This is what should be expected of brethren devoted to their work, in such circumstances; and it may be hoped that some of our various Home Missionary Societies will interpose, to sustain them longer at their stations.

" To aid in determining the duty of the Board in respect to this field, a series of inquiries was addressed, early in the present year, to each of our three ordained missionaries among this people, and from these brethren answers were received, which, copied out in a fair hand, together fill one hundred pages of manuscript. The last of the responses was received as late as August. The question is,— Considering the state and prospects of the work among the Cherokees, and the claims of other missions, and of other parts of the unevangelized world, whether the Board may now properly retire from the field, and expend elsewhere the five or six thousand dollars required for the support of this mission.

" 1. *The Cherokees are a Christian People.*

" This mission is one of the oldest under the care of the Board, having been in operation about forty-three years. It has employed 18 clerical missionaries, 29 laymen of different occupations, and 66 female assistant missionaries, or 113 in all; and $356,421 have been expended in it from the Treasury of the Board.

" As the result of these and other kindred efforts, the Cherokees have been elevated from the savage state to their present degree of civilization. Doubtless, among the ignorant portions of the people, there are remains of superstitious notions and habits, greater than are found in older Christian communities; but the people, as a body, give the common proofs of being a Christian people. However low may be the standard of their Christianity, it is their only religion. The people are generally, as with us, ranked in one or another of the evangelical denominations. And they are accessible to Christian preachers, and listen to them with the same deference as do their white brethren in the adjoining States. They inhabit chiefly the eastern section of their territory, which borders on the State of Arkansas; extending north and south about one hundred miles, and east and west about seventy-five miles. The Cherokee people are supposed to number about 21,000. Our three missionary brethren, residing among them, concur in the opinion, that they reckon themselves, and are to be acknowledged, a Christian people.

Mr. Torrey says : 'Christianity is recognized among them, as much as in any portion of the United States. Their Constitution provides [Art. VI. Sec. 1] that no person who denies the being of a God, or a future state of reward and punishment, shall hold any office in the civil department of this nation.' Mr. Ranney says: 'The nation, as such, I presume, would claim to be called a Christian nation. Some laws have been passed by the Cherokee Council, which have recognized Christianity as the religion of the nation. This has been done incidentally, rather than directly and positively. I suppose that, almost universally, they would desire to be called Christians.' And Mr. Willey bears a similar testimony. 'I think,' he says, 'that the Cherokees, as a nation, may justly be called a nominally Christian nation. The Constitution of the nation recognizes the Christian religion, and requires a belief in it by all who hold office under the government. All teachers in the public schools are required, by law, to have the Bible read in their schools daily ; and when they are prepared for it, they are requested to pray daily in their schools.'

"2. *How far the Cherokees have the Gospel Institutions.*

"'In this territory and population,' Mr. Torrey says, 'there are probably, of all denominations, including native pastors and exhorters, not less than sixty licensed preachers, or one to about every four hundred inhabitants. Of these, sixteen are white men,—namely, three missionaries of the American Board; three Moravians ; three Northern Baptists ; two Southern Baptists ; and five Methodists. There is probably no citizen of the nation who is not within a convenient distance of occasional religious meetings. There are, I believe, thirty public school-houses, all of which are used more or less as preaching places, and probably more than double that number of other places of worship.' The stations of the Board are in the southern section of this territory. The Moravians have two or three stations in the northern section ; the Northern Baptists occupy the eastern side ; while the Methodist circuit-riders, and a portion of the Baptists, perhaps mostly from the South, range through the territory. 'The Methodists,' Mr. Torrey writes from Park Hill, 'are building a large brick church on the hill opposite ours, and in full view of it, about two miles distant, to cost $3,000.' Mr. Ranney, writing from Lee's Creek, says : 'The Baptists have built a meeting-house within about half a mile of the station, where they frequently have preaching.' Mr. Torrey thinks there is no part of the country that is not frequently visited by preachers from the Methodist or Baptist denominations. Mr. Ranney supposes that all can hear some kind of preaching, at least occasionally, from some one of the denominations ; but that only a very small proportion have opportunity to hear the preached Gospel statedly and regularly on the Sabbath.

"Mr. Torrey reports the church members as being more than three thousand in number, constituting more than one-third of the adult population. Of these, the Northern Baptists have the largest number, or about fifteen hundred ; the Methodists the next largest ; the Southern Baptists the next ; and the Moravians about two hundred and fifty. Of the actual piety of this large membership,

we may not speak confidently. Where so many have opportunity
to attend only three or four meetings in a year, even though these
meetings be protracted, we can hardly look for much religious
knowledge, or effective Christian character, especially as the larger
portion of the native preachers are said to have but little education.
Our brethren declare, that no members have been received into
either of our own churches, without first giving what they deemed
to be credible evidence of repentance and faith in Christ. In this
there has been exact conformity to the principle recognized by the
Board : — 'That credible evidence of repentance and faith in Christ,
in the judgment of the missionaries and the churches they gather,
entitles professed converts from among the heathen to the ordinances
of baptism and the Lord's supper; those ordinances being evidently
designed by Christ to be means of grace for such.' Mr. Rau-
ney regards the members of his own church, at Lee's Creek, as
furnishing the same evidence of faith and repentance, as did the
members of a church in Vermont, where he labored as a minister of
the Gospel before going among the Cherokees.

" 3. *Difficulties in the way of further Operations by the Board.*

"Whether it be possible for a missionary society, situated like
the Board, to revive this mission, and to prosecute it vigorously for
a succession of years, is a matter of considerable doubt. One of our
brethren thus writes : 'To one who looks upon the surface, the
position which your missionaries now occupy among this people
amounts to this. They are laboring under a complication of disad-
vantages ; at a great expense — greater, I suppose, in proportion to
the extent of their operations, than that of any other denomination ;
shut out, at least for the present, from adding to the number of their
stations, or exchanging them for more promising localities ; regarded
with jealousy by a very influential portion of the community ; with
no active native preachers; with small congregations; with very
few young persons connected with their churches ; with a membership which has not materially increased for many years, and with
scarcely any promise of future accessions : and competing with other
sects, who occupy, indiscriminately, every part of the country, have
a large corps of native assistants, and count their audiences at times
by thousands, and their accessions by scores.' Looking deeper, this
brother sees 'something under this weak and despised exterior,'
in its healthful influence on the piety and morals of the nation,
'that is really worth all the cost and contumely which have attended this mission for the last ten or fifteen years.' This is probably true of the past. Yet among a people situated like the Cherokees, and with such an all-pervading inroad of other denominations,
it must be difficult for the Board to regain its ground ; mainly because so many other professedly Christian teachers occupy it. The
proportion of the people now reached by our ministrations is comparatively small. The audience at Park Hill is not far from forty ;
that at Fairfield (a monthly meeting) is sixty ; at Dwight, it is from
sixty to one hundred ; and at Lee's Creek, seventy-five. Moreover,
all the missionaries preach through interpreters. If it were possible, as it is not, to procure native pastors for the small churches
at each of these places, the people could not be induced to support

them; 'since other denominations,' as we are assured, 'would very readily take the support of these churches upon their hands, on condition of receiving them into their fellowship.' Elsewhere, the same writer speaks more fully on this important point. 'Unlike most nations emerging from heathenism,' he says, 'this people have, from the memory of the oldest, and I do not know but always, been entirely exempt from taxes. They are able to give but little at the best, and they think themselves less able than they really are. Their idea of public money is money paid to them, for their benefit; not by them, for the public good. As to eating and drinking, they are liberal, and will share the last loaf with the needy. They will often provide entertainment at camp-meetings, at no small expense of labor, time, and property. But to persuade them to carry these same provisions quietly to their minister, to be used frugally for his family's necessities, would be no easy task. Again, the moment these stations are deserted by the missionaries, there are at least three denominations, who are ready to furnish them with preaching free from all expense, except an occasional contribution and camp-meeting; and who would take our educated young men into their service (if they would consent) at a salary higher and surer than they could possibly secure from the people, under the most favorable circumstances.' These are facts which should obviously have much weight in determining the future duty of the Board. Churches that are to be always dependent, in lands which have become professedly Christian, can have but a slender claim upon institutions that exist for the propagation of the Gospel among heathen nations. Until the churches shall enter more readily and fully into the work of missions, such investments cannot be wise.

"Should the Board occupy new districts in the Cherokee country, there is reason to believe that other denominations would follow us, and there render it as impossible for us to make headway as they do where we now are. And in obtaining new locations, in forming new relations, in starting anew in every thing, with such obstacles, and with the disadvantage of prejudices, however groundless, against us as a Northern society, — prejudices, so prone to start periodically into life and vigor, upon the recurrence of our national agitations during the Presidential election, — our prospective embarrassments are too great, and our success is too doubtful, to warrant the attempt. 'I suppose,' says one of our brethren, 'that to attempt to establish new stations without an act of Council, would be simply to forfeit our expenditures; and I have no idea that such an act could be obtained.'

"The national law on this subject, passed September, 1889, is as follows : —

"'Sect. 2. Be it further enacted, that in future, no missionary school or establishment shall be located, or erected, without permission being first obtained from the National Council for such purpose, and the place designated by law for the same, with such other general regulations as may be deemed necessary and proper, either as conducive to its particular usefulness, or conformity to national rights and interests.'"

"4. *The Mission Discontinued.*

"In view of these facts and circumstances, and for the reasons thus briefly stated, or suggested, and for no other or different reasons, the Prudential Committee have deemed it expedient to discontinue this mission. To this end, they have recently adopted the Resolutions that follow — namely :

"*Resolved,*— 1. That, in the adoption of the Christian religion by the Cherokee people, and the recognition of it by their government; in the general diffusion among them of Gospel institutions, though under different forms; in the introduction and permanent establishment of the principles and practices of piety, though of course under many imperfections; and in the creation, notwithstanding formidable obstacles, of a regulated civil community, from one of the largest aboriginal tribes of our Continent,—the Prudential Committee gratefully acknowledge a work of divine grace, amply rewarding the exertions and expenditures which have been made, by Christians of different names, in this behalf.

"2. That while the spiritual renovation of the Cherokee people is confessedly imperfect, the Committee regard the appropriate work of the Board among that people as having been so far accomplished, and the further successful prosecution of its labors as, at the same time, so far impeded by the intervention of other denominations better situated for operating there than ourselves, as to render it proper and expedient for the Board to withdraw, and expend the funds hitherto devoted to this field in other more needy portions of the unevangelized world, where it can now work to better advantage.

"3. That, accordingly, the mission of the Board among the Cherokees should be, and it is hereby, discontinued.

"4. That this does not at once terminate the personal relations of the members of this mission to the Board, but leaves them at liberty to make such arrangements for the future as they shall severally judge proper; and the Committee will recognize their claim to such pecuniary aid, whenever they retire from their connection with the Board, as its rules, usages and means enable it to afford.

"5. To prevent the possibility of misapprehension, it is further resolved, that the mission is not discontinued because of any unfaithfulness on the part of our brethren in that mission; they having been exemplary, so far as is known to the Committee, in the discharge of all their missionary duties." — pp. 137–142.

"The Cherokees," say the Prudential Committee, " are a Christian People"! — and, in some concluding reflections, designed to fix this idea, by repetition, in the minds of their readers, they sum up the matter thus : —

"The mission is not abandoned ; but *our* appropriate work is done. The Cherokee people have been Christianized, through the divine favor, and what remains for building up and sustaining the institutions of the Gospel — which is every where a work never brought to a close — must be left to others ; for the reason that our appropriate work is no longer there." — p. 145.

The details above given by the Prudential Committee do not give us a very exalted idea either of the quantity or quality of the Christianization thus claimed. But, to see *how* small is its quantity, and *how* poor its quality, even according to the Prudential Committee's own standard, we must collect those scattered evidences which form the basis of the assertion that the Cherokees (acknowledged by the Committee to number "about 21,000") are "a Christian people."

First, as to quantity. Here are the numbers, given in a statistical table, (p. 143,) of the Cherokees who are church members at the four mission stations of the Board in that nation : —

At Park Hill,	83
" Fairfield,	24
" Dwight,	59
" Lee's Creek,	20
	186

The Annual Report for 1859 (p. 149) tells us that of the twenty-four church members of the meeting at Fairfield, (a *monthly* meeting,) the "average attendance" is "only four or five." The average attendance of communicants at the other three stations is not given.

By counting in the white communicants and the colored communicants in these four churches, the entire number of the Board's church members in the Cherokee nation is raised to 183. But it is upon the 136 *Cherokee* church members that the claim must stand (if at all) that "the [21,000] Cherokees are a Christian people."

There is, however, one more chance for the Prudential Committee's claim to be substantiated. If a large proportion of the nation are punctual and devout attendants upon the preaching of a pure Gospel, thus manifesting their respect for Christianity, and their allegiance to it, they may, perhaps, in the judgment of charity, be called a Christian nation. To judge fairly of the claim that the Cherokee *nation* is Christianized, we should look, not at the number of church members only, but at the size of the *congregations* which the missionaries report as usually attendant on their Sabbath services. These are given as follows, pp. 140, 141, of the Annual Report for 1860 : —

Audience at Park Hill, ... 40
  " " Fairfield, (monthly,) . . 60
  " " Dwight, "60 to 100," say . 80
  " " Lee's Creek, . . . 75
                 ‾‾‾
                 255

It is, then, on the strength of four Sabbath audiences, amounting in all, church members included, to 255, that the 21,000 Cherokees are declared "a Christian people"!

It is true that the Prudential Committee bring, in aid of their comprehensive claim of a Christian character for the Cherokee nation, sundry statistics respecting the "licensed preachers" of other ecclesiastical bodies (chiefly Baptists and Methodists) who are operating in the Cherokee country, and who have gathered churches there. But when we remember (even apart from the fact of their being inveterately pro-slavery) that the bodies by whom these preachers are "licensed" are the very ones which have been charged by the Board with "a lamentable defection from some of the first and most elementary ideas of Christian morality," (p. 17 of Annual Report for 1858,) we shall find that this specification, instead of helping the claim of the Prudential Committee, hinders it; instead of showing, as the heading of their paragraph would deceitfully represent, "*How far the Cherokees have the Gospel Institutions*," it only shows another effort on their part to mislead the readers of the report, and to claim a Christian character for a pro-slavery system, outside as well as inside of their own operations.

Having looked at the *amount* of the thing claimed as Christianity in the Board's four churches in the Cherokee nation, let us next look at its *quality*. Perhaps its ardor, its devotedness, compensate for its small numerical amount. Perhaps the number was kept *so* small because only eminent Christians were admitted to the Church. Let us see.

The first thing to be noticed is, that what they called Christianity included a recognition of the holding, the buying and selling of slaves as entirely unobjectionable; as something, the right to do which was to be upheld by law and custom, in Church and State.

But, passing by this consideration, let us test them by *the Board's* standard of Christian character; namely, their practical use of church membership; their appreciation of "the privileges of the sanctuary." To do this, I will quote the statements respecting the spiritual condition of the 136 Cherokee Christians, from the last four Annual Reports of the Prudential Committee, including that which records the "discontinuance" of the mission.

The Annual Report for 1857 says—

"The history of the churches under the care of this mission for several years has been singularly uniform. . . . . The total membership of the churches remains very nearly as it was in 1851. . . . . The interest in the Cherokee churches in the services of the sanctuary does not seem to have deepened. At some of the stations, the number of worshippers on the Sabbath has slightly increased; but, on the whole, no certain improvement in this particular can be reported."—p. 149.

The Annual Report for 1858 says—

"The brethren of this mission, with one exception, are unable to report any religious interest which can properly be called a revival. Mr. Ranney has admitted four persons to the church at Lee's Creek. . . . . A few additions have also been made to the church at Honey Creek. But the reports from Park Hill and Fairfield are less cheering. The past year, Mr. Worcester writes, has unhappily been one of sad apathy in regard to the most interesting of all concerns. My preaching thus far, Mr. Torrey says, has been attended with but little apparent profit. I have some reason to believe that two or three persons have been led to indulge a hope in Christ through my word. Whether their hope is well founded or not, remains to be seen. . . . . The grace of liberality is not largely bestowed upon the Cherokees."—pp. 128, 129.

The Report for 1859 says—

"The past year cannot be regarded as one of special prosperity. The additions to the number of communicants are only seven; so that, taking into account the annual loss by death or otherwise, the churches have received no accession to their strength."—p. 147.

"The amount contributed for benevolent purposes cannot be reported with accuracy. It is presumed, however, that there has been no advance upon the liberality of former years."—p. 148.

"In speaking of this church, one year ago, Mr. Torrey stated that, of twelve colored members, none resided within eight miles of him; and that, of thirty-one Indian members, only fourteen lived within six miles of him; the rest being entirely, or almost entirely, beyond his reach. The average attendance of communicants at Fairfield is only four or five. It was not till a few weeks since that he could report the first direct, tangible, satisfactory case of conversion connected with his labors. As there is no reason whatever to call in question the fidelity and earnestness of this brother, the Committee are not clear that, in the present state of the world, the Board should prolong its efforts at this station." — p. 149.

The suggestion made in the sentence last quoted was carried into execution, and the Annual Report for 1860 announced that the Prudential Committee had closed their work among the Cherokees. The statement in that Report respecting the spiritual prosperity of that year was as follows : —

"The past year has not been one of ingathering to the churches ; though they have preserved their general good estate, as compared with the other religious communities in the nation."

Which is to say, (if we "put that and that together,") — that, though there are no *more* Christians than last year, the previously existing ones show nothing *worse* than "a lamentable defection from some of the first and most elementary ideas of Christian morality."

Thus it appears that the real basis of the claim of Christian character for the nation of 21,000 Cherokees is the existence of 136 Cherokee church members, of the sort above described, and the attendance of 119 more persons, on Sundays, upon those means of grace which *converted* the 136.

The next inquiry to be made is — What action was taken by the Board, in their Annual Meeting, October, 1860, upon the decision of the Prudential Committee to discontinue the Cherokee mission ? What did the Board say to the declaration of the Prudential Committee, manifestly false, that this relinquishment had *not* been made on account of slavery ? What did they say to the declaration, alike false and preposterous, that the real reason of the relinquishment was that their efforts to Christianize were not needed there, because the nation were already Christians ? What did they say to the details of evidence adduced in support of this hypothesis that the Cherokees were a Christian people, namely : that 136 of them, out of 21,000, were members of churches, these churches agreeing to recognize slaveholders, equally with others, as Christians : that this church membership comprises "very few young persons," that it "has not materally increased for many years," and that it has "scarcely any promise of future accessions"; that these Cherokee Christians have "no active native preachers" : that even the *audiences* (church members and others, Cherokee, white and colored,) which usually assembled at their four stations, were only 40, 60, 80 and 75, making but 255 *hearers* of the Board's Gospel out of 21,000: and finally, that "if it were possible, *as it is not*, to procure native pastors for the small churches at each of these places, THE PEOPLE COULD NOT BE INDUCED TO SUPPORT THEM!" What did the Board say to *this* sort of evidence that "the Cherokees are a Christian people"?

They said nothing! Even the Committee* to whom, in the ordinary course of business, this portion of the Report of the Prudential Committee was referred, said nothing, either of the double deceit therein practised by the Prudential Committee, or of the absurdity of claiming a Christian character for the Cherokee nation upon such grounds. On the contrary, they "*recommended the adoption of the following resolution*, AND IT WAS ADOPTED" by the Board: namely—

"*Resolved*, That the action of the Prudential Committee in reference to the Cherokee mission be, and the same is hereby, approved by the Board."—p. 16.

Immediately after this record in the proceedings of the Annual Meeting in 1860, comes the following, from which it appears that certain members and friends of the Board, Orthodox Congregational Ministers forming the General Association of Illinois, had made one more effort to induce the Board to purify itself from complicity with slavery:—

"RESOLUTIONS OF THE GENERAL ASSOCIATION OF ILLINOIS.

"The Business Committee reported that certain Resolutions of the General Association of Illinois, on 'the relation of the Board to the Cherokee Mission,' had been brought to their notice, and recommended that they be referred to the Committee to whom the Report of the Prudential Committee, respecting that mission, had been referred. This was done accordingly. The Resolutions are as follows:—

"'1. *Resolved*, That the cause of Foreign Missions is vitally connected with the spiritual prosperity of our churches, and entitled to hold a leading place in their Christian affections and charities; and that its appeals to their sympathies, prayers, and self-denying bene-

---

* The Committee on the Cherokee mission consisted of Rev. Dr. Beman, Judge Jessup, Wm. C. Gilman, Esq., Rev. Dr. Asa D. Smith, Rev. Dr. Sabin, Rev. Wm. A. Nichols, and Rev. J. G. Davis.

factions, were never so loud and urgent as, in the providence of
God, they are at the present time.

" '2. *Resolved*, That we most gratefully acknowledge the good
hand of our God in the foreign missionary work which, during the
last half century, the American Board, the pioneer of our benevolent societies, has been enabled, through the divine blessing, to
accomplish; in the information which it has collected and diffused
throughout Christendom respecting the heathen world; in the com-
passion for the perishing and the zeal for Christ which it has kin-
dled in the hearts of his disciples; in the spirit of self-denial and
self-sacrifice which it has quickened and fostered; in the blessings
of a Christian civilization which it has conferred upon the benighted
and degraded; in the many trophies for Christ and heaven which it
has won from Paganism; in the impulse which it has given to the
great cause of Christian benevolence; and in all the forms in which,
at home and abroad, it has advanced the triumphs of the Redeemer's
Kingdom among men; — and that we desire that the Board may
enter upon the second half century of its career with fresh unction
and fresh power, relieved of every disability which may impair its
moral influence, cripple its energies, diminish its resources, or obstruct its widest usefulness.

" '3. *Resolved*, That we regard it as demanded alike by the Gospel
and humanity, and an object of intense desire, in view of the existing
state of the national mind, the demand and associations of the approaching jubilee, and the highest influence and success of the
Board, that the divorce of slaveholding from Christianity be completed at once in the churches of the Cherokee nation, and that a
full declaration of principles against slavery be sent forth to the
world, as the testimony of the Board to that great cause which now
involves the deepest interests of humanity.'

" The Committee subsequently reported, that 'the action of the
Prudential Committee, and the statements contained in their
Report with reference to the Cherokee Mission, taken in connection with previous declarations of the Board, have satisfactorily
answered the requests of the General Association of Illinois; and
no further action of the Board is deemed necessary.' This report
was accepted by the Board." — p. 17.

It appears from the first paragraph of this monstrous report, that not the Business Committee, but the Committee
which had just echoed the relinquishment of the Cherokee
Mission, are to be held responsible for it. No where in the
whole action of the managers of the Board (I am aware that
this is a very strong expression) has there been a more
palpable and impudent fraud than the assertion of this
Reverend Committee, that the cutting loose of the slaveholding Cherokee churches from the Board has " *satisfactorily*
answered the requests of the General Association of Illinois,"

which were, first, "that the divorce of slaveholding from Christianity be completed at once *in the churches of the Cherokee nation*"; and next, "that a full declaration of principles against slavery be sent forth to the world as the testimony of the Board."

It is by their accustomed careless acceptance and adoption of reports like this, (the endorsement of a reputable merchant upon a forged check,) that the Board enable the fictions, elaborated by complicity of the Special Committees with the Prudential Committee, to pass current as truth in the community.

The next action, in the Annual Meeting of 1860, was in regard to the foreign slave-trade, a memorial against which, presented by Rev. Dr. Cheever to the Annual Meeting of the previous year, had, after discussion, been shoved out of the way by a reference to the Prudential Committee. (See *ante*, p. 216.) As this body hoped now to get the whole subject of slavery off their hands, they brought up this branch of it also, to receive its *quietus*, as follows—(it will be observed that they avoid mentioning *who* presented the memorial):—

"THE SLAVE TRADE.

"At a meeting of the Board in 1859, a memorial on the subject of the African slave trade, which had been presented for adoption, together with the whole subject thus brought before the Board, was referred to the Prudential Committee. In their Report upon the Gaboon mission, (which was referred to the Committee on missions in Africa,) the following statements are made upon this subject, and, information having been called for, were read before the Board:—

"'It is gratifying to learn, from recent statements, that the French Government have promised to discontinue their "emigrant" traffic after the present season. This traffic, at the Gaboon, has been less than usual during the year, and it has less affected the operations of the mission than heretofore.

"'The Committee were instructed by the Board, at its last meeting, to take such action concerning the slave-trade, in this and its other form, "as in their judgment its relations to their work, as a Board of Missions, shall seem to demand." No time was lost in attending to the duty. Mr. Walker, of the Gaboon mission, being then in the country, and being one of the best authorities on the subject, was consulted. His opinion as to the "emigrant trade" corresponded with the facts above reported, and he thought more harm than good would result from memorializing the national Government at present. In this opinion, the brethren at the Gaboon subsequently concurred, as the Committee were informed by Mr. Bushnell. It was also the belief of Mr. Walker, that the slave-trade, in its customary form, is not now directly affecting us. The Committee embodied these views in a report, which they placed on their files, and do not think it incumbent on the Board to bring this matter before our Government under existing circumstances.'

" The report here mentioned as having been placed on file by the Prudential Committee, which is dated November 8, 1859, was put into the hands of the same Committee, on the African missions, and was also read to the Board. It is as follows:— ·

" ' The sub-committee to whom was referred the memorial on the slave-trade, which was presented to the Board at its late meeting at Philadelphia, and by the Board referred to the Prudential Committee, have considered the matter, and report :

" ' The question now to be considered is this : Is it expedient for the American Board of Commissioners for Foreign Missions, or for the Prudential Committee in the behalf of said Board, now to memorialize the Congress of the United States, or the President of the United States, on the subject of the African slave-trade ?

" ' That this trade is an enormous evil, wherever it exists, there can be no doubt. It pollutes whatever it touches, and desolates wherever it goes. And this is probably just as true of the exportation of "free emigrants" from Africa, under the authority of the French Government, as it is of the general slave-trade.

" ' Great, however, as the evil may be, it is our clear conviction that neither the Board, nor its Committee, ought to memorialize the Congress or the President of the United States, unless the trade, in some of its forms, evidently interferes with the proper missionary work of the Board. This missionary work is now carried on among the Zulus, upon the south-eastern coast, and at the mouth of the Gaboon, on the western coast of Africa.

" ' The foreign slave-trade, in either of its forms, has not directly interfered with our missionary work among the Zulus. The trade does not exist in that territory, and will not be likely to enter it, as the territory is under British authority.

" ' Neither has the Gaboon country been disturbed by the general slave-trade for years, the nearest market for the purchase of slaves being at the mouth of the Nazareth, about one hundred miles south of the Gaboon. The trade in "free emigrants," by the French, has, however, been established and carried on at the Gaboon. Mr. Walker, one of our missionaries, says of this trade : " It is not different from the old slave-trade, except in name and profession of philanthrophy, and the presence of a naval officer aboard each vessel, to protect it from the English cruiser on the coast. But these things only intensify it, and make it more effectual for the accomplishment of evil." If, then, there is a strong probability that this trade will be long continued at this point, it would seem to be proper and expedient for the American Board to address the President of the United States, in the endeavor, and with the hope, of securing the influence of this Government with the French Government, in favor of the discontinuance of this trade, because of its interference with their missionary work. Mr. Walker, however, is of the opinion, that this traffic will not be long continued at the Gaboon. He says : " I see that this traffic is suspended by Government order on the east coast. It has also been abandoned in Liberia. Last month, Mr. Best wrote me that the trade in the Gaboon had met with so strong a competition from the increase of English trade there, that the vessels were preparing to leave for other parts of the coast. But dates of a month later speak of the vessels as still there. I do not think the trade is to continue. The present arrangement terminates in about two years, and from the fact that it has been withdrawn from the east coast, and the constant opposition of the English Government, as well as English trade, I do not think the arrangement will be renewed. I do not think that the French emigrant system is to affect us in the Gaboon, or any other missionaries on the coast, seriously."

" ' We regard Mr. Walker as the very best authority on this subject, and with his testimony and opinion so clearly expressed before us, we cannot think it advisable to address the President on the subject at the present time. If it shall be found, in the course of events, that the expectations of Mr. Walker are not realized, and that this traffic is likely to be continued, to the injury of our missionary work, a suitable appeal will of course hereafter be made by the Committee to the President in this behalf.' " —pp. 17–19.

The Prudential Committee place their refusal to act in this important matter on the ground of the opinion of Mr. Walker, one of their missionaries, whom they represent as " the very best authority on this subject."

Mr. Walker is a very hopeful man. Thirteen years ago, (1848,) writing from the same mission, he announced that the slave-trade was already " broken up." In the Prudential Committee's Annual Report for that year occurs this report from Mr. Walker respecting " King George's town " : —

" The people there are debased, suffering through the influence of the slave-trade ; which, however, has been broken up by the activity of English and American cruisers." — p. 134.

Mr. Wilson, also, another missionary of the Board at the Gaboon, has shown himself unduly hopeful upon the same subject. In the Annual Report for 1852, Mr. Wilson says—

" The English squadron has very nearly put a final end to the slave-trade. All its strongholds in the vicinity of the Congo have recently been abandoned. Indeed, I know of but three points on the whole coast now where it is still continued ; and these, I have no doubt, will be relinquished before the close of the present year."

In another statement, (subsequently written, though in the same year,) Mr. Wilson says, (p. 218) —

"It will be gratifying to the friends of humanity to know, that the slave-trade on the coast of Africa is virtually broken up, *and probably will never be revived again.*"

Coming down to the year 1859, Mr. Walker's confidence becomes somewhat less positive. In their Annual Report for that year, complaining that at the Gaboon "domestic slavery is extensive *and increasing*," the Prudential Committee state that—"Mr. Walker thinks the French slave-trade *cannot long continue.*"

In the quotations from Mr. Walker in the Annual Report for 1860, which we are now examining, that gentleman's confidence seems yet further diminished. Speaking of the trade in "free emigrants" by the French, which, he declares, "is *not different* from the old slave-trade, except in name, and profession of philanthropy," his ground for encouragement is that "the present arrangement terminates in about two years," and *he does not think it will be renewed!*

What an insult is it to the common sense of the community—a community which has heard the energetic expressions of Southern determination to have the foreign slave-trade speedily revived, and which has seen several books and pamphlets recently published, by clergymen and others, in direct advocacy of such revival—what an insult to our common sense is it for the Prudential Committee to say, immediately after the passage last quoted from Mr. Walker—a passage also bearing in the very opposite direction—

"We regard Mr. Walker as the very best authority on this subject, and, with his testimony and opinion so clearly expressed before us, we cannot think it advisable to address the President on the subject at the present time."

Even this perversion of Mr. Walker's testimony is not the worst of the deceit here practised by the Prudential Committee. In the face of his testimony, (in 1859, that the French slave-trade still existed in the Gaboon, and in 1860, that "the present arrangement" for it was to continue two years longer,) and in the face of their own lamentation, (p. 40 of Ann. Rep. for 1859,) that slavery in the Gaboon was *increasing*, and that much of the *property* there is in the form of slaves, they now say —

"Neither has the Gaboon country been disturbed by the general slave-trade *for years.*"

This statement is made in the hope to persuade the community that "neither the Board, nor its Committee, ought to memorialize the Congress, or the President, of the United States, unless the trade, in some of its forms, evidently interferes with the proper missionary work of the Board"!

If it shall seem incredible to any one (for want of having the Annual Reports at hand for reference) that this body of grave and reverend seigniors should make an assertion which could be proved a lie by abundant recent evidence out of their own mouths, such doubter should remember, first, that these gentlemen, having long been accustomed to an implicit acceptance of all their statements as correct, by the patrons of their missionary enterprise, have already had a large experience in finding *mis*-statements thus accepted; and next, that much was to be risked, at this particular crisis, in the hope of now seeming to become entirely free from their long-continued complicity with slavery, and of covering their long course of mendacity with the mantle of the past.

If the Prudential Committee can make it appear (truly or untruly) that the African slave-trade causes no *direct* interference "with the *proper missionary work* of the Board," their purpose is answered; outside of this boundary, they seem perfectly indifferent as to the immense threatened enlargement of crime in the whites, and of suffering in the blacks, which would necessarily attend the threatened revival of the foreign slave-trade. As their confidence in the "excellent" Mr. Byington seems undisturbed by the fact that he suffered one member of his mission-church to burn another alive without instituting discipline in regard to it, preaching against it, or treating it as an offence in any manner whatever, so their confidence in the system of complicity with slavery, which they have now maintained for more than forty years in the Cherokee and Choctaw churches, seems not to be in the least disturbed by the recent developments of inveterately pro-slavery character in those tribes. Nay, so accustomed have the advocates of the Board become to sub-

stitute implicit confidence in the Prudential Committee for
the exercise of a moderate prudence in "putting that and
that together," that even the Editor of the *New York Evan-
gelist*, in printing (March 21st, 1861) the following instructive passage of history, probably did not even think of the
responsibility of the Prudential Committee for their forty
years' course of missionary instruction leading to it. Here is
the passage : —

"THE INDIANS. — The Cherokee, Choctaw, and other Indian
tribes of the Southwest, nearly all of them slaveholders, are evidently under the influence of secessionists. The principal Chief
of the Choctaw Nation has recently convened the local Legislature
in council, for the purpose of consulting as to the action to be taken
in view of the secession of the Southern States. The message of
the Chief reviews the 'grievances' of the South, and the history
of the slavery agitation in the Northern States, and declares the
position of the Choctaw Nation to be that of a sovereign and independent State, and not of a territory of the United States, with the
right to make treaties, and to do all other acts and things which
a sovereign State may do. He declares that all the sympathies
and feelings of the Choctaws are with the South, having been born
and nurtured on its soil, and having institutions in common with
the Southern States. He deprecates the division of the Union,
and holds the example up as a warning to his countrymen never
to let contention and discord enter into their internal and domestic policy. He recommends that Commissioners be sent to Washington city to look after the money interest of the Nation, and to
take counsel and advice from the President of the United States.
He also recommends that a General Council of the Chickasaws,
Creeks, Seminoles, and Choctaws, be held at the central point, for
the purpose of adopting some line of policy, 'necessary to their
security.' The General Council responded to the sentiments of
their Chief by passing resolutions expressing the views of the
General Council of the Choctaw Nation in reference to the political
disagreement existing between the Northern and Southern States."

Later intelligence (*Journal of Commerce*, August 12th)
tells us that "the Choctaws, Creeks, Seminoles and Chickasaws have given their adherence to the Confederates, and
probably the Cherokees are divided on the question."

The Prudential Committee have just certified that these
Indians are a "Christian people." After a course of forty
years of missionary teaching from the "excellent" Mr.
Byington and his colleagues, they are graduated — Christians !
Their "sympathies," it is true, are with the South, in the
present contest, and their "institutions" are in common with

those of the South. But the excellent Mr. Byington has taught them (assuming to teach *from the Bible*) that slaveholding is perfectly consistent with the Christian character; and, no doubt, they will exercise church discipline upon those brethren and sisters who burn their slaves alive, as soon as they are assured that such was " the practice of the Apostles "!

The foregoing record of facts, supported by full documentary evidence drawn almost exclusively from the Annual Reports of the Prudential Committee, may be summed up as follows : —

1. The missionaries who were sent by the Prudential Committee to evangelize the Cherokee and Choctaw Indians chose to recognize the slaveholding of those tribes as an indifferent and entirely unobjectionable thing, and to honor that wicked " institution " by the early and free admission of slaveholders to their churches as Christians.

2. The Prudential Committee not only neglected to warn their missionaries, at the outset, against entering into this complicity with slavery, but they saw the process begin, and go on for many years, without a word of remonstrance, or the least sign of dissatisfaction.

3. When some of their patrons, the givers of the funds which they had thus perverted, remonstrated against their allowance of this sin, they refused to interfere for its removal; and when a large body of their missionaries from another station added their protest against slavery, this Prudential Committee suppressed their testimony, and imposed silence upon them by a law which has been ever since enforced, and which still stands (No. 42) among their " Regulations."

4. When, in subsequent years, the remonstrances from members and patrons of the Board so increased that they could no longer be disregarded without risk to the treasury, argument was attempted in opposition to them ; and the special committees to whom these remonstrances were referred, not only defended the existing policy, and recommended its continuance, but did so by various sorts of misrepresentation, not unfrequently including direct violations of the truth.

5. The reports of these special Committees, while refusing to interfere with the admission of slaveholders to the mission churches, nevertheless made large admissions in regard to the evil character and the pernicious influence of slavery; and they seemed to aim to please both parties, talking against that sin in the strain of the remonstrants, even while in action they maintained the policy against which those remonstrances were directed.

6. The Prudential Committee acted upon the hint thus given; and ever after, in the reports they made, the correspondence they held with the missionaries, and the deputations they sent to examine and report upon this subject, the *action* recommended (always favorable to the policy of the pro-slavery missionaries) was invariably accompanied by a strain of voluminous description and pious reflection *un*favorable to slavery in general. And they took advantage of this verbal characteristic of these reports — the fact that very much of the *phraseology* contained in them was adverse to slavery — to refer back to these documents, in subsequent years, with the claim that they were *really* in opposition to slavery, and that they proved the Board free from complicity with it.

7. The Board, leaving all these things with implicit confidence in the hands of the Prudential Committee, voted, by large majorities, whatever they chose to recommend, and rejected, by equally large majorities, the action against slavery and the slave-trade occasionally proposed by Dr. Cheever, and the few in that body who sympathized with him.

8. Meantime, slavery was bringing forth its natural fruit in the Cherokee and Choctaw communities and churches, as well as in the slaveholding communities and churches around them; the very pleas of the missionaries in behalf of it — such as the extenuating statement, (p. 95 of the Ann. Rep. for 1848,) that if the Indians treated their slaves badly, they treated their own children badly also, and that no better was to be expected of them, under the circumstances — showing the corruption which a tolerance of slaveholding was already working in the churches. Until finally, when the utmost extremity of wickedness and cruelty was manifested by a slaveholding woman in one of those churches — the murder of

a sister in the church by burning alive, without a particle of legal evidence of her guilt, and in spite of her declaration of innocence with her dying breath — this mission *church* showed itself precisely on a level with the profligate slaveholding "world" of Missouri and Arkansas, by hushing up this enormous sin, and treating it as a necessary part of the discipline indispensable to the maintenance of slavery. Nay, they went further in this line of wickedness than the unregenerate "world" *could* do, going on as usual with the administration of "the Lord's Supper" to the murderer!

9. After the system of tolerance of slaveholding in the mission churches had brought forth this fruit, (though Mr. Secretary Treat says the Prudential Committee had not been informed of the slave-burning, and though it is quite probable that the "excellent" Mr. Byington, to whose "fidelity" and "devotedness" they had given unbounded praise, had avoided reporting *this* fruit of his labors,) it was suddenly found, in the Annual Meeting of the Board in October, 1859, that the Prudential Committee had discontinued the Choctaw Mission. They had stated to the missionaries, as the reason of this change, "the unceasing embarrassments and perplexities connected with the mission," specifying afterwards an expected diminution of receipts from the churches if the connection continued; to the public, in the Annual Report then presented, they stated also, that they *could not tell* all the reasons of this change, and that "the whole case" was not there; but to neither of these parties did they frankly say, that this trouble had come from their own guilty complicity with slavery; neither has the mysterious unknown reason, unfit for publication, by which they found themselves "greatly embarrassed," ever yet been explained to the public.

10. In the succeeding year, 1860, the Cherokee mission also was discontinued. This, the Prudential Committee said, was *not* done on account of slavery, but was done because the Cherokee nation was already Christianized, and thus their appropriate work in it was finished.

11. The Prudential Committee, admitting that the Cherokee missionaries were adverse to the discontinuance of the mission, nevertheless represented those missionaries to "*concur in the opinion*" that "the Cherokees are a Christian

people." The paragraph in which this declaration occurs (p. 138 of the Annual Report for 1860) shows how accustomed the Prudential Committee have become to a confidence, in their readers, so implicit as to take no note of the most glaring discrepancies and contradictions in their statements. Immediately after the statement above mentioned, that these missionaries *concur* in the opinion that the Cherokees should be acknowledged a Christian people, the testimony of the three missionaries themselves is given ; and *not one* of the three takes the ground ascribed to them by the Prudential Committee! Not one of them "concurs" in the opinion that the Cherokee nation is a Christian people, any more than in the opinion that the Board may properly retire from that field of labor.

12. The details of evidence fail to establish the ground assumed by the Prudential Committee as thoroughly in the case of the Cherokee people as in that of their missionaries ; for, on a careful scrutiny of the evidence, the Christianization of the 21,000 Cherokees is reduced to the following rather inadequate basis, namely; — the alleged facts, that 136 Cherokees are members of the mission churches; that 255 persons (church members and others, Indian, white, colored, and mixed) are attendants on the mission preaching; and that an average of 80 pupils irregularly attend the mission schools. As to the morality of these Cherokee church members, they may all hold, buy, and sell slaves, if they will. As to their piety, it is admitted (p. 141) that they do not care enough for the preaching of the Gospel to support it at their own expense, even when able to do so. And the first intelligence that we have of this slaveholding nation, after the certificate of its Christian character publicly given by the Prudential Committee of the "American Board," is that, sympathizing with the manners, customs, and "institutions" of the Southern secessionists, they are considering whether to join *their* movement for the extension and perpetuity of slavery !

13. The unfair and dishonest treatment which the Board have always practised towards the remonstrants against their complicity with slavery, has never been more glaring than in their reply to the last request of this sort, made by the General Association of Illinois; for the petition of this

body " that the divorce of slaveholding from Christianity be completed *at once, in the churches of the Cherokee nation*," was declared by the Board to be " satisfactorily answered " by the dismissal of these churches from their charge, with the certificate, published to the world, that the continuance of their slaveholding was no impeachment of their Christian character.

14. The fact, in the position of the " American Board," which now most emphatically challenges the attention of the civilized world, and especially of that part of it which cares for the propagation of a pure Christianity, is that they have deliberately chosen to bear a testimony practically in favor of slavery, and to refuse a course of action practically adverse to it, even when proposed by clergymen, their friends and allies; that they have refused, now as well as heretofore, to purge the Cherokee and Choctaw churches of the enormous corruption which their missionaries, with their consent, introduced and perpetuated in them; and that, in dismissing from their watch and care these corrupt churches, and the yet more corrupt nation to which they belong, with the volunteered certificate that both are " Christian," they have insulted the common sense as well as the religion of this age, and have interposed the most fatal of obstructions to the progress of the Gospel of Christ.

In the forty-two years of the Board's maintenance of the Cherokee and Choctaw missions, they have *connived* at slavery, avoiding, by various dishonorable and dishonest contrivances, the hard duty of reformation. Now, they go a step further, spontaneously and publicly vouching for slaveholding churches as *Christian* churches, and for a nation upholding the worst form of slavery as " *a Christian people.*" Will any Christian in the Northern churches, will any of those men in the free North who now see the revelations, more and more hideous, which slavery is constantly making of its own character, continue to support a Board which has thus deliberately taken its position on the side of slavery? Will any man give another dollar for the disposal of that Prudential Committee, until they shall have retracted that shameful testimony respecting the Cherokee nation, and commenced a course of reparation in regard to it, doing something really to Christianize those whom they have corrupted?

The guilt of passing a forged note is small compared with the sin which these men have been committing, and persisting in against vehement remonstrance, for forty-two years. Pretending to teach Christianity to an ignorant people, they have imposed upon them, under that venerable name, a religion which allows and favors slavery. Just as surely as it is the duty of a repenting forger or pickpocket to undo the wrong he has done, and just as surely as it is needful for those around him to require confession *and reparation* as indispensable among the evidences that his penitence is real, just so surely should this Prudential Committee be required to make both these sorts of atonement.

They have not merely wasted the money intrusted to them by the churches, but they have misused it, in the worst possible way, sowing tares instead of wheat in the consecrated ground which they had undertaken to cultivate. To look at the matter from the pecuniary stand-point, the least important of all, in a matter involving spiritual interests, the union of the Cherokee and Choctaw Indians with the rebellious States of the South, in the war now commenced by them for the maintenance of slavery, will cost this nation fifty times the sum already expended upon those Indians by the Prudential Committee; but their union in this movement for the defence and extension of slavery—their enlistment in this warfare of barbarism against civilization—is the natural tendency of the sort of missionary teaching which the Prudential Committee has furnished them; whereas, a faithful use of their access to those tribes, and a preaching of true Christianity among them for forty-two years, would certainly have tended, and might perhaps have fully availed, to make them refuse such shameful companionship, and stand fast in the liberty with which Christ makes free.

What wonder that their churches were always small and poor! There was no purity, no conscious internal elevation, no spiritual nobleness within, to counterbalance what their parishioners "without" esteemed the advantage of open indulgence in profaneness, theft, drunkenness and fornication. Their church members gave up the *license* of some sorts of sin, without at all attaining "the glorious *liberty* of the children of God." What wonder that only 136 out of the 21,000 Cherokees thought it worth while to join the mission-churches! What wonder that only 255 of the same nation thought it worth while to attend the mission-preaching! And what wonder that neither church nor congregation thought *such* preaching worth paying for! It did not come near enough to Christianity to *be* worth paying for!

We sometimes read of a repentant sinner who can find no peace until he has sought out those whom his evil teaching has seduced into dishonesty or intemperance, and persuaded them also to repent and reform. Just this reparation the Prudential Committee are bound to make to the Cherokees and Choctaws. At whatever expense of personal humiliation and self-sacrifice, they are bound to try, at least, to undo the mischief they have done, to retract their libellous representations that Christianity allows the holding, buying and selling of slaves, and to supply truly Christian teachers for the instruction of that misguided people. Not until they have done this, and made confession, besides, to their re-monstrating patrons, of the dishonest contrivances by which those remonstrances have been counteracted and neutralized, should they be held acquitted of guilt for the past, or entitled to a renewal of confidence in the future.

APPENDIX.

THE following letters give all the further evidence that has appeared up to this date (August, 1861) of facts and incidents relative to the slave-burning in the Stockbridge mission station, in January, 1859, (erroneously stated, in the first letter, to have been "some time in 1860.") The suggestions of Prof. Bartlett in regard to this evidence — in regard to its admissions, direct and indirect, upon some points, and its ominous silence upon others — are worthy of most serious attention. The first of these articles (with no responsible name signed to it) appeared in *The Congregationalist*, of this city, May 3, 1861. The comments of Prof. Bartlett appeared May 17th, in the same paper.

For the Congregationalist.

SLAVE-BURNING IN THE CHOCTAW NATION.

Some time during the past winter, there appeared in *The Independent*, and (I believe) in *several* of the religious papers, a letter from Prof. Bartlett, of Chicago, relative to the burning of a negro woman in the Choctaw Nation some time in 1860. The tenor of Prof. B.'s letter seemed to imply that there had been a culpable silence on the part of the missionaries in that Nation, upon the point, and that the mission church were guilty in winking at the sin of participation in the affair. Having spent some five years us an assistant in mission labors in the Territory, and knowing somewhat of the trials that gather so thickly about the weary way which the beloved brethren and sisters laboring in the Territory have trodden for the last ten years, I was grieved for their sakes, and enclosing a printed copy of Prof. Bartlett's letter to one of the brethren, requested an explanation. The following is a copy of his reply. The original I still retain. If you will give it a place in your columns, I think you will confer a favor upon the mission. It proves what I had supposed in reading Mr. B.'s letter, viz., that the whole affair was conducted by a *lawless mob*, with whom the national authorities, even, dare not interfere. How, then, should our mission brethren meddle with them? While I detest slavery as thoroughly as Prof. Bartlett can desire any person, Christian or heathen, to detest it, at the same time, I do say to my Christian brethren at the North, Have a care, my friends, that in your zeal against slavery, you lay no stumbling-stones in the pathway of those who, amid trials and self-denials that home Christians know little of, have toiled on for years, to give the Gospel to those who had it not. Should we not rather, at this hour, when to trials and self-denials are added dangers also, give them our prayers in large measure, rather than our censure?

Yours, respectfully,

A Former Member of the Mission.

P. S.—Will you allow me, through your paper, to request *The Independent* to do us the favor to copy this article?

Choctaw Nation, March, 1861.

Miss ——: In regard to the inquiry respecting the burning of the slave woman, I have only to say, that Dr. Lowrie's letter to Rev. S. C. Bartlett contains the substance of the facts in the case. The public meeting was composed only of the relatives,* the Harkinses and † Pitchlyns, "Capt. Whiskey" presiding, as usual on such occasions. They constituted judge, jury, and executioners, and conducted things in precisely their own way. The only free member of the church, in good standing, who was present, and took any part in the transactions, was Mrs. Harkins, wife of the murdered man. There was one other free member of the church present, but he was *not* in good standing, and it is not known that he took any part, except as a spectator.

Now, what would Mr. Bartlett have us do in a case of this kind? Shall we discipline those members who took a part in the affair? That has *already been done.* ‡ Mrs. Harkins voluntarily gave herself up to the discipline of the church, made all the confession which the most fastidious could desire, was restored to fellowship, and now leads a consistent Christian life. What more could be done in the way of discipline?

Would Mr. B. have the church, or any member of it, institute a *legal* process against the parties? Such a measure, in this country, and in case of the *families in question*, would be simply ridiculous. Some of those very persons have since been tried for the murder of a *free white* citizen of the nation, and acquitted.

Would Mr. Bartlett have the church, its pastor, or any of its members, from the pulpit or the stump, bear a public witness against the sin of such proceedings? That would have been about as wise as to preach a sermon against the supremacy of the Pope, beneath the walls of the Vatican.

This is a land of liberty! The broad stripes and bright stars wave over us yet, or did then, at least, and we are still under the

* The relatives of the murdered man, Col. Harkins.

† It should be borne in mind, that the national authorities would not molest a Pitchlyn, their standing in the nation being such that to hold them amenable to law would require as much courage in the Territory, as it would now for a native of South Carolina to arrest J. Davis for treason. Let it be remembered, also, that while the United States exercise a certain supervision over the Territory, all civil and criminal affairs are left to the discretion of the Council and National authorities.

‡ Mrs. Harkins was represented in the letter of last winter as a daughter of Col. Pitchlyn, which is, I suppose, correct, though I do not certainly know.

protection of that government which guarantees to us freedom of speech, and freedom of opinion, but actually there is no more freedom of opinion here than there is in Spain. On any thing pertaining to slavery, we have to conduct ourselves just as we would under the most despotic government in the world.

Would Professor Bartlett have us publish to the world the matter? We can see no good that would arise from such a course, nor any necessity for us to take it, while there are so many men in the North ready and willing to save us the trouble.

The action of Northern men, of a certain class, in respect to the Choctaw Mission, often reminds me of a flock of turkey buzzards. You know with what indifference they flap their lazy wings over the most beautiful landscape. The purling stream, the waving trees, the blooming flowers, have no attraction for them. But show them a dead carcass, and they pounce upon it at once. So certain Northern men can see nothing of the *good* that has been effected here by the Mission. They take an extra grip on their purse strings, and look with cool indifference upon the members we have educated, the general good that has been effected through our labor.

But show them a dead negro who has been put to death by a set of men who fear neither God, man, nor the devil, any further than suits their convenience, and they are all down upon us at once.

I can only speak as an individual, but I think I hazard nothing in saying, the Mission would be *exceedingly obliged if some one*, of that class, Mr. Bartlett for example, would *come down here*, and tell us precisely what we ought to do, and *show us* precisely *how to do it.*

Yours, truly, —— —— ——.

While I write, a friend suggests that *such* a mission ought to be *cut off*. To such I can only say, what Christian man will take the responsibility of shutting out the Gospel from a people just struggling into the light of Christianity and civilization, amid the worst of surrounding influences? If for the sin of those who rule, the preacher and teacher shall be removed from the people, what shall be done with *us*? When the Lord hath so dealt with us, then let us shut out the living preacher from our brethren who know far less than we. Till then, let us beware how we shut out from a still ignorant people, the little light that, with God's blessing upon the labors of toilworn men, and wearied, patient women, is beginning to gleam upon the darkness of those Indian homes and Indian hearts. Would that those who would do so, could see what I once saw among them — a converted Indian, whose crisp hair and black complexion bore testimony to the fact that African blood mingled largely with the Indian in his veins, standing beside the communion-table, and with tears rolling over his face, pleading with his people to listen to the teaching of these very missionaries. "While," said he, "on one side one white man brings you whiskey, and on the other, another teaches you to gamble, and to practise every wickedness, these men, and *these alone*, have given us the words of life through Jesus. Listen to them — listen for your life, for they alone have cared for our souls. They only teach you what will save you from temporal and eternal ruin."

It is vastly easier to sit quietly at home and criticise, than to share the difficulties of our Indian missionaries. Were it not an act of common courtesy to allow one who will go to them, and, sharing their trials, their discouragements, their toils, *practically showing them* "a more excellent way," to be the one to "cast the first stone"? Were it not more Christ-like to thank God for what He has condescended to work out by them, than to hinder them in their work, because of what they cannot do?   JOTA.

Correspondence of the Congregationalist.

THE SLAVE-BURNING.

MESSRS. EDITORS:—Your paper of the 3d instant contains a communication concerning the sad tragedy to which I called attention several months since. All information concerning it comes slowly and painfully. Although the subject is now eclipsed by the greater events of the hour, I will ask space to say, that the attempted explanation is very unsatisfactory—both in its mode, its tone, and its statements.

A member of Mr. Byington's church was burned alive. Another member of that church, then and now in good standing, it is admitted, was accessory to the murder. No distinct allusion to the terrible deed was ever made by the mission or the missionaries in their Reports to the American Board; and when they were transferred to another Board, there was nothing but a passing notice, ending with the deceptive statement, "It was a terrible affair, but the mission and the church here are not responsible for it." Letters addressed by me to those Boards brought out only the information which they had; and a respectful letter of inquiry to the pastor of the mission church received no attention whatever. At length, after about three months waiting, a public call for information was made. Then only, the missionary pastor wrote, refusing to give me any information or explanation, but saying that he had at length (two years after the event) reported to the Presbyterian Board, and that they could explain if they chose. A respectful appeal was publicly made to that Board; but no word of responsible and official information was given—and no authentic and detailed statement has been furnished to this day. After several months of waiting, however, we get one *anonymous* letter, wrapped up in another anonymous letter, answering our respectful inquiries in a case of admitted murder with meager statements and hard names. I think the Church is entitled to a better account, in a more responsible shape.

The tone of the communication is far from satisfactory. A murdered church member is only a "dead negro"! A Christian brother, asking a simple explanation of the murder, is a "turkey-buzzard," pouncing on "a dead carcass"! The missionary who can think and write thus of the objects of his Christian labor—to say nothing of his Northern brethren — should be blest with friends wise enough to suppress his letters.

The statements, too, are unsatisfactory, besides awakening other painful inquiries. "Actually there is no more freedom of opinion here than in Spain;"—and Mrs. Harkins belonged to one of two "families," against whom even a legal process "would be simply ridiculous." These statements are certainly distinct — whether intended to be *frank* or not — and they only intensify the demand on those brothers to show that they have not compromised the doctrine and the discipline of Christ's Church. The facts purporting to be given are guarded, and apparently defective. "The only free member of the church, in good standing, who took any part in the transaction, was Mrs. Harkins." But how many members not free were there, and what of them? "One other free member was present, not in good standing." What was his standing, and what of him? The process of discipline "has already been done. Mrs. Harkins voluntarily gave herself up to the discipline of the church, made all the confession which the most fastidious could desire, was restored to church fellowship, and now leads a consistent Christian life." A score of questions rise on reading this blurred account. When was it — before or after the call for information? Was any notice taken of the case before the next communion? Did Mrs. H. then partake with the church? Who took the initiative, the church or Mrs. H.? — and how much is contained in that word "*voluntarily*"? What was the discipline? Was Mrs. H. debarred from the communion? — and how long? Is a simple "confession" all that is necessary to restore to church fellowship *a person who has taken part in a murder?* Is the murder of Christian slaves by "Christian" masters too trivial or too common an affair in the Choctaw nation to require even a passing allusion, in communicating information from the mission to the Board that employs them?

I am sorry to say that I am not satisfied with the explanation of that letter. It awakens more doubts than it solves. I presume the public will speedily learn the facts more fully from another source. Meanwhile, I gladly take my leave of a subject on which I have said more than I could have desired.

Yours, truly,   S. C. BARTLETT.

CHICAGO, May 6, 1861.

www.ingramcontent.com/pod-product-compliance
Lightning Source LLC
Chambersburg PA
CBHW030814020726
47499CB00006B/1913